DEANNA

RUIN & ROSES

Ruin and Roses

Book One of the Cursed Kingdoms Series

Deanna Ortega

First paperback edition Mar 2022

Formatting by Deanna Ortega

Art by Madeline Drury

Map by Joshua Hoskins, Hoskins Cartography

Cover images by Cover 2 Cover Author Services

To all the bad decisions we've made in our lifetimes, and the ones we've yet to make.

CONTENT AND TRIGGER WARNINGS

//CW: Violence (Graphic), Death, Mature Content, Mature Language, Sexual Content, Mental Abuse, Physical Abuse, Misogyny, Suicide (Mentioned), Sexual Assault (Mentioned), Death of a Parent, Child Abuse, Animal Death//

PRONUNCIATION GUIDE

Places:
- Anwyn: ANN-win /ˈænwɪn/
- Lunasa: LOO-nah-sah /luːnæˈsɑː/
- Ellesmere: ELS-meer /ˌelsˈmɪr/
- Luhne: LOON /luːn/
- Karhdaro: cahr-DAHR-oh /kɑːrdɑːrəʊ/
- Weylin: WAY-lin /weɪlɪn/
- Faery: FAIR-ee /ˈferi/
- Gralahran Mountains: grah-LAH-ren /grəˈˌlɑːren/

People:
Lunasa: Lunasians loo-NAS-ee-uhns /luːnæsˈiːəns/

Royals:
- King Certis Serpen (*King of Lunasa*): SUHR-tis SUHR-puhn /ˈsɜːrtɪs/ /ˈsɜːrpən/
    - †*Queen Elyse Serpen (True Queen of Lunasa): EE-lees / iːliːs/*
    - †Queen Kore Serpen (*Jane's mother*): kor-AY /koːreh/
- Prince Oliver Serpen: AH-liv-uhr /ˈɑːlɪvɜːr/
- Princess Olivia Serpen: oh-LIV-ee-uh /əˈlɪviə/
- Princess Driata Serpen: dri-AH-tah /drɪɑːtɑː/
- Prince Ciaran Serpen: KEE-ren /kiˈren/
- Princess Gemma Serpen: JEM-mah /dʒemə/
- Princess Jane Serpen: jAYn /dʒeɪn /

Nobility:

- Lord Keeper Baltazar Tellyk (*Keeper of the Crown*): Bal-TUH-zar TELL-ick /ˈbæltɑːzɑːr/ /tellɪk/
- Duke Vellum Tellyk: VEL-uhm TELL-ick /ˈveləm/
- Liam Tellyk (*Baltazar's Brother*): LEE-ahm TELL-ick /liːəm/
- Duchess and Duke Tilby (*Rulers of the Barrens*): til-BEE /tɪlbiː/
- Lord Weemble (*Of Luhne*): WEEM-buul /wiːmbʊll/

The merry band of misfits:

- Lux: lUHKs /lʌks/
- Louisa: (Lou): loo-EES-ah (LOO) /luːiːˈsɑː/
- Kaleb Dower: KAY-leb DOW-uhr /keɪlʌb/ /ˈdaʊwər/
- Tessa (Tess) Dower: TES-uh DOW-uhr /tesæ/
- Gwyn/eth Dower: gWIN-uhth DOW-uhr /gwɪnəθ/

Karhdaro: Karhdarans cahr-DARH-ens /kɑːrˈdɑːrens/
- King Blair *(King of Karhdaro)*: bLEHr /bler/

Weylin:
- Queen Orabelle *(Queen of Weylin)*: ah-RUH-bel / ˈɔːrəbell/

Ellesmere: Ellesmerans els-MEER-ens /ˌelsˈmɪrəns/
Royals:
- King Maveri Alistair (*King of Ellesmere*): may-VER-ee al-IS-tehr /meɪˈvəri/ /ˈælɪstər/
- Queen Aurina Alistair (*Queen of Ellesmere*): ah-REE-nah / ɑːriːnæ/

•Prince Arius Alistair (*Prince of Ellesmere*): AHR-ee-uhs / ɑːriːʌs/

•Swineston: SWYN-ston /swaɪnstʌn/

Guards:

•Zander: ZAN-der /zændər/

•Commander Jenson: JEN-suhn /dʒɪnsʌn/

•Captain Gialanos: gee-ah-LAH-nos /dʒiːəlɔːnəʊs/

•Codis Wallin: KOH-dis WAH-len /kəʊdɪs/ /wɔːlɪn/

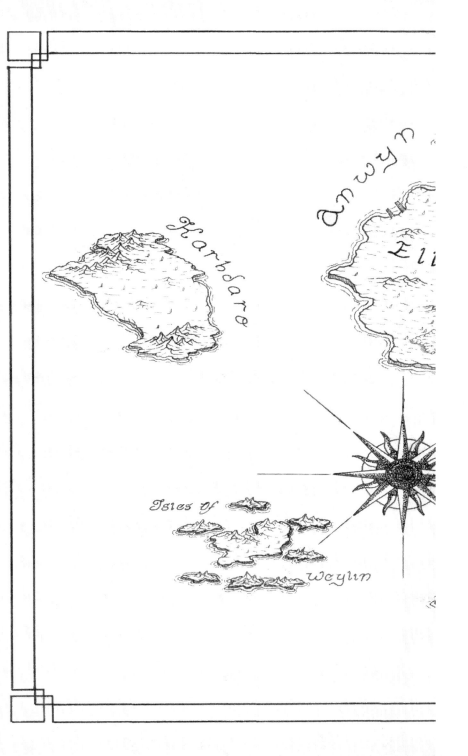

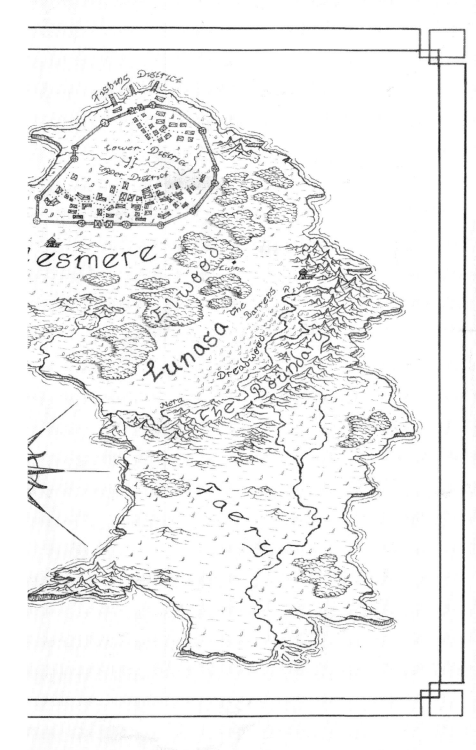

CHAPTER 1

The tinted skylight's glass nipped at my fingers while a cloud-peppered sky shadowed the reflection staring back at me. I looked like a fucking idiot. An absolute moron. One that would punch Baltazar in his smug face for calling this a simple mission.

A supposedly simple spell would solve both of our problems and make me better at my job. But no—I was on a turret, risking life and limb for King Maveri's blood crown.

Squinting, I narrowed in on my target. It sat in the middle of the treasury, rubies glimmering even in the low light. Fragile cases and trunks—containing the kingdom's most treasured heirlooms and jewels—surrounded my mark.

The guards wouldn't be in there. They were busy scouring the palace for explosives. A diversion that had taken me days to cultivate. Baltazar didn't see fit to teach me how to magick my way into and out of a building, but his seemingly useless lessons on changing my voice worked.

1

One whisper into the right ear, in the right hall, at precisely the right time... And you have a bomb threat while another royal family was planning to visit.

Visit—I thought dryly. That was my mind oversimplifying at its finest. It was more fitting to call it what it was, a transaction. But regardless, a breach of safety was terrible for politics.

"The devil is in the details," Baltazar had responded when I suggested the plan. *"You can't have a bomb threat without an explosion."*

He was right, of course—he was always right.

The clock tower gonged in the distance. My pulse thundered in my ears. "Three..."

My muscles tensed as I cinched the rope around my waist and thighs. "Two..."

I pressed my aching palms against the glass, scraped and cut from scaling the stone wall. Rubble spilled into the treasury. "One—Ruptus." *Break.* The glass splintered.

The window gave way, and I was plummeting. The cord fibers ripped into my hands as I slammed to a stop. With my shoulders screaming and teeth grinding together, I looked down at my feet. The mirrored image of my dangling soles above the marble floor mocked me while my heart battered my ribs.

I was inches away from shattering my legs.

The thudding of my boots echoed around the chamber as I dropped down.

Shattered glass and the dangling hawser were the only sign that an intruder had entered. I gazed down at my hands, ripped open from my descent.

"Inritum facio." *Undo.* The glass shards floated up to the ceiling, clinking one by one into place, repairing the damage my previous spell had wrought. The rope coiled back around my waist, tucked neatly under my cloak like I had never used it.

Dipping my head to appreciate the valuables surrounding the crown, I groaned.

Baltazar ordered me to break into the most heavily guarded castle in Anwyn, and it wasn't even to steal away with riches.

His instructions had been clear. *"Remember, Jane. Take nothing else."*

Dread clawed at my gut. If Baltazar found out what I did with my cut from each job or that I sometimes took extra... There would undoubtedly be consequences. Though, even that was shading it lightly.

Concentrating on the task at hand, I pushed a weighted breath through my nose instead of focusing on a possible future that may not come.

Focus, Jane. Get the crown and get out.

Maveri was a paranoid lunatic if you asked me. The sigils etched around the room marked the place to detonate if a person not of the royal line decided to paw the king's favored things.

Huffing a sigh, I eyed the wards. Leave it to the mad king to prefer his precious items destroyed rather than in the hands of another.

I reached for the dagger I kept tucked in my boot while mentally reciting the spell Baltazar taught me just before I left Lunasa.

My mentor rarely explained why he was teaching me a new incantation, but I long since learned that he trained me as the need arose. His needs, not mine. Surely. My eyes darted to the fixed skylight high above, and my cruel mind imagined what sound my body would have made if I cut that rope any shorter.

Baltazar's voice filled my head as if he was in the chamber with me, chastising me while I cursed him. *You rely highly on magic for someone who was born without it.*

Gritting my teeth to silence the reminder, I split open the drying wounds on my palm with my dagger. "Illusio."

I needed to believe—to imagine—the illusion of the mad king of Ellesmere was sliding around me, clinging to my skin and clothes. My flesh tingled as my hips spread wider, and my frame drooped toward the ground. My dagger felt weighted suddenly, far too heavy in my shorter and fattened fingers—ones free from calluses or marks of any labor.

My lip curled back from my teeth at the thought of the man I embodied, and I stifled the disgust, nearly forcing me to recoil out of the illusion.

Focus. I could drop the spell as soon as I got out of there, but why hadn't Baltazar told me exactly how real it would feel?

I suppressed a shudder as I moved forward, and the stomach that hung well over my buckle jiggled.

No wonder the mad king had his own line of executioners. I was sure he struggled to get up from his throne, let alone be able to wield a weapon. But, of course, it didn't make him any less fearsome, what with his penchant for bringing death upon an indiscretion as simple as an insult.

"My King?" My back was to the prince, but the voice had haunted my dreams since he came to visit my family's home. The fact that he called his father only by his title and not something more endearing spoke volumes.

Why is he here? I pulled my dagger closer to my chest, praying to the lost gods that he didn't see it.

"Arius." The king's voice rumbled from my lips, not bothering with the same formalities his son used. Maveri respected only his title. "Why have you come?"

"You asked me to pick something for my *betrothed's* arrival." He spat the word. If I wasn't already disgusted myself, I probably would have been offended by the way he wielded it like a curse.

"I wish to be alone with my riches. Come back another time." No dismissal, no niceties, a clear command designed to be spoken by a man that thought he was everyone's better.

"Your soon-to-be family certainly is that pompous." The voice changed as he spoke, the pitch deepening, and I turned, realizing why.

Oh, Gods...

Curly, raven-colored ringlets and eyes like chips of silver greeted me as his one annoying dimple popped up with his full-lipped grin.

Liam, Baltazar's second in command and younger brother, stood before me.

Of course, it was him. My day hadn't been trying enough. The gods needed to punish me for some unknown slight. I would much prefer they strike me down.

Despite my training, my face flushed at his nearness and ability to deceive me. I swallowed down all the words that rushed up when he was around. He would only laugh, that pitiless laugh of his, and mock me for them.

"You can't be here," I hissed, my voice seeping into the king's as his presence unraveled my hold on the spell.

I could feel my body lengthening, no longer standing in Maveri's stout frame. It was a relief but also terrible because I wouldn't be able to redo the spell. My leathers settled over my skin, replacing the feeling of the king's fine silks. I hated Liam with every ounce and every fiber in me. I hated him. But gods dammit if his eyes roving over me didn't make me want to tear his clothes off.

My fist clenched at my side to avoid just that.

Liam's narrowed eyes tracked the motion, but his gaze stayed fixed on my left hand—no, to the glittering ring on my finger.

"*He* wanted to ensure you didn't mess this up." His eyes finally lifted, and he noted the disappointment lining my face as it fell and my spell faded. I watched Liam's face light with my failure.

He made me fail. His lips twisted into a cruel smile at the triumph. "He always seems to have the foresight that you will."

It was part of the strategy Baltazar created for everyone— even his second—to believe that I was useless. But really, I was his hidden weapon, his defense. But that smug look on Liam's face threatened to make me unravel carefully laid plans.

My rage boiled within me, forcing me to reign in my control as I kept my lip in a pout. "You'll get us both in trouble."

"How boring." He tilted his head to the side, his silver eyes examining me. "Is that the human in you?"

He wanted a reminder to rush over me of the time before. A time when he hadn't cared about my breeding. But I wouldn't —couldn't—allow it. So I shoved the memories and the inevitable feelings they would raise—away—down as far as I could before they could consume me and cloud my judgment even further.

"You're a bastard." It was true. A cheap shot, but true. Both he and Baltazar were the sons of some absent duke and—if rumors served—his maids. They came to Lunasa when Liam was only a boy, back before Baltazar reached his position in society. Long before my mentor's frankness impressed my father, and Baltazar quickly ascended our society's ranks.

Liam's lip curled back from his teeth at the mention before settling into a dangerous smile. "Perhaps, but bastard as I may be... My parents are both alive."

Even though my jaw felt like it was grinding to dust, I coached my shoulders to relax and my eyes to roll. "You do know your way around a nerve, don't you?"

His light eyes darkened, a smile tugging at his lips. He raked those damned, too familiar, eyes down my front—slowly. As if to paint a picture of my body in his mind. Or perhaps to compare it to one that haunted him. Perhaps, my traitorous mind quietly hoped one that stained his memory the way the sight of his night sky darkened skin did mine.

Fuck.

Finally, dreadfully, he met my gaze, and regret didn't cloud his face but more a catlike satisfaction. "Good that you remember."

My breath caught while a curling sensation rolled low in my stomach.

"Get out of here, Liam." I ignored the flash of heat that coursed through me, the indecent thoughts threatening and rippling the edges of my mind.

Choosing to focus instead on how his name tasted like bile

on my tongue, and there was *nothing* I could do about it. Not without exposing myself, but I imagined it. The look on his face the day he realized I wasn't worthless. But I had to let him believe it, even if I no longer wanted to pretend.

"No. That's not how this works." His smile laced with an arrogance that turned his eyes into pools of molten silver. "I'm here to clean up your mess and retrieve the crown."

Stop focusing on his fucking eyes, Jane.

With one word, one word, I could shatter his bones. But that wouldn't do. It would blow my cover. To the world, I was Jane. Just Jane. Plain Jane. Mundane Jane. The clumsy, part mortal Jane. It didn't matter how much harder I studied in private. How much stronger and faster I had become. What mattered was their perception of me, whether I had a choice or not.

And I already guaranteed Baltazar the blood crown, from my hand, and mine alone.

Baltazar would tell me to *think*. He would have insisted I use the human part of my brain to outwit my opponent. To do so without them even knowing they had lost. Liam's being there complicated the mission but didn't prevent it.

I pulled in my shoulders, knowing the movement would draw attention there.

My chin dipped into my chest, and I let out a gasping sob. *Too much, reel it in.*

Feigned tears cast a watery filter over my vision. "I—I need this win. Especially before... Before I have to marry him." There it was—the card I had against Liam. The one thing that should have made him back off.

"No."

It took me a moment to process the word and the hollow, unfeeling laughter that followed. Finally, my eyes met his, and I saw something there. A flicker of genuine amusement as the corner of his mouth twisted slyly to a grin.

Liam knew, somehow... He knew that was a scam.

What would Baltazar have me do? Would he want me to destroy my cover further or allow Liam to steal my triumph?

Liam reached for the talisman hanging from his neck.

Neither.

My nails bit into my palms, and warmth seeped underneath the crusted blood. His lips parted in a chuckle. Already relishing in ruining or taking over the heist, I spent weeks carefully crafting.

His mistake.

Under cover of that laughter, I whispered, "tempus modero." *Time control.*

The amusement on his face paused.

Liam still stood with his hand gripped around his charm, and a mockery of his laughter echoed in my ears, but the room was silent.

My heart echoed steadily, beating in my ears. The migraine from not using enough blood to maintain the spell already clanged around my skull, and white spots burst over my eyes. I was one party trick away from passing out unless I got some rest.

I regarded the jewelry, weapons, and finery around the space, knowing I couldn't chance taking anything else. Nausea roiled through me, and the corners of the room went fuzzy as I pressed my hand against the case.

"Ruptus."

The case shattered, imploding slowly, almost imperceptibly. The ground beneath my feet trembled, and I prayed that when the room went up, it would force the detection spell to falter.

Shards scraped against the back of my hands and up my arm as I grabbed the crown. I yanked it off its cushion just as an inferno sparked up in the back of the room. The floor beneath my feet splintered and widened, and my mouth fell open in a silent scream.

Or maybe the cracking floor was too loud for me to hear. My ears rang with its echoes.

Shit. Guards would come.

The case stand spun, dislodging stones and hurling them around the room. I dodged them, tucking the crown deep within the folds of my coat. A bead of sweat licked its way down my face at the fire, burning hot enough to devour jewels and bones.

Trunks of gold turned molten and bubbled over, and the wood casing splintered and ignited. Gems disappeared in the white flames as the glass and stone from the skylight pummeled us from above.

Liam's mouth twitched—

I needed to move faster. The spell would run out soon. His grating laughter was cut off by a gasp just as time started again. "What the—"

"Go." I shoved both hands into his chest, propelling him away from the doors as the flames engulfed them.

His arm wrapped around my waist before gripping his talisman, and the blinding blaze around us disappeared. Darkness wrapped around us in a sulfuric gale. Bursts of starlight danced in my vision as a droning filled my ears. Far—

He was taking us too far away, and he wouldn't be able to control it. The fire must have thrown him off course. My hair whipped around me as the breath was stolen and returned to my lungs. It felt as though we were careening through the worlds.

There was nothing— Then warm light seared my eyes. We tumbled from the sky through gnarled tree limbs. Still bleeding, my hands gripped the fabric of Liam's shirt while I screamed. My ribs slammed against a branch, and pain lanced up my side into my back. My vision faltered, and my body crashed into the earth. Liam huffed out a breath below me. My eyes adjusted to the light leaking in from the trees of the Elwood. I saw my fingers first, still knotted in fabric, blood soaking through the white material. Then, I felt a heartbeat that was steady and as familiar as my own.

I tilted my head to see Liam's features lined with fear and staring at me. He checked my face, seeming as relieved to hear a second heartbeat as I was. But that didn't make sense. And when his eyes narrowed, they confirmed it. "Get the hell off me."

"Uh...yea. Okay." It hurt to move, and a whistling sound swept through my body when I breathed. I need to get to Baltazar. He would be with my father's traveling party. He would heal me.

"You're injured," he said simply, as though stating it was a warm day. But he stepped closer and pressed his fingers under my coat. The opposite side to the crown, thankfully. And while the air filled with the smell of sulfur again, my lungs felt lighter and ached less when I breathed.

"Thank you," I whispered, not realizing I spoke until he stepped away again.

"My brother will be disappointed that you failed." There it was—the proof that he didn't realize I won. His belief in my ineptitude was so deep that he probably would think it was an illusion if I presented him with the crown right then.

"My brother will be disappointed that you failed." There it was. Proof that he didn't realize I won. His belief in my ineptitude was so deep that he probably would think it was an illusion if I presented him with the crown right then.

"Why?" I wasn't sure why I asked it or even what I was asking. Why had he healed me? It was probably his orders. Baltazar's insurance that the weak human wouldn't die. Why did he hate me? I couldn't be asking that, though. He would never answer that.

"You have an engagement party to prepare for." His voice had grown cold. Devoid of even satisfaction. Then he turned on his heel to walk away.

It was like time had slowed again, watching the trees and shadows devour his silhouette. I wished, only for a moment, I could tell him it had been my father's plan and not my own.

Then I wanted to go after him and punch him in his arrogant, careless mouth.

But the mission was successful. I patted the welt pocket of my jacket, appreciating the curvature of the crown, tucked away there.

My temper settled as I once more wondered, *why this*? It didn't matter, though. Not really. It wasn't my job to ask questions, only to deliver. And it was a milder job, even with the encounter with Liam. No matter how he made my blood boil, he was no match for an ogre guarding the last phoenix egg.

No—that was the gig. Danger. Stealing. Lying when the need arose. Using magic that others thought I couldn't grasp.

When you're the only part-human born into a family of witches, they don't know what to expect. And often, my father asked, or my siblings tortured me about my magic. Or rather... My lack of it.

Constant questions didn't do anything but make me feel even more hopeless, and they certainly didn't encourage traditional magic to come to me any more freely.

Though my father tried to be much more polite about it— even if it came off condescending.

Part of me hoped my lacking was also due to his curse and, in some way, even more, his fault. The curse had drained Lunasa's traditional magic down to its husk. Nothing more than parlor tricks. And each time they questioned or prodded, I would evade them or produce a quick lie.

I was a puzzle, the mistake my father made with my mother. But she was gone, and I lived on as a constant, prodding memory of that mistake.

And for that, my father doted on me—favored me even.

More so worried over me, I thought dryly.

Honestly, the more he pressed and my siblings tormented me, the more I wanted to prove them wrong. But the only magic I'd learned how to use was the same magic that made me more of a criminal than the heists I performed.

I would be convicted. Worse, Baltazar would.

No.

I couldn't tell anyone. I wasn't sure what my father would

do if he ever discovered what I was doing instead of preparing for my new life. Especially if he learned about my use of the blood magic, most likely, I would be convicted as others had before me who'd risked too much and stupidly got caught.

And even if I didn't care about myself, I couldn't watch them take Baltazar. I couldn't watch guards string him up and mark him as a traitor to the crown before they took his life.

So I hid my magic and the secret life I led despite the very real responsibilities I had been committed to as my father's daughter and a representative of his crown.

Responsibilities that would take away the already small freedoms I had.

I hadn't wanted any of this. I was fulfilling my duties as a princess, despite what I would have chosen... Or who.

Some princess— I bit down on a humorless chuckle. *How very royal—to be traipsing through the shadows with a stolen crown from my impending father-in-law's treasury.*

My father would probably collapse in shame if he knew. But I silenced the guilt gnawing at me. He didn't deserve it. No. There was much worse he could be suffering. My guilt would be wasted on him when he was the cause of our people's suffering. People who starved and wanted for everything while he lounged in borrowed finery and pretended the curse that ravaged the lands outside of our gates wasn't his fault. While he fed his rotting body, not sickened by the guilt that drove me after my mother's death, everyone else suffered.

No, my guilt served our people much more than it would go to waste on him.

I reminded myself of what Baltazar had taught me early on.

The first of many valuable lessons and arguably, the most important one.

One I reminded myself often when I started to regret the new life I led under the guise of my proper duties.

"Your humanity is a weapon. But like any weapon, you must learn to wield it properly, lest the first person you wound is yourself."

So I barred my heart against my father's feigned niceties, my siblings' horrid acts, and against Liam's eyes—those that used to melt me that had turned cold and against my humanity. Of every word, every detail of advice Baltazar had given me over the last year—that was the one I clung to most.

CHAPTER 2

After seeing one of the markings I had left on the trees surrounding my camp, it hadn't taken long to figure out Liam had dropped us about half a mile away from it.

I hadn't flinched when Baltazar tasked me with stealing the crown. It was easy enough. Not the simplest task I was ever given, but not impossible. My father's guilt aided my mission. He didn't question my refusal to join his caravan or my choice to ride ahead of his traveling party. No, he was all too aware of the choice he had taken away from me.

And paired with the necessity of this joining, he wasn't willing to have the most rebellious of his children bail on the deal he had stricken.

Maveri's continued support in exchange for my father's youngest daughter's hand.

Mine.

Maveri's son hadn't wanted one of my siblings.

He wanted me.

With no warning, aside from clearing his throat, my father announced my newest role at dinner as though he was announcing the next course. The only signal of his nerves had been his darting gaze.

His eyes had pinged off each of my siblings before landing on Driata. The loveliest of my siblings and the one far more suited for a crown than the rest of us. Her hand had choked up on her silver fork in a way that looked like it may snap the metal clean in half.

Her jealousy of the future proposal was evident in the rigid set of her features. And if she had only asked, she would have known I didn't even come close to wishing for this. But she was probably too consumed by her own years of failure in securing a suitor for her hand.

My other siblings had been quiet, their eyes boring into their plates while the clinking of their utensils on the porcelain echoed around the great room.

They were each as inclined to fulfill their duties as I was.

But Driata, she wanted it. So she greeted the masses of men who pooled at her feet with a timid smile and grace. But despite being the only one of us that wanted to be, she was unchosen and unwed.

But Arius chose me. And though I would gladly hand the prince's wretched ring over to her, I hadn't been given a choice.

I had to agree for the safety of my people, for the meager means of support Ellesmere's king offered.

But that didn't mean I was happy about it.

So I accepted Baltazar's mission, as I had each one he had ever offered me. And while the trip was challenging on horseback, and I had to push my mare harder than I ever had, I managed to arrive ahead of everyone else to collect the blood crown.

And perhaps a part of me was grateful for the risky mission. Perhaps I welcomed Baltazar's orders because it may be the last one. And if it was to be the last thing I accomplished for him... Hopefully, it also fucked over my family-to-be and my father.

Baltazar's need for the crown would only match Maveri's want for his riches to remain within his grasp.

And maybe... That small, insecure voice whispered in the back of my mind. *Perhaps this would convince Baltazar he needed me and that I could continue to play my part and work for him.*

Because I needed this, I needed him--to be useful to him. I amended quickly, ignoring the confusion that laced around my thoughts of him.

He was my mentor, my friend. No more, no less. But he gave me something I'd never had: the means to feel useful. I couldn't lose that.

I shook my head. Trying to stave off the feelings, I always worked to convince myself didn't exist.

I was exhausted, obviously. And though Liam had healed my injuries, my body was still sore. The magic I expelled hadn't helped, and the walk back was excruciating. I could feel the thrum of my pulse, like a lullaby willing me to sleep.

My father would be arriving by late day, and he expected me to meet up with him on the outskirts of Luhne. There I would be bathed and dressed before the rest of the journey. But first, I had to meet with Louisa.

Jett, my favored mare, whinnied with excitement as I

approached. Surely, she hoped I had nabbed her a snack on my ventures, despite the empty patch of soil surrounding where I roped her to the tree. One that proved that she had eaten her fill.

My cloak was torn and muddied, and my breathing labored by the time I reached her. The bright and hopeful sparkle in her eyes diminished as she realized my hands were devoid of treats. She let out a derisive snort and kicked up dirt around her like a petulant child throwing a tantrum.

"Sorry, girl." Another huff of resignation followed me as I pulled the parchment with my sketches of the treasury from my torn pants pocket. I unfolded them, looking over the plans one last time. Examining the contours of the walls, I wondered if I missed anything and hoped I hadn't.

In theory, the magic I used shouldn't have left a trace... Hopefully. I studied the king's sigils and each ward. They would track talismans and the imprints that one might leave behind.

The cocky king hadn't thought to guard his treasury against blood magic... Unless I missed something.

Tossing the pages in the embers, I watched them ignite the same way the room had— slowly, then all at once.

When they turned to ash, I worked to cover my makeshift fire pit with dirt and break down camp quickly.

I strapped my bedroll and satchel to Jett's saddle and emptied the remaining wine from my canteen into my mouth.

I didn't want to be sober if I had to do this.

Gripping the length of the horn, I placed one boot into the stirrup and threw my other leg over her back.

Traveling horseback instead of a carriage was hard, but I

preferred it. I grew used to the ache in my legs for days after. It was worth feeling the wind on my face. The beat of Jett's hooves jolted through my body as she pushed on faster, trampling the ground beneath us.

I think she fancied it, too, the freedom over being kept in the stables. It was the only time we weren't both made into show ponies, strutting about to impress the gawkers of Lunasa and the other kingdoms.

The trees of the Elwood thinned, and I saw the billowing plumes of smoke and smelled the savory meats my father's traveling party roasted.

Of course, they wouldn't stay in Luhne but on its outskirts. My father *would* prefer a tent to the wasteland of our kingdom's capital. I kept far away so we wouldn't be heard or seen over their revelry as we passed. Once we reached the opposite edge of the Elwood, it wasn't much further to Luhne.

The cobblestone streets of the capital were a chaotic hell of poverty.

Babes cried out for food that wouldn't come, peddlers

shouted about wares they sank the last of their savings into obtaining, and courtesans begged for company when they only craved a night in a warm bed.

I clung to the familiar comfort of the shadows. Tucking my change purse deeper within the folds of my cloak, I was under the guise of trying to shield myself against the bitter cold. The smell was one I didn't know how anyone got used to, with waste bins of trash spilling over in the streets.

Lunasa was dying, rotting from deep within the earth, leaving food and even something as simple as firewood in short supply for commoners. When the nobles relocated—away from the towns and cities within their control and supposed care— they took with them their attention and their ability to answer their citizens' pleas for help. My father did nothing to prevent it, and many of them couldn't make the trek to complain with the castle sequestered so far away in the mountains.

Because I didn't want to notice any faces that would be missing the next time, I let my eyes unfocus and kept them to the ground. Only when I got closer did I fix them on the alley that led to the back entrance of the dilapidated pub house.

The door groaned open, and the smell of stale wine filled my senses even as the darkness gobbled up the thin streams of sunlight warring against the clouds.

Each time it made me uneasy, having nothing to cover the squelching sound of my boots on the tacky floor. I would never get used to being out in the open. Bodies crammed into the place, sucking away the oxygen, making my cloak unbearably warm. And though their bloodshot eyes were probably unsee-ing, a boozy film distorting sight and sound, I couldn't risk being seen. Not even there.

I couldn't bring myself to judge the men and women who spent their nights there, running up tabs they could never pay. The place provided a retreat from reality and enough ale and body heat to stay warm. But it wasn't my place to judge when I wanted for nothing and couldn't empathize with just trying to survive.

Louisa hummed as she wiped down the bar with her tattered rag, never looking directly at me but always knowing when I arrived. Her ribs showed through her threadbare dress, even in the darkness. She twisted to a part of the bar, cleared of the drunkards who inevitably would pass out on top of it.

"Drink?" She never looked up from her task, and I never met her eye.

"Golden ale."

A nod.

Careful not to rattle the coins, I untied the heavy pouch at my waist and handed it to her across the stained and rotting bar.

She nodded, still looking through me, and slammed down a glass, splashing me with a skunky-smelling liquid, before turning away. It wasn't personal, the way she dealt with me. No, quite the opposite, she was the closest thing I had to an ally in Luhne, and the lack of communication served as a form of protection for us both.

Louisa would give the gold to those most in need, and I would keep providing it to her. A man whose illness could that the right poultice could cure, a mother whose children wouldn't make it another night without food, and so on.

Sucking down the glass to the dregs, I did my best to stifle a gag that bubbled to my throat at the rancid taste. Then, when there was only the sheen left of condensation, I stared into it—

not wanting to focus on anything, allowing the stupor to seep into my veins.

Only once my limbs were numb with it, and the warmth of the bar had sweat licking at my skin, I stood and stumbled back into the street.

It was an hour's ride back toward the royal camp, and before that, I had to make it to the smattering of trees outside the courtyard where I left Jett grazing.

Carts lined the square, some with busted wheels barely attached to rotting wood. Others who traveled further distances and sold in more fruitful locations had banners, marking them as the ones with favorable wares. Their meats were fresher, typically caught and killed on their journeys, their fruits shiny, polished as if newly plucked. While the stench of perished foods mixed with the smells of Luhne from the older, more worn-out carts.

It was quiet for a market day, but I supposed that's what happens when you try selling to the poor. One doesn't try very hard.

"Vegetables," one peddler tried weakly as I walked past, but when he realized I wasn't biting, he returned to flipping through the book he was reading.

A boy and a girl, him no more than ten and her looking at most fifteen, were shoving each other near a busted cart. The thing sat on one bent wheel, weeds bursting through the pavers and growing up around it. Its condition told me the hobbled cart had been there for a while. Dirt dusted a few carrots, some potatoes, and a bag of grains. But even over the street's stench, I could smell fresh bread.

The girl noticed me first. A scrawny thing that reminded me

of a twig with all of its newly grown leaves plucked off. Her messy, plaited hair nearly met her thigh, and though her face was dirtier than the boy's, I saw her brow bend in suspicion. "Whaddaya want?"

"Gwyn, mama warned you about scaring people off," the boy—only as tall as his sister's shoulder—whined and nudged her shoulder. His hair stood in all directions as if it were trying to run away. His face still had the roundness of a babe, even though I saw how bony his frame was under his torn coat.

"Is that bread?" I asked, aware that the sister—Gwyn—looked ready to attack me for bothering them. Surely, she thought I was going to haggle them.

"Made fresh this mornin'." The boy bared his missing front teeth in a smile. "And the veggies are from our garden. They won't grow very big here."

His smile fell slightly, and Gwyn straightened her shoulders, gaining another inch. "Biggest and freshest you'll find grown here."

I tapped my chin as if I were thinking it over, already sold on helping them as much as possible without drawing attention. They looked near starved and possibly like they were trying to sell the only options they had for a meal. "I'll take a bread roll and a carrot."

Gwyn was already shaking her head. "We don't trade. We only take gold. The real stuff."

Louisa had most of my gold, but I kept a few pieces just in case. More than what a lump of bread and a palm-sized carrot were worth. Gods knew they needed it more than I did.

I reached in my pocket, lumping the six coins together in

my fist, and held it out to her. Her eyes went wide at the weight but settled back as she turned, and I watched her bite a piece.

"Go on and serve the lady," she urged her brother, deciding the gold was real, while she quickly placed the rest of the wares back in a basket.

The boy took a bit of cloth and wrapped up the largest carrot and a piece of bread before placing them in my hands.

He gave me another gap-toothed grin and whispered excitedly, "I think mama will cook tonight."

A sharp whistle echoed around the nearly empty space as the two kids ran off. "Meat pies! Fit for a king!"

I took off in the opposite direction, as quickly as remaining in the shadows would allow, toward the outcropping of trees.

Jett ate the offered carrot greedily while I loosened her reins from the tree.

I waited for her to finish while I swallowed the lump of bread and distracted myself with the view. Dirt and patches of stubborn, yellowed weeds covered the peaks of the mountains in the distance.

My siblings used to tell stories of when the lake the rocks guarded beyond my father's castle was so clear you could see the sapphire-like gems at the bottom, smoothed by time alone. But time and rot had filled the lake a putrid brown, leaching out its very essence. To the point that I had a hard time believing it was ever anything other than ugly. A testament to how far the kingdom had fallen.

The clouds above were festering with the bitter rain that would soon pour out of them. My father often likened it to them weeping over his lost magic. My lip pulled away from my teeth. Disgust filled me at the thought that the lands gave a shit about him or his magic.

The sulfur smell thickened, letting me know I didn't have much time.

Looking at the black expanse of Jett's back and its sheer distance from the ground, I leaped. My leg barely made it over as land blurred beneath my feet. I regretted it each time I drank, never heavily enough for my body to grow accustomed to how it made my insides burn.

The ride back was excruciating, and if I hadn't known any better, I would have thought the stubborn mare was making things more difficult for me. The liquid in my stomach sloshed around with each movement of Jett's legs. I noticed her veering in the road to the bumpier sections or hopping over a fallen log more than once. The pounding of her hooves seemed louder, too, as if she wanted me to suffer for my behavior.

But she didn't seem to grasp that I didn't care. Part of me wished to be thrown from her back, injured in a way that the prince wouldn't want me. I hadn't asked for him, and being the youngest, I surely shouldn't be marrying first. But my father had the match in his head years ago, when I turned fifteen.

We could run. Jett and I could take off in the opposite direction and distance ourselves from everything the way my mother had always wanted to before…

But where would I go? My allies consisted of Louisa and my horse. And I was pretty sure the barmaid only tolerated me for the gold I gave her.

And what about Baltazar? Could I abandon him without a word? Even as I thought it, I was shaking my wine-fogged head.

I knew too keenly how that felt. And my people needed the continued alliance.

No, I needed to stay even as everything in me begged to run.

My chest slammed into Jett's neck as she came to a skidding halt at the edge of some ivy-coated rocks overlooking the travel-beaten road to Ellesmere. I clenched my jaw to bite back on the curse I wanted to bark at her.

She nickered while I slid from her back and mismeasured the distance to the ground. Mud splattered my face as I caught myself with my hands.

I wiped them on the sullied fabric of my cloak and ushered her toward the path as the earth around us shook with the grumbling thunder rolling above.

Hopefully, my father's party was ready to leave soon— though I wasn't excited about our destination, I damn sure didn't want to get stuck out in the storm brewing.

Wheels ground against stone, and the patter of hooves signaled that my father's traveling party was near.

I directed Jett to the meeting point, both of us tired of traveling. I knew my father had requisitioned his woodworkers to make pullable stables so the horses could rest in rotation. She would be comfortable with all the treats she desired.

We looked down on all-white horses, with lavender and yellow roses braided into their manes, pulling seven gold-lined carriages. Four guards wearing chest plates inlaid with gems flanked each.

My siblings, who undoubtedly wanted to be there as much as I did, were probably within the confines of their own rides or fawning over my father.

My father's royal carriage sat proudly in the center of the gaudy display. Carved from raw amethyst—thinned and hollowed to be light enough for the horses to pull. Even still, the carriage alone had six horses hooked to it, the largest from our stables. A plume of peacock feathers flared off the back as though it would take flight. Carvers etched Lunasa's castle into the shining exterior walls.

My father made sure to bring only the best: the best-looking carriages, the best-looking courtiers, and probably the best-looking servants and courtesans. I huffed a sigh through my nose, which Jett copied in solidarity.

Even the horse knew my father was pretentious.

Servants covered the fires, and the tents had already broken down. They were apparently waiting for me.

A stable hand in a cloak of cream and silver darted out to take Jett's reins, only after bowing deeply.

"Gods, Alec. The only one you should be kneeling for is Gemma. Get up." I ground my teeth together even as he tried to tuck his head deeper into the hood of his cloak to hide his scarlet cheeks. I pulled my bags from her saddle.

"I'm to inform you we will be leaving as soon as His Majesty Oliver returns." No sooner had he spoken than he was turning and nearly dragging Jett away as fast as his booted feet would take him.

Right, okay.

Where had my brother gone? I wondered as I looked at the line of carriages.

My feet carried me closer to the procession, and any concerns about Oliver drifted, suffocated by thoughts of how long I'd gone without seeing Baltazar and needing to give him the crown.

I could have lied to my drunken mind and perhaps convinced myself that I didn't want to burden myself with keeping the stolen item any longer than needed, but that wasn't entirely true.

Time spent away always drove me toward him when I returned. It was mortifying and one of my wicked and careless inside thoughts. I would never admit it to him unless he were to reveal the same to me first.

It wouldn't be hard to figure out which carriage would suit the king's keeper. And, of course, my father would want him close, so he would surely be with the travelers. But Baltazar would also wish to keep his dealings private.

There.

Beyond the rolling stable, a carriage carved of pine was behind the procession. The top corners had been gilded and marked with spirals, Baltazar's sigil.

"She's busy?" I heard Baltazar's rumbling voice, even muffled by the fabric-lined walls of the coach. The timber made my body ache, drawing me forward at the thought of being nearer to him. I thought again of my time away. Days, it had been days since I saw him in person.

Over the sound of my heart thudding in my ears, I heard another voice. "I lost the blood crown."

Liam?

"I told you to *distract* her. Not fail the mission." Baltazar's words were each followed by the echoing sound of pounding and the hiss of a surprised indrawn breath.

"I'm sorry, brother. I will not disappoint you again."

Distract her? What the—

My chance to process the interaction was cut short by the sound of footsteps.

I was sure whatever they discussed wasn't meant for me to hear, and one of them catching me eavesdropping wouldn't go in my favor.

"Wait." Baltazar didn't often fail to dole out punishments for missteps. His tone warned he wouldn't begin leniency then.

Liam's halted response spoke of his recognition of just that. "...Yes?"

"Break your hand." Baltazar's command chilled the blood coursing through my thumping heart. My own hand flew to cover my mouth to repress my gasp. I would have thought it a cruel joke save for the lack of laughter. The lack of... Any emotion at all.

Sure, Baltazar wasn't an easy man to please, but this was... Cruel and wicked in a way that I had never seen--at least not with Liam and me. Others, of course. Ones that disappointed him a fraction too often. But not us.

"Wh—what?" Liam's voice cracked.

"You've broken something that is mine." I could picture my mentor clearly. He would place his hands behind his neck as he leaned back and propped his feet up. A look of calm indifference would mask his face, except for the one eyebrow he cocked just a bit higher than the other. "Now, you break something that is yours. Surely you remember our father's rule."

"Baltazar." Liam sounded like he was already in agony—as if he had already experienced the pain.

The chair groaned as Baltazar leaned forward. "Either you do, or I will."

I expected a word to be my warning, but he used traditional

magic. There was only the sound of bones crunching. Then a muffled scream, as if something had confined the sound. I glanced around to see if anyone else had heard or had noticed what was happening.

Should I have stopped this? Would I have been able to?

My flustered mind's questions ceased to matter when Baltazar spoke again. "You're dismissed."

Baltazar's cocked eyebrow would have relaxed, and he would adjust further back into his chair.

Footsteps grew louder and closer as the brass knob on the door spun.

My heart beat a furious rhythm in my chest. I had nowhere to go.

I dashed around the carriage and crouched to see Liam's boots as he stepped onto the rocky trail. I waited until the crunching sound of gravel faded behind the clopping hooves and snuffs coming from the stable before moving to the door.

"I didn't think you'd come back—" Baltazar's words paused when I swung the door open and clicked it shut behind me, feeling the rough wood rubbing against my clothes. "—So soon," he finished smoothly.

But of course, I wasn't supposed to know that. He was lounging as I expected, lying on a velvet, green chaise. The one eyebrow rose again, and his hands rested underneath his neck. It was his way of putting others at ease, so they would be in their most relaxed state when they inevitably disappointed him.

I tried not to let my distaste for the putrid smell of traditional magic show. "There was a small hiccup."

"Don't tell me you couldn't retrieve the item?" His slanted, honey-colored eyes narrowed on me while he used the same tone he had with Liam. The one before he made his brother break a hand. Anger, laced with frustration. And it made me wonder, how much was a façade? Because he already knew what Liam knew. That we destroyed the crown along with the treasury.

I pulled the blood crown from my coat. Despite what I just heard, I smiled, pleased with myself at his widened eyes even if he immediately composed himself. "I always deliver."

"You most certainly do." He stretched and rolled off the chaise, a corner of his mouth lifted. "Then what, may I ask, was the hiccup?"

Your brother and second in command—on your orders, I thought brazenly. But the nearer he got to me, the faster my thoughts muddled, and my heartbeat quickened. The smell of tobacco and cedar wrapped around me. My neck heated, and I was sure it would be rosy if I looked in a mirror. He was several years my senior, but witches aged... Very well.

Baltazar is your mentor, I reminded myself. His rough hand slid up the side of my neck, and he stroked my cheek with his thumb. It threatened to unravel me—to do away with any secrets I was withholding and loosen my tongue, which was precisely his goal. He had to know the power he held over me.

How much do you know? He seemed to ask without even speaking, meeting my eyes. A crooked grin flashed. Long enough to show me he was pleased before taking the crown from my hands and pulling away.

He may as well have splashed ice water in my face. I grappled for words that wouldn't give away how flustered I was. He needed to value me. Despite his orders for Liam... Orders for his brother to distract me... There was a reason. "Liam. He distracted me. Or tried to."

"Ah, but a pretty face did not so easily sway you?" His expression was a cold, emotionless mask again. I should have asked why he wanted me to be swayed by his brother—especially since he was the one to set up the encounter. But I felt that if I mentioned it, Baltazar would be furious. And the center of my emotions for him--at the very core of them--lay a bit of fear.

Every lie must be grounded in truth. I heard the lesson in my head. "At first, yes. But he underestimated me."

Baltazar dragged a hand through his white hair while watching my mouth, feeling the weight of my words as I said them. "Do you fancy the boy?"

"Wh—what? No." I hadn't thought about Liam like that in years...

Was that why Baltazar sent him to distract me? Had he wanted to test me?

He waved his hand. "Go."

"Excuse me?" He hadn't even asked me to give him my report... He was supposed to offer me a drink while I gave him the details of my heist.

He schooled his expression into a blank, unreadable stare and went back to lounging in his chaise, eyes closed. "You're excused."

A dismissal.

CHAPTER 3

Stepping from the carriage was agony setting my insides ablaze.

He dismissed me. Why did he care if I gave a shit about Liam? I didn't, of course, though I could recognize his cruel attraction. But I put that to rest years ago, and my focus was only on the plan, Baltazar's goal, which he needed *me* to fulfill.

Gooseflesh spread along my skin at the thought. A white-hot flame licked its way up my arms and neck just thinking of him.

I suppose he would miss it with his duties as my mentor. *Or maybe*, my mind whispered, *it's because you're human.*

No. I thought, even as my heart thudded against my ribs. My mentor never cared about that. *But neither had Liam.* I banished the treacherous thought as my fingers brushed my cheek where his thumb had been. He so rarely touched me, even in lessons, that he may as well have branded me.

"Jane." Gods, I hated that name.

My mother once told me the name was the mortals' most plain name.

Why then? I asked. Why name me that way? She had paused as if wanting to snatch the words back to avoid that conversation.

"Because Janie," my mother had flicked her eyes around the library, looking for the spies she swore watched her. "I hate magic."

"But you're magic. I'm magic." I touched the charm on my necklace to hers. Our talismans.

She gave me a wicked smile she used to save just for me. "Maybe you won't be."

Then she died, I thought, bringing me back to the present. Leaving me torn between hatred for magic that was my birthright and my desire to succumb to it in all its danger and beauty.

"Jane..." My sister, Driata, huffed a breath as if she sprinted all the way from the castle though she couldn't have gone more than a few yards. "Meeting...messenger...Ellesmere" Another gasp of air. But I knew what she was going to say. "Under attack."

My eyes widened, and I pulled from the real emotion I was feeling to make it more believable. I *was* shocked that they had figured it out so quickly. I obviously knew the treasury had been robbed. But under attack? They would never suspect me— plain, mundane Jane.

"We have to go." Driata gripped my wrist, and her free hand grabbed the ruby dangling at her throat. Even if he were less than twenty feet away, she would use magic—like she was rubbing it in my face. "Father is furious."

I closed my eyes; the rotten smell of sulfur filled the air as her magic surrounded us. She didn't need words. No, she only needed her talisman. Mine—the one my father gifted me on my sixth birthday—was a dud... Or I was. Until Baltazar took me on as his student and taught me a cleaner magic. One that wasn't paired with the putrid rotting smell of traditional magic, making me wonder why it was frowned upon.

"People tend to fear the things they don't understand instead of learning how to master them," Baltazar said with a light in his eyes that I'd heard others whisper was crazed. I didn't think it was lunacy, though. It was inspired.

Opening my eyes, I tried to squelch the urge I had to empty the contents of my stomach. They were all there, all five of my siblings. There was Oliver and Olivia, twins and two halves of one whole, partners in malice by far the worst of all my siblings. Then there was Driata. The one with more suitors lined up than the rest and entertained each one with cunning and a coy smile. Ciaran, who desperately aspired to be like Oliver, would fall on his own blade to prove it. And Gemma, who didn't care for any of us.

It was hard not to notice how similar they were, born of the same mother from different times when they were gathered like that. Sure, Oliver and Olivia's cheeks were sharper, Ciaran's nose a bit broader, Driata's skin a tinge more bronze, and Gemma's cheeks rosier, but ultimately the resemblances to their mothers were uncanny, with our father's genetics barely pitching an effort. I had the same red hair as them, though mine was fairer. But my eyes were green where theirs were hazel.

Moreover, my frame was wider and shorter, while they were all tall and lean.

I looked at Driata's auburn hair pinned to hide her ringlets, which she claimed hating to tame, and wondered how the gods must laugh. Wherever they were—it had to be one of their grandest jokes to make six people look so alike but think and act so differently.

I peered at the frail vessel of my father, sitting on his makeshift throne. His face showed his years, and his bones jutted through the layers of clothes he wore to stay warm. It was a task to set my features to neutrality as he smiled at me. But was that kohl under his eyes? Rouge on his cheeks? Had he done it to make himself appear less far gone?

The curse would wear him down until the next reincarnation of my grandmother was born, aged, and remarried to him. Part of me wished he turned to dust before then. I didn't want another reminder of my mother or another sibling to torture me, though it was by their own father's mistake that I was born.

My father stood using Sefar, his favored sword's scabbard, as a cane and stepped forward. "My children. There has been a great defilement of Ellesmere."

He didn't *look* furious, though I wasn't sure he had the energy left in him to be angry. He motioned for Oliver to step forward, his eldest son, his heir. My brother bowed deeply and held out a piece of crumpled parchment to my father.

As my father cleared his throat, I heard the first smattering of raindrops pelting the carriage roof. "We received a message from King Maveri, stating Ellesmere's attack. The treasury is in shambles, as well as one of his castle towers. He has invited us to visit but has requested to postpone the premarital celebrations."

"The prince probably did it himself to avoid his engagement to Jane."

"They're already engaged, idiot."

"Though I'm not sure it was a fair match."

"I'm not staying in a demolished castle, father!"

"Certainly not for *Jane*."

"The scandal this sham is causing already."

"This attack makes the mad king look weak."

"Are you sure you would want to be allied with him?"

I looked out the window as my siblings spoke over each other and watched the edges of the glass begin to fog. We needed to decide what we were going to do quickly. The roads would flood soon.

"Enough." Though his voice was as frail as his body, it still managed to echo around the cab. "We honor our commitment and aid our ally as they have us." He narrowed his eyes and looked each of his children in the face. His expression softened when it fell on me.

If looks could maim, the one Oliver gave me would have flayed me alive. "Father, I have taken upon myself to requisition more servants for our journey. Maveri's letter mentions several of his are indisposed with the cleanup."

"Level-headed and always thinking ahead, my son." My father patted Oliver's shoulder and allowed a small smile before resting his head back on the wall. Slowly as it was, we all knew what it signified. He released us until someone had more information. My siblings magicked themselves away, and my nose scrunched.

I didn't know if I could ever get used to it. I couldn't understand how they seemed so unfazed. The scent, especially when so many people used magic at once, was overpowering and nauseating. My stomach turned while my head throbbed.

Needing to get out of there to find my carriage, I reached for the door. Once I got there, I could go over everything that had happened.

"Janie." My feet felt leaden. He wasn't supposed to call me that, and he knew it too. It was my mother's pet name for me. But nothing stopped him. Not me demanding he stop, not the names my siblings tortured me with in response.

Slowly, I turned back to face my father. His eyes, set into the hollow sockets on his face, twitched to the left of me where Oliver still stood. "Leave us."

Oliver looked as if he wanted to protest, but he raised his hand to his talisman, a crow carved from emerald hanging on a studded chain.

He vanished, but the smell of magic lingered as if in a warning.

"I have things to attend to." I didn't want to play the game. My palms still burned from the rope that had bit into them. I dug my nails in any way.

He tapped Sefar's scabbard on the floor. "You have plenty of time."

Shrugging, I inched closer to the door.

"Still no magic?" He leaned forward, hoping I would tell him my powers had come overnight. Perhaps it gave him hope for his own.

My lip curled away from my teeth. Despite the king's gentleness with me, I could never forgive him for what he had done and caused. "You understand the devastation of being powerless, so there's no need to discuss it further."

"Do you think you need a new talisman?" He fingered the owl pendant at his throat, a near copy of the one he had made for my mother.

He was already speaking again as I shook my head. "Perhaps, I can have one made before you move to the other side of Anwyn."

The only good part about my arranged wedding was that I would be permanently on the other side of the continent.

"No."

"It's been three years since—" I stopped listening, already knowing what he would say. I wouldn't have him blaming my acting out on my mother's death.

I spun on my heel, my mind whirring with all the ways he could punish me for leaving. All the ways he would have if he weren't a shell of the man, he once was in a time before I knew him. I stomped from the cab, ignoring him as he shouted for me to wait.

Desperate for escape as I was, I ran straight into Oliver before I saw him.

"What could the king possibly need to speak with you about?" He grabbed my chin in his hand and forced me to look up at him.

"Magic. Always magic." It would never change. Well... Perhaps that wasn't exactly true. He would probably lose his focus on me when he took a new wife.

His lip curled, no doubt thinking how pathetic it was that I still wasn't presented with the craft. "He's not suggesting you call off the wedding?"

Coaching my face neutral, I reminded myself there was no

chance of that. When my father had his mind set on something, he was relentless. "Why would he?"

"You remember that cheap replica your mother had made for him?" His lip curled away from his teeth at the memory.

A glass sword. A miniature replica of Sefar. It sat amongst gold and gems in an aged trunk in our own treasury back in Lunasa. Cast away and aside. My father hated the replica, saying its mere existence had blasphemed Sefar's existence, which was exactly why my mother had it made.

"I'm trying to keep up, dear brother, but I can't fathom where you're going with this." A muscle in his jaw ticked as I spoke. Perhaps because I mentioned our familial ties. How could he have a family member that was so powerless?

"Father said the Sefar replica was a mockery of the real thing." His nails dug into my cheeks as he spat each word. "But I think you—a spiteful child—know what it truly is. A mockery of the fantastic. A spitting image of something magic. Like you. You look like us, but you will always be ordinary. Uninspired. Useless, like that wasted piece of glass."

My face bruised under his grip. I wanted so badly to spell him, but I could barely move my jaw.

Don't let him win but let him think he has bested you. Baltazar's voice echoed in my mind. I bowed my head, every bit the fragile human my brother believed me to be.

"Get out of my sight." He shoved, and my shoulder slammed into the wall of the carriage. My nostrils flared, and I bit down hard enough on my cheek to draw blood.

Not now. Not yet.

The rain splashed onto my face, cooling my heated cheeks. I

focused on my squelching boots on the muddied ground as I counted my breaths.

I needed to get away before I used the blood flooding my mouth to do something I regretted. I hated all my siblings, but Oliver... Gods. I wished I could tally the days until his death.

Three carriages behind my father's sat an all-white carriage save for its gold door. Carved feathers framed a cursive J.

Mine then.

Never mind the fact that only one of these carriages could probably feed the entire populace of Luhne if my father sold it. That didn't matter to my family, and I supposed it wasn't supposed to matter to me. My mind wandered to the pair of children I met that day in the square. Dirty, hungry, the girl so young to have her trust in the world broken. The boy still had a light in his eyes that I hoped the world wouldn't extinguish. But I feared just as quickly that it would diminish with time.

The wind from the growing storm chilled the golden handle, biting my fingers as I twisted it. The golden handle was chilled from the wind of the rising storm. I pulled the door open and stepped into the lavish cab. The air was warmer, with coals burning low in a metal tray by the door. Though curtains darkened the space, lanterns hung from the ceiling at different lengths casting almost a feigned starlight on the walls. Straight ahead was a copper tub, steaming with water and smelling of fresh lavender. Clearly just drawn and heated by one of the servants. Towels and soaps lined shelves and bars that circled it. Draped over a rack, near a floor-length mirror, was a silver gown. No doubt it would be as extravagant as everything else my father had brought for the trip.

My eyes widened when they landed on the bed where Liam

was propped up and examined me like a starved viper, and I was a cornered mouse. Heat spread from my chest up to my neck. What was he doing there? He was casually sitting amongst the decorative pillows on my bed.

I looked back out the door before swinging it closed behind me.

He couldn't be there. If anyone had seen him... No, he had to go.

"You—" My hands clenched into fists at my sides.

He pulled one of the white, fur throw pillows into his lap and pulled at the threading absently. "I take it the wedding is still moving forward?"

"Of course, it is."

"I just assumed since the bride-to-be blew up several parts of the castle..." He shrugged as if the words he was saying weren't damning. "The princeling may have reconsidered."

"Keep your voice down," I hissed, trying to listen for sounds around the carriage over the rain.

"What's with the worry, Princess? We're alone." He lifted his shoulders again, and I tried to tell myself that meant nothing.

Alone. The word thudded around my empty mind. I tried to summon an ounce of the courage I saw Driata use when she dealt with suitors.

Explosives? Sure. A heist on my future family's treasury, yea. But I didn't know how to react to the man being in my bed... again. How had he even gotten there without being noticed? Though I supposed he wouldn't have used the door.

"Liam." I wanted to match his unfeeling tone. But his name

came out as more of a question. "Tug on your talisman and get the hell out of here."

"What happened to your face?"

"What?" My fingers touched my jaw before moving to my cheeks. Blood had dried in half-moons where Oliver had grabbed me, and his nails had dug in.

"What happened to your face?" His words were clipped with anger underneath them like a sharpened blade.

What happened to your hand? The question was at the edge of my tongue as I glanced down at his curled, disfigured fingers. But he wouldn't answer, and I already knew.

Instead, I told myself I was protecting Oliver from Liam, not the other way around. I drew my shoulders inward. "It must have happened in the heist."

He cleared the space between us almost faster than I could blink. Pillows scattered on the floor in his wake. I could smell the spice of bourbon on his breath. "You think I wouldn't notice if something had marred your face?"

His thumb brushed the blemished skin on my face. Somehow, he knew I was lying. He could always tell, despite my training. Despite my multiple attempts to keep him out of reach, he was always there. Watching. Knowing.

Fuck.

"Who did this to you?" Liam's face was inches from mine. His body pinned me to the door as if he could see the fingerprints left by my brother if he only got close enough. "Baltazar? Oliver?"

"A branch—It must have been a branch on my ride." Lie. He knew it, too, if the flash of rage in his eyes told me anything.

Another lie—one I was telling myself? I was breathless

because he was crushing me against the door, not because he was that close.

"You don't want to tell me? Fine." He shoved away from me. "I might remind you that we have eyes everywhere. And it's my family's pockets that pay them."

I could tell he would leave as his anger shifted from the person who harmed me and directed toward me instead. "Liam, wait."

"When I find out who did this...he'll die." He lifted his hand to his talisman, but his eyes never left me.

"I never even said it was a man." He had left me breathless, and I thought he would go before I got out the words. But as soon as I said them, I wished I could take them back. To him, it was more a confirmation than if I just kept my mouth shut.

Liam nodded, even as his silhouette faded. "Your cut is on your nightstand."

It was as if I had imagined the pine and spice scent of him and the way his body had touched mine. Yet, it was as if he had never been there at all.

My knees nearly buckled, and I told myself it was from the adrenaline of the heist or the ride. But that's the funny thing about lies... They don't work as well when you tell them to yourself.

I dragged myself toward the bed, not bothering to pick up the discarded pillows, and kicked off my boots before climbing under my heavy covers. I wasn't expecting to get much sleep that night, but when I closed my eyes, I dreamed.

"No." My voice was raw, dripping with fear as the word slipped free from my tongue.

Blood. Bright, crimson-colored blood. Fresh blood, and there was so much of it. Coating the ground, splattered on my cheeks, and caked underneath my fingernails. My mother's blood. Her life's blood had confettied out of her like some sick pinata. I tried to run, to push off the pavement, to scream. But I had been screaming for what felt like hours.

No help came.

Taking a rasping breath, I pressed my scraped palms against the cracked concrete and lifted my chin. My eyes narrowed, and my jaw hurt where I had been grinding my teeth together. "If you're going to kill me, do it."

"I never wanted it to come to this, Darling."

"I don't even know you. Stop calling me that."

"Elyse. You know me, as I do you. You must feel them—the memories washing back over you as they have in the centuries before."

"I don't know what you're rambling about. My name is Kore."

Throwing my hands up, I blocked the red light flashing from the arms of his robes, searing my eyes. "Who are you? What are you?

His voice vibrated against my skull as he grew nearer. "You may be repressing your truest self here, in the lands of the mundane, in a world of mortals. But you'll remember when I bring you home."

"I'm not going anywhere with you." My jeans frayed at the knees as I scrambled backward. "You're a murderer. A lunatic."

The light pulsed, blurring everything and scattering the darkness before it consumed me whole.

Gasping breaths of the jasmine-scented night air felt like jagged glass in my lungs and throat. Sweat coated my forehead, and I noticed my tangled sheets as I stretched my back. Rubbing my shaking hand against my drooping eyelids, I tried to collect each fading piece of the fragmented dream.

That my mother's stories still haunted me was unsettling, but what bothered me more was my inability to retain more than small pieces each time I opened my eyes. She had always favored the dark over the lovely.

She never told me stories about a band of dwarves or a kind-hearted prince saving the princess. No, she told me one story on repeat, about a crazed king who killed her mother--his reincarnated queen and stole away with her bastard daughter.

Gooseflesh rose on my skin, and I realized that the lanterns and the coals must've burned down sometime during the night.

I stepped into my boots and walked to a lantern on my shelf. I turned the knob, and it cast an orange-tinted filter around the room.

My stomach let out a low rumble, reminding me I hadn't eaten dinner. The swaying, rocky movement of the cab reminded me exactly where I was. In a carriage, bound for Ellesmere.

The rain had died down, but in the quiet, I could hear the sloshing sound of the wheels rolling through puddles. The hooting call of an owl searching for its prey. I sat on the end of my bed and readied myself for a long night.

CHAPTER 4

Just before sunrise, the carriage jerked to a stop. I drew back the curtains hours before, far too alert to sleep. A knock on the door sounded, and I glanced at the sack of coins Liam left beside my bed the night prior. Grabbing them, I stuffed them in my satchel and stood.

Twisting open the door, I couldn't move my feet as panic coursed through me. Three women stood below the step, looking at me. Two I didn't recognize—who stumbled over each other in deep curtsies—one with greyed hair and crinkles around her eyes, the other with a sharp nose and a whiskered chin. The third... Louisa stood slightly behind them, her brown hair braided over her shoulder.

None wore talismans, marking them as commoners. Nobles and royals were the only ones allowed to wear the magic-wielding jewels.

My eyes widened in shock and question, but it was the older

woman who turned to me with a smile. "The crowned prince and guards came to Luhne for new workers."

The younger one gave me a wide-toothed grin. "Offered us more gold daily than we'd make in a year."

Ah. "And what are you doing *here*?" My eyes flicked to Louisa, but she focused on the plant on my nightstand.

"We're your new handmaids." The old woman smoothed her tattered skirts and looked at the floor.

"Sent by Oliver?" Two bobbing heads answered me while Louisa turned to me with brows drawn and a tight frown.

Spies.

"Alright." I could've sworn I heard the elderly woman sigh as I agreed. "What are your names?"

Louisa cleared her throat. "I'm Lou. I'll be your seamstress."

It was the most I had ever heard her speak, causing me enough surprise that I forgot there were others around. "You sew?"

"Yes, *Your Royal Highness*." Her words were curt, followed by a stiff but dramatic curtsy.

Lou and I never shared pleasantries. So much so that I didn't know she preferred the name Lou. And she thought that I was simply a thief. I never told her my title, but in fairness, she never asked.

"Edera, and this is Agatha. Kindly met, Your highness." I noted that the younger woman, Edera, spoke more confidently than Agatha.

I walked to my desk, and sat in the cushioned chair, sighing before speaking. "Please, call me Jane."

"We couldn't—" Agatha started, but I held up my hand.

"I won't respond to anything else."

Another nod.

"Your Highness—Jane," Edera corrected herself, as her shoulders pulled inward. "We're supposed to see that you're ready."

"For what?" I straightened. Even as I asked, I knew.

An exchanged look between the two as if they were pulling straws for who would tell me.

Agatha lost. "You'll be the head of the royal procession today."

For a moment, I saw red. Focusing on a blank stone, I worked to control my breathing. It wasn't their fault, any of theirs, that I was being forced to go through with it. It wasn't their fault that I didn't want to. Though, in fairness, had I put up much of a fight? *No. Because my father always gets what he wants. My mother was proof of that.*

My breathing steadied, and I looked down at my clothes that were still in shambles. "I do need to bathe."

"We'll draw you a bath." Agatha smiled, and though she was his spy, I saw the pride there. The seemingly silent promise that she would not shirk her responsibilities and wanted to earn her living.

They needed the money, probably to feed their families, maybe to pay their tabs. I didn't know, but I wouldn't stop them from earning it.

I would have to be more careful, but them being there didn't change anything. And though the thought of being waited on and watched made my stomach clench, I would give them bits that they could give back to Oliver. Nothing I couldn't afford to lose, but enough that they would be thanked generously by the crown itself.

After the women stripped me of my clothes and threatened to toss them into a raging fire, they plucked, scrubbed, filed, rubbed, and primped some more.

Agatha sucked in a breath when she saw my hands and rubbed a burning salve on them before rinsing them away. I hissed at her like a feral cat, but the pain in them subsided quickly, taking away the sting of an almost infection.

Only after my body pruned and smelled like jasmine on the night air did they declare that they worked their own form of magic and allowed me to step out.

I pulled on the silken robe that Agatha held out, trying to tell myself that everything was okay and that it was normal. But with six eyes on me, I felt my neck heat and tugged the straps closed even tighter.

"You two may leave. Only one of us needs to tie the ribbon." Lou made a shoo-ing motion with her hand.

Agatha and Edera only looked between each other, then at me. "Go. I'm sure Oliver has other tasks for you."

It was cruel, taking even the slightest joy in the way they scurried from the room like they were mice, and I caught them while holding a broom. But they *were* spies.

Not very good ones either, by the way, their whispering voices slid right through the door like it was made of parchment.

"What do we do now?"

"Speak with the prince."

"About what? She's done nothing but soak."

"Yes, but did you see the state of her when we walked in?"

"As if she'd been romping in the woods with brutes."

"One minute Jane," Lou shouted right in front of me,

throwing her voice to the door. "I forgot my pins. I'll just run out and get them."

My hand slapped over my mouth to hide my laughter until I could no longer hear the pair running away from the carriage.

The barmaid turned seamstress spun on me, forgoing all pleasantries and smiles as she drew her face inches from mine. "What are you trying to do?"

"What—nothing? What are you doing here?" I whispered, hoping she would take the hint.

"Me?" Her voice raised higher, and my eyes darted to the door considering the handmaids could walk back in. "Tell me, Princess, how many years would you serve for treason?"

"Lose your business? The pub? You're risking it to be here?"

"I risked it by helping a thief. One that I thought cared about the people when she stands in her tower smelling like petals, wrapped in silk."

"I'm not—I do." I grappled for words, for anything to explain that I did care. But my fumbling mouth settled on, "Why are you helping Oliver to spy?"

"The *money*, Jane!" She threw her hands up as she screamed. "The gold you give helps but isn't enough. It's never been enough. The money could feed the people who come to the pub. Warm their bellies with more than just stale, watered-down ale."

Feeling like she slapped me, I realized she was right. Of course, she was. It was the reason I let them stay. They needed the gold Oliver offered, and it was more than even I made in a year, surely.

Lou seemed calmer now, resigning herself to believing she

hadn't been found out. Our secret and very illegal dealings remained just that. Her shoulders sagged as she pulled a cushioned pedestal into the center of the room. "Stop standing there stupidly and let me do my job. Give me something I can tell him."

Embroidered gems stabbed into my bare feet as I stepped up. "I can't. There's nothing I can give you that won't put the little I'm able to do under scrutiny."

"What about your clothes? Why *were* they torn?" Lou rifled through a trunk by the door before apparently finding what she was looking for. She stood carrying a stiff piece of folded fabric.

"I don't wear corsets." My ribs ached just imagining the bruising from the first and only time I was forced to wear one.

"I've been informed you don't have an option." Lou grimaced, clearly as pleased as me when given orders. "The gown won't fit otherwise."

"Pants are preferable anyway." I pulled the ribbons on the robe tighter around my waist, feeling the smooth fabric riding up on my thighs.

She shrugged her shoulders, and a frown tugged at her lips. "No one packed you any pants."

I forced my fingers to loosen on the fabric and sucked down a deep breath. Probably my last one of the day. "Alright."

The barmaid turned seamstress walked over with her face scrunched in thought. "Why they're forcing you to go to all this trouble when he'll see what's underneath on your wedding night, escapes me."

"Because by then, it will be too late." I hadn't thought much of the wedding when I could avoid it, let alone the wedding night. It wasn't that I hadn't been with a man. I had.

And some jobs had taken me out of Lunasa, and I had encounters that meant nothing at all. But how could it mean nothing if we were married?

Lou yanked the laces on the back of the corset, and I sputtered a cough. Just as I caught my breath, she tugged again. "One more deep breath."

"I can't retract my ribcage." As it was, my breaths were short, labored.

"Right, okay," she grunted, securing the ribbon. "You never answered me, though. Give me something I can tell the prince."

Avoiding looking at her, I glanced down at my midsection, but I could barely see my feet over my breasts spilling out of the top. Gods, why was that considered the only way to be beautiful? All I could think of was how my bones would be aching by the end of the day.

Lou lifted the silver gown over the steam from the tub and shook it out before crossing back over to me while pulling pins out of the front pocket of her stained apron. The same one I saw her wearing each time I went to the pub.

In that lighting, I could tell where the white was browning and fraying. How the pocket was close to coming off, and she restitched it with colorful threads and patches of fabrics. Lou clearly fixed it with whatever she had on hand.

"You should tell Oliver that Agatha and Edera are right." She gave me a questioning look as she gestured for me to step into the fabric. "I took a half-wild lover, and we've been rutting in the woods like animals."

She sucked in a breath that turned into a heaving, snorting laugh, and I nearly fell from the stool when I joined her.

When she righted herself, she fastened buttons and secured

the bodice with thread. "That wouldn't bother you? The thought of your family thinking you a whore?"

I shrugged, gaining another prick to my arm. "It's better than the alternative."

She gave a sharp inhale and placed her hand on her chest. "That they think you're celibate?"

Unable to bring myself to laugh at her joke, I met her eyes as the weight of my answer settled on my chest before I even spoke the words. "That they know I've been robbing them and giving the money away."

Her head jerked in a nod. She knew the dangers and would be implicated if anyone ever followed me.

When she finished dressing me, she stepped back and scrunched her nose. "I didn't make this one."

I didn't even cast a glance at the mirror. Frankly, I didn't want to know. I gestured my thanks and swung open the door to the carriage, stepping out in the sunlight.

The bodice on the gown paired with the corset was so tight, that I could barely breathe, let alone bend naturally. I stumbled when I reached the ground and sputtered when my lungs could not fully refill with air.

If I died because of a gown, I would consider it a personal slight from the gods. I stomped towards the royal carriage, readying myself to see my father and the others. I would never understand why my siblings worshiped my father the way they did.

They treated him as though the life he cursed us all to was normal. My siblings, as full witches, had already lived longer lifetimes with more time still. And each had suffered through their mother's death. But how were they okay? I would never understand how someone could accept such a loss even as time passed.

Five lifetimes. My father had been alive for five lifetimes. Far longer than most, but had he really lived when his curse stole the life of his queen over and over? The First Queen died the youngest. My father and his original wife cast their spell when they were twenty-five. She passed the very next day.

My grandmother was the only other incarnation to pass before her time, at only thirty-eight when my father killed her. His ignorance of aging in the mortal realm created confusion when he fell upon my grandmother and her nineteen-year-old daughter. Or perhaps it was only wishful thinking that fueled his lunacy when he struck down his true bride.

I shook my head to ward off the memory. I couldn't think of that when I was about to deal with *them*.

The door swung open, and Driata offered me a small smile that I didn't bother returning. She knew I didn't want to be there, marrying a man I hardly knew.

"It could be worse," she had offered before I left the stables with Jett five days prior. *Arius was crafted of a maiden's wet dreams.*

"In those dreams, are they being wed against their will?" I threw my leg over Jett's back, not wanting her answer.

"Some women fantasize, I'm certain." A small, knowing smile tugged at her mouth.

Not me. *"I'm the youngest of four sisters far more suited to this arrangement. Why not one of you?"*

"Father wanted to see that you were taken care of without your magic...and after—"

I ushered Jett and ridden off, not wanting to hear the

excuses again. It was political and unwise politics if anyone had cared to ask me.

"We're waiting for you." She waved her hand towards the carriage's interior, and I pulled my lip between my teeth.

If I climbed in, that was it. We would be heading to Ellesmere, and the engagement would be official.

"Come along, *Jane*," Gemma whined from within. "You may as well finally show us the ring."

Leave it to the hopeless romantic to not care that Arius proposed, but care about the ring.

Ciaran feigned a whisper. "He didn't even offer it to her. He sent messengers with it. Probably worried that her hideous face will make him run off with the help."

"That feels self-deprecating given that you all look alike." Liam's voice was gruff as if he was waking.

Driata offered her hand again, and when I took it, she hauled me into the carriage. I only realized my mistake in giving her my left hand when she started squawking about the size of the ruby. She waved my arm back and forth at our siblings, and my father like it wasn't attached to me.

I looked up in time to see my father's beaming smile. Though, he didn't direct it at me but the man who sat beside him.

Baltazar sat between my father and Liam, staring at the rock on my finger with narrowed eyes. No doubt he was trying to figure my way out of it.

"In all the years you've been my advisor, this is by far the grandest idea you've ever had." My father's words directed at my mentor sucked the air out of my lungs and left the cab stifling.

Baltazar simply nodded his approval before turning his focus to a scroll he had in his hands.

"Have you and the prince talked about children? You'll be the first of us." Gemma's voice held a touch of dreams and an ounce of bitterness, but the words bounced around my skull.

I couldn't breathe. I was a pretty bird, with a painted beak, bred for breeding. While it was political, I hadn't considered it had been Baltazar's suggestion. What was his goal? Why had he kept it from me? We kept secrets from others, sure, but not each other.

A warm hand grasped mine, but my eyes were still on Baltazar's tilted head, on the crease in his forehead that told me he was deep in thought. Whatever was on the scroll was awfully important at that exact moment.

"A ring fit for a queen." Liam's tone was soft, almost imperceptible, as the pad of his thumb ran along with my fourth finger.

I snatched my hand from his, and my eyes darted around the space. I moved to steal a seat nearest the window on the other side of the cab, smoothing my shaking and sweating hands over the skirt of my gown.

"The servants prepared breakfast. You should eat something." Driata offered me a silver plate with eggs, bite-sized bits of meat, and a bread roll.

"If I eat that, I'll explode from this gown." It was harder still to breathe while sitting, but I took the plate and sat it on my lap.

"Yes, and Gods forbid the princeling knows you breathe." Liam sighed while looking out his window. "The horror."

Baltazar looked up finally, glancing at my gown, then the plate in my hand. "I think she'll be fine without the extra food."

And just like that, I was no longer hungry though I hadn't eaten since the day prior. He was right, of course. There would be plenty of food in Ellesmere.

CHAPTER 5

I t wasn't long before the screeching sound of metal filled the cab as the gates into Ellesmere palace were opening.

"Remember children..." my father began, trailing off for us to finish his thought.

"Presentation is key," we chorused. Though each of us seemed to wish we could jump out of the carriage for opposing reasons.

He looked us each in the eye as he spoke, a clear warning in his tone. "This engagement will bode well for each of you when it comes time for matches, and it would serve you all well to remember that."

He looked nervous. I couldn't recall a time his posture was so rigid or his jaw that tense. Gemma patted his arm absently, proving she could sense it too. Perhaps he was worried my siblings' hatred of me would cause them to make a mockery of the meeting.

Truthfully, I had never hoped for anything more.

It wasn't fair to Arius that I hadn't given him a chance. I understood that. He could have been the perfect gentleman—and he had been the one time we met before.

The day I turned fifteen, Maveri Alistair and his son had come to my father's blessings ball—the celebration dubbed such due to my mother and I sharing the same days of birth. Arius had asked me to dance, I had accepted, and Liam had pummeled him afterward. You can't really beat the shit out of a prince without consequence.

Unless you were Baltazar's brother.

The pair sat so close and yet looked like the forest we rode through had grown directly between them. They dressed up, both in black suits with satin lapels. Baltazar's had a pin with his swirling sigil, marking him as my father's right hand.

In contrast to their night-colored attire, my family was outfitted regally, all in shades of gold. The gowns my sisters wore were glittering, possibly with shards of it. And my father and brothers looked as if their seamstresses had spun the thread from thousands of coins.

Looking out the window, I saw the canopy of trees casting a feigned twilight upon the drive. Moss curtained above and magically kept a carpet of marigolds in bloom along the path no matter how many wheels or boots tracked across it.

Like everything else the mad king did, it was extravagant.

My *visit* had taught me that the palace lay at the end of the tunnel, sitting tall on a cliff overlooking where land met the sea.

"Don't be nervous," Driata whispered as if we weren't crammed in the cab with too many other ears.

"Everything's fine." I released a breath through my nose as the corners of the cab blurred. Perhaps I should have opened the window to allow some fresh air. *Maybe I wasn't fine...*

"If I were you, I would be worried the prince had found a stone more entertaining." Ciaran snorted a laugh while glancing toward Oliver and Olivia. When their stiff faces gave way to no amusement, the laughter quickly turned to a feigned cough.

The twins ignored their eager devotee for some reason, and they had been unusually quiet for the ride. If I looked closely enough, I thought I saw some slight purpling on the peak of Oliver's cheek, but it could have been the lighting.

"I don't think he'll have trouble with Jane amusing him." Gemma tilted her head to the side as she spoke. "That dress makes her look like a lady of the night."

My father choked out a cough in surprise, his cheeks turning ruddy at the implication. He wouldn't correct her, though. Of course not. Even as she insulted me, she was doting on him, fixing the cuff of his sleeve.

What would he think of his sweet daughter when he found out about Alec, the stable hand?

"Funny you should say that," Liam said with a chuckle, pausing to tip a glass flask to his mouth. The brown liquid sloshed inside as he twisted the cap back closed and leaned around his brother to look at Gemma. "I was going to ask you if the gown was yours."

My brows rose in shock, even as a muscle ticked in Baltazar's jaw, and he snatched the container from Liam. "Apologize."

"For what exactly?" Liam offered his brother a tight-lipped smile, almost looking genuine in his curiosity.

My father cleared his throat, clearly done waiting for

Baltazar to step in further. "I do believe you just called a *princess* a *whore*."

"Apologies, Your Majesty. But I do believe Princess Gemma called a princess one first." Liam leaned forward, propping his chin in his hand and leaning out of Baltazar's eye line.

"Baltazar." My father clicked Sefar's scabbard on the cab floor, seemingly to get his keeper's attention. "You told me he would not become a problem. Did you not?"

"Forgive him. It's been a long journey. The boy must be tired." I didn't watch Baltazar as he spoke but Liam, whose mouth twitched as if he had more to say.

He seemed to give up altogether, huffing a sigh. Then his silver eyes met mine. There was no cruelty in his face for once, not even a witty smile. Instead, his mouth pulled down in a frown, and his broad shoulders sagged down.

I wanted to force my eyes away, feeling the thick tension within the cab. The silence was a deafening drumbeat as no one spoke. Not even Ciaran, with his constant need to hear his own voice.

An arm wrapped in black fabric reached around Liam's back, making it seem like Baltazar was comforting his drunken brother. But I knew what it meant. He spoke out of turn, perhaps even embarrassing Baltazar, which wouldn't do. A lesson in etiquette was coming.

I glanced at Liam's lame hand, curled in his lap, having not been healed. Why hadn't he healed it? And more importantly, why would I care?

The carriage rolling to a stop silenced my thoughts.

My thoughts were silenced as the carriage rolled to a stop.

"Princess." Baltazar's voice cut through me as he nodded in

my direction. It was always strange hearing him use the title. I much preferred my name when spoken from his lips. "—escorting your father."

"What?" Heat spread from my neck up towards my cheeks. What had he said?

"You will exit with me first, Janie." My father's use of that cursed name washed away any of the thoughts I was having about my mentor. "Your fiancé is supposed to greet us."

I unfolded myself from the seat. Dread was pooling in my gut. There was no backing out now, nowhere to run.

Hands smoothed my copper-colored coils gently from behind, and I tensed. Driata murmured as though only for me, "smile, Jane. You're so beautiful when you smile."

I was overly aware of my face. Too conscious of the grimace that formed on my mouth. I looked at Baltazar, hoping to find a smile of his own. One I could mimic. I only had to pretend. How hard could that be? I did it all the time.

But I found him turning to Liam, his fist white-knuckling the back of his brother's jacket.

Bony fingers pulled at my wrist as my father wrapped my arm through his while using Sefar to balance.

Sunlight washed over the cab as the door swung open from the outside. A servant dressed in shades of cream and silver offered me a hand.

I smoothed down the front of my skirts and tucked my fingers into the servant's hand while standing straighter.

Prince Arius' head of sandy blonde hair and eyes the color of cinnamon met me. He had grown and kept a beard since I had seen him last, maintaining it trimmed at his jaw. He had aged and looked like a man, though I met him when he was just under eighteen.

Driata was right. He was handsome. He stood almost as tall —though his shoulders were less broad—as Baltazar. And my mentor was only challenged in height by Liam, who had outpaced my mentor in height and width by the time he turned sixteen.

Dipping into a curtsy, I fluttered my eyelashes at him.

My mind wandered to the first time Driata had tried to give me the talk. I thought about how mortifying it had been that she hadn't known my mother had given it to me years before. Or really that she was speaking on it at all.

The thoughts made my cheeks flush with embarrassment. The prince would think it was modesty, perhaps even nerves. But, if he were like most men I knew, he would attribute my blushing to his own good looks.

Good.

I knew the part I had to play, the role I was supposed to paint on my skin. Arius couldn't possibly know that I was bold enough to consider running. The match was more to my benefit than his own.

"Merry met, Princess. The rumors of your beauty do not disappoint." As he spoke, I offered him my knuckles and tried not to think of the hike I would have to make on foot if I took off right then.

"You're too kind, Prince Arius. Thank you for allowing my family and me to visit your home." If I didn't focus on it, perhaps I could forget the taste of bile in my throat.

He's being polite, I reminded myself. *It's only fair if you give him a chance.*

But I had been called beautiful before, and it ended in a broken heart.

"After an inconvenient occurrence, the palace is under...*renovations*. I want to extend the invitation for you to join us for a late lunch though we had to move it on short notice." My stomach chose that moment to rumble its need to the entire courtyard, and Arius only smiled, offering me his arm.

It didn't matter that I hadn't eaten any food in a day and a half. I wouldn't be able to fit anything through the corset and bodice of the gown. And despite my comment in the cab, I thought it would probably be frowned upon if I found myself bursting from the dress.

Praising myself mentally for only pausing for a moment before tucking my hand into the crook of his arm, I offered him a timid smile. "Do you often greet all of your guests personally?"

The prince barked a laugh that seemed genuine, and I found myself gazing sideways at him, taking in his strong jaw and the smattering of freckles on his nose.

"I felt it was only right to see my ring on this delicate hand of yours since I could not be there to offer it to you in person." His fingers grazed mine, nestled against his forearm and skimming the ring I wore.

"Ah. And what was it that kept you from proposing yourself rather than sending a messenger to do your bidding?" I couldn't keep the bitterness completely out of my tone, but I swatted his arm playfully as if it were our own inside joke.

He paused, his body stilling for an almost imperceptible moment before seeming to decide to turn down a different path. "Allow me to assure you, I would have given anything to be there with you at that moment."

My slipped feet padded on the grass with the turn as we veered off the cobblestone path toward a white, ivy-coated arch ahead.

Seeing such vibrant greenery in Ellesmere was strange compared to Lunasa. I wanted to touch the green sprigs of grass flourishing everywhere and dancing in the gentle breeze. Our gardens thrived at the castle through the sheer will and magic of the gardeners, though my father had to change his own laws to allow each of them talismans.

"There were matters more pressing, then?" It was an assumption, but he was avoiding the point.

He stopped us at a fountain of two lovers locked in a passionate embrace. My back stiffened, not even at the statue's nudity, which put the couple's bodies—ample breasts and asses —on display for every passerby, but instead because of the white rose bushes surrounding the trickling fountain. His sun-kissed cheeks dimpled as he gave me a full smile, one that I'm sure normally melted hearts and gave him the skeleton key to chastity belts, but I was no maiden, and though I gave him a small smile back, I was unimpressed.

He plucked a rose from the bush and snapped off the thorns quickly, without a thought, and my heartbeat hammered in my ears. "I was traveling to Weylin in preparation for your surprise."

He mentioned the rocky island passively, dismissing the ships that splintered against its shores in the thousands.

"You prepared a surprise before you proposed?" It took every ounce of will in me not to step back. I couldn't, not with my family who had followed us, watch. Not with Baltazar and Liam standing just behind my brothers. Baltazar was busy aligning his cuff sleeve, but Liam's eyes bored into me. No. Past me, at the prince's hand raised to tuck the rose stem behind my ear.

I tilted my head to the side and down as if too shy to allow Arius to touch me but allowing him access all the same. Liam didn't look away, a muscle in his jaw flicking, and my stomach plummeted.

Arius' fingers trailed over my jaw and cupped my face. He stole my gaze, hopefully not noting where it had strayed. We were close, and it was intimate enough to feel as if we were alone.

But we weren't.

Driata sighed dreamily when Arius finally answered. "I had a feeling you would say yes."

Of course, he had. And really, what choice did I have in the matter? No one would suspect I was any more than the role, and even if they had, they would find a way to squeeze me back into it.

He smirked, taking my silence as agreement, and placed his hand on the small of my back. Then, turning me away from the fountain, the roses, and even my court, we walked toward a curtain of hanging marigolds that hid bronze doors leading into the palace.

We entered through an alcove that could have been a service entrance, and I wondered why we hadn't been received in the main hall and really... Why had Arius bothered greeting us at all?

Was he being genuine when he said he wanted to see me

wearing the ring? Or was I right to believe there was something wrong there?

My teeth sliced into my cheek as I silenced my thoughts. There was no reason to assume Arius was anything less than a gentleman, and perhaps he was less pompous than I thought if he would risk someone seeing him roaming the service parts of the castle.

That would be a surprising and welcome difference from my father and even his own gold glutton of a king.

Maybe it wouldn't be as awful as I thought.

We passed through corridors with intricate carvings of the royal crest, a boar's head donning a crown of flames and rubies.

The blood crown. So named for the king's penchant for violence—including the massacre of his father and eldest brother so he could take the throne.

As tasteless as his rise to power had been, Maveri had been my father's strongest ally at a time when the rift between Ellesmere and Lunasa had been great. Maveri's father, Rikerd, sought to have my father dethroned for the spell he and the First Queen had cast all those years ago. It defied nature, and even with the curse running rampant in Lunasa and my father's veins, Maveri's father thought Lunasa deserved a better king.

Maveri, of course, stopped that when he allied with my father to seat himself on the throne of Ellesmere.

Arius' voice pulled me from my thoughts. "What are you thinking about?"

"Hmm?"

"You've been gnawing at your lip and staring off at vacant walls for the entire walk." He stopped us in front of another carving—one of a hog reared up on its hind legs. The more I looked at the image, the more its features seemed more human, its chest more defined, its legs thickening...

Magic. There was magic in the carvings.

"Your grandfather." I should have lied, perhaps even tried to save face, and pretend I was admiring the castle's stonework. But I was curious, and though I had been instructed by my father not to bring up our kingdoms' pasts, I wanted to see what the man thought. The way his mind worked and if he supported his father's ways.

"My grandfather was politically minded," he said, though it seemed like a half-thought.

"I can't tell from your tone if you approve of that or not." I glanced back at my family, far enough away to give the new couple their privacy. I wondered if they could hear us.

He paused. One blink, then a second while he stared at me, his head slightly tilted as if he were trying to figure me out too. "Who am I to stand here and tell my almost bride that her people would have been better off if her father gave up his kingdom?"

"And who would I be to ask if you think it's wrong that your father butchered his own blood?" I should have kept walking. That wasn't an approved topic. The weather, my travel, the flowers, and tapestries, yes. But *that*...no.

"My father was able to get Lunasa access to ports again and help feed starving villagers." My breathing hitched as he paused to touch the rose he had tucked in my hair. That was the moment where he would show his undying loyalty to his king. Murderer or not. "But he bathed in blood for that, and I'm sure there was another way."

What? Had I been so judgmental to assume he was like his father?

Words evaded me. My normal quick wit had run off with my tongue.

I settled on a nod, turning away and pacing forward as if I had a clue where he was taking me.

He seemed to accept it, joining me in my silence and tucked my arm over his.

It was strange. The feeling that in a few months-time, Ellesmere was supposed to become my home... I wasn't sure I ever had one, not really. Not since my mother *left us*. That was what everyone called it. Too afraid of the curse that was the word death.

Death was final, unchanging. Save for the people who survived you, those who loved you that would forever be changed.

Swallowing the lump in my throat, I looked anywhere but at the prince while I waited for my shining vision to clear. First, the polished marble floors, then up to the gold-spun tapestries and ornate lanterns lining the stone walls.

My steadying breath caught the scent of meats that permeated through the halls despite the flowers hanging from all the walls and sitting on every intricately carved wooden table we passed. It made me think of Driata and her choice years ago to abstain from meat. She must be in agony there. Smelling what she would call the rotten odor of unnecessary death.

I glanced back at her and caught her curling her lip back from her teeth while fanning her face with a kerchief.

Her eyes widened in signal as she met my eyes as if asking how I could bear it. I gave her a slight shrug in answer.

Did it smell like the kitchens overflowed with animals? Yes.

But she knew Ellesmere was known for their seasonings and their meats. The Elwood was rife with hunters willing to kill for their king. It's how Maveri maintained enough riches to control the ports. And the reason why the alliance between our two kingdoms needed to remain firm.

Baltazar would have coached her on how to act and pretend she was enjoying the foods they offered... But she needed to get in control of her face. Our entrance into a great hall captured my attention.

An aged butler dressed in a suit with a fluffed collar announced our arrival to the several people already milling about. They turned, with flutes of champagne and small plates of skewered meats in their hands. "Prince Arius Alistair and his betrothed Princess Janai Serpen of Lunasa."

I cleared my throat, though it was much louder than intended, causing the crowd to stop clapping. "I—uh. It's Jane."

The butler turned to me, his soft blue eyes framed by a delicate web of lines and wrinkles. "My apologies, Your Highness. Would you like me to reintroduce you?"

"No!" My voice echoed around the room. I sighed, quieting my tone as the man flinched again. "I'm sorry, no. That won't be necessary."

I felt a tug on my arm and moved out of the entryway.

"King Certis Serpen of Lunasa is accompanied by his five eldest children: Prince Oliver Serpen, Princess Olivia Serpen, Princess Driata Serpen, Prince Ciaran Serpen, and Princess Gemma Serpen." My siblings swept in with my father, and the butler paused. Then, "Keeper of the Crown, Lord Baltazar Tellyk and his brother Liam Tellyk."

"You don't apologize to the help." Arius' voice was a whisper in my ear. Barely loud enough for me to hear.

"I didn't mean to yell at him."

"He got your name wrong." Arius swiped a flute from a tray as a masked waiter walked by and placed it in my hand. "It's not as if he has many tasks to excuse the mistake. Now come. There are some people you'll need to meet."

CHAPTER 6

I had never met the other royal families.

They weren't fond of my father, but that didn't stop him from trudging into the room, gripping Sefar's scabbard for dear life, and grinning like he wasn't a walking skeleton.

Perception is key.

He had to pretend like his kingdom was on the line, and maybe it was. They were firm supporters of Maveri's father in ousting him.

The nearest to us was a man with women and men alike fawning all over him, tipping back flutes of champagne and offering him bites of meat and cheeses I figured from descriptions I had heard of his size alone that he had to be the King of Karhdaro. But it wasn't his supporters, dressed in the thinnest pieces of lace, that caught my attention. Instead, it was that he dressed in such contrast to the fine gowns and suits that everyone else in the room wore.

His *shorts* were nothing more than briefs, barely concealing his bulging manhood, and his tanned, inked chest was on display for the entire room to see. His thighs and tattooed arms rippled with lines of muscle that easily measured the same width as my waist.

As Arius escorted me toward him, one of the king's scantily clad admirers whispered in his ear something that made his chest heave with laughter that bounced around the room.

Nearer, I saw his thick, dark hair met his shoulders and framed an exquisite face. The closer I got, the more details I noticed. The way his full lips held an easy grin and his eyes were the color of the sea glass found on beaches after a storm. He was a precise kind of beautiful, and it was no wonder his hangers-on flocked to him in the dozens.

"Merry met, Princess." He aimed those eyes at me, and his mouth curved in a slow smile, making my fingers itch to reach for pencils and paper to sketch him. His flock of followers parted enough for him to bridge the gap between us as he stooped low in a bow beneath his status. His hand swallowed mine entirely while he placed a kiss along the back of it. "What I've been told of your beauty...it does you no justice."

His accent was thick and one I rarely heard on the continent, giving me pause. I did my best to recover quickly, dropping in a curtsy and giving him my most demure smile. One that I knew my sisters didn't have to pause before giving. One that was a natural extension of their faces.

Even Olivia had mastered it early in age.

"You're too kind, King Blair," I managed finally, as I straightened. The foreign monarch still had a hold of me and pulled me close to his chest. "Merry met."

"I imagine you have had your share of admirers," he whispered, feigning a kiss on my cheek. "Why you chose this one is beyond me."

He leaned away, dragging me instead into his gaze. His face was young, tinted by the sun, and pinched with a worry that couldn't be for me. Heat rose from my neck into my cheeks under the intensity of that stare. Bowing my head, I felt the curtain of curls fanning my cheeks, hoping one shade of red would hide the other.

"Come." Arius' voice was harsh in comparison to the dulcet tones Blair had spoken, but I took it as an invitation to escape the king's too-heavy stare.

He led me toward large glass paneled doors that I hadn't noticed though they dominated nearly the entirety of the back wall.

The smell of salt on a chilled breeze greeted me and cooled my too-hot face. I wanted to soak it in, and I wished for fewer clothes so that I could feel the sun competing with the sea air for space on my skin.

The view was breathtaking. We stood on a balcony constructed of aqua-colored glass, which distorted the rocks jutting from the side of the castle. The bright noontime sun hung high in the sky and reflected its blinding light off the calm sea, whose waves lapped at the sand far below.

I squinted to try to separate the cloudless sky on the horizon from the boundless sea, but the colors blended almost perfectly together. I never knew such calm or such beauty. If I had any breath to spare in the too-tight, hard boned corset, it would have stolen it away.

"Do not think you will receive such warmth from me,

daughter of death's deceiver." The voice was cold, feminine, and edged with ice.

I turned to find a woman wearing a crown of... Ivory bone? Or an excellent replica. Her face had such gaunt angles that my mind trailed to the harsh strokes of my pencil I would use to recreate her image on paper. Her silver hair whipped out behind her as though the briny breeze was a storm she alone controlled. My eyes trailed down to a gown that looked to double as armor, glinting turquoise in the sun. It looked to be composed of scales of some sort...

"Orabelle—Queen of Weylin." Arius introduced her as though they were old friends, and though I hadn't taken my eyes from her, I could hear the smile in his voice. "Orabelle, Jane. Jane Orabelle."

"Jane." Her mouth formed my name as if it were foreign, and her lip curled as if she got a taste of something bitter. "How...plain."

I straightened further, keeping my cool, unfeeling mask in place. "If you would like to insult me, you'll have to come up with something far more creative than my father's indiscretions and my boring name, I'm afraid. Neither was a choice I made."

Orabelle's mouth twitched up at the corner as if I had made a joke. "And would you have chosen differently?"

It felt as though she switched topics without informing me, and I didn't know how to react. My stomach twisted with nerves. "It will never matter what I choose."

The queen of the isles smirk vanished. "And here I for a moment thought you were more than a delicate, plucked flower."

"She certainly would be the most enticing in a garden,

though would she not?" Arius chuckled in my ear, and it was everything I could do not to jump. How had I forgotten he was there? And why did his confirmation of her words make my skin crawl?

"I'd like to think of our princess as something far more interesting." Liam's voice carried out over the balcony. "Perhaps a poison?"

May the gods smite me where I stand. The man was everywhere. I turned to him where he stood only an arm's length away from Arius, whose face held barely concealed annoyance.

"And who might this be?" Orabelle's tone was much huskier than she'd used with me or even Arius. She sounded like a cat that was content with a belly full of mice.

Liam brushed past me, not flinching at the jolt of pure static that seemed to pour through us at the contact.

Maybe he hadn't felt it. But I had, and it seemed to wake me up and make me more aware of each of his movements. There was a slight stumble in his gait, and his hand hung limp at his side. His blue-black curls were mussed as if someone had ripped their fingers through them.

Orabelle's icy eyes met mine, then tracked back to Liam as he strode toward her.

She gave him a toothy smile, and I was struck again by how severe her features were even as they softened before my eyes. Her cheeks appeared less gaunt, her lips fuller and pinker. The eyes watching him widened and were framed by impossibly darker and longer lashes.

What the?

Liam bowed at the waist, grasped her hand in what felt like

a near intimate gesture, and glanced up to meet her stare as he kissed the back of it.

"Isn't that a friend of yours?" Arius asked, his breath brushing the arch of my ear.

"No." Yes. Definitely not. Maybe. Nope. I worried my teeth would be ground to dust before the interaction was over.

"Then you need not tell him that Orabelle has gained the most notoriety for feasting on her lovers after they bring her pleasure."

Excuse me, what? "I'm sure that can't be true."

And it didn't matter. Liam wasn't going to *sleep with her*. Had he not seen her morph in front of his very eyes by the work of some strange magic?

"The bones in her crown are from the only husband she ever took." The prince let out a soft chuckle. "Picked clean on their wedding night."

"And you find that rumor to be amusing?" My eyebrows arched. The only bit of emotion I would allow to leak onto my face as I stepped back through the door while downing the champagne in my glass and exchanging the empty for another on a server's tray.

That one followed the former into the scarce contents of my stomach. Only then did I grab a plate filled with bite-sized bits of buttery fish and garlicky beef. Though there wasn't much room in the dress, I would find a way.

The bubbles felt heavy in my stomach, even as the rest of me felt lighter. I picked up the joke of a fork that was no larger than my forefinger and plopped a piece of crab into my mouth.

Delicious. I followed that with a bite of cheese. Sharp. Dry.

I felt the presence near me before I had a chance to react. Oliver crowded my line of sight.

"That fiancé of yours has grown bored already, then?"

"Prince Arius is entertaining guests." I ducked around him, only to meet with a wall of bodies created by none other than Olivia and Ciaran. *Gods above, have they got nothing better to do than follow him around?*

"Can I help you?" I laced my voice with sugar to douse away the bitter thoughts. I may not be excited to marry, but I was certainly not complaining that I had to see my siblings less often.

"I'm not sure you can," Olivia said, her eyes narrowed, and looking over my gown and the crumbs of bread I hadn't noticed had fallen on the bodice.

Brushing them from my chest, I made my hands shake, so it looked like I was wracked with nerves. "Then I should go find Arius."

"On a first name basis, are you?" Oliver's voice was too close behind me. And while I was sure I could get out of the situation with little violence and no injuries on my part, Baltazar would want me to maintain my guise.

My chin dipped toward my chest as I lowered my eyes. "He's to be my partner. Am I supposed to call him by his title?"

"You need not forget you barely hold a position yourself, sister." Olivia spat the last word as though it pained her.

"You would be better suited ending things like your mother." Ciaran may as well have struck a physical blow. Wincing, as though he had, I wished for the conversation to end.

Gods, the moment Baltazar permitted me, I would gut him.

"No," Oliver said, his mouth a cruel line. "She would much rather pretend to be one of us."

"And pretend we would ever let her wear even another kingdom's crown," Olivia added, flicking my nose.

"We would sooner see you dead." The threat was there. Even when Oliver moved away and the others followed, it hung over me still. He didn't realize I didn't give a shit about a crown.

I didn't even understand why he let himself get so excited and obsessed with the idea of one. There wasn't a point in being an heir if our father was apparently never going to die.

More wine, I needed something to wet my mouth. I aimed myself toward another server, but Blair intercepted me with a heavy arm around my shoulders. "Hello there, sweetness. It looks like you could use some fresh air."

"Not on the balcony," I grumbled, preparing to battle my way through bodies to get away from everyone.

"Of course not." The sulphury scent of magic hit my nose, and the bubbles in my stomach rose as we tumbled into nothingness.

We landed on a plush carpet of grass and pine needles, and I heard the soft nickering of horses. My eyes focused on the ivy-coated white stables, nearby.

Blair plopped down a few feet from me, gesturing to the ground that he wanted me to do the same. I crossed my legs as I squatted and finally reached the ground... Despite being unable to bend my torso.

"Did one of those boys do something to you?" The timbre of his voice lowered, and a fit of uncovered anger pinched his brow.

"What do you mean?" I looked to the stables to avoid meeting his eye, trying to think of Jett and wondering if she was in there. "No, of course not."

He clicked his tongue, clearly not believing a word I said. "One leads you out to the balcony, and the next follows. Then you're draining booze like it's a lifeline and quickly sinking."

"And you care because?" I couldn't hide the irritation in my tone, though if Baltazar knew I let my control slip, he would be furious. But what was I supposed to do? Keep acting forever? I felt like I was a dam fit to burst and wouldn't be the only casualty.

"That's a question I've been asking myself." There was a question in the pitch of his voice and raised brows. As if he were surprised to admit it. "But I also saw through your façade the moment you stepped into that hall."

How could he know? I had everyone else fooled. Even the ever-suspicious Oliver couldn't prove anything he suspected of me. But the man sat there half-naked and accusatory.

Shit. "I'm not sure—"

"Don't do that," he cut over me with his palm raised. "You are quite clever, but those in my clan are rather good at detecting bonds between people."

"So...you can tell I don't care for Arius." I shrugged, trying to pull back together the torn shreds of my cover. "A lot of wives don't care for their husbands."

He shook his head vigorously, trying to clear my words from the air. "You've got to ask the right questions."

"What do you want from me?" I was half tempted to get up and run away back to the castle, but I was worried—if not also a bit curious.

"There are certain things at play, pieces I'm unable to move." He steepled his hands together between us. "But if *you* were to move one, I would be forced to move too."

His eyes were wide with honesty or *maybe lunacy*.

"My fiancé will wonder where I am." I don't know why I said it, though I knew it was true. And it would not do for him to think I was romping with another man on his grounds.

"Who worries about Arius fucking Alistair?" The king dragged his fingers through his hair and expelled a heavy breath.

Uncertainty flooded me, even as I stood and dusted grass from my gown. "I don't have a choice." The strange conversation sobered me and made me wonder what *questions* I was supposed to ask.

"Your secret is safe, and the image of your chastity remains unsullied." He waggled his eyebrows, losing the grave face that had plagued him only moments before. "I assumed the task of escorting you to your surprise."

"That itself isn't inappropriate?" I asked, not caring, and the king smiled in turn.

"I can do as I wish." He offered me a conspiratorial wink. "Ellesmere needs what I provide."

He didn't elaborate and gave no impression that he would, so my brain trailed back to the surprise.

In all the chaos, I forgot Arius had said there would be a surprise. But I assumed and hoped it was lunch. Wasn't all of that strangeness enough? "There's more?"

"The boy prince seems to be under the assumption that you'll enjoy the spotlight. He would never guess you thrive in the shadows." Blair's smile made him seem younger than me somehow as he yanked the white rose from behind my ear and crushed it under his boot.

He offered me his arm, and as I looked down at the crumpled petals, I wondered if maybe he did know more than he could say.

CHAPTER 7

It was a pleasant surprise when Blair didn't immediately whisk us away using his carved talisman. He explained that he found more peace in nature than rushing from place to place.

"Are you going to tell me what the surprise is?" I asked, hopeful that he wouldn't be vague in all things.

His eyes shone with amusement even as a muscle feathered in his jaw. "I was sworn to secrecy. And a man is only as strong as his word."

I couldn't fault him for it, though I wasn't sure why it was so easy to speak with him—to hear the truth in his words. "Why do I feel like I'm going to hate this?"

"Because you most certainly will."

I let the silence grow between us, never becoming a tempest beast but a comfortable companion as we walked. I took my slippers off and carried them in my hand to feel the soil, so rich compared to Lunasa, and the grass—thick and verdant with life

85

under my feet. The sun was lowering in the sky and had cast a tangerine and fuchsia glow around us.

Blair led us over a hill, past the castle's east side, and away from the sounds of horses and their handlers. We reached a hedge three times in height taller than the monarch at my side. Impressive, given how my neck ached each time I met his eye from craning upward.

It was lush, with vibrant red flowers and green leaves. It may as well have been a stone wall for all you could see through it. "Is this the part where you actually decide to murder me? Just as I think we could become friends?"

Blair chuckled, the sound low in his throat. "Sweetness, if I wanted you dead, I would have done it in a room full of people."

"That's..." My eyebrows raised as I craned my neck to look at his toothy grin. "Comforting."

"I've no doubt you would go down valiantly." He shrugged. The gesture showed how little he meant his statements but also proved he might as he tugged me through the arched flower-coated hedge.

Musical notes floated toward us on the sea breeze, and I sighed. How many times have I had an opportunity to run away? But there we were, walking into a hedge maze toward what sounded like a party though I was content with no cele-bration. Especially not one to commemorate a rock I wore on my finger and a contract that would sign away any future or hope I had of freedom.

"Do you think I should go through with this?" It didn't make sense, asking a near stranger if I should play my part. But he was a monarch —an unbiased one, it seemed—and I had a feeling he would answer to his ability.

"I think if you had a choice, you would have ridden off today and not looked back." The frankness of his words startled me. When I didn't respond, Blair continued, "but you're here, and the cards have been dealt. Your only option is to play."

"Talking in code like that makes you seem like an asshole." I laughed, realizing how strange it was that I was so unguarded with him.

But there they were, hanging between us as the giant king doubled over in a fit of laughter. Then, through gasping breaths, "You would fit in well in Karhdaro. All of them are over my bullshit too."

"Then give a straight answer for once."

"Straight is boring. Look at the predicament you're in."

"I already told you, I have no choice in the matter."

"The day you realize that's a lie, I'll make sure I'm in the front row to watch you burn it all down."

Why did it feel like I had known the man for years?

Hearing the music draw nearer, the notes louder and more distinguishable as a flute, a harp, and so on, I reminded myself of my place. I relinquished the king's arm and fell into step a bit behind him. And while I kept my back stiff, my chin dipped.

That was what Baltazar wanted. *Let them see you as feeble. Make them believe you are nothing but grateful for this opportunity.* But how could I pretend to feel thankful as I wanted to crawl out of my own skin and slither away?

It only worsened as we stepped through the final arch leading to the center of the hedge maze. It was a massive glass atrium lined with copper and gold arched high above, filtering in the waning sun. Dozens of people milled about. Faces blurred together, and my heartbeat pounded in my ears to the beat of the music.

I wasn't meant to be a spectacle. Blair was right: I had surely secured my place in the shadows. But there I was—framed in white roses of all things, I realized as I recognized the scent and looked around.

Blair hissed under his breath, just loud enough for me to hear, "too late to run now." The bastard leaned back to shove me forward with his massive paw of a hand.

I stumbled, but he caught me by the back of my bodice, and I sucked in a jagged breath as it pinched my ribs. Rude.

"Princess Jane. I would like for you to meet my father, my King." Arius' voice rang out over the soft music, and I wanted to scream, to duck back through the maze until I found Jett and never look back. But Baltazar had a plan. He had to. Which meant I had to keep my part.

I looked up in time to see the blonde walking past a group of courtiers fanning themselves and giving him bright, too-white smiles, hopeful for a glance their way, no doubt. And while I couldn't care any less if he looked, he apparently only had eyes for me. Dear Gods.

Further beyond him, a throne carved of citrine and latticed with blooming jasmine stood tall amongst the people in attendance. But lounging, with his rotund stomach on display and a grease-coated leg of some poor animal hanging from his maw... The mad king himself. King Maveri Alistair.

His wife Aurina was absent, though I hadn't really expected her to be there. The queen had never been seen outside of their castle, had never been painted or carved or molded. Some said the mad king had made her up altogether. Others said she was magnificent, and he was far too selfish to share her with the world.

Unfortunately, the *rare beauty* was missing, and her disgusting king sat alone.

I would sooner feed myself to river hags than approach Maveri for no reason. But I had a reason. The plan—Baltazar's plan.

What was the plan again?

Right. Meek, timid, thankful.

The small portions of food I ate were turning in my stomach. How hadn't I thought of the heist all that day? What if he knew it was me?

What if the elaborate party was his web, and I was the helpless fly he was about to devour? My gaze trailed around the faces in the darkening atrium. Still wearing their unadorned masks, servants set to work lighting sconces and mini fires around a flower-strewn dance floor. The music had picked up its tempo while people swung their partners in twirls of fabric.

But around the space, almost imperceptible, were stoic faces of men who looked uncomfortable in their evening wear. More likely used to the armor they wore when they wanted to be conspicuous. One, a sandy-haired man tugged at the collar of his shirt while lines of discomfort bracketed his mouth.

Guards.

Baltazar would have warned me... If we had—I had been caught. Right?

I hadn't realized I faltered back until I pressed against Blair's hard stomach. I froze, unable to move, even as his hands came down on my shoulders. A deep chuckle rumbled through his chest and up rumbled up my spine. "Sweetness, that's your cue."

Overly aware of my face, I pulled my lips into a smile and wished for one of the servants' masks to cover my creasing brow. But none of the guests had them on. I supposed that's how they were distinguished as *the help* as my fiancé called them. The thought alone raised bile in the back of my throat.

Arius crossed the distance between us and intertwined his fingers through mine. His hands were clammy, and I stifled my urge to cringe away. But, no, my mask couldn't slip... Not tonight.

He guided me through the dancers, who—though lost in their own world of music notes and flirtations—still managed to part for us as though it were their duty. And maybe it was. Perhaps the prince had hired them for just the task because I was sure we did make quite the spectacle. Traipsing across a bed of reblooming flowers with fabrics of silk and lace framing us as though it was our wedding night, and the performers were forming our aisle.

I would perish. I would certainly pass away--my heart would stop mid-step if that were Arius' plan.

We reached his father, who didn't deign to look up at us as I curtsied. Who really cared that my lungs were near collapsing at the movement?

"My King." Of course, Liam was right; that was how Arius addressed his father. "I would like to introduce you to my fiancé, Princess Jane Serpen." Gods, that name. The title. I think I preferred being named Plain.

"Merry met King Maveri. Might I express my absolute pleasure at my future as your daughter-in-law?" Drool dripped down the king's chin as I spoke. It plopped onto his hair-coated chest as he licked and sucked the grease from the meat off his fingers.

A snort of laughter rang out in the crowd's silence as even the musicians stopped playing.

The remainder of my life flashed before my eyes as I waited for the gluttonous king to speak. Arius and I would perform a fertility spell—the only way our peoples could conceive—and we would have three potbellied children. They would take their height from their father, their thighs from me, and their stomachs from their grandfather. They wouldn't be particularly athletic, and each would die in increasingly embarrassing ways.

The first, choking on bones he's inhaled at dinner, the second in an asthmatic attack, and the third would sink to the bottom of spring while attempting to catch his dinner for spite. Then, finally, Arius would start shrinking in his grief and morph into the image of his father sitting before me.

The terrifying daymare receded at the sound of the king clearing his mucus-coated throat.

"Jane." He smacked his lips together around my name as if tasting it and dragged his eyes along my body up to my face. "I can't tell if, under all those clothes, you have the hips to bear me grandchildren."

"She's built like a prized boar, father." Arius' smile was proud and beaming, and I wanted to break every single one of his too-white teeth. How was that considered a compliment? "Speaking of prized boars." He waved his hand, and two masked servants came strutting up the dais holding a leather strap tied to the largest pig I had ever seen. Its squeals of terror echoed through the atrium, and my spine clenched.

"What is this?" Surprise, fear, confusion. One of those emotions took hold of my voice and raised it to an octave I never imagined I could reach. My façade was slipping, no... Running away as the pig stared two black beady eyes in my direction while thrashing its neck back and forth against its captors.

"Our dinner for tonight. A roast fit for the future Queen of Ellesmere." As Arius spoke, a shriek cut out over his voice and the pig's cries.

"No. Have you lost your mind?" Bodies swarmed toward us while Driata barreled through the crowd. "This-- This is to be your dinner? Why don't you just cut one of your guests open and watch them bleed? He has a heart." The last word caught up in a sob as she threw herself over the pig, shielding his eyes from the devastating fate and offering herself up as a sacrifice instead.

"You realize boar meat has provided us with the fortune that supports your kingdom in their troubled times?" King Maveri was spitting mad as he attempted to lift himself from his throne.

Driata ignored the king, turning pleading eyes on Arius instead, who surprisingly offered her a kind smile. "What would you have us do with him instead?"

"Keep him." Driata stood, seeming for the moment content that she saved the thing. And even the boar looked calmer as my sister grasped Arius' hands between her own. "What a thoughtful gift it would be to Jane."

Excuse me? *Has she seen that thing?* "Uh—"

I couldn't speak fast enough as the prince silenced me by caressing my chin like he hadn't just compared me to the five-hundred-pound hogtied up before us. "That could be lovely, giving us something to care for together."

I would rather die, not that he asked me.

"Then it's settled!" Driata clapped and threw her arms around Arius, who returned the hug as if they had known each other since they were babes. He should marry her. They would be much better suited for each other and could raise the pork to be a fine young gentleman.

"Take him to Jane's rooms." Arius used not one please, offered no gratitude—and my what? *That thing was going where?*

"Um...thank you." My words were weak, and even I didn't believe them, but Arius beamed as if it had been his idea all along.

The music swelled once more as servants dragged my new pet off to sully my rooms. *You'll be going home in a few days*, I reminded myself. Not soon enough, though.

"Would you like to dance?" Not likely. But I fluttered my lashes at the too-charming prince anyway. Play the game. Master the part. Demure. Controlled. Docile.

"It would be my pleasure." I dipped into a curtsy while offering him the back of my hand, and he swept me into his chest. He led, which was customary for him, and I followed despite wanting to rip out his arms. He spun us until I was dizzy and until the smell of cedar and tobacco wrapped around me like a blanket. Baltazar stopped us mid-spin with a pat on the prince's arm. "May I cut in?"

Arius' laugh seemed empty, and his eyes darkened even as he took a step away. The clammy touch of his hand on my lower back lingered. Even as Baltazar stood in his place. I looked up at the golden eyes of my mentor as he pulled me in close, and the tempo of the song shifted and slowed. He tucked his head closer to my ear, and as he whispered, I felt the caress of his breath. "Excellent job. If I didn't know better, I would think you're enjoying yourself."

Excellent. Any praise was high coming from a man who was so easy to disappoint. But excellent? That was unheard of.

"I would rather be anywhere else, but apparently, you wanted me here." I managed to keep my voice low and speak into his chest, but I knew at least he had heard me with how his posture stiffened.

"It was a necessary step."

"*Of course*, it was. It always is." I sounded bitter, even as tears burned the backs of my eyes.

"Come to my room at half-past midnight." There was no way I heard him right. Was he inviting me to his bed? No.

There was no time to ask because he flung out his arm to twirl me, and I landed square against a substantial and bare chest. "Sweetness, I'm offended you're giving so many others your attention."

"And just when I thought I had seen enough of you, you pressed my face into your nipple." The words came out muffled against skin that smelled like grass and salt, like the earth after it rained.

His laughter rumbled through me, and my toes curled in my slippers. "There are other things I can press against you if you like."

"King Blair. Is there something you're trying to imply?" It was the role of a lifetime not to burst into the fit of laughter that threatened at his insinuation.

"Just Blair, Sweetness. Please, you insult me with titles." He sighed as he swayed, and I did indeed feel the press of him against my stomach. "And I don't need libations to be liberal with my love."

At that, I laughed and stole a look at the king's aqua-colored eyes. He caught me, offering a smile. A *genuine* smile, and when he licked his lips, I realized his offer was genuine.

What is going on with the men at this party? Except for Arius, my fiancé, I reminded myself. You know, the one who called you a pig.

When I didn't answer, Blair spoke again. "Many guests at this event may be more open to speaking due to liquid courage and its enticing abilities."

"I would rather go to bed." It didn't matter that it was just after sundown, and the revelry had just begun.

"Leaving so soon?" He pulled away a bit to see my face as he posed his question.

My head bobbed in a nod. "I'll have to sneak away if I can and find my rooms."

"I hope you won't be offended if I stay and don't escort you?" Blair asked, sounding as if he would change his mind if I even hinted that I wanted the company.

"I'm sure I can find my way." Patting his arm, I pulled away, but he held my hand.

"Causing distractions is one of my strongest qualities." He winked and let me go. "Take a left when you exit the atrium."

Metal tinkling sounded as Blair ripped free his shorts, which were apparently clasped together at the sides with tiny buttons. His tanned ass was on display for everyone to see. "Who wants to see how we celebrate nuptials in Karhdaro?" he bellowed as he strode through the crowd. I watched a woman faint, simply fall over as she caught sight of his front side.

Gods. Okay, to the left.

I walked as quickly as possible without drawing attention to myself, though I wasn't sure anything was taking attention away from the naked king.

Finally, I reached the rose-coated arch and darted into the darkness of the hedge maze. A dim lantern cast shadowy light on the cobbled path every few feet.

I wasn't sure how I was supposed to remember my way out of there when others had magicked their way through.

Perhaps I could find a servant.

No sooner had I thought it than a suited man in a mask came barreling around the corner, tipping back a flute of champagne to his lips. I wasn't sure the servants would be allowed to drink. But I was no one to stop him.

The man stumbled, and the glass shattered against the stones splashing its last remaining drops on the skirt of my gown.

Fuck's sake, I wanted the night to be over.

He didn't speak, didn't stoop to clean up the glass though someone, perhaps the naked and frolicking Blair himself, would surely get hurt. Instead, he just stared at me—trapped in the darkness between lamplights and lunged.

CHAPTER 8

The man smelled like pine and spice. Like a forest, if someone soaked it in bourbon. He trapped my hands above us in one of his and pinned me against the hedge. Sharp branches sliced through the fabric and my exposed skin.

I needed to move, to get away from the overly drunk man—before I did something stupid like killing someone near witnesses who could walk out any moment.

He dropped my hands but trapped them between our chests as he reached behind himself and freed a silver dagger.

As he spoke, I recognized the sultry whisper and why he only used one of his hands. "I've grown tired of watching you take half breaths."

Liam dragged his blade down the fabric of my gown, slicing through cloth and the cording of my corset. My breasts burst free, nipples peeking at the chilled night air. I sucked in my first full breath of the night as I worked to cover them with my fabric-trapped arms.

He hadn't stepped away, and barely an inch lay between him and my exposed skin as he used his blade to push up his mask. His wide eyes caressed and devoured me as they trailed from my neck to the gown pooling at my waist.

"You're drunk." I inched backward, the brambles of the hedge digging deeper into my curls and flesh.

"*Drinking*," he murmured, sliding the flat edge of the blade over the curve in my breasts. "But not drunk."

The cold metal bit my sensitive skin, and I drew a ragged breath. What had gotten into everyone tonight? What did it say about me that I didn't want it to end? I had spent far too many nights with unknown men, or my own hands gripped between my thighs, thinking of the way Liam used to bow on his knees and worship me.

"How do you manage it?" I asked. My heart jumped into my throat as Liam glided the point of his blade between my breasts. Maybe I should've been terrified, but gods dammit, he was so close and smelled like home— If I made a home of singed and ruined memories.

Somehow though, I knew he wouldn't hurt me. Not physically, at least.

He paused, the blade resting in my cleavage. It drove me to madness as he pressed his body closer against me, aligning his hips with my waist. I couldn't surrender another step. There wasn't one to give. The smooth material of his suit teased me, and gooseflesh spread all over.

"Manage what?" Liam said finally, an afterthought.

"Being alright after... Well, everything." I wouldn't react

and would not rip his clothes off despite every thought in my traitorous mind.

"I'm meant to protect you. But only you can protect your heart." The freezing blade was removed and tucked away, and he gripped my arm as darkness stole away everything.

We tumbled into a room before I processed the sulfuric smell and realized he magicked us out of the hedges. He dropped my arm as if the contact burned him, and I wished it had.

How was I supposed to move on if he was always right there? It was torture. I was readying myself to say just that when he spoke instead. "Half-past twelve. The rooms are across the hall to the right. The final door."

It felt as if he doused me with a bucket of water.

Business then.

It was always business.

An animalistic squeal tore through the air behind us, and I whipped around. Lou was there, grunting and wresting the giant pig into a pile of orange and gold linens.

"The princess and I are having an affair," Liam offered calmly. A lie meant for Lou, who overheard his instructions. He threw it out rashly, considering she probably knew the rooms Liam gave me directions to were Baltazar's.

Lou scrunched her brow, clearly not believing him, but it didn't stop him from leaving without another word. But it did prevent me from explaining to him that the seamstress already knew about my illegal activities. Not that it would spare her if Baltazar suspected there was a witness. However, knowing Baltazar, she was probably already in his pocket along with the other spies that Oliver had hired.

Only when my back slid along the door and I felt the wood on my skin, did I remember that I was still half naked.

Louisa let out a low whistle between her teeth. "You want to talk about that?" Looking up, I saw that she was pressing her lips into a tight line, physically restraining herself from laughing.

"Can you tell me where my things are so I can grab a robe?" There. I acknowledged my nudity. But that was all, no more, no less.

"Agatha and Edera have already run you a bath. You'll want to hurry. They'll be back any moment." She motioned toward the back of the room to an arched doorway.

I stripped the gown off and tossed it into Lou's outstretched arms, already moving as she worked on tucking it under the sleeping boar.

My feet padded across the ornate rug, and I tried not to notice the orange and gold furnishings.

Hideous as they were, even the tangerine embroidered settee was much newer and made with richer fabrics than the ones we had in Lunasa.

The finery filled room contrasted the unadorned tower I took over back home. My father had wanted me closer to everyone else, but I declined. It distressed him even further when I refused his decorators and design teams. I didn't need the spoils of his selfish lifestyle. But, unfortunately, it didn't seem I had a choice in Ellesmere.

The door leading into the rooms from the hall creaked.

Shit.

I sprinted into the bathing room, splashing into a curved, ivory tub. The readied water scorched my skin, and I gulped back my protest at the sudden heat. The smell of eucalyptus and sage slapped me in the face, burning my nose and stinging my eyes.

"She sounds like a ton of bricks," Agatha huffed from the sitting room, already sounding annoyed.

"What's she doing in there?" Edera added. "Learning to swim?"

I squinted through watery eyes and the steam wafting off the water while they gossiped about how early I left my engagement party.

White, marbled tiles and red brick framed the bathroom. Faint, silver etchings marred the otherwise sterile-looking tiles, and I tried to focus on those instead of their rude banter.

"Must have upset the prince."

"You'd think she would be grateful for the opportunity."

"And her sister! That pig would feed many of us through the worst of the year."

"Not that we have good parts of the year anymore."

Lou was quiet through the exchange, even as they got closer to the bathroom.

"Your highness—Jane," Agatha corrected herself. Her tone softening the moment she walked through the tiled arch. "I'm told it was a lovely party."

"Quite," I bit out, keeping my tone and face neutral. The fact that these women scoffed behind my back wasn't new to me, but it was alarming how quickly she could switch. It would make Baltazar proud, really.

Edera trailed behind her, dragging in a squeaking cart full of lotions and soaps. "And he got you a pet. That is rather romantic."

"It's a bit committal for someone who doesn't know whether she's nurturing or not," Lou said as she entered, carrying a stack of towels. I wasn't sure if it was a jab or in my defense. I couldn't read her... Which could prove problematic.

"Oh, I'm sure the princess will make a fine mother." Without warning, one of the women dumped fresh and near burning water over my head. My hair filled my vision and covered my ears, muffling whatever was said next.

Edera's fingers scraped along my scalp while Agatha scrubbed a soap bar along my arms.

My stomach clenched at Edera's suggestion, and the image of three helpless boys flashed in my mind. I never considered bearing children, though I guess some part of me knew it would be part of my responsibilities. But would I actually rear a child? To what end? So I could eventually be driven mad like my mother?

I looked up, perhaps to give light to my questions, just in time to see Agatha with another pitcher of water. I clenched my eyes and mouth but not quickly enough, and the water flooded my face.

Gods dammit.

Edera yanked my arm, hauling me to my feet and pulling me from further descending into my worries.

I pulled my lip between my teeth, reaching for a towel to cover my too-exposed flesh. Agatha swatted at my hands, yanking the warm fabric out of reach as chills spread over me, and I stood like a soaked, feral cat. She huffed, patting me down, even as my body—already rosy from the steaming water—flushed further.

The pair of fussy women aided me over the tub's wall, and I stepped out into a silken black robe Lou offered.

Edera worked quickly to coil my newly tamed hair into braids that hung damp at my back while Agatha tucked my feet into fur-lined slippers. "Is there anything else we can do for you?" They asked in unison, giving me pause.

"I'm still hungry, actually." And as soon as I voiced the thought, my stomach grumbled its agreement.

"We'll leave a tray by the door." Agatha—clearly having assumed she was in charge—nodded at the door, dismissing Lou, Edera, and herself.

The latter two curtsied while Lou pressed two fingers to her forehead in salute as they departed.

I took in the empty sitting room and sighed.

It was such a relief to breathe.

"I've grown tired of watching you take half breaths." His words warmed my cooling skin, and I dragged the tip of my forefinger between my breasts where his blade had touched me. Even wrapped around a blade's hilt, his hand had been so close to my skin...

Those icy eyes focused only on me... Fuck.

My thighs clenched together at the very thought as a familiar ache built low in my stomach and crept down.

A burst of knocks pulled me from the building fantasy, and I crossed to the door, hoping it would be anyone except Agatha and Edera. The nosy women were starting to drive into my nerves, and despite knowing better, it wouldn't be long before I snapped.

But when I opened the door, only a cart holding a silver hooded tray and a bottle of leftover champagne greeted me. I glanced both ways down the hall, expecting one or both to be spewing their nonsense about me.

Silence.

Rare, but I would accept it gladly. I wheeled the cart through the sitting area, ignoring the oak table and chairs. Instead, I beelined to the last doorway, tucked to the other side of the main room, and half hidden behind lace curtains.

The pig snuffled and snorted in his sleep as I passed, and I tried not to think about the implications of such a thing. We could raise it together. I winced as Arius' words played back in my mind.

Gods, I should have the thing sent to Driata for spite.

Turning, I used my hip and back to shove open the heavy door and yanked the cart along after me.

Another sigh escaped me as I took in the ridiculously over-done space.

The sleeping room was double the size of the other rooms combined, though it had been decorated by the same gaudy hand. The designer chose pale gold paper for the walls, smattered with orange blossoms. Gigantic wooden posts were inlaid with citrine and draped in chiffon curtains that framed a pillow-laden bed. The sheer fabric billowed in the jasmine-scented breeze drifting in from open balcony doors. The furnishings all held the same gold and orange notes that I realized were a theme.

Gods, imagine someone told the castle's staff that those were colors I enjoyed. A pig to care for and shades of orange to stare at for the rest of my life. Lovely.

My stomach growled, alerting me of its displeasure at being confined all day instead of filled.

Pulling my focus away from the garish room, I removed the tray's lid. Yellow and white shades of cheese formed a flower in the center of the dish, fanned on one side by various warm slices of bread and on the other by golden, flaky meat pies and shell-fish cakes.

Not a fruit or vegetable in sight.

My satisfaction in Driata's torment during our stay may have been wrong, but so was her causing my first son to be a bristly fucking hog.

I plucked up a few cubed bites of cheese, tucking them into my mouth and noting a bit of white and thin black cylinders poking out from behind the tray. Someone had stuck pencils and a parchment there.

I plopped two more bits, one saltier and one sharper, in my mouth.

Could I? Should I? Did I have the time before my meeting?

I seized a meat pie and bit into it. The steaming, buttery crust melted while the garlicky meat roasted my tongue.

How long had it been since I'd drawn just for the sake of the art? When was the last time I let the smearing of lead color the side of my hand as pencils detailed the lines and shapes of my inspiration?

I took another bite of the pie, chewing slowly as the heat gave way to herbs—hints of rosemary and thyme being brutally suffocated by garlic. I swallowed, and my hand was already reaching for the drawing supplies.

Just a few minutes, I cautioned myself, knowing the desire would win out. But only for a few minutes because I needed to focus on the tasks at hand—ones that served Baltazar.

I looked at the massive bed. It would swallow me whole if I scaled the edge of it and sank into the mounds of pillows.

Shaking my head, I pivoted, deciding to drag the cart onto the balcony instead.

Wide, wooden-backed chairs greeted me. The fire pit they surrounded burst to life as I stepped onto the wooden planks—a detection spell of some sort. An iron railing edged the long space's expanse, allowing one to overlook the waves crashing against the royal docks in the distance. I guessed, by looks alone, which of the ships were the foreign king's and the ones that belonged to the cold queen.

Orabelle's fleet and Blair's were as different as the pair of rulers. Hers were unpainted steel meant to survive the treacherous rocks surrounding the Isles of Weylin. Blair's simple structures appeared to have never had much time in the sea or too much. Builders crafted them of wood with great, velvet textured sails.

Music swelled on the night air to my left, much at a much faster pace than when I left it and not meant for proper dancing at all. Instead, the music was seductive in its thumping, thrumming, pulsing beat. I could only imagine the nobility being drawn to Blair in flocks as they shed their evening wear and inhibitions before inevitably letting the night take them away.

Jealousy simmered at their lack of inhibitions even as I propped the sketch pad on my thighs. I worked to focus on the ships in the sea and started sketching out vague arching lines.

Despite trying to quiet them, my thoughts wandered to the lust and dust-darkened pubs I would need to visit on my next job.

It had been too long since I'd let a nameless face sate me,

even partially. And if I were to get through the ordeal my life was becoming, I could at least find joy in being able to make at least those decisions for myself.

Sloping lines formed under the pencil tip even as my eyes grew heavy and eventually fell closed.

The heavy tolling of a clock tower shook me from the world of dreams.

Shit.

I started, my fogged brain trying to wake the rest of the way. Pencils clinked as they scattered with the parchment on the deck.

What time was it?

I glanced down at the drawing I intended to be of Blair and Orabelle's ships. Instead, it was a perfect replica of Blair's ass. Shading and all.

I snatched the paper, crumpling it, and stuffed it deep into my robe pocket. Then, scrubbing a hand over my face, I rushed back into and through the rooms, heading for the door that led into the hallway.

Sleep coated my eyes as I yanked open the door wishing I could silence the creaking. But when I craned my neck out, peeking along either side, the carpeted hall was blissfully empty.

Careful of where I placed my feet, I began my dimly lit excursion down the hall. I wished for a change of clothes, even as I tugged the ties to my robe tighter and yanked the folds of fabric more firmly around my chest.

Night was my favorite time. I didn't need to stick to the shadows because the world was made up of them. I kept my feet on the cushioned rug to avoid making noise and relaxed a fraction.

The hall's silence was interrupted by the clinking of iron and grunting coming from further down.

Lights brightened an archway, where a door was propped open.

The nearer I got, the more clearly I could tell it was a training room. Perhaps for guards on shift taking their breaks on this side of the castle.

Like everything in Ellesmere, the area was superior to the one we had in Lunasa. More so than even the makeshift one Baltazar had created below our dungeons.

A padded sparring area spread along the left side of the space. And enough weights for a militia to throw around filled the other. My eyes moved to the back of the room, where punching bags and—

Liam.

He was shirtless, and his broken hand—his sword hand—was pinned behind his back. Muscles rippled as he swung, over and over, landing perfect blows. Sweat glistened in the magicked lights hovering around him. He flexed and parried invisible attackers.

My face felt hot, and my heart hammered against my ribs. I couldn't look away, even though I wanted to run. I was staring.

Gods, Jane... Turn around and walk away.

Liam shifted, and I tucked my body behind the wall, breathing hard. Metal scraped, and I peered around the corner again. He grabbed one of the long swords, extended his arm, and rotated it slowly, letting the weapon's weight settle in his muscles and bones.

"He will not break me," he whispered to no one.

I pushed myself off the wall, moving past the doorway as quickly as possible, wishing I hadn't seen him that way... Working so diligently to avoid being broken.

For a second, only one, I considered going to him. But I wouldn't—couldn't. Trying to sort through Liam's issues had long since stopped being my place.

I reached the final door in the hall and twisted the handle without knocking. The hinges creaked as it swung open, and I flinched away from the sound breaking my quiet. But a tea kettle screamed in an answer on the other side.

My eyes darted up, tracking my mentor, sitting half-dressed, hunched over a desk. Baltazar didn't look up as he scribbled furiously on a scroll. The raven's feather on his quill brushed the strands of sleep-mussed hair dangling about his face as he scraped the pen tip along the paper.

Baltazar adjusted, and I thought he had noticed me, but he only squinted down at whatever he was working on. The movement sent his pale hair tumbling further into his face, making him look younger despite the dips and swells of muscle in his bare tension-lined shoulders.

Was there a clothing shortage I hadn't been made aware of?

I shifted my weight back and forth, knowing better than to interrupt whatever he was doing.

His room was much smaller than mine, consisting of only a bed, a kitchenette, and a desk. It was the chamber of a man who didn't want to be waited on. Or perhaps, for some, too lowly to be served. I had no doubts that he arranged to have it that way.

Deciding it was better to wait for his attention, I turned to the kitchenette. My time was better spent distracting myself from his naked chest, and food was as good an option as any.

Was he pissed? Did that mean I was late, after all? I hadn't waited to hear the rest of the clock tower's peals to know if I was. On the other hand, who knew, maybe I was early?

I still didn't know what he wanted from me, but for him to ask me to join him in the middle of the night and devoid of half his clothing... Perhaps...

An open cabinet door swung, and I jumped back as one of the trainees stepped into view from behind it.

Fox, named for the shape of his face and not his quick wit. I supposed Baltazar must have brought him along.

But if he were there, it confirmed I misread my mentor's invitation to his rooms when I thought he was making a pass...

The scrawny thing pulled away with a roll of sweet bread hanging from his maw and a pile of them in his arms. He saw me and flinched, sending the rolls flying.

"Clean it up," Baltazar commanded without looking up from his desk.

Fox scrambled around the small room, picking them up. "On it, Boss."

I nudged one toward him with my foot and went to the abandoned cabinets. Then, grabbing a teacup and the last roll, I shot daggers at Fox over my shoulder.

The boy was at most fourteen, Baltazar's newest recruit, and he ate like an animal. But mostly, he just quietly stared at me every time I wound up around him. This time though, he drew in one of his heavy, wheezing little breaths and nodded his head.

I eyed him, confused until he nodded again. As though he was encouraging himself.

"I heard about the explosion today. Riva said that was you." Only after he finished, his voice pitched with excitement, did I fully process that he was speaking to me.

"Yea." I knew it was rude that I barely listened or cared what he said. The recruits always knew too much, in my opinion. Riva was another training to be a spy and hadn't yet been given a name. I scooped tea from the counter and plopped it into the cup.

"That's legendary." He bobbed his head, and more rolls spilled from his arms onto the floor.

I poured the boiled water over the chamomile, and the scent wafted up into my face. I watched the color deepen, and the leaves expand, refusing to move my eyes from the cup. I knew where I would look if I did.

Seconds ticked by as the steam created a haze over the yellowing liquid.

My focus was so unbreakable that I was sure I hadn't blinked. Once it fully steeped, I walked carefully to the table.

I wasn't hungry, even as I ripped the roll and let it melt on my tongue. But it was doing what I meant it to—distracting me. A few more bites and the tea would be cool enough to gulp down.

Fox plopped down in the chair across from me, apparently done with his task. "I have my first trial run with Scoot coming up."

Ah, Scoot. Not one I would have paired with a trainee. He earned his name from vanishing at any sign of trouble during a mission.

"We're going over the boundary." Fox had quieted his voice. With good reason, but it only served to catch my attention finally.

"What do you know about the fae?" I asked, taking another bite of my roll.

"They're dangerous." His fingers tapped nervously on the table. Good. He should be scared.

"Jane," Baltazar called. He still hadn't looked up but crooked a finger and angled it at the chair opposite his.

"Take devil's nettle with you, tuck it in your shoes. And if a faery glamours you—and you somehow realize it—rub salt in your eyes." I finished my roll, lifted my cup in salute at the boy, and moved at my mentor's command.

Baltazar pushed around some papers before looking up.

The muscles in his shoulders flexed, and my mouth went dry. I grabbed my teacup, choking down the liquid, leaves and all, even as it scorched my throat. It was all I could do not to cough it back up as I sat the cup on the desk.

"Fox was about to be sent for you."

So I *was* late, and he *was* annoyed.

I focused on a spot in the center of his forehead, coaching

myself not to look down.

He steepled his hands. "I have a job for you."

"So soon?" I could no more hide my shock than he could his disproval with it. He usually gave me a few days before a mission.

"Tonight."

"Of course, what is it you need from me." I knew better than to question him though he should have given me time to plan. And there was the minor issue of my not having pants... A fact Louisa hadn't been shy about pointing out as she stuffed me into the corset and gown.

Baltazar folded the paper he had been scrawling on and sealed it with wax. "I need you to deliver the blood crown to the King of Karhdaro's main ship."

"Blair was your client?" So much for knowing better than to ask questions.

"No." His answer was simple, curt. A warning, really, for me to tread lightly and consider my place.

If Blair wasn't his client... I was, what? Planting it?

Baltazar wanted to frame Blair or one of his clan members. It was a simple job, one my mentor had given a hundred times —to his spies. "Isn't there someone better suited to this task?"

Blair had been kind to me. I felt like myself for the first time in a long time, and dammit if I wasn't tired of pretending.

"Since when do I not know what suits you?" His brow knitted, and I knew without looking that his mouth had formed a line, and he would have clenched his jaw.

My eyes met his, and I lost every inch of will I had when I considered what was below them. The expanse of uncovered muscle, probably tightening with anger.

Don't you dare look.

Forcing a smile, I nodded. "Where do you need me to plant it?"

"Good girl," he purred, and any indignation fled me. "Somewhere he won't notice, but guards can discover it easily. He leaves at dawn, so be sure to see the task completed when you leave here."

My fingers curled around the bottom of my seat, hard enough that I thought the wood might splinter, even as I bobbed my head in a nod.

Baltazar pulled a black canvas bag from a drawer within his desk. Unlocked, of course. He was confident no one would ever betray him. "There are supplies here too. Rope and two daggers."

I was entering an unknown king's ship to frame him for stealing a crown, and Baltazar gave me two daggers and a rope? *Was he trying to get me killed?*

Nodding again, I uncurled my fingers from the seat and stood, dragging the satchel with me and aiming for the door. "On it, Boss."

"Oh, and one more thing," Baltazar said as I reached the door.

I hummed, barely listening over the ringing of my own death knells in my ears.

"When you're awake this late," he continued. "I'd much rather you train than eat."

Not tonight, I thought, yanking open the door. And it took every ounce of my will not to rip it off its creaking hinges before it closed behind me.

CHAPTER 9

The realization that the armoire in my chamber held nothing—save for elaborate gowns with too complicated straps, ties, buttons, more frilly robes, and a drawer filled with slips and lacey, nearly nonexistent underwear —was crushing.

A glance into the canvas satchel told me what I already knew. There were two gorgeous daggers—both with carved wooden hilts. The first looked like a bear's head, while the other was a mountain range. But, aside from the daggers, the bag only held a long, wrapped-up piece of rope and the blood crown whose rubies shone in the moonlight streaming in from my balcony. But, of course, nothing that would cover my ass.

My bag from my travels wasn't in my room either, meaning Baltazar probably had someone take care of anything that could implicate me in the explosions and the burglary that followed.

Shit.

Dropping the satchel at my feet, I tore through the clothes

again, hoping for something thicker than the silk I wore. There was another black robe, but this one had fur-lined cuffs. Wishing above all else that I had a single pair of pants, I tugged it from the armoire.

Trying to avoid any reflective surfaces, I lifted the bag's strap over my shoulder and neck, letting it fall between my shoulder blades.

The length of the robe would be problematic, hanging just about midcalf. But I didn't have time to worry about it as the clock tower tolled. That time, I would pay attention to it.

I darted for the balcony, knowing it was the fastest and most unfortunate way to the docks. I lifted myself onto the iron rail on the balls of my feet and prayed it would hold.

The bell pealed for a second time. Thankful to be wearing slippers instead of boots but angry at myself for having nothing but the housecoat, I slid my feet down and gripped the ledge with just my hands. My palm scraped on jagged stone, and my fingers found purchase between two bricks at the edge. I bit back the sound climbing my throat as my nails cracked.

I shifted my hips, stretching my legs in search of a foothold.

The wall was too smooth.

The muscles in my arm and back screamed as I let go with one hand and reached, trying to find a lower handhold.

Nothing.

I reached upward again, gripping the edge with both hands once more. My fingers spasmed, and I wanted to bash my own head against the wall.

The rope—I should have used the rope from my bag. And this was a great example of why I needed time to plan.

Looking down while I dangled there filled my stomach with

lead. But the chambers were on the third floor—I could manage.

I tilted my foot, letting my shoe fall off, and it rustled in the bushes below. It wasn't *that far* to fall.

The clock tower gonged a third and final time, and the silence echoed around me. The music from the party had stopped.

Okay. I could do it.

I released a fraction of my grip on the wall and let my hands slide down the stone.

My breath caught in my throat as the stone under my hands cut and singed as the ground grew nearer, and I couldn't grip onto anything.

Finally, blissfully, the tips of my fingers caught on a bit of crumbling brick. My teeth slammed down on my tongue.

But it held.

I breathed noisily, my entire body tensing as I forced my hands to let go again and landed in the bushes.

Brambles tangled in and ripped the fabric of the coat, and I stumbled. My back slammed into the ground, and I grunted a curse, then another—the first for Baltazar and the other for the cruel gods.

I closed my eyes briefly before pushing up to find my shoe. Brambles had encased it as though they had a will and wanted to spite me. I tucked my foot back into it and prepared myself for the rest of the horrid, unplanned job. I hung close to the wall, well into the shadows, until I reached the open expanse between me and the pier.

I adjusted the strap in the bag where it rested between my breasts, the crown's weight weighing me down. Place the crown

—don't think about the implications of framing a would-be friend and get out of there. Simple. But then, why didn't it feel simple at all?

Banishing the last bit of the thought, I ran for it, eating up the distance between me and the shadows. The fabric of my robe tangled between my thighs, and the cool night air nipped at every inch of exposed skin as I moved.

When I reached the docks' creaking wood, I noted that the ships' had even more differences up close. Orabelle's armada was slimmer and sleeker, crafted to destroy and consume vessels that dared to venture near it in the sea. Blair's appeared cobbled together by hand, and I honestly didn't know how it could even stay afloat.

It reminded me of Lou's apron, homespun and patchy. Not knowing the king that well, I felt he had a story for each marking and hole. I gnawed at my lip, reminding myself that the two conversations I had with the man didn't mean we were friends.

But it didn't stop me from feeling like what I was about to do was a betrayal. And the act itself, feeling treacherous, didn't stop me from having to do it. My loyalty was to Baltazar, the man that had picked me up from the shattered pieces I was after my mom died and gave me a purpose. And if this was part of his plan, then it was necessary.

I yanked the satchel around and pulled out the dagger with the carving of mountains, feeling its weight in my hand before pushing the bag back behind me.

Slicing the blade against my outer thigh, I worked to reveal any detection wards the king may have put on his fleet. "Reperio." *Detect.*

Nothing happened—

Did I do the spell wrong, or did the king trust his allies enough not to have any wards? After what had happened to King Maveri's highly protected treasury and given what I was about to do—it probably wasn't such a good idea.

Usually, I would have much more time to plan it out. I would have time to figure out where to stash bloody clothes and weapons, map an escape route, etcetera. But apparently, the task would be on the fly. As my blood dripped into my fur-lined slipper and soaked into the material of my robe, I realized I was probably going to have to ditch my clothes in the sea. Which meant I would have to dash back to my room naked, especially with Agatha and Edera there to inspect me and watch my every move.

Great.

I was one gust of wind away from showing my rounded backside to the whole of Ellesmere castle.

Get it together, Jane.

Pulling the rope from the bag, I fastened it around the end of the dagger even as I slunk more profound into the shadows cast by the ship's side. I needed to work quickly and quietly. If I got caught—oh Gods, if I got caught breaking into a foreign king's ship with the stolen blood crown—no, I couldn't think that way. I had until dawn to get in, place the damn thing, and return to my chambers.

Loosely looping the rope in large circles, the dagger hanging free, I let my hands get used to the weight. The salty air coated my nose as I worked to slow my breathing and observed the ledge high above me. I shook my shoulders and stepped back, allowing the unweighted end to fall under my shoe.

The rope whipped out as I swung my arm, once, twice, a third time before letting it loose, and heard the clunking of metal on wood. Tugging the rope to test it, I made a mental list of everything I needed to forever have on my person as I started my ascension.

A grappling hook for starters, though that could draw attention. I could use some gloves—the rope ripped through my calloused and scarred palms. A weathered board stuck out, and I pressed my slipper onto it. *Boots, the list needed boots.* I lifted my leg higher, gripping the rope to hoist myself. *Pants—speaks for itself, really.*

How the boat kept itself together in the sea was a mystery in and of itself. Water-worn holes and dents larger than me riddled the wood. What were they running into out in the ocean?

Finally, I reached the top rail of the boat, where I was met with a life-sized, wooden carving of a naked man, his back arched as he met the breeze. Blair was strangely liberated for a king—I bet he would have no objection to a woman wearing pants.

And yet I was about to frame him or one of his people for a crime that would surely end in someone's death.

"I was sure you would be too busy thanking Arius on your knees to come for this mission." Liam's voice at my back startled me, but I only yanked up the dagger from where it stuck out of a plank and turned.

Liam gave me an arrogant grin while propping his elbows on the ship's wall. "Though by the looks of it, you must have just finished."

His gaze, much clearer than before, trailed down my front. Those damned silver eyes tracked every inch of the ridiculous fabric I wore while I looked at the reflection of the stars in them. My thoughts trailed to what I saw of him in the gym... Nope, not going there.

"I wasn't given much choice in clothing." Did his eyes narrow at my words, or did I imagine that? I hadn't slept with Arius, especially not to thank him. For what? Calling me a pig or gifting me one? No, thank you. But maybe my words didn't outright deny it either. What did Liam expect—the man was my fiancé, my duty.

"Too busy *squealing* for him then, were you?" Liam asked casually, though a muscle flexed in his jaw.

"You're an ass." I started to brush past him, hoping to get the job over with, though the thought of what I was doing set my teeth on edge. There was no reason to ask him why he came. He always would, even when his presence compromised the mission every time.

Because it compromised me.

"I'm an ass, and you're a boar. Between us, we're halfway to a petting zoo." There was a smile in his voice as he mocked me. I don't know what came over me then, but my hand lashed out and made a sickening sound as it contacted his mouth.

"When did you become so cruel?" I spat, even as I backed away from him, my fingers tightening around the bag's strap.

Get in, get out, get back to your room.

His tongue dragged over the bead of blood on his lip, even as he cracked a crooked smile. "Well, alrighty then."

No surprise, no shock. Baltazar was going to kill me for showing my hand. Weak, feeble, a general fuck up. Then why did my mentor constantly test me by pairing me with Liam?

I huffed a breath through my nose and turned my back to him.

Stupid, inconsiderate, intolerable ass.

I looked around the empty ship, taking in the wooden beams, the busted sail dangling from the mast, and yet... There was something. Memories painted over the fading mahogany. So different were the old planks in comparison to the Orabelle's pristine silver fleet I could still see nearby.

If anything, it looked like a fishing ship, more than one fit for a king. But Blair hadn't acted like a king either. A pang of guilt hit me even as I tucked the dagger away in my bag with the rope and pulled open the creaking door to the ship's lower level. He had been strange but kind. And yet... There I was. I never felt guilty stealing, spying, or even killing in the name of Baltazar's cause. I never even questioned him about the cause's specifics—a better world. But even as much as I wanted that, I liked what he had given me more.

The walls had paintings of Blair pinned on them with many cheeky grinning faces. They blurred as I walked down the stairs and remembered the day I met Baltazar for the first time.

I met him on one of my family's outings to the square. During one of the trips, my father would force his children to go on each year to demonstrate strength. He said it was to display kindness, and in truth, the blessings we bestowed were always generous donations from the very treasuries I learned to steal from. But each of us knew the truth. The trips were a grandiose display of his power even without his magic.

I had been to years of training and lessons before I met Baltazar on that trip. My brothers and sisters had tormented me about my magic, threatening to leave me with commoners that would still reject me despite human blood because of my unearned title.

In truth, I thought about disappearing into the crowd long before he mentioned it, but staying was far more spiteful.

Because of that spite, Oliver, my eldest brother, beat me before magicking me through a wall into a musty pub house. I was kneeling in spilled ale and weeping when Baltazar walked in.

Heat rushed to my cheeks when I considered the shameful thoughts I had when I saw him. His hair had fallen in his face as he leaned down to offer me a hand. His lip curled at the sulphury scent of magic still lingering around me. "Let me buy you a drink."

Sitting at the stained and chipped bar, he whispered that he could make sure no one ever used magic on me against my will again. I helplessly agreed after just a sip of a burning cocktail a red-nosed waitress had handed me at his request.

I knew the risks, what the Tellyk men were capable of, and was so embarrassingly willing to be hurt again.

I thought he might take advantage of me. Or worse, try to exploit the fact that I was a Serpen, and maybe despite his ties to my father, he didn't realize how little power I wielded, magic or otherwise. Instead, he taught me to wield my humanity as seamlessly as he trained me to use magic.

Echoing footfalls behind me brought me out of the memory, and I turned to lose it on Liam—

Blair. The king—wearing his too-small shorts once more—stood behind Liam, looking all too amused. "To what do I owe this pleasure?"

Shit on it. We were so screwed.

Liam turned, a cheshire grin forming and his dimples on full shine. I wasn't the only one with a mask in place. "Ja—the princess and I were looking for some fun."

Some... What? Blair's eyes darted over Liam's shoulder. The tight stairwell felt as if it were shrinking. His eyes drank in my robe. I watched them drop to my exposed thighs and drag upward to the curve of my breasts. When he met my gaze next, he offered me a grin that hinted he knew how much of nothing I was wearing underneath the useless fabric. "Is that so?"

Liam gave me my new role without any direction. I refrained from pulling the material closed and let my posture relax as I let my lashes fan my face and plastered on a sugary smile.

I hadn't spoken when Blair's eyes narrowed, and he glanced between Liam and me. "What are you really doing here?"

"The truth is," Liam began as he held his palms up toward the king. *Right. That's where it all went out the window. No one would come to my funeral. Or perhaps my father would make my siblings show up for the public eye.* "Jane is a fantastic fuck, and I thought you should experience that before you leave."

The thought of breaking his spine crossed my mind only twice before I swatted it away. His first compliment in years, and that was what he said? *Better than being called a hog*, but not by much.

"Sleep evaded me when I thought about your offer." I not so subtly shoved Liam against the wall as I walked up the steep stairs and more faintly jammed my elbow into his ribcage. "Maybe I shouldn't have come."

As I walked, I ensured the material rose higher and higher

on my thighs. It was easier to color my cheeks red when I thought of what I was implying.

How far would I go to see the mission complete? Gods, would I sleep with him? More jarring still, why did I know I would enjoy it?

Blair's hand rose, the back of his fingers brushing over the curve of my jaw, then down. Chills followed their trail even as his hand rolled and grazed my shoulder through the thin material of the robe. "What's in the bag?"

I blinked—once, twice, a third time.

What?

"Toys!" Liam blurted when I didn't answer, sounding like he was holding in a fit of laughter. "I told her not to bring hers, that you'd have plenty. Let me take—"

Faster than my eyes could track, Blair ripped through the satchel's strap and backed away, already undoing it.

"Hm...daggers. Not usually something I'd bring to the bedroom, but I'll try anything once. Funny thing is... I had one just like this made for my guard... And the other one's identical to the one I misplaced when I got to Ellesmere. Rope. Fun. And would you look at this?" He let the blood crown dangle from his index finger, and I thought my heart would explode from my chest.

If Blair didn't kill me and I managed to survive, Baltazar surely would end me for trying to rip his skin off. The King of Karhdaro's stolen daggers? Smite me now.

Blair rapped on the wooden door at his back three times, and the ship lurched in the tide. I stumbled back, losing my footing, before warm hands and a solid body caught me. But Blair used the distraction and Liam's busy hands to his advantage. The king lunged at him and snapped the cord on his talisman.

I steadied myself as he motioned at the darkened stairs below us with the dagger before pointing it at me.

Turning, I saw that Liam was already descending.

Coward.

The cool, pointed tip of the dagger pressed at my spine.

As surely as I knew my name, I knew we would die there. Slowly, painfully in some sort of hellish dungeon while the careless king bled me out. Probably in a room splattered with the transgressions of others who sought to wrong him in the past.

But I had nowhere to go, no one to save me, and no choice but to begin the trek down.

CHAPTER 10

No one spoke as we walked. The only sounds were the crashing waves, our footfalls on the steps, and the thundering sound of boots on the deck, rattling the picture frames on the walls.

That must've been the members of his clan readying the ship for sea. That far down and away from the castle, I couldn't hear the clock tower to tell how far off we were from dawn.

If they set sail before Liam and I managed to get off the boat... Gods, I couldn't think like that. My eyes darted around the darkened stairwell as I tried to find anything to prevent whatever was about to happen. I blocked out the images of carnage while I noted the lanterns bolted into the wood-paneled walls. Those wouldn't do. But what about the frames with the painted, smiling faces? Faces that mocked us as we walked down to our execution.

Could I shatter the glass? Blair pressed the tip of his blade into my robe in warning, like he heard my thoughts. *Don't do it, don't think about it.*

What chance did I stand anyway? The monarch was massive, crowding the space behind me and matching my pace. He was much bigger than me and stronger based on the width of his arms. And he had my dagger—well, *his* dagger that Baltazar gave me.

I wished desperately for a different reality, one in which the job had been easy, Liam hadn't shown up, or I had altogether refused Baltazar's request. Or, at the very least, Blair hadn't taken my only weapons. I didn't want to die in a frilly robe at sea.

My jaw clenched as I forced myself to *think*. I couldn't fight the king hand to hand. But I could probably outrun him.

And where would I go? My mind taunted, thinking of his people on the deck above and the one behind me blocking the exit. *Down?*

We had no weapons, Liam's hand was still ruined, his talisman gone, and there was nothing to draw blood—making my magic useless. Even if I managed, the blade at my back was a warning. If I tried anything, Blair would surely end me swiftly. We were going to die there.

Our echoing steps banged around my skull like gongs. They sounded final—thunk, thunk, thunk. The sound our coffins would make as they nailed them shut. That is if he didn't just dump us at sea.

I could talk my way into and out of any situation. I just needed to play the proper role. But, then again, what was it he had said at the party? *If I wanted you dead, I would do it in a room full of people.*

How had I found that funny only the hours earlier? It was lunacy.

Liam reached the final step and turned, and worry pinched his brow. He looked over my head, exchanging a glance with Blair before the king spoke.

"Final door at the end of the hall." The king's voice was gruff, maybe because he was straining against his pressing anger by putting off the inevitable.

Sighing, Liam turned on his heel and continued his slow pace. We followed, the knife not budging—even as I felt Blair nearly fold in half to avoid hitting his head on the ceiling when he ducked out of the stairwell.

We passed rows and rows of wooden doors before reaching the final one, standing alone on the far wall. No one had marked it in any way—but somehow, even closed—my mind couldn't stave off the images of a torture chamber below the worlds.

"Go in." His words sent my heart hammering against my ribcage. I was going to die. As nice as he had been at the party, Blair was going to kill me.

The door creaked when Liam opened it, and though I couldn't see much around his torso, I saw an oversized bed.

Blair nudged me in after Liam, and I grew even more confused. I noted the shining silk sheets, dulled by the shadows of the pillows piled on top of the mattress. It took up most of the space, though the ceiling reached far higher than I would have imagined. Coals burned low in a grated fireplace to the left side of the bed. Someone had obviously tended them before our arrival to keep the room warm. A wide pipe stuck out its top and reached up to the ceiling, releasing the smoke somewhere outside of the ship.

Liam sat down on a metal trunk at the foot of the bed, quietly watching my panic rise.

Thick curtains layered the walls, ones I had seen in seedier buildings in Luhne. They usually hung in the back rooms to muffle sounds.

I didn't understand... There were too many questions pinging through my head. I was so focused on figuring out what was going on that I moved too slowly when Blair pulled the dagger away.

I spun, but he'd already backed out of the room and closed the door between us.

The thick wood muffled his voice when he spoke. "I'll have to delay departure." It sounded like he chuckled. "Don't go anywhere."

A click told me what wriggling the knob confirmed. Blair locked it from the outside. Before turning to Liam, I placed my forehead on the smooth door for one slow breath.

He was shucking off his jacket and cuffing the sleeves of his white shirt before finally tilting his head back onto the post nearest the fire.

I moved quickly, assessing the room. First, I checked behind the curtains—just in case. But the walls had no windows and no means of escape. Someone had bolted the grate covering the coals shut. And while it was obviously someone's chambers, there were no trinkets or baubles that would be of use. Even the dimly lit lanterns were far too high up to do me any good. I doubted the fluffed pillows would serve me against Blair or his men.

My heart took up a furious beat in my ears. I couldn't let my emotions get out of control. I had to keep a close rein on my panic, even though it felt like it was creeping into my veins. I had to think. To get us out of there. Then what?

Liam smirked at me then, and I realized I was pacing like a pinned animal. The familiar gesture weighted my feet to the stone, and my chest tightened. "How did we let this happen?"

"My guess would be the robe." He shrugged, his brow pinching. "It's...distracting."

I gritted my teeth against my quick retort. We couldn't fight. Unfortunate as it was, if we were going to get out of there, we would have to do it together.

When I didn't respond immediately, he let out a weighted sigh and relaxed his face forcibly. "Anyway, you should rest."

Panic rose, tightening in my chest. Warm tears stung the back of my eyes despite urging myself calm. "No one will come for us."

And it was true—Baltazar wouldn't risk exposing himself, not for his brother or me. I knew him well enough to know that.

"*Jane.*" The way Liam said my name made me think he had said it more than once. "I swear, I will do whatever it takes to get us out of here."

My feet depressed slipper-sized imprints into the layered rug as I paced. "He's going to kill us."

"Blair is not going to hurt you." I could feel his eyes tracking me as I moved.

"How do you know that?" I wrung my hands, feeling wholly helpless for the first time in years. "We tried to frame him. He's at least going to get Maveri."

"He's not."

"He's probably on his way to fetch the guards."

The door swung open behind me as I spoke, and Blair entered the room. He clicked it shut behind him as I rounded the bed to put distance between us.

The dimly lit lanterns and low-burning fire cast an apricot hue on his tanned skin. He shot me a wicked grin. "I much prefer to do my own dirty work."

I scanned his body for weapons but didn't see any—no sign of even my bag. His chest was bare, save for his own carved talisman.

Gods, he filled up the room's small space so thoroughly that I was grasping for a dagger at my thigh that wasn't there. Despite the warmth from the fire, gooseflesh spread all over my skin as his eyes trailed over me. The aqua-colored flecks in his eyes seared the flesh from my hairline to my chin. They dipped lower to the parting panels of fabric that made up the damned robe.

My fingers rolled into fists at my sides, and I pressed my fingernails into my palms. But despite the pressure, they'd broken and chipped. No blood welled.

I couldn't use my blood in front of the king anyway. Baltazar would kill me.

Fuck.

"Since neither of you admitted to what you were really doing here." The king turned narrowed eyes on Liam. "How about you tell me exactly what Baltazar ordered you to do?"

"Nothing. We just so happened to be on the ship...." My panicked lie trailed off as Blair's hand rose to silence me.

He wouldn't buy it. How had I not thought of a backup plan?

Because Baltazar sprung this mission on me, and Liam ruined everything—again. But despite his always being a nuisance, he had never made me fail.

But there we were, obviously about to be slaughtered by a foreign king.

I assessed the king and noted Liam's amulet resting on Blair's knuckles. The smoky quartz seemed dull like it needed polishing. But Liam kept it... How had I not noticed it was the same one I gifted him after his last one broke in training? I picked it for the color—the same shade of his eyes in the dark.

The cord was wrapped tightly in Blair's palm. Was there some way I could get it back? Then Liam would have hope of magicking us away...

"Now, Liam," Blair said, interrupting my sure-to-fail plans. "Tell me exactly what orders Baltazar gave you." Every step the king took, the trousers he wore tightened and loosened around his thighs.

Liam glanced at me, his eyes widening in panic. "I... can't."

"Tell me the parts you can share in front of our Jane."

"I'm to keep you on our side."

Blair moved once more, standing chest to chest with Liam. The breadth of the king's shoulders was wider than his, but they were matched in height.

I had no doubt the king's clan members weren't far away. There was no way we could fight our way out.

If I could just reason... Blair was so friendly at the castle. But that was before he caught us planting evidence on him.

"King—" I began as I closed the distance and wedged between the pair.

"Blair. I told you to call me Blair." He spoke over me, then turned my body away from him. His hard chest was flush against my back, and the too-thin fabric of my robe gave way to the heat of his skin.

Focus, Jane. "Blair...okay. I know this looks bad, but I can explain." No, I couldn't. And if I didn't come up with something soon, I was sure the situation would only end in bloodshed—mine and Liam's.

"I want Liam to explain how Baltazar ordered him to keep me docile if I caught you." Blair's thick accent was sultry though there was no trace of his calm arrogance or riddles.

"By doing anything to keep her safe. Even if my life was forfeit." Liam didn't waver, even as he shared breaths with the large king.

My brows nearly met my hairline with my shock.

His pointless mission was to clean up my messes and ensure I didn't become compromised—but to trade his life for mine? There was no fucking way Baltazar ordered that. Liam would have never agreed to it.

"Would you say..." Blair rested his chin on the crown of my head, twirling a lock of my hair around his finger. The red strands rested against Liam's talisman, still cuffed around his knuckles. "That is the command that takes the most precedence right now. Above all others?"

"Yes. I have to protect Jane." Liam's voice strained. Was it paining him to admit his orders? Of course, it was.

Why would Baltazar task Liam with protecting me when he

knew our history? It was awful enough that he was always there, hoping I fumbled.

Not to mention, I was *usually* perfectly capable of defending myself. "We wouldn't even be in this situation if it weren't for you."

"Sweetness," Blair placed his inked hand around my throat. He clicked his tongue in disapproval, brushing a thumb against my lower lip. "I haven't asked you to speak yet."

Liam moved closed to grip Blair's wrist, and the warmth of another body in front of me was overwhelming. "What are you doing? Blair, you're not going to harm her."

How was he so sure?

"What will you do?" The king squeezed my neck, and Gods above—it was too much. The gentle pressure and being pinned between the two men. "With no magic and a broken hand. What *would* you do to save the girl?"

I knew that I should have feared the death threat. But instead, I squeezed my thighs together, wishing for friction to ease the growing ache between them.

"Anything. I'll do anything." Liam's voice was desperate as he worked to pry Blair's fingers off my neck. But the king moved faster and soon pinned Liam's hand beneath his own, pressing it into my skin.

Blair turned my chin and tilted it up to Liam. "Kiss her."

Wait, what? A strained laugh escaped me, sounding all wrong.

He wouldn't. He would sooner let me die. And Blair... He was my *friend*—or could have been. Was it all some game to torture us, then kill us later?

A muscle flexed in Liam's jaw when he looked down at me,

and there was a war in his darkened eyes. The calluses of Blair's palm scratched the sensitive skin on my jaw.

My instincts told me I should fight. Fight my way out or die trying. At least there was honor in trying. But... Part of me was curious, dammit. What would he do—how far would he go to keep with Baltazar's orders? And maybe a part of me wanted him to want it. To ache for it and crave it the way I so desperately did.

I needed to suffocate those thoughts, but I couldn't stop them from flooding in. My posture slackened as I shook off the impulse to fight.

Their pine and rain scents encased me, caressing my skin, sinking through my flesh and into my bones. The king didn't need to urge me—I angled my head, meeting Liam's silver-colored gaze.

I still wanted him to have a way out, even as the curling low in my stomach increased and pulsed in time with my short breaths.

My throat ached against their rigid grips. Even more so when I forced out, "no one will fault you if I die here. You can let me take the blame."

"I don't want you to die."

"Because of Baltazar's orders?"

"No."

Then, why?

I hadn't spoken the words, but they hung between us. Maybe I should have asked. Perhaps given the circumstances, Liam would have told me.

His eyes darted between mine and my lips. If we hadn't been so close, I wouldn't have heard him whisper, "do you want this?"

Wedged between the two of them, I nodded. "Do y—"

Before I could finish my response, his lips found mine.

Lightning struck our bodies, undoing and re-piecing back together all that we were. Blair loosened his grip, and Liam slid his hand to the nape of my neck, knotting his fingers in my hair to pull me closer.

The king shifted behind me, pressing his hard length against my ass. He tugged down the fabric covering my shoulders and tasted the skin there. Liam didn't falter, didn't pause with another man's hands on me.

Did I hate that? Not really. It felt as though my body would combust with my growing need. Liam seized control of my mouth with his tongue, and any thoughts, regrets, or concerns drifted out to sea.

I wanted to taste him and explore this with him. Even after all those years, I needed to remind myself why he still held such power over my desires. Heat stirred at the center of me.

Blair's hand still around my neck and Liam's tangling in my hair... It was too much and not enough. I moaned into Liam's mouth as his tongue swept over mine. I tugged at his belt, and the smooth leather slid free of its clasp.

Blair's free hand explored the planes of my skin, my shoulder, the curves of my breast, my waist, over the dip in my navel. Then lower still, and my stomach twisted, tightening when he shifted to grip my ass instead. He hoisted me so my legs hooked around Liam's hips.

Thighs spread, I whimpered, my slick center grinding against the bottom ridges of Liam's stomach.

Blair steadied me with his chest, his decadent chuckle

rumbling through my back. Blair wrapped his arm over my chest, and his fingers crept down again until they trailed over my entrance.

I gasped as the king teased me, feathering over my core but not filling me. I rocked against his hand, frantically urging him on.

"No panties?" Blair asked, his teeth grazing my ear. "Maybe Jane did come to play."

I bit Liam's lip as my back arched, willing him to touch me too. He dipped his head in response, his teeth closing around my nipple through the thin material of the robe.

Gods.

Blair yielded at last—swiping his thumb once, twice, and a third time over the sensitive bundle of nerves at the apex of my thighs. Finally, blessedly, he plunged two fingers into my aching body. With his other hand, he ripped off the ties to my robe. "Do you want us to fuck you, Princess?"

Liam bit down harder, cupping my bare ass, and my only answer was to moan again. He lifted his silver eyes—darkened even in the well-lit space—and gave me a villainous grin. "I'm going to need to hear you say it."

The breath left my lungs as he looked at me so intently, those smoke-colored eyes filled with his own desire. I couldn't answer, not with words, but I cried out, riding Blair's hand. Liam smacked my ass and gripped the delicious hurt.

Suddenly, his hands were gone, and Blair slipped his fingers out of me. I squirmed while Liam sank to his knees.

The transition was so smooth that I didn't know what was happening. The king lifted the back of my thighs and splayed them.

Liam's tongue and teeth explored the skin on my upper thighs. He moved higher and higher, licking and nipping before meeting my center. I whimpered, my whole body buzzing and throbbing. I bucked my hips, rocking against his mouth, and he slipped in two fingers without warning.

"Fuck," Liam groaned, his teeth grazing over my clit. "You taste better than memories."

Blair leaned closer, nibbling and sucking my shoulder while stroking his rough palms along the backs of my thighs.

I moaned, gripping his hair in my fists and rolling my hips while I ground down against Liam's face. I held him against me, even though the pleasure was so all-consuming that I could hardly breathe.

Climbing... Reaching... Crashing... I gasped an unintelligible string of curses and came undone for them. Sleepy gratification rushed through me as my head fell back on Blair's shoulder.

The pair flipped my wrung-out and trembling body. Liam's pants rustled behind me as my knees thudded on the plush rug. He slid under me, creating a vise across my breasts with his muscled forearm, and tugged me against his chest.

Liam's voice was no more than a growl. "*Say it.*"

He was right there, the proof of his arousal pressed into my ass cheek. If I said one word, all of it would end. But fuck if I wanted it to stop.

"Beg for it," Liam whispered, tempting me to fight him. "Beg us, and we'll make you come."

Stringing thoughts and words together as my legs shook and my chin tilted so I could look at Blair—who was ripping free of his pants—was a task, but I managed, "please."

I wasn't sure it was enough, but I couldn't give them any more than that—wouldn't. It was all the pair needed, though. Liam buried himself inside of me. I panted at the size of him filling up my already pulsing core while he rubbed my clit. I moaned, anticipation washing over me once more.

My eyes moved to Blair, stroking his hard dick while watching us—watching me bounce on Liam—as if he too was gaining from it.

The king stepped forward, and I braced, taking his length in my hand. I rolled a thumb over the bead of precum on the head of his thick cock, looking up at him once more before licking the divot in the tip.

Sinful, he tasted positively sinful.

Slowing his pace, Liam settled inside me, and I ran the pad of my tongue up the bottom of Blair's shaft and slid my lips over the head. I worked him with my hand as I lowered my mouth.

Liam chose that moment to stop holding back. He grunted, surging into me, and I steadied myself as I moaned and screamed around Blair. With every thrust of Liam's hips, Blair went further into my throat. My watering eyes slammed closed, and I never wanted it to end.

"Look at me." The king commanded, and I blinked, lifting my eyes to meet his gaze while he shoved himself deeper still and let out a growl. "I want you to see what you do to us."

Blair's throat bobbed as he swallowed, pulling his lower lip between his teeth and biting down.

He grunted, an immoral smile tugging at the corners of his mouth while his eyes traveled over my head to Liam. "How wet has she gotten from sucking my cock with that beautiful mouth?"

Liam groaned as he slipped out of me before shoving back in. "She's drenched, dripping. There's nothing she loves more than being on her knees."

Bouncing my ass in time with Liam's pounding thrusts, I stroked the king to his base. I pulled back and flicked my tongue over his head to catch my breath before taking all of him back in. He drove his hips forward, slamming into the back of my throat.

"Gods dammit, Princess," Blair murmured, the sound itself threatening to push me over the precipice. "That tongue is going to get me in trouble."

My nails bit into the king's firm ass, and his dick thickened in my throat as he thrust deep and came hard, his cum rushing out. My cheeks and throat tightened around him while he groaned my name.

Licking the evidence of him from my lower lip, my eyes followed as Blair backed away. His smile was full of male arrogance as he stared at my bobbing breasts through hooded lids. I lifted off Liam on shaking legs, who grunted in protest.

"Down." Not taking my eyes off the large king, I pointed to the bed in front of us. He laid down while I climbed up to kneel over his throbbing dick. Leaning forward, I met his mouth as I arched my back to offer up my pussy to Liam once more.

Liam didn't waste time. Raking his hand down my spine, he lined himself up at my entrance before slamming into me.

Blair's mixture of a groan and a chuckle against my mouth nearly sent me tumbling over the edge again. "You'll pay for making him wait."

Just as the king spoke, Liam dragged himself out of me to the tip and volleyed into me again. His hand clapped my ass, knocking me down on Blair's chest. The king fisted his already rising dick and rubbed the tip of it against my clit.

My thighs quaked while pleasure rocketed through me, and stars danced in the corners of my eyes. Every muscle in my body went taut as I panted and begged them not to stop.

"Do you know how good you feel, Jane?" Liam's words were warmed leather, sliding across my skin.

I cried out a combination of their names while Liam yanked my head back by my hair—exposing my throat to the king, who propped up to drag his teeth along it.

Gooseflesh spread along my skin, and I plummeted over the ledge of ecstasy, unsure how I would ever recover. I clawed at Blair's shoulders, his dark laughter, and my orgasm tumbling through me.

Gasping and blinded by the overwhelming pleasure, it was all I could do to keep myself braced on my elbows and knees as Liam's grip tightened on my hips.

My muscles constricted around his base, and he spilled himself inside me with a grunt.

He kissed the bottom of my spine and pulled out while warmth seeped out of me. My inner thighs twitched, and I nearly collapsed on top of Blair.

Eyes heavy, the king tucked me into his side while my legs clenched and shook. His laughter reverberated as he whispered, "I was told we would have the use of toys."

"The first time is meant to be gentler." Liam offered as the bed dipped with his weight, and he slid in on my other side.

It was strange how I managed to be embarrassed, in contrast

to the confidence I had just displayed. But my face grew hot with it anyway. I wondered what the appropriate amount of time was to wait before killing Liam after he just shattered me so delightfully.

But one more time couldn't hurt. I bobbed my head in a nod, wondering what I had done to deserve such sinful torment.

CHAPTER 11

Gulls squawked on a salty breeze as I woke from the deepest sleep I had ever experienced. Chilled, silky sheets tangled around my legs while I instinctually stretched my deliciously sore body in search—

Memories of what Blair, Liam, and I had done well into the night, coloring my cheeks scarlet as heat rebuilt in my core. But I cracked my eyes open to take in the empty expanse of the bed surrounding me. Then beyond the wooden and amethyst frame of it, to the low burning fire... I realized I was alone.

With that painful realization came others drenched in doubt. What had I done? On the night of my engagement party, I slept with a foreign king and—Liam. Oh, Gods. I had the most brutally glorious sex of my life. And judging by the coldness of the bed—they left?

As doubts plagued me and embarrassment flooded in, so too did a tinge of anger. I grappled with the slippery sheets and tugged them around me while I climbed out of bed. The fabric pooled on the plush rug at my feet as I walked over to the oak door.

Tugging it open, I remembered the shock on the man's face who had brought in food hours earlier. I worked to think only of the delicious pastries he presented us rather than the naked scene we were displaying.

The rugs underfoot concealed my steps as I walked on, looking at an open door toward the end of the hall.

I told myself I wasn't snooping if I was looking for Liam or Blair. Small, pretty lies. Whatever I looked for, lie or not, vanished as I stepped into a space that felt all too private.

It was spotless. Not a speck of dust floated in the air in front of me or tainted a single piece of paper in one of the most beautiful art studios I had ever seen. It felt unused. The papers and sketch pads flipped open with pencils and pastels in every section, just waiting for a touch of inspiration to hit so they could be of assistance.

The room's far wall was a curved glass window that looked out on a still sea. An easel accompanied the view, propping up a large, empty canvas.

Blair's booming laughter pulled me from the trance the room had placed on me.

I followed the sound out of the peaceful space, further down the hall.

The floor dipped into wide stairs until I stood outside a dome-shaped room. The walls looked like someone carved them from the stump of an ancient tree. There were veins and swirls in the white wood. Fragments of light shone through cracks sealed over with a clear polish.

Liam lay in the center of the space, face down on a small bed with his arm extended while Blair—his back to me—held a buzzing tool over the new ink he was infusing into Liam's skin with magic. More confusing, though, were the lines and swirls of the dark tattoos that already peppered Liam's body—even from a distance—so similar to the ones I had seen on Blair's skin.

I ducked back, pressing against the wall where they couldn't see me, and peeked in.

"You don't think I could take a wolf in a fight?" Liam grunted as Blair moved the humming needle on his arm.

"We're talking about without magic."

"I'm aware." Liam lifted his muscled shoulders in a fraction of a shrug. "And I'm saying I could do it, a swift kick to the chest as it lunges for my throat."

Blair's chuckle echoed throughout the room. "What about a bear?" The boom of laughter deepened, sounding a lot like a growl.

"Maybe I'm not walking away from it, but I'm taking the bear down—" Liam's words cut off as a hiss of pain left him.

Blair's large palm slapped against the back of Liam's head. "Sit still."

"You really shouldn't have healed it." Liam's mended hand flexed, and I realized someone had righted his bones.

"I didn't. I'm aware of the rules." The king lifted the needle, pausing his work. "Besides, what will you do now? Re-break it?"

The pair locked eyes as Liam lifted his head. "I may not have a choice."

Gods, why would he do that to himself again?

"The pain was a nuisance." The buzzing started again as Blair flicked his tool back on and resumed inking Liam's arm.

"It'll be far worse if he finds out," Liam whispered, but I heard him all the same. Who were they talking about—Baltazar? Would he be pissed to find out his brother had figured out how to heal his hand before he thought the lesson complete?

Blair's fingers tightened around Liam's arm, his knuckles turning white. "He can't know."

"She's going to read into this." I blinked hard as Liam changed the subject, still trying to wrap my head around everything.

"Why shouldn't she? I performed gloriously." The king let out a dark laugh that made a familiar desire curl low in my stomach with the memory of that sound between them.

"She has to know it means nothing. I was only trying to protect her." My gut bottomed out as Liam spoke the words. "Thanks for that, by the way."

I bit down on the inside of my cheek, hard enough to taste the copper tang of my own blood. I was a reckless fool. How could I have trusted him again?

"Blair wouldn't have killed me." I don't know why I said it —I wasn't even sure I believed it.

"Mm... Hello, Jane." The king dropped the tattoo needle and stood, clearing the gap between the center of the room and where I stood at the corner of it as I gripped the edge of the sheets. He said my name in a way that made me like the sound of it. Nope, I was not going there. Not again.

"I'd like to be taken back to my rooms now." That stopped his movement toward me. I would not allow them to look at me like I was some lovestruck fool, not after only one night and a few gasps of their names. Pleasure was pleasure, and nothing had to come from it.

I coached my face neutral, hoping they didn't ask how long I had been standing there. Praying they wouldn't ask me what all I heard.

"Princess, surely you can't be wanting to leave while your bare flesh is still tangled in the material of my sheets." Blair offered me a smile, handling his surprise.

"I would be in clothes if you hadn't managed to tear through mine." It was hard to keep my eyes above the planes of his chest and the lines of muscle pointing down to what lay beneath his cotton pants. But I was trained in masking my emotions.

Liam strode across the rich carpet, and I noticed the inking on his body vanished. His mistake. I knew they were there, and if I squinted, I could see past the concealments he had placed. Why had he covered them up? I would figure that out when the two imposing men didn't surround me. Preferably when everyone was wearing more clothes.

"Blair would have killed you, and it serves you to remember that. He could have snapped your neck." His eyes narrowed as they bounced between the king and me. Blair looked at him then, attempting to convey some silent knowledge, but Liam ignored him as he looked at me.

"If Blair were going to kill me, he would have done it while my back was bare to him, and his name was on my lips." I squared my shoulders, wanting for some desperate silly reason to make him see that he had a choice even as bile rose to the back of my throat and humiliation burnt my face.

"I saved your life by fucking you."

"And what were you doing the fourth time then? Because I very well could have choked on your dick and died." I couldn't pluck the words from the air—they left me and filled the space around us with my hurt. But dammit, he shouldn't have that power over me. He couldn't.

Blair snorted a laugh, finding something funny in that. But the more I thought about it, the more vindicated I felt.

Perhaps the first time was to *save* me though even that felt untrue. But what of the others? And when they wore me out, my body throbbing and aching... Liam had curled next to me on the king's bed, and I fell asleep in his arms. What danger had I been in then?

"You've never been a disappointing fuck, Jane. So forgive me if I ran away with your feelings." Liam's mouth was a cruel line that I wanted to slam my fist into, but I refrained if only because my hands were the only things holding up the gods damned sheets.

"I feel nothing for you." Lies. I was a liar, and he got under my skin. That didn't stop me. "Don't let an orgasm fool you. I've been capable of giving them to myself for years."

"I'd like to see that." My eyes cut to Blair. The king grinned like a child in a room full of sweets, despite the palpable tension in the room.

Squaring my shoulders and ignoring Liam's jaw grinding, I looked only at the king. "I would like to go home. My fiancé is probably wondering where I've been."

"Understood." His smile vanished, but he bobbed his head in a curt nod. "You will tell no one what we have done, I hope.

And I will keep the crown and pretend I know nothing of your involvement in it."

He looked at Liam then, the pair sharing a glance I had no hope of understanding before Blair spoke again. "Go retrieve clothes for her and her bag. I would sooner carve out Arius' eyes than let him see her this way."

My stomach flipped at the suggestion even as Liam said nothing and exited the small room.

"It's not strange?" Old insecurities slipped into my voice as I spoke, and I hoped Liam had gone far enough not to hear me. "What we've done here?"

"I felt as if I had you to myself." Blair smirked and reached in his pocket. He pulled free the dagger with the bear carving and the thing dwarfed in his hand. He held it out to me. "Keep this. It will make whatever story you choose to tell more believable."

I thought of denying him, but his face warned it would do me no good. I accepted it, gripping the material of the bedclothes tighter over my breasts.

"I snooped." Unsure of why I admitted it but feeling bold enough to do so, I continued, "I saw your art room."

"If you like that one, I would be delighted to show you the much bigger one I have in Karhdaro." His smile was a slow, edible thing—like he knew something I didn't. "You could come back with me."

Ignoring the last part and focusing on the first, "Do you draw?"

Thinking of the marks he had been inking on Liam, I thought of how ridiculous my question was, but then his answer confused me. "No, of course not."

He hadn't said it in a silly joking manner, and my nose scrunched with confusion.

"Here." Liam returned fully dressed and practically tossed the soft clothes in my face. I ran to the back of the room and yanked them on, leaving the sheet in my wake, but the clothes made little difference when I realized I was swimming in them. They were a man's clothing, and judging by their rain-soaked earthy scent, they were Blair's. *Great. More evidence to destroy.*

Not to mention, I would surely have to lie to Baltazar, which I had never done. And that lie would have to match up to whatever Liam would tell him, even though the last thing I wanted to do was speak to him. *Grand.*

"We dropped the anchor when we were out of sight. Your magic should be strong enough." Blair clapped a hand down onto Liam's shoulder.

"Anchor?" I asked like the confused little parrot I was.

"My people advised us to sail out," Blair explained, and my eyes shot wide. "Otherwise, it could have looked suspicious, which would have foiled our fun."

I crossed back to the men that had brought my body to ruin while I was supposed to be on my mission. *Focus Jane.* "Our magic doesn't work like the other kingdoms. It's not as strong. What if we can't make it back?" Panic started working through me. How distracted could I have been not to notice the ship setting sail?

"Liam's is plenty strong enough, I assure you." Blair winked at Liam while the latter scowled in turn.

"Right." Though by my tone, I didn't agree as I turned to Liam. "What are you going to tell Baltazar?"

He paused, a muscle in his jaw flexing. "We'll tell him we

were successful though Blair nearly caught us. We had to lay low until we were certain the king left."

While I didn't want to agree with him, I couldn't deny the quality of his plan. "We can say we stayed in the servant's tunnels because we saw one of Maveri's guards."

"Your father-in-law's men are all over the palace after the burglary," he agreed readily, but his silver eyes cut to Blair's aqua ones. "One more thing, though."

My arms crossed over my chest. "Well? Out with it."

"You need to break my hand."

"Absolutely no—" Blair started, even as I cut in, my voice a screech.

"Are you out of your mind?"

"He'll know. I wouldn't have fixed it, and Jane hasn't learned how." He flexed his fingers, so recently repaired, like he was saying goodbye to them.

But he was right. Of course, he was right. Baltazar would know, and the whole plan would go to shit. I looked at the dagger Blair had gifted me.

If I did it... There was no going back. Blair would see me use blood magic, and that alone had its own set of consequences. "Why can't one of you do it?"

"Blair won't." Even as Liam said it, the king was already agreeing by backing away with his arms crossed. "And my way is... Much more painful. You try to hide your abilities, but I've seen you make clean breaks in glass."

I couldn't hide my shock at his knowledge. *Has nothing ever gone to plan?*

His eyes pleaded with me, and worry creased his brow. Of course, Baltazar would punish us for failing, but how much more would he punish Liam if his hand someone healed his hand?

"Why do you look like you're about to do it?" Blair's deep voice had increased an octave. "Fuck's sake. You are. Okay, well, I'm going to see about breakfast. Jane, it was truly a pleasure. Come for me anytime," he said suggestively, even as he paled a shade and backed out of the doorway.

That solved the problem of him seeing the blood magic. Who knew the large man could be taken out by the thought of someone else in pain?

I released a breath, grasping the dagger's hilt tighter, and took Liam's rough hand in my own. Then, slicing the back of mine while he cradled it, I thought of the tiny bones in his fingers, connecting to the ones in his palm. "Ruptus." *Break.*

A roar of pain echoed from the hall as Liam flinched away from me, agony streaming from his mouth.

I'm sorry, I thought, but I didn't say it. Maybe I should have, but my lips stayed sealed even as tears blurred my vision. I scrubbed my hand over my face, wiping them away.

My heart broke even more as Liam stepped forward once more, the hurt I just caused him lining his face.

He grasped his talisman and touched it to my wound, and it sealed over. "Let's get you back to him."

He meant Arius, or perhaps Baltazar. Pain cleaved through me, despite or possibly because of all that happened on the ship. As the sulfuric tint of magic filled the air and transported us back to Ellesmere, I couldn't help but think I was leaving a piece of me on the sea.

CHAPTER 12

W e landed in my guest rooms with a thud.

Liam's jaw was tight, his eyes squinting, and I wondered how he could bear the pain. It took effort not to ask him if he was okay.

Obviously, he wasn't alright—I broke his damn hand.

Forcing my mind away from his suffering, I adjusted the loose clothes. It was easier not to feel sorry for him when I thought of his reckless and rude words on the ship.

"Jane is a fantastic fuck."

"You've never been a disappointing fuck."

They lanced through me, and as my anger steeped, my imagination conjured the exact pitch he would scream if I broke the rest of his bones.

"We should—" he began, but I silenced him with a raised hand.

"Get out." Turning away from him, I crossed to the armoire. Blair's pants sagged lower on my hips with each step, and I tugged them up, tangling my fingers in the side, so they didn't fall.

The air stirred behind me as Liam followed me instead of leaving. I tightened my grip on my dagger and the fabric at my side.

"If you don't leave, your hand won't be the most pain you feel today," I whispered furiously.

Agatha and Edera could come in at any moment. I needed to change and remove any evidence of what I'd done.

"Jane—" he started, but I whipped around. Anything he would have said choked off as I lifted the dagger, pointing it at him.

I needed him to leave my name out of his mouth so I could forget how he had groaned it only hours prior. "Go."

Liam answered by shaking his head, and I moved forward, ignoring all warnings that I should put distance between us.

He stumbled back one step, then another as I leveled the blade's tip with his neck.

I followed his retreat until he neared the wall. He glanced back stupidly, and I lunged forward. The sharp edge lined up against his throat, nicking him and drawing a fine line of crimson.

But instead of looking unsure, even with the fury so clearly painted on my face, he offered me a ridiculous smirk. "If you wanted me pressed against a wall, all you had to do was ask."

Though he murmured it, his voice was too loud, and fuck, we were too close. I focused on his neck, my steady hand, and my breathing. I wouldn't notice how his scent clung to me or how my heart thrummed in my neck despite all logic urging me calm. And I certainly wouldn't focus on his words.

"I don't want to be around you," I spat. *Because then I would think about what we did. And how much I enjoyed it.*

"Be angry if you like, but we need to see him." Liam shrugged as if it didn't matter... But Gods, it did.

My posture slackened, and a knot twisted within my stomach.

I had to lie to Baltazar.

I looked up then, and something softened in Liam's face. Then I blinked, and it was gone. His eyes were steel when the corner of his mouth kicked up. "Scared of disappointing your master?"

Any hopes that we could face Baltazar together withered with that damned smile.

I shifted, releasing Liam and running to my armoire. His body heat left me, and the absence chilled me even through the borrowed clothes.

Even as I ripped open the armoire's doors, I knew what would greet me. Frills, lacey things—nothing that would be useful to me, but I needed to figure it out.

I tossed my dagger to the back, covering it with the floral train of a gown I hoped to never wear.

My fingers released their grip on the hilt, and Liam grabbed me, yanking me against the hard planes of his chest.

Was he—

The sulfuric tinge of magic seared my eyes as he whisked us away into nothingness.

A hollow pit tore in my gut as we landed elsewhere, and before I opened my eyes, I knew.

"Where have you been?" Baltazar's smooth voice wrapped around me like a blanket, even though my fear of him at that moment should have made it much less comforting. "And what the fuck are you wearing?"

My eyes snapped open, and I looked down at the clothes Blair had offered me.

"She had no pants for the mission, so I loaned her clothes," Liam answered when he noticed my mouth apparently didn't work. "So unprepared."

I found my voice and added, "and we were spotted, so we had to hide while sweeps were being done."

"But we handled the guard who saw us." I refused to look at Liam as he spoke. Instead, I maintained eye contact with Baltazar, drilling my focus on keeping wholly still.

Handled. Was Liam implying we killed a guard? Surely, Baltazar would look to see if any were missing.

"Very well." Baltazar stood, dragging a gilded letter opener off his desk.

The sound it made carved through my resolve. Was he... Going to hurt us? Here?

But Baltazar didn't move toward us. Instead, he cleared the space between himself and the door leading to the hall. "You two obviously need more training if you can't do something as simple as this without being caught."

"Of course, sir," Liam agreed like Baltazar wasn't condescending, and his tone alone hadn't implied his disbelief of our lie. But I forced myself to nod along.

Baltazar waved his hand in front of his face, muttering a word and slicing open his hand with the opener.

My ears popped, and a dull ringing pealed before... Nothing. The absence of sound was startling. I couldn't even hear my own heartbeat though I could feel it kicking up its pace in my chest. My eyes felt wider, trying to compensate for my other lost senses.

A silencing spell, one I'd seen him use a dozen times... On others.

His mouth moved in a mockery of speech, and the blood in his hand pooled, glistening in the lantern light. But the crimson brightened, emanating a crimson-hued light of its own.

He pressed his hand in the center of the door, sliding it down and smearing the glimmering blood. He shifted away, and the liquid swirled around the door, taking its shape.

My mouth fell open on a silent question as Baltazar backed away from the fully glowing door. He waved his hand, allowing sound to rush back in. The flicker of the lanterns' flames, my heavy breaths, my heartbeat. It was too much and too sudden.

"Go ahead," Baltazar said, and I flinched at the gruff tone.

He held out his hand for Liam to heal it, despite being fully capable himself. But it was a demonstration of power, and Liam went through with it. He pressed his fingers—still ruined —into his brother's wound, stitching it back together with magic.

Baltazar's eyes narrowed on me and flicked toward the door.

He wanted me to go first, perhaps to prove something, but it only served to piss me off.

Nothing about a glowing door screamed fun. On the contrary, it looked like something that old fae tales warned against.

Leaning, I stretched my arms out, keeping as much distance between myself and whatever lay beyond it.

The icy knob bit into my palms as I twisted it, and the hinges whined as I pushed it open and stumbled away.

It swung open to nothingness. A swirl of black darker than the night sky and even less fathomable.

"We're going in there?" Despite the rising confusion I felt gnawing at my insides, I kept my tone calm.

"Yes, Jane." He enunciated his words slowly as if I might not understand. "We're walking through the portal."

It was mental, really. My affinity for doing everything my mentor asked of me. He owned my mind and body, even if I questioned my actions.

Blair's ship, a lust-warmed skin, panting breaths, a stolen crown. Flashes of the one set of orders I'd ignored.

And our lie to cover it up.

Cigar smoke filled my lungs when I stepped forward despite my pressing thoughts. The blackness faded into a grey haze coating the air of a lounge. Velvet settees circled around a small table where someone had spilled a deck of cards. A dark stained wooden bar wrapped around the back wall and was draped in shadow so thick. The faces of people propped on bar stools when darkened with shadows. Some sort of magic.

A door on the far wall, framed by light-filtering windows, chimed as two more patrons entered. I couldn't make out their faces either.

Some sort of magic, then.

"There's a cloaking spell in place that protects everyone who steps into the businesses in this plaza." Baltazar's voice came from behind me, but it sounded...off. Different but still recognizable to me.

"I can tell who you are." My own voice was garbled and deeper like I had spent years smoking the cigars being puffed at the bar.

"Because I want it that way." He walked ahead, not motioning for Liam and me to follow.

The lounge was so different from the seedy bar in Luhne that it was shocking. Even with the tobacco smoke, it was clean and not overcrowded with nearly lifeless bodies. I crossed over to the large windows thinking I wouldn't be able to see beyond them given how little light they let in. But when I got to them, they were so clear that I reached up with my fingertips to touch the glass and check that it was actually there.

Cold, hard glass pressed back against my fingers. The same cloaking magic guarding the people inside must have coated the window. Strange.

My eyes wandered at the perfectly placed orange and white tiles that made up the streets and not that far in the distance— the marble gates of the castle. A plump woman in a pale blue gown raced by the window with a man in a fitted black suit at her heel, holding an arm's worth of shopping bags. Young children weaved around the couple, pretending to fly fluffy stuffed animals and a wooden horse. I couldn't hear them, but I saw the man's broad smile.

It looked like they were laughing.

A sharp, blade-like ache twisted in my chest. Unable to look on anymore, I pulled away.

Baltazar—cloaked in thinner shadows than everyone else, including Liam, who I lost sight of—tapped the bar. Once, twice, a third time. The barkeep clicked his tongue and yanked a chain hanging by liquor shelves.

Under the faint hum of music, the shelves groaned and slid away, revealing a plum-colored curtain. Baltazar flicked his wrist, and I moved toward him. A person holding the tidied cards stood. They cut the deck before slapping them back down on the table. I passed them, and they shuffled around the table's edge, trailing behind me to the bar. Liam.

As we reached him, Baltazar pulled back the curtain to reveal a winding staircase. He led our descent with a sure gait.

Lanterns sputtered to life with each step. I gripped the iron railing like it would protect me if the steps suddenly dropped off ahead of us.

Baltazar was being strange—more mysterious than usual and I couldn't focus on anything but the cold iron in my fist.

The steps went on forever, but we were finally met with a curtain that matched the one above.

Baltazar flicked it open, strutting inside with his shoulders straight.

The stairwell opened to a large chamber three times the size of the bar above. All manner of weapons lined the stone walls— everything from maces and gauntlets to bows and quivers of arrows. The floor beneath my feet was squishy and padded. Grunting sounded from different areas of the room. Shadowed people lunged forward with blades and fists in combat.

My mentor cleared his throat, and the fighting abruptly stopped as all the shadowed fighters turned. Thumping echoed on the stone walls as they slammed their fists against their chests in unison and dipped low in bows. Then the people launched back into their practice drills as if they hadn't stopped.

There had to be hundreds of them.

Sweat licked the back of my neck as I realized they were bowing before Baltazar, the apparent king of criminals. I'd never seen so many of his workers in one place. Back in Lunasa, I had only met a handful. And they bowed?

A door I hadn't noticed at the back of the training space swung open, and a giant shadowed body stepped out. Movement at the person's feet made me look down to see a chubby orange person's heels. Its legs were too short for the size of its body and sagging gut, but it puttered around the giant person's legs and mewed.

The person mimicked the others' salute but didn't bend when they reached Baltazar. "Merry met, Lord Tellyk."

Only when Baltazar nodded did the person twist toward me. "You're with me today, kid."

"And you are?" I asked, trying to see through the enchantment.

A raspy chuckle from a voice I didn't know. "A bit offended you don't recognize me."

"Your face is literally shielded."

"Lux has quarters in all of my strongholds," Baltazar cut in. "He's simply indispensable."

Lux's size should have hinted, but I hadn't expected to see him until I returned to Lunasa. He was a mountain of a man—the biggest I had ever met, with shoulders broader than Jett's and standing taller than seven feet. Lux had chosen his own code name. Which was for the best because the one we picked out for him would have been Ogre or Troll. His eyes were more intimidating than his size, though. I couldn't see them through the spell, but they were so dark brown they almost looked red when I could.

Though the men were sure to not see it—I felt a smile tip the corners of my mouth at Baltazar's third in command and my trainer since I joined the ring.

While my missions usually remained limited to thievery—I

went on one mission with him early on. His were... Of the finishing and information gathering sort. Needless to say, he killed three people on that mission and tortured a fourth. I still wasn't sure what information had been important enough for Baltazar to send an assassin, but that was the job. No questions.

I was more curious about the fat little pet trailing Lux's every move. Crouching down, I scratched the thing's chin, and it rubbed its face into my palm. Half the cat's tail was singed, and she had two different colored eyes, one green and the other blue.

"This is Ginger. Her last owner became..." Lux paused and clicked his tongue as if thinking of the right word. "Unavailable."

The sweet name was comical, given that Lux was a massive sword-wielding assassin and potential psychopath. And the fact that he most definitely had killed Ginger's last owner.

"It's good to see you." I stood, clapping Lux on the bicep in greeting before turning on Baltazar. "But I—I can't train here. There are too many people, even with the concealments."

My eyes subconsciously moved to Liam, who had never seen me train but had a strange amount of knowledge of my skills that no one besides Baltazar and Lux was supposed to have.

"No one knows who you are." He gestured at my face shrouded in shadows.

"But—"

He held up a hand to silence me. "You can't stay hidden forever."

But I had to. Not only would it be essential for my duties as princess...but I was his secret weapon. That was my importance to him.

"Is this because of the wedding?" My heart pounded in my ears. "I'm of no use to you anymore?"

"This is not the time or the place for a discussion." The shadows around his face thickened as if shrouding him from my growing anger.

When would the ideal time be? We barely had a chance to speak since I found out, and things were changing too quickly. "You're the one who arranged it."

"That's enough." He started walking away, dragging Liam by the collar of his black tunic toward another group of fighters.

"You've kept me hidden and all of this from me." I waved my arm to encompass the space, the weapons, and his followers. How had he kept all of that from me?

"It's only now become essential for you to know about this location." His voice grew quieter as he continued to walk away.

The sound of Lux humming caught my attention, and I looked back at him. He gestured at my clothes. "That won't do."

Looking down, I remembered the borrowed clothes. The ones I told Baltazar I borrowed from Liam. The clothes scrunched and sagged all over because they were far too large on my frame. "I've got nothing else."

Lux turned without responding, and I wondered if it was his rude way of dismissing me. He crossed to the left of the room, and I followed, convincing myself I wasn't above begging.

He couldn't skip a lesson I wasn't given a choice in attending. But he stopped in front of another curtain hanging between rows of weapons.

Silently, he revealed the racks of clothes that lay behind it. Starched maid's uniforms, guard's regalia, formal gowns, aprons. Everything one would need to go unnoticed in a castle's setting and beyond.

Rage simmered through me. I had gone on my last mission in a gods damned robe.

"I'll wait here and make sure no one enters," Lux said, barely pulling me from the depth of my anger. "Choose whatever you like that fits."

I stretched out on the far side of the room. The tunic and pants I chose tightened and loosened around my limbs while Lux examined one of the weapon-filled walls. Trying to decide just how to torment me, I supposed.

We wouldn't use magic. Our sessions were for physical and combative skills. Lux wouldn't allow it—he didn't even use it himself. He had refused Baltazar's lessons and broken the talisman he was offered—saying it would never be as reliable as a blade.

I straightened as Lux returned with two blunt poles. He spun one over his knuckles and tossed the other at me. "We're working on disarming today."

The wood slapped against my palm as I snatched it out of the air. Lux lunged, jabbing me in the ribs. "Fatal."

"I wasn't ready."

"An opponent isn't going to wait for you to finish braiding your hair."

My nostrils flared as I scrubbed the forming bruise.

He swung for my ankles, but I leaped aside.

Anger weighted my attack on his midsection, but he brought his staff down hard on my shoulder. I crashed down onto the padded floor.

"Dead." His voice held no hints of humor or exertion when held out a hand in offering.

I kicked my foot out, cracking it against his knee. My arm shot out, slamming the staff into his chin. "Dead."

He chuckled as he stretched his jaw. "Foul play."

"You wouldn't help an opponent up," I argued, using his logic against him.

Lux's staff stabbed into the ground where I had been, but I was already moving, rolling out of reach.

My thighs tensed when I raised to a squat and circled around him. I darted forward—staff aimed to strike—but he met the blow with his own.

The power behind it rang up my arms and into my neck. I danced back, and Lux followed.

Though I couldn't see the entirety of his face, I could feel his eyes locking on his prey. "Stop fighting with your emotions. Use your mind, calculate the best way to attack."

Lux flicked his wrist, spinning the staff again over his hand, speeding it up until it blurred.

But I was used to the overconfident prick's games. It was nothing more than a distraction. Lux kicked out a booted foot—meeting air as I used my staff to propel over the attack.

I spun, my teeth grinding together as I smashed the wood against his shin, then up into his wrist.

Lux's bellow, and the sound of cracking bone splintered the air around us. His staff thudded, rolling across the mat.

Laughter, surprised and bright, bubbled out of me as Lux chuckled. "Well done, kid."

Pain lashed against my back, and I tumbled forward. My face smacked into the ground, and my teeth clacked together. White spots flecked my vision.

Wood cracked against bone again, and I rolled. My breathing hitched as my weight fell on my bruised back. I blinked, trying to clear my eyes, and saw Baltazar standing before my trainer. My mentor held the assassin's fallen staff just out of reach.

"What the fuck?" I spat, unable to hold my tongue—damn the consequences. Baltazar didn't turn to me, though, and spoke to Lux as their concealments thinned. "Coddling the pretty bird will do her no favors."

Baltazar fucking hit me. Nausea swept through me while warm tears cast a film over my eyes.

Lux's words were strained, and I squinted. Blood dribbled from his nose down onto his tan shirt. "I wasn't—"

Baltazar gestured for Lux to stop talking and turned to me. "She isn't capable of disarming you."

"Yes, sir." The darkness swelled around Lux's head and dipped with his nod.

Had Lux... Had he let me win? Why?

"Get up." Baltazar wielded the staff like an extension of his arm, motioning for me to rise. I did as he commanded, using my own weapon to help prop me. My body protested stiffly, and I bit back a yelp at the stabbing feeling along my spine.

"I don't understand why you're angry with him." Or why you struck me, I tacked on silently. He never had—

"Your multiple failures are unbecoming." He shrugged, tossing the staff from one hand to another.

"I was successful in both my mission and in disarming Lux."

"Why is it that Liam goes with you on missions?" Baltazar tilted his head, and the shadows followed.

Because the gods hate me. "For safety?" I offered instead, wishing I could see his face. Maybe then I would understand what he wanted from me.

"Because I can't trust you to be competent without supervision."

"That's bullshit." Silence rang out as weapons and bodies stilled. I was losing control of my temper.

"Attack me." His casual stance was so at odds with the aggression in his tone. And—I couldn't hurt him. I couldn't imagine a world where I would want to. But I also never refused him.

Which was why I stunned even myself with my answer. "No."

My mentor's concealments dropped, and he blinked. The sluggish response only worked to emphasize his shock.

"If you won't listen, it's time for you to leave." Baltazar dropped the staff, and its weak thud paired with the emotionless words in a way that left no room for arguing. "Enter through the gates. If anyone asks, you've been enjoying the town in your absence."

Then, without so much as pausing, Baltazar walked away.

What had I expected? Anger? Disappointment? Either really, or maybe both... But nothing?

Lux offered me a slight wave before leaving me to my tumbling emotions.

My cheeks burned—both due to the encounter with Baltazar and Lux's doubts about my abilities.

I could have won on my own merit.

Why would he *let* me win?

Praying the concealments would mask my welling tears, I quickly exited. My muscles strained as I sprinted up the stairs and spilled through the lounge's door and onto the cobbled street.

Magic tingled as woven illusions rippled over me. I turned back to see the lounge was gone, replaced by an abandoned shop. Boards covered the windows I looked out through before my lesson.

Strange.

That was why I worked with Baltazar. The magic his blood was capable of was incredible. With his training, I hoped to be even a fraction as powerful. But at what cost? I wondered, veering toward the imposing marble gates. The welts covering my body twinged in answer.

I needed to heal them, to change and erase all memory of my time in Ellesmere if I could manage it. Though I hated admitting it, I had hoped I would love it in a new kingdom. A fresh beginning despite so often being swarmed by my past.

Ellesmere was so different from Lunasa. The clean street lined by polished shop windows so close to the castle gates proved just that.

Even if the ride to Lunasa's capital didn't take several days from our castle, our gates were almost always closed.

I supposed Ellesmere's ability to feed and sustain its people played a role. They didn't have to bar citizens from the castle if they didn't have to worry about an attack caused by desperation and anger.

But their castle *had* been attacked, and though I saw guards patrolling the grounds, no guards were stationed at the gate. Instead, there were iron benches on either side. An elderly woman sat on one, tossing corn kernels to a swarm of birds.

Ellesmere's people were so well fed they could literally toss food away. My people begged and died in the streets. Much like my motive for working with Baltazar, one cause drove me to fulfill my responsibilities to Arius. I could no longer watch my people suffer. So I would simper while any selfish hopes withered if it meant Lunasians had a shred of hope.

Resting my forehead on my bed chamber door, I let my lids lower as I finally started to give in to my exhaustion. It would be short-lived. I knew that even before I heard the door from the hall creak open.

My eyes popped open, and I stared down at the casual clothes I'd gotten from the training room.

Voices carried through the door, and I held my breath against a building sigh.

Agatha and Edera.

"I have it on good authority that her fiancé has been looking for her."

"Her whole family has been looking too."

"Surely, she's run off."

"Prince Oliver sent their brother to check the stables, and her horse is still there."

"Half the guard is looking for her."

Their voices jumbled as they put more distance between themselves and the door separating us. The soft squeals and snuffles of the hog eating told me they must be feeding it. What did that thing even eat?

"He's got quite the temper, hasn't he?" Agatha sounded like she was right outside the door.

If they took one look at me in my chambers like that... Word would spread through the castle, and probably all of Ellesmere, by midday.

I yanked a robe free from my armoire while stepping out of the training clothes. Then, pulling on a paisley-patterned fabric, I ran to the fireplace and tossed in the evidence of my outing.

As the fire flared up and grey smoke puffed out of the fireplace consuming the clothes, Agatha stepped into the room with wide eyes and a handful of crisp sheets. "Your Highness—Jane. You're back."

I turned my nose up, acting every bit a royal bitch. "What do you mean?"

She dropped the sheets on the bed, still looking like she had seen a ghost while she wrung her hands over her apron. "We—everyone has been looking for you. Your father and fiancé are in a tizzy."

Well shit. What could I say when I didn't know where people had already looked?

Baltazar had told me to come through the gates, so hopefully, no one had searched the town for me.

I huffed an indignant sigh, making sure it was heavy with the stress of my position and pinched the bridge of my nose. "I told Baltazar where I could be found."

Gods, when could I stop acting? It was exhausting, and though they were a pair of gossips, they didn't deserve to be talked down to by me. Certainly not because of a title and my breeding.

"The keeper?" Agatha tilted her head, examining me—

probably trying to figure out if this new information would be valuable.

"The *Lord* Keeper," I corrected, lifting my chin.

"Ahhh. The Lord Keeper did mention you were curious about the town." The woman didn't seem convinced, though. And all other thoughts fell away as I focused on making my lie more plausible.

"I find it fascinating the castle gates are left open." My voice was sure as I wove truth into the tale. Brief as my walk was, I had been in town. "And the stores are so clean."

"Oh." The crease in her forehead relaxed, and I let my heart rate settle.

At least Baltazar had covered for me...kind of. He probably regretted that after he saw Liam and me. And suspected us of... what? Hopefully, nothing close to the truth.

"—Run you a bath if you'd like?" I hadn't realized Edera was behind Agatha until she spoke. "We already have the pails heated by the fire. Just in case you came back."

"No, that won't be necessary." I waved them off with my hand, thinking of the bruises marking my body that I hadn't had time to heal. Then, gritting my jaw against the rosy flush that was no doubt coloring my ears and neck, I turned away from the two nosy handmaids. "Someone should tell my fiancé I've returned."

The two women clamored at the opportunity, each rushing to tell him first. Curses and a near brawl carried in from the hall as the door closed behind them.

I peeked around the wall, into the empty—save for the giant hog—sitting area, and dashed for the washroom. The stark tiled room was warmed by a marble fireplace with silver pails sitting in front of it.

I quickly dumped them into the tub and glanced at the unlabeled bottles of soaps, scrubs, and herbs on the cart. I grabbed a handful of what I had seen the chatty pair grind into my skin and splashed them into the heated water with a sigh.

I rubbed a yellow paste that Agatha had put on my previous injuries along the marks on my arms, the curve of my ass, my thighs, my hips... Anywhere that fingers had grabbed, teeth had bitten, and the newer ones from my lesson. But each touch took me back into the embrace of the two powerful men who had dominated me and then soured with the weight of Baltazar's blow.

The marks healed with the magic laced in the salve, and I wished that with each dissolving ache, the balm could erase the reminder of each touch. When the welts and bruises faded and my skin was pink from the hot water, I furiously scrubbed at my skin and hair. Partially hoping to forget the awful lesson but mostly praying the smells of citrus and rosemary would cast the mixture of the two men's scents from my mind.

How was I supposed to look Liam in the face again after what we did? How was I supposed to focus and get through each day leading up to my marriage? How was I supposed to marry a man like Arius when the memory of Blair's and Liam's hands and bodies were trapped in my skin?

I would pretend everything was okay, even as it felt like my world was crumbling.

CHAPTER 13

As if my thoughts had summoned him from the castle's depths, Arius' voice boomed through my rooms. "Princess?"

My hair dripped around my face and down my back as I climbed out of the tub.

I yanked the robe on, cinching the ties while the water leaked through the thin fabric and closed the distance between myself and the open door.

"There you are." Arius' smile was a slash of white teeth that didn't quite match his eyes. His fingers curled around my upper arms, not gently, but not quite bruising. "I've looked everywhere for you."

"I had no intention to worry you." My eyes widened, the guise of caring if he were mad at my absence sliding into place.

The prince ate it up, sighing contentedly. "Had you wanted to see the town, you could have told me, and I would have swept you away."

"I wanted to see it without frills and finery."

"You deserve no less than that which you were born for." He paused, and his face scrunched in contemplation. "You didn't go to the lower district, did you?"

"Lower district?"

"A place not suited for a fine lady like yourself, lest you have to mingle with the undesirables." He tucked a sopping lock of hair behind my ear.

Had I seen only the frills and finery? I pulled my lower lip between my teeth. Was there more to how his people were living than I saw? More than the cheerful, wasteful people?

I made a mental note to find out more and changed tactics, aiming, instead, for distraction. I dropped my gaze, allowing pinkness to spread into my cheeks. "It's unladylike of me to have you here without a chaperone."

"You're no less mine now than you will be the day we sign the contract, so who cares what people think?" The way he said it and the slide of his hands down my arms made me want to rear away from him, but I kept my feet locked in place.

"While that's true." Bile coated my tongue. He was so polite... But Gods, there was something about the man that made my skin crawl. "I worry your honor would be tainted if mine fell."

"Then we shall go take a stroll on the grounds." He locked his fingers in mine as he tugged me toward the door. "I want you all to myself on your last day."

"Let me dress." I yanked away from him and almost forgot to add a girlish laugh, so he thought I was being playful. Smite me where I stand. This is going to be a long day.

"I'll send servants up to have you fitted in orange." He winked. "It's my favorite color."

Nodding, I held my breath until he left the room, and only then did I groan. A long day, indeed.

Lou burst into the sitting room—alone and out of breath—looking as if she sprinted the whole way.

I raised my brow at her in surprise and question, and she shifted my bag from behind her. "I took your things to be laundered, but Aggravating and Exaggerator were on their way down."

"And you look like you've been chased because?" I glanced behind her to the closed door, wondering if Agatha and Edera—whom I assumed she was referencing—were following her.

"Prince Arius," she said the name with more distaste than when speaking about the handmaids. "He was looking for them, but I intercepted him. I figured you'd want my company more than theirs."

"Well, praise above for your swift feet." I loosened a breath of laughter as she shooed me to my room.

She shuffled through the armoire, pulling out a garish orange gown the color of a ripened fruit, and my nose wrinkled. She turned so I could see the monstrous thing, so much tulle and ruffled fabric that I couldn't see the woman holding it.

"By the gods, this is the ugliest thing I've ever seen." Lou's voice was muffled by the layers of material covering her face. "And that's saying something. My uncle's rumored to have been sired by a troll."

She snorted a laugh, though the laws of our kind were clear about crossbreeding.

It simply wasn't done. I learned the lesson early when a woman was brought in for questioning about her son—a shifting boy with bark for skin in the city of Luhne. My stomach clenched at the memory of my father beheading her while my siblings, mother, and I watched. Even as my mother begged my father for mercy for the woman's sake. Even as I tried to run toward her son, Oliver had nearly broken my arm to hold me back. The boy died that day, no older than seven years old.

Lou stumbled, bringing me back to the present as she walked straight past me and tossed the gown into the flames. Then, ripping an iron poker from the mantle, she prodded the beast of the dress while the fire devoured it.

"Well, this is interesting." Driata's voice was too loud against the crackling flames.

"It fell," I said too fast, far too fast for something to be innocent.

Lou pulled away from the fire with the poker still wrapped in her fist. She seemed unphased by Driata's presence. Even if my sister chose to wear her tiara like a second skin. The barmaid didn't care that she was amid royalty.

"I'm only scheduled to dress Jane today." Her eyes roved over Driata's body, and my proud sister, the one who had been known to bring multiple suitors to their knees, was the first to look away. "But I can make time for you."

"If the scraps you're wearing indicate your worth as a seamstress, I'll pass." But despite the cruelty of her words, there was no menace in them. Like whatever she saw in Lou's assessing eyes snuffed out her bite.

Lou chuckled, seeming to note it, too. "Suit yourself, Highness. But if you ever find yourself in need, let me know first."

Driata's mouth gaped open. "I need to speak with my sister —alone. You're excused."

If Lou could rattle the rest of my family the way she so effortlessly had Driata, maybe her being there wouldn't be so bad.

She exited without so much as a curtsy which sent Driata into a huffing rage. "Oliver has hired *heathens*. Absolute heathens. What is this about?"

What would happen if I told her they were spies? Would she be angry? Relieved? Melt into a puddle of her own fear-riddled tears? More likely, she wouldn't believe me and would go directly to Oliver.

"Morale?" I shrugged. It wasn't a complete lie. I was sure his image did benefit from the new jobs he created.

"You're not stupid, Jane." She sighed and flopped on my bed. "Oliver is up to something."

Stepping toward my armoire, content with dressing myself, I crossed my arms. "Is this what you've come for? To gossip about the new servants?"

"No," she said, her eyes moving to the door. When she

spoke next, she cast her voice lower. "I wanted to talk about your absence the night of your official engagement. You were barely present, and then you went missing. It's all very upsetting."

Anger had my hands fisted at my sides. "Well, if that's all."

I took a step back, giving a clear view as I motioned toward the door. I didn't want to deal with any of it. Not then, probably not ever. She would inevitably tell me I wasn't grateful enough for my position, and I would have to care enough to pretend.

That was Driata's niche, making those around her fall at her feet.

"I'm sorry you don't want this, Jane." She didn't move from where she was lounging on my bed. "It's not that I don't understand why you wouldn't want to go through with it."

My eyes narrowed. "If you understood it and had taken my side, I wouldn't be here."

"Not long ago, you had far different plans for your future. And you've never had the classiest options in your life." She held up her hands in surrender, even as her words stripped me bare. "I get that. But your magic hasn't presented itself, and after your mother... Well, father just wants to protect you."

"Do you hear yourself?" I didn't bother to make my voice pleasant or to acknowledge the second part of her statement even while it ripped through me. She didn't understand. Not at all. "That's why you think I don't want this? I don't have enough class?"

Maybe it was my tone or how my jaw clenched in a way she couldn't ignore, but Driata straightened. "I just meant—"

I held up my hand. "You meant what you said. *Get out.*"

"Jane..."

"*Out.*" I never screamed—at her or any of my siblings. Despite how they acted, of all of them, she was the one I was closest to. She was the first to come to me after my mom died. She was the one who held me even as the others spat their cruelty. But all that, and she thought my lack of class made me want to retreat...

Her eyes were wide and shining with tears even as she grabbed her talisman. I saw the realization hit her as she vanished.

When the last tinge of sulfur faded, I searched the wardrobe for the simplest gown. I dressed quickly and nearly snapped my arm to lace the ivy-colored fabric myself.

If I had to marry a man I didn't love... I was going to be the best damn bride Ellesmere or Lunasa had ever seen.

Arius waited for me in the entrance hall. I nodded my thanks to the servant who found me wandering about, lost and a bit frantic, and escorted me to the sweeping staircase. The marble steps were inlaid with gold—because why wouldn't they be? And so polished that they reflected my gown as I descended.

The prince greeted me with an empty, preening smile. "Did I not mention the orange?"

"There was an accident with the dress." I shrugged.

"I'll have it cleaned so you can wear it for our departure." He laced his fingers through mine, and I worked not to flinch away.

"It burned—" It took me a moment to hear and process what he had said. "Wait... Our departure?"

"I'm coming back to Lunasa with you until the wedding. No one informed you?" He tugged me toward the doors that two stern-faced guards dressed in gilded leathers were already opening.

Shaking my head, I thought of the trouble that would cause me. Having the freedoms I had in Lunasa without my fiancé around was something I didn't want to give up. It's why I agreed to visit. To ease any tension caused by my not moving to Ellesmere immediately. *But now, the man had offered to uproot himself, and what was I supposed to say? No?*

"There will be no more disappearing, though." He chuckled, the sound low in his throat, and I forced a smile, even as tension wound through my gut. "I'll be keeping track of you from now on."

"What is a woman if devoid of mystery?" I offered, trying to piece together the scattered remnants of my secret life. How could I shut it down?

"You no more need mystery than I want it," he said as we stepped out into the grand drive. Flower petals scattered on a gentle breeze as we followed a footpath that Arius knew by heart.

Which—of course, he did. He grew up there. But he had only been to Lunasa once. Could that work in my favor? I could evade him and give him enough of my time that he thought he had all of it. But that would be easier said than done. And if I could stall him coming...even better. Glancing around, I committed every tiny detail to memory so I could sketch it out when I returned to the guest rooms. Every stray stone, the path's curves, and each trimmed shrub some poor gardener had groomed to look like animals. A boar, a bear, a rabbit, and so on.

"Are you doing it now?"

I hummed, barely hearing his words. I would have preferred to skip out on his company and work on planning.

"Trying to be mysterious?" My thoughts halted, and I realized I had been suspiciously quiet along our walk.

"Apologies, my Prince. If I'm being truthful, you make me very nervous." All lies should be based on truth. And it was true. He made me nervous, not because he was irresistible, but because he was as nosy as Agatha and Edera.

"Understandable, really." He squeezed my fingers within his own. "How often are you granted this much attention?"

He was right. And at the same time, he wasn't. Most of my siblings didn't pay me half a mind, but I grew accustomed to my own company. Then there was Baltazar and his ring of criminals. They became sort of a second family to me, or really, a first. Working on magic and learning to fight had bonded us in a way that only my mentor had power over. He picked each of us for our abilities to fade into the background.

And that all felt as though it was fake too. How much was Baltazar hiding from me? Did he care at all?

"Rarely," I answered, despite myself. If only because I knew it was the answer the prince craved.

He clicked his tongue at that. Like it displeased him even though he was the one to bring up the line of conversation.

We talked nonsense while we walked, with his time and again directing the conversation to me. He asked me about my favorite things, from food to my favorite day of the week. Having that much focus on me was uncomfortable. It felt like he was trying to prove some point, though to who—it was only the two of us walking together—was a mystery.

I noted a crack in the castle's outer wall, where small pebbles of stone had chipped away. It was surrounded by a smattering of apple trees which I found most interesting since I hadn't seen a single bite of fruit since arriving. Guarding the small orchard was a statue of a beheaded king Rikerd. A grotesque display that Arius said his father had commissioned straight after he killed the fallen king.

Arius reached up to pluck a ripened apple and polished it on his sleeve before continuing our stroll. "Have you named our pet?"

Don't let him realize you're disgusted by it. Instead, humor him like the simple-minded princess you are. "My Prince, I thought you deserved that honor."

He turned in to me, chuckling. The length of his body pressed against mine. "I suppose it'll be good practice. In preparation for my naming our children."

Merciless Gods above. Maybe Driata was right. Maybe I just wasn't made for courting. Perhaps I should have asked her how she kept such a straight face when men stroked their own egos right in front of her.

A small smile and widened eyes met his gaze. Like I was in awe of him. My head was an empty vessel for his thoughts to reside. "You'll be naming the children, then?"

"It is how things are done." He shrugged, tapping my lower lip while I did my best not to recoil. "We wouldn't want them to have frilly, useless names."

Right, I nodded. *Leave the big thoughts and big ideas to the strong and competent men.* I tilted my chin downward, allowing color to fill my cheeks. Too shy to be touched that way. On cue, the prince backed away with a frown.

Leave it to men to be easily manipulated by wide eyes and a dumb smile.

"Winston," Arius said with shoulders pulled back in a proud stance as he handed me the shining apple. "A strong name for an exceptional beast."

"I would have chosen Boaris. Or perhaps Wilboar. Though Hogry and Theoboar would have been contenders too." My laughter died on a cough when Arius stared at me straight-faced, with one eyebrow raised in confusion.

"Probably best if you leave the names to me then."

Well... I would call the pig Swineston in private then.

I nodded. "Of course, my Prince."

"Your Highness!" A guard sprinted through bushes coated in blooming violet-colored flowers toward us. Arius turned from me and steadied the man by the shoulders.

He wasn't a tall guard compared to the others I had seen posted at the doors and patrolling the castle grounds. He was still a bit taller than me but had to crane his neck to make eye contact with Arius. He wore a baldric strapped over his gilded leather vest. Two short swords—was he not strong enough to hold a full-sized sword, or was it a preference?

"Commander Jenson, how can I help you?"

Jenson sucked in a breath as if he thought it may very well be his last, and his eyes darted to look at me. "There's been a development with the intrusion."

My attention piqued at that, though with little difficulty, I managed to maintain a bored expression as I took a noisy bite from the juicy apple. Crisp, tart. Not like the sweet ones we imported back home.

"Well, out with it. What's this development?" If I wasn't mistaken, I was sure Arius' voice had deepened. I slowed my chewing to stifle a smile that tried to creep into my face.

The commander cleared his throat. "Apologies, Sire, but your father has asked that this only be discussed with you and him."

A long sigh left Arius, and he seemed to cool his temper with that one exhale. "Very well."

Part of me wished to object, to be privy to whatever the *development* was. But the other—more logical part, understood that it would only stand to raise suspicion.

Arius turned to me and brushed his knuckles over my sun-warmed cheek. "I'll take you back to your rooms."

"I'd like to stay—if that's okay. And explore my new home." Asking for his permission made me want to sever my own tongue, but I did need to know as much about the grounds as possible to work out my plan.

Arius smiled and nodded, agreeing to allow me the freedom of the grounds. He kissed my hand before stepping back to grip Jenson's wrist. "I'll come back when I've finished."

The sulfuric smell hadn't yet dissipated before I was jogging. I moved quickly but soundlessly back in the direction we came, searching for the apple trees and the fracture in the wall behind them.

Rustling and panting carried on the afternoon breeze. Chills spread across my body as recognition flooded me. I knew the voice the same way I knew my heart was shattering all over again.

I crested the hill against my better judgment. The cement wall was coated in honeysuckle vines, their orange petals crushed by Liam's back. His head tilted up toward the too blue sky. A girl wearing a saffron-colored dress was kneeling in front of him in the dense grass. Her red hair bobbed as she sucked his dick, and for one horrifying moment, I thought it was one of my sisters.

But she looked up at him—her voice husky like he had been fucking her throat for hours. "Are you close?"

And luckily, the voice wasn't one I recognized.

Liam looked down, his lip curling back from his teeth. "I asked you not to talk."

He moved to rest his head again, except his hooded eyes seemed to focus for a moment...on me. I stumbled back, even as that icy gaze locked, and a wicked smile tugged at his mouth. "It's your lucky day."

"Hm?" she asked, around the length of him.

My mouth went dry, my nails biting into the flesh of the nearly forgotten apple. I wanted to be anywhere else, but my feet were rooted to the earth. Liam leaned down, lifting the woman up until her legs gripped his waist. Her girlish giggle cut into me while he continued to meet my eye.

I opened my mouth—to what? Object? Liam winked at me and thrust into her as she gasped his name.

Her white apron flipped over her head, marking her as a servant. She writhed and wriggled while moaning loudly as he plowed into her with reckless abandon.

"You like that?" He mouthed my name, and my thighs clenched. Dear Gods, what was I doing?

"Yes." She dragged the word out in a groan of ecstasy, but she couldn't see his face. She couldn't see the expression of hunger as it bored into mine. My skin heated as I watched her come undone for him.

"What is wrong with you?" My voice was too loud when their mingling breaths and grunts of pleasure had been the only sounds in the space.

The girl screamed, clamoring away from him. She adjusted her dress and panted. "Your Highness, my Gods. I apologize for the indecency."

Her face was like mine, but different. Her cheeks were a tinge sunken, and her skin a bit paler. I twisted to gape at Liam, hoping against reason that he would answer my question. Perhaps he could tell me what was wrong with him. But he only shrugged as he buttoned himself back into his pants. Like he wasn't bothered by me walking up.

He owed me nothing.

Perhaps he was in a relationship with the woman, I thought, my stomach sinking. Did I owe her an apology for what we had done with Blair? That didn't stop my hand—still clutching the apple—from rearing back. It didn't stop me from launching the apple through the air. And it didn't stop the poor servant girl from jumping in front of the asshole to protect him.

The crack of her nose echoed over the distance. It pissed blood through her fingers as she howled like a cat in heat. The magic woven around her face dropped away, and her curly red hair turned to stringy, blonde waves.

"I—I'm sorry. I was aiming for him—" The woman's sob cut off my words as she sprinted away, clutching her face.

He *laughed*, glancing to where the servant had so abruptly departed. "You were enjoying the view enough to let me finish."

My teeth ground together, and I wished the damned apple had found its mark. "Did you conceal that servant to look like me?"

"She didn't look like you."

"Liar."

"You're not the only woman in the world with red hair, Jane." Liam crossed his arms over his chest and leaned back into the wall.

My nails sliced half-moons in my palms as I coached myself not to cross the distance and punch him in his face. "Look me in the face and say the words then."

"If I wanted to fuck someone who looked like you, I'd simply choose one of your siblings." He shrugged. "They all hate you enough to do it."

My mouth fell open in a gasp. "You prick."

"At least I don't pretend to be something I'm not."

"What are you talking about?"

"Prince Arius! I'm a vapid, insecure damsel who needs your particular protection." He held up his hands in surrender as he imitated my voice. His stupid magic made it perfect.

"*I'm* doing what is required of me." I wasn't sure if I was telling him or myself.

"No." His eyes narrowed as he kicked off the wall and closed the distance between us. "I'm doing what's required of me. You're extinguishing yourself before you've had a chance to burn."

"You don't know what you're talking about." The words were barely a whisper. He stood so close that the scent of pine and spice enveloped me.

"I can't wait for the day you realize how much power you hold." When he vanished, it felt like he took my breath with him.

CHAPTER 14

Finding my way back to the castle was much easier than I thought, and I was thankful I didn't need to wait for Arius to show up and save the day.

I wasn't the damsel I pretended to be. It was a role required of me and no more than that. So who cared what Liam thought?

Obviously, me, my traitorous mind whispered.

Walking quickly past the guards at the doors as I could without drawing suspicion, I made my way to the grand staircase. Three flights of stairs, a left, two rights, and a long hallway, and I would be back to my rooms.

I could sketch and strategize all I needed in private. So long as the meeting kept Arius away long enough. Then hopefully, my plan would keep him away from Lunasa for a while.

Rounding the third turn, I ran into Lou's stiff chest. "Oh! I was just coming to fetch you."

"For what?" My tone was sharper than I meant, and it didn't escape her. She raised her brow in question.

Shaking my head, I gestured for her to get on with it. It wasn't her place to worry over my hurt feelings.

"He has requested your presence," she said, her voice hushed. Liam, my father, Maveri, Arius, Andras? How many men could she be referring to... All of them, really.

My face must have given away my confusion because she mouthed the name of the one person I hadn't suspected. "Baltazar."

One mention had my heart and my stomach switching places. I considered but hadn't confirmed my mentor would ensure any valuable spies were in his pocket. I nodded, and she turned on her heel, not waiting to see if I followed. She knew I would. If Baltazar had hired her, he would have only done so after demonstrating the consequences of disappointing him. Like he had with me earlier that day.

We made it to his chambers in half the time it would've taken me to get to mine, even though they were a bit further.

I cast my eyes up and down the hall to check if we were clear before I swung open his door. But what I saw made no sense. The room hadn't changed, but who I saw and the clap of magic I felt filling the space was altering any sense of normalcy and reality I had ever held dear.

Driata stood, holding Baltazar's bloody wrist while the crimson-stained the sleeve of her gown. Why would he be initiating her?

"What the fuck?" Only when my sister jumped did I realize I'd cursed in front of her for the first time.

Baltazar gave me an easy, all-knowing smile. "The princess

and I talked over lunch, and I think she could prove to be quite an asset with the proper training."

He blew it. My cover, my life, my secret. In one breath, he damned it all.

"No." It wasn't her I was objecting to. Or maybe it was. But it was more important that he was replacing me. He crafted a new life for me to marry Arius—who was no more exciting than watching plants die—and he found the next available princess to trade me for.

"Excuse me?" I knew the tone. He was an inch away from losing his temper, and a punishment would follow.

"You heard me. No." My words were clipped as I squared my shoulders, closed the distance between us, and prodded him in the chest. "You are not to recruit her."

His hand gripped my finger to the point of pain. A threat and a warning. "I will swear in every single member of your gods damned line as I see fit."

I snatched my hand away from his, narrowing my eyes. "You can't."

He dipped his face until only an inch separated us, and his whiskey-scented breath warmed my face when he spoke. "I can do whatever I please. Especially when the spare I have can't complete a simple task without going missing for a day and a half."

His words cut into me, especially as I realized it was a punishment in and of itself. Maybe not for failing, but for not succeeding fast enough. For not coming to him straight away. And if he suspected what really happened...no. That penance would be much worse.

"If you do this, I'll never forgive you," I breathed. Hot tears burned the backs of my eyes, and I willed them away. Even as my throat clogged with emotion.

"That's where you're confused, Jane. I don't need your forgiveness. I only need you not to fail me," he spat, turning. The coldness of his words and distance swept through me. They climbed deep within me, burrowing in my soul.

"Driata," he said her name casually as if he had never called her anything else. "You'll be shadowing Jane for the foreseeable future. Where she goes, you go. When she trains, you learn, and so on. Am I clear?"

"Yes, sir," my sister chirped at my mentor like a happy little bird. Clearly not seeing that my world was exploding, and she was at the center of the blast.

Loosening a breath and squaring my shoulders, I reminded myself that Driata would have to be the next day's problem. Right then, Arius traveling to Lunasa was the biggest threat to my way of life. I knew what he was having her agree to. Driata couldn't out us, but Arius sure would grow suspicious if I regularly disappeared for days.

"I need a potion." Abrupt, to the point, and looking Baltazar square in the eye.

"What type of potion?" His brow raised as he stepped back, realizing I calmed myself down.

"A potion, or the ingredients for one." I rubbed my hands together as my plan started unfolding. I was itching to sketch it out, to see the images before me in my mind.

Baltazar scratched his chin, recognizing the excited gleam in my eye and knowing it meant I was readying for a mission. "What's the potion for?"

"A distraction." I shrugged, even as I bounced on the balls

of my feet. "My fiancé is planning on traveling with us back to Lunasa. I can't have that—not yet. I'll create a reason for him to stay here."

"Jane," he said my name like a caress, placing his hands on my shoulders. "What kind of potion is it you need for this distraction?"

"An explosive one." The grin that slashed across my face was immoral and promised chaos. And if I concentrated, I could pretend I hadn't heard Driata suck in a gasp. Like it was just me and Baltazar, planning...even though it definitely wasn't.

But he didn't return my smile—his face pinched with something I couldn't decipher. "I can't allow that."

"Why?" Gods, I was trying so hard to keep my emotions in check, but the day was getting the better of me.

"Because it's not part of the plan."

"And yet, part of the plan is bringing Driata into the fold." I crossed my arms over my chest to trap my hands. Not that I would strike Baltazar...right? Right.

He released a long-suffering sigh. "The decisions I make are none of your concern."

I took a step back, so his hands fell from my shoulders, and looked between Lou and Driata. The pair seemed concerned. Their only concerns should have been why they were still standing there. "Then the things I do when I'm not working for you are none of yours."

His mouth pursed. "You're always working for me."

"I'm doing this, Baltazar." Uncrossing my arms was a task, but I had to prove to him and myself that I could stay calm. "So, you can help me or get out of my damn way."

"So be it." He gave me an abrupt nod and spun on his heel

to walk toward his desk. A few moments of him rifling through the drawers filled the room with awkward silence.

I could hear Driata shifting from foot to foot and Lou patting the pockets in her apron, the contents rattling in the desk—

"Ah. Here." Baltazar swirled a glass bottle of chalky liquid, and the contents mixed, giving off an iridescent lilac-colored glow. He held it out to me, and I took it carefully. "Break this bottle where you want your blast."

"Thank you." A copper tang filled my mouth before I realized the bite I had taken from the inside of my cheek. But I barely noticed it. He stood beside my sister while she nodded like his good little lap dog.

Oh... Are they fucking?

"You only have ten minutes to get away once it's oxygenated."

"Fine." I turned, not having anything left to say and not wanting to see Driata standing in my place next to him any longer than I had to.

"And Jane," he called after me as I grasped the doorknob—inches away from freedom. "When this fails, I expect you to never question me again."

Avoiding a probing fiancé for the rest of the day wasn't easy. It did, however, allow me to explore what would be my home.

I drew in my sketchbook everywhere I went. Tucked behind hedges, in the crook of a bent and ancient oak, by a crystal-clear lake I found past the apple trees, and lastly, feeding some of the crisp apples to Jett in the stables.

The insatiable mare was crunching through her fifth apple —core and all—as I sat atop a hay bale. I knew my legs would burn with the itch of it later. There was something so peaceful about sitting in the quiet stables with only the soft stomping of hooves and horses snuffing to keep me company.

Careful of the potion tied securely to my thigh, I adjusted my skirts, gnawing on the back end of the pencil I used to sketch out the crack in the wall. The split in the foremost tree marked the spot, low at the base of the castle's infrastructure. Vines coating the wall nearly concealed it—but my eyes were trained to see the little things.

Like how Liam's legs parted right above the fracture... And how pollen and bruised petals had scattered over his shoulders where he rested them. The servant girl's hair was the same shade of orangey-red as the dress Lou had burned. Liam hadn't quite gotten the shade right, just like her face had been off too. But that was the risk one took when using magic to look like someone else. Nothing would ever be spot on.

Jett snorted at me, and I tossed her another apple, which she caught between her teeth with a chomp. "You're going to get fat."

She flipped her mane at me and turned her head away.

"The gods know I won't miss a meal if I can avoid it." I held up my hands in surrender. "I'm not judging."

I glanced down at my sketch, filled with abject horror. My imagination had led to a wandering hand. There, sketched in finite detail, was a pollen and petal dusted Liam pinned against the wall I was planning to destroy. Except the woman he lifted had curls that fell in a pattern I couldn't help but recognize. A head tilted back in lust revealed heavy lids covering what would only be my green eyes. And the building's stonework had become a silky texture that I gripped in my hand.

Pressing my knees together, I worked to banish the feeling of silk sheets slipping between my fingers. To eradicate the smells of earth and pine that washed over me like they owned me and kill off the lingering aching emptiness I had felt in my core since I left Blair's ship.

The sound of the page tearing from the binding of my book was jarring. The shredding and tearing that followed were the acts of a lunatic—a woman being driven mad. I jumped up, kicking hay and sawdust over the scraps of paper.

Sex couldn't be mind-blowing enough to make you lose your actual mind... *Could it*?

No. And I wouldn't think about it anymore. I would file

the thought away, the same way I had the creeping feeling that my sister was sleeping with my mentor. It was the only thing that made sense, though it also made no damn sense. *Why her?* I wanted to scream...

But the *why* made perfect sense. I wasn't blind, nor was I stupid. Plain and unappealing weren't things that accompanied thoughts of Driata. I tucked my sketchbook under my arm, empty of any evidence, and caressed Jett's proud face. "We'll get out of here first thing tomorrow, girl."

I could've sworn for a minute that she huffed a sigh, and I couldn't have agreed more with her. But the sun was dipping, and my stomach was rumbling. I'd only fed it the fruit Jett was willing to spare—which wasn't much. It was time to face everybody and perform one of my best acts yet.

CHAPTER 15

Having an explosive potion strapped to your thighs probably wasn't the best way to show up late for dinner. But I reminded myself that no one knew. Well, except Driata—hovering as close to me as she could get, despite the bodies I kept trying to wade through to get away from her. And Baltazar, who paid me no mind.

Starving for his attention had become a pastime, and I tried not to let it get to me. I always put him first and made his word my own strict law. So what had that gotten me? A giant rock paired with a commitment as large as most of my family's egos.

It was strange how the Alistair's took their meals standing, though I did wonder if it was different when there weren't so many people. While Blair and his clansmen had left early morning the day prior, Orabelle's small fleet had stayed behind. Though—for the life of me—I couldn't figure out why.

Driata cleared the appetizer table, stifling her need to flinch over the meat. But I ducked around two servers and one of

Maveri's guards, grabbing rolls and shrimp along the way, plopping them into my mouth.

Could I avoid her forever? No. But could I avoid her until the next day, when she would sit her ass in a plush carriage, and I would ride Jett back home? Yes. It would be several days before I had to deal with her again. All I had to do was evade her tonight.

She stomped her foot like a child and walked briskly to Gemma and our father, gathering food from trays for him. Gemma acted as if she had to be his caretaker when it was he who sealed his fate for himself.

Conversations swarmed around but fell on deaf ears. Baltazar would've wanted me to listen. To spy. *You're always working for me.* But that night, I didn't care what he wanted. His mission—that I blindly followed—had made me a pawn. Only for him to find a replacement as soon as it suited him.

I ate until I was fit to burst, psyching myself up for the task ahead. Until a freckled, angry-looking face popped into my line of sight.

"Hello, my Prince." He preened like a peacock at my use of the title, but his pursed lips hadn't settled.

"Where were you?" Arius asked, with his voice a harsh whisper, meant to not draw attention, as he nudged me toward the back wall.

I didn't answer immediately, chewing on my lip, but that only worked him into a fury. His fingers gripped my forearms, tight enough to bruise. "I said no more disappearing."

"I'm right here." *What would his face look like if I slammed it into the bowl of cocktail sauce just out of reach?*

"What did I say? I'll be back for you." His nails bit in, close to drawing blood through the sheer sleeves of my gown. "I looked for you."

Maybe I *had* lost my mind because that was the most interesting the prince had been since I arrived. "You didn't look hard enough because I'd only gone to the stables."

Tempting fate, was I? Maybe I should have stayed away. I was in no mood to play my part. The role had never benefited me anyway. Perhaps I had lost my head because right then, as his nails drew dewdrops of blood, I knew I could hurt him. Maybe I wouldn't live. But neither would he.

Anger unfurled in my core. Hot, putrid rage like I had never felt. Why was I being trained to fight if I was always to play the simple, helpless princess?

"Were you with him?" His eyes were bouncing between my own, hoping he might be able to detect the truth there.

"Who?" But I already knew what he suspected. Liam and my history preceded us. But, gods, Liam had broken Arius' nose over a dance.

"Lord Tellyk's bastard brother," he spat, though every eye in the room weighed on us as they watched the barbaric display.

"I told you. I went to see Jett." My jaw clicked, and I ground my teeth together hard enough that I wondered if they would turn to dust. "You actually gave me the idea to take her apples."

Oh. He didn't say it, but I saw the word in his face and loosening posture. I could feel it in the exhaled breath on my cheeks, in him letting go of my arms. He took a step back.

I straightened my spine, still playing my part, even if it shifted. *Now I was a pissed-off princess.* I tugged at my sleeves— as if I were self-conscious of the spectacle he made us into—

although the crescent moons could still be seen. Then, without another word, I stepped away from him and into the swelling crowd.

A clinking sound came from the side of the room where my father had been sitting. The group, made up of Maveri's supporters and Orabelle's, were so embarrassed and disgusted by the display between Arius and me that they let me pass through easily.

Generally, if my cheeks hadn't heated naturally, I would have forced them to do so, another symptom of the feeble character—

My father's raspy voice butchered my line of thought. "I have wonderful news."

The crowd quieted, if only hoping for fodder to mock him with later.

"Queen Orabelle has decided to bless us with her union to my heir. They set sail later today to announce this new alliance to the people of Weylin."

Hushed voices raised to deafening until Arius shouted above the commotion. "Wondrous news, indeed. It seems love is contagious. My future bride and I extend joyous congratulations."

Was it not him who told me the queen's last husband was eaten by *her*? And *love*? I didn't think that love had anything to do with what was happening. But despite my feelings on the matter, Arius' words had calmed the confusion. Glasses were raised, the marriages were toasted, and a revelry commenced.

I had half a mind to warn Oliver what he was getting himself into but quickly dismissed the notion when Olivia announced she would be traveling with them. Was I hoping they were consumed? No, of course not. But it would be nice having two of my tormentors across the sea for a bit.

Not to mention, with the celebrations at foot, I had the perfect exit strategy. Fade into the crowd, execute my plan, then pop back in as though nothing happened.

I moved closer to the arched doorway with every pat on the back that Arius and Oliver received. It seemed to become a competition—a pissing competition of masculinity and royals. Who could receive more praise and boast the loudest of their love? *One doesn't fall in love in a day or two, so I was confident neither of them could win that.*

"I told her it would bring potential to you and your siblings." My father chuckled as I swept past them in a flurry of bodies that had swarmed him.

"You did, father." *Was it just me, or did Gemma look less enthralled than usual?* The swell of support that our father was receiving did nothing to amuse her, which surprised me. I would have thought she would be overjoyed.

"First the heir and then the spares." Ciaran was clapping Oliver on the shoulder. How it should have been all along."

Had he just called us all spares?

I shook my head, realizing Oliver's back was turned away from the exit.

That was my moment. Ducking into the hall, I was plunged into my comfort place of shadows.

Dodging guards would have been easier if they weren't posted in every part of the castle. Probably due to the last incident I caused. It was okay, though. Arius had taught me the way through the service tunnels that first day.

Couples had split off and sneaked into alcoves and dimly lit corners to shower their partner with affections. Good for them, I supposed. Though with less alcohol, they would have realized that they weren't well-hidden, and the vulgar fountain I passed had less ass and breasts on display than I saw walking through the halls.

"Jane! Wait," Driata yelled when I passed the garden's entrance. The gods had either forsaken me or laughed at my misery.

I could continue, but that risked her hollering louder.

I turned sharply and waited for her to catch up. Her loud-winded breaths alone told me how well the night was going. "Go back to the party, Dri."

"Baltazar told me to stay with you." Her hands were on her hips, shoulders back. The way she stood when dealing with the mouthy nobles or a suitor who didn't want to take no for an answer.

"And I'm telling you that you're meant for the light." A low throbbing began in the base of my skull.

My sister shook her head, and I assessed her, trying to see a world in which it could work. She was wearing a pale pink gown that puffed out at the waist. Her perfect, straight hair was braided down her back, and her nose was pointed at the star-filled sky.

"No more puffy gowns. They're too loud and too unreliable." I whispered to her. "Tonight, if you must follow me, you'll watch to make sure no one catches us."

She bobbed, surprising me by not complaining. "Who am I watching for?"

"Anyone. Guards, servants, nobles, stray animals. And don't make another sound unless you see something."

"But what if—"

"No." I turned, not giving her another opportunity to speak as I moved across the night-coated grounds.

She was probably going to try to connect with me, but honestly, she could save the bonding for Baltazar. Which I certainly wasn't going to let myself obsess over.

We reached the apple trees quickly and only passed a handful of partiers that had spilled into the gardens and surrounding grounds. They were far off, though, within the torchlight just outside the castle and the drive.

To the unsuspecting eye, Driata and I were just two more nobles taking a moonlit stroll.

"Stay here." I motioned to the farthest trees and grabbed an apple from the lowest branch to hand her. "If you see anyone, say '*what a marvelous night to celebrate love*', loudly."

"Is that all? You don't want me to tussle with them?" She held her manicured and polished hands in front of her, rolling into little fists. I choked out a laugh before I realized she wasn't joking.

My eyebrows rose almost to my hairline as I shook my head. "No. Don't *tussle* with anyone."

Pulling up the skirt of my gown, I untied the glass vial and walked back toward the crack in the wall. The honeysuckle had already righted itself from being crushed. If I hadn't been so busy committing a crime—I would have been more fascinated by the gardening magic that kept the flowers in bloom.

I reared my hand back to toss the bottle at the center of the fractured stone.

"What a marvelous night to celebrate love loudly." Driata's

voice was quiet, and I scolded myself for not being more concise with my wording.

Crouching low and monitoring my footfalls, I approached her station.

"You're not scared of being out here all alone?" A deep voice I recognized as Commander Jenson asked.

"I—I'm not alone."

Dammit Driata.

"Right. Because I'm here."

"No, I'm here with a suitor." Her confidence was unwavering. "We're playing cat and mouse."

"And are you the predator or the prey?" Something about the way he said it made my skin crawl.

"I'm the mouse, and I must insist you go." Bitchy princess entitlement dripped from her every word. "You'll spoil it if he sees you here."

But I needed to *think*. He saw her, and my plan hinged on not being seen. I should have made her hide or stand further away.

"Well, I've gone and found you. Do I get a prize?" My stomach turned. He would never speak to her like that if there were someone around.

"Sir! Do not touch me." My heart hammered in my ears as I sprinted through the trees.

When I reached them, Jenson's back was to me, but I saw him pinning Driata against a tree. Pink fabric puffed around him, and she let out a garbled scream.

"Get your hands off of her." I gripped his leather vest and slammed my foot into the back of his leg.

His knee buckled as he cursed and fell into Driata. Before

he could right himself, I yanked the buckle fastening his baldric, and his swords clanged to the ground. The commander turned, his features warring between shock and anger as he saw me.

He lunged, but I ducked low and threw my fist into his stomach.

"*Bitch.*"

"That's no way to talk to a lady." Driata popped out from behind him with her face pinched in outrage. She flung out her clenched fist, but I noted how her thumb hung loose as her knuckles smashed into his cheek. She sucked in a breath, and cracking bone echoed in my ears. Her thumb jutted out at an angle.

Yikes—a nasty break.

"Driata, get out of here," I said through gritted teeth. He spun on her, and I tightened my grip on the vial. I could not let that thing shatter. Not yet.

"He ripped off my talisman," she whined, clutching her broken hand to her chest and diving away from him.

"Then *run.*" I wanted to shake her.

How could she allow herself to rely so thoroughly on magic?

I kicked upward that time, planting my foot at the apex of Jenson's thighs, and he grunted a curse, pitching forward and cupping himself.

Relying on magic is a weakness, Baltazar had said. *You're at an advantage because you survived without it all these years.*

It was why he refused to teach me any, except in stages. *First, you learn how to disguise yourself, then you learn how to defend yourself if you're caught. You learn how to protect yourself by*

*learning to fight and wield a weapon. Then and only then do you
learn how to escape.*

*"Why?" I asked, angry that he wouldn't teach me something
that would make my missions easier.*

*"Because," he had said with a crooked, arrogant smile. "If you
need magic to escape, you've failed your other lessons."*

A sharp pain stole my breath, and I realized my mistake a
moment too late. Driata screamed as blood soaked through the
bodice of my gown. As if in shock, Jenson slowly pulled his
short sword from between my ribs.

"What the fuck?" Liam's voice was a gut punch on top of
what was already a shitty night.

"They attacked me." Jenson was shouting, though it
sounded pretty quiet over my heart pounding.

"He *stabbed* her," Driata sobbed, kneeling in the grass
looking for...something. Warm hands grabbed me as the ground
swelled up toward me. Or was I falling? I coughed, but it was
wet. Thick. Red. Blood. That wasn't a good sign.

"I have you." Liam. Grey eyes. Storm clouds. His eyes
looked like storm clouds.

"Can't let you heal—" Jenson leaped toward Liam, and I
raised my hand to—what? Glass shattered in my hand as it
slammed into his temple.

Liquid splashed over Liam and me as the commander
slumped to the ground. My brain was running too slow, even as
my breathing became more manageable and less stunted.

Not good. I sat up, nearly slamming my forehead into
Liam's face.

"Lie down." He tried to push my shoulders back into the
grass. "I haven't fully healed you."

"Bomb." I flexed my empty hand, feeling the glass splinters in it. "Ten minutes."

"Jane. He's covered in it. You're covered in it." I looked at Driata as she spoke. Her index finger wobbled, her eyes brimming with tears as she pointed to Jenson.

He was unconscious next to us, and the same purple liquid clinging to mine and Liam's clothes were splattered all over him from face down. His forehead dripped blood where I smashed the bottle.

Shit. "We have to move him."

Liam lifted the commander easily and carried him through the trees at my direction, tossing him down in front of the fractured stone wall.

"What now?" He tried to wipe his hands on his pants, but the potion clung to him.

Grabbing his arm, I hauled him toward the lake I saw that afternoon, running faster than I ever had. The water was icy, and I ignored Liam as he protested, dragging him deeper and deeper until even our heads were fully submerged.

Opening my eyes, I watched a tiny stream of bubbles float out of his mouth and tried to memorize the planes of his face. I pulled off my soiled gown, kicking it away from me. My legs tangled in the fabric even as I ripped at the buttons of his shirt. He caught on quickly and tugged off his potion-soaked pants.

If it didn't work—it had to. My eyes roamed over him, then myself. I didn't see any more of the potion.

His fingers brushed my ribs, and finally, the pain from my wounds caught up with me. My hand throbbed, but my side felt like it was on fire. I wasn't sure how much longer I could hold my breath even as his healing magic flowed into me.

A low rumble sounded as the water around us vibrated. The pressure popped my ears. I looked at Liam and down at myself. Giant bubbles steamed from my lips as I pushed out a sigh. I kicked off the rocky floor and breached the surface.

"You're alive." Driata bounced from foot to foot excitedly at the shore as she scrubbed her hand over her tear-streaked face.

Plumes of black and grey smoke billowed toward the sky beyond her, and angry white and orange flames ate up the trees and licked up the side of the castle.

Guards and people shouted in the distance. They wouldn't be far off.

I didn't think about what the explosion meant for Commander Jenson. Instead, I motioned for Liam to follow me ashore.

Driata threw her arms around my shoulders and wept into my slip

"We have to get out of here."

Wishing I asked Liam not to bring me to Baltazar, I knew it was unreasonable. But it was only as my mentor paced in front of me like a caged animal that I understood the gravity of my error. "If you didn't need me, why are you standing in front of me covered in blood?"

Sweat pooled at the nape of my neck.

"It's done, isn't it?" I had never spoken to him like that.

"You *killed a guard*, Jane." His eyes never left my face, even while the tap, tap, tap of his shoes echoed around the room. "He has a wife, children, and a dog."

"He tried to assault my sister."

Baltazar twisted, so he was standing in front of me. "And what about the others who were injured in the blast?"

"There was no one else around." I shrugged. *Shrugged* at the leader of a seedy group of criminals. Maybe I had a death wish.

His eyebrow rose a fraction. "In the building?"

"That side of the castle holds Maveri's trophy rooms. The only things harmed were the carcasses of dead animals he collects." My shoulders reacted at the words as I said them aloud. I had triple-checked that part of the building. It was six floors of creatures the king boasted about killing.

"How are you so sure?" A muscle ticked in his jaw.

"I obviously had a plan." No one would mourn me if he killed me for my insolence.

He strode towards his desk and sat, like putting himself behind it would give him back power over the conversation. Over me. "What's gotten into you?"

The question rocked me more than a physical blow would have. Because what *had* gotten into me? Was I only angry about Driata? If I was being honest with myself... I had been mad for days. My impending marriage was his idea.

He made me plant evidence on the one person I met in Ellesmere who gave a damn about having a genuine conversation with me. Evidence that could very well get the king killed. Then—as if that all wasn't enough—I was confident he was having an affair with my sister. And even if he wasn't, he brought her in on the one thing I had to myself that my siblings couldn't touch or taint.

"You're giving me away." My voice broke, and I didn't care even as both of Baltazar's brows shot up to his hairline.

"Excuse me?" His brows pinched, and the mask snapped back down.

"Don't do that." My fingers gripped the edge of his desk as I leaned into his face. "You're the one who coordinated the wedding. Why?"

He didn't respond and flicked his eyes pointedly behind me. But I didn't care who heard. I wanted to hit him, to force him to show anything other than his calm, unaffected stare. "Whatever game you're playing at—it ends now. I'm *done*."

Baltazar's hand shot out and grabbed my wrist as I went to turn, holding me in place.

"Go." But the word wasn't directed at me. Creaking sounded, followed by footsteps.

Driata and Liam left me there with him. Alone.

Cowards.

Baltazar stood, never lifting his hand from my wrist, and walked behind me. He lowered his mouth and trailed his fingers along my arm. They drifted over my chest, sliding up until he wrapped them around the base of my throat and tilted my head back. His breath warmed my neck and the curve of my ear when he spoke. "It is a game, Jane. And we aren't done playing yet."

Speech was lost to me, but he spoke before I tried.

"You are mine." He stepped closer, pinning me between his body and the desk. My breath hitched, and he was near enough that I knew he heard it. "No bauble can change that."

"What?"

"You're playing a part. One that you've played well up until tonight. But never forget who owns you." His rumbling voice rolled over my skin, down my body, and to my center. But it didn't soften his clipped, harsh words.

I leaned forward to suck in a breath of air that didn't smell like him, but he pressed firmer still. I lost track of everything but his touch, where his body met mine. "You."

"Good girl." His words threatened to undo me. My rage ebbed out of my body, leaving only need and desire. How was his voice so calm when I heard my heart beating in my ears?

Baltazar stepped away, and cold air swarmed all the places his warm body had been. That one careless move was his greatest mistake. It was the first time I realized my mentor was manipulating me.

CHAPTER 16

The king didn't understand until I told him my mother's name. And then he was consumed with grief.

He shouldn't have been allowed to mourn her because it was his blade she fell on. Sefar.

So, I told him what I wanted to do each day since he had killed her—what I was left holding back for years. He didn't love her. He didn't get to lament for her. The loss he felt was his magic.

And instead of longing for her, he waited for the day he regained his magic, his eternity.

Waking was always disorienting after I dreamed of her. I lost sense of time—days, months, years, always half expecting her to be sitting there on my bed, patting me awake with a wicked gleam in her eyes.

That morning was no different. My eyes squinted open against the morning light, and I reached for her, readying myself to tell her that dawn was far too early. And she would respond by saying that the flowers were their most glorious at sunrise.

But my arms came away empty. She was gone. She wasn't coming back. There would be no more morning strolls through the gardens. I slipped into my robe. I couldn't—wouldn't think about her.

There was too much to be done. That morning, I would trade one type of purgatory for another. Ellesmere for Lunasa.

The unknown enemy for the backstabbing friend.

"Oh good," Lou said at an octave that was much too chipper. "I was afraid I'd have to wake you."

Fabric rustled at the foot of the bed as she tossed something there. I adjusted the pillows to sit up and rubbed the sleep from my eyes. Pulling the small pile of clothes toward me, I winced. "What's this?"

"Clothing." She enunciated it slowly as though I was incapable of understanding. "While you're always in states of naked... Normal people often cover up in public."

She gestured to the slip I wore when I arrived at my rooms the night before.

Lacing my hands at my front, I smiled at her rudeness. "Why are they on the bed and not being packed?"

"I've fixed them."

"And what was wrong with them?"

"You had so many useless dresses." I snorted at her assessment, and she continued, "but I figured you could spare some. So, I turned a few into pants."

I leaped from the pillows' plush confines towards the pile, pulled each pair up, and examined them. They were practical and feminine...and pants. How those three things fit so well together made me feel Lou had some of her own magic.

The first pair was crafted from a sapphire gown, and I

stepped into them without waiting to look at the others, which were a shade of cream and a dark grey. She managed to cinch the waist. I still had a figure in them—and didn't look like a dumpling the way I looked in men's pants—but my legs were completely mobile.

"Thank you." I could've kissed her, but I settled for a hug. When I pulled away, though, she was trying to hide a frown. "What's wrong?"

"They're gifts." She pointed to the pair I was wearing, then the two on the bed while her teeth worried her cheek. "Farewell gifts."

My face scrunched. "What is that supposed to mean?"

"Prince Oliver left for Weylin. But before that, he told us we'd all been less than useful and not to bother being there when he gets back." Lou shrugged as if it weren't a big deal. "Agatha and Edera left with the others last night to travel back home."

"Isn't this job helpful to you?"

"I don't want your pity, Jane."

"Good thing I don't pity you." I placed my hands on my hips. "Is the money you're making helpful to you? Or is being away from the pub an issue?"

Picking at the frayed end of the apron, she wasn't meeting my eye. "It's helping keep the pub running. I send the money home anyway."

"Then I'll pay you. So long as you keep making it worth-while." I kicked back a leg in a pose to show her how versatile and fabulous her creation was.

Lou smiled then, showing me all of her teeth, before running to the armoire and pulling out my canvas bag. "I helped the servants pack this morning, so they didn't rifle through your things."

She tossed me a coat, and I slung it on, buttoning it up to my collar sternum, while I tucked my slip into my pants like it was a blouse.

When she spoke next, her voice was barely a whisper. "Now, do you want to tell me what happened last night when you blew up half of the building?"

"Barely a quarter." I double-checked my bag. Sketchpad, old dagger, new dagger—thank you, Blair—and a set of worn-out men's clothes. All there. "And everything would have been fine had that guard not shown up."

"Driata told me he got handsy with her, and you took him out."

"You talked to my sister?" Since when were they on a first name basis?

"Princess?" His voice was muffled through the door, and I calmed myself like I hadn't just been talking about my role in the explosion.

"Yes, my Prince?" I was already crossing toward the sitting room and made sure to close the door behind me, hiding Lou and the bag I left open.

"A servant told me you had gone to bed last night, so I wanted to be the first to tell you what's happened." His face was grim, and I didn't need to pretend it may be good news.

"Is everything alright?"

He shook his head. "There's been an attack on the castle."

Drawing on a bit of my residual panic, I widened my eyes. "Again? Is anyone hurt?"

"We've found no injuries yet, but the west wing is in shambles."

I touched his arm gently, with worry. "I'm so sorry someone has done this to your home."

"Our home." He corrected me while dragging angry, frantic fingers through his sleep-mussed hair. "It was a surprise, but that was to be redone as a nursery."

The thought of the death-drenched animals in that wing hovering over one's newborn babe was enough to turn my stomach. I grimaced, hoping he would see it as pain over the delay and not for the disgust it really was.

"There's no way I can travel right now." He sighed, his honey-flecked gaze meeting mine in apology.

Not excited, I coached myself silently. *Saddened. Slumped shoulders, shaky breath. Pop that lower lip out a little further.* "I understand."

"You could stay." His hands slid around my waist, and I felt his fingers lock together behind me.

"No offense, my Prince." I offered him a soft smile, trying and failing to make it meet my eyes. "But I don't exactly feel safe here while the castle is under attack."

Arius' lips pursed together, sending a tick through his jaw as deep lines formed between his brows. He said nothing, hadn't even moved. But I knew. The anger and hurt in his face betrayed his disbelief. Something I said or done, maybe not even that day, but since I had arrived.

My toes sank into the plush rug so I could gain the height needed to reach his face. I used my fingers to smooth the lines on his forehead, watching his face soften under my touch.

He tightened his grip, pulling me toward him until our lips

met. I hadn't even had a chance to close my eyes—but he opened his further. It was like he was assessing me, watching for cues of my reaction. I slammed mine closed and moved my lips against his, trying to ignore his scratchy beard and forget the memory I was creating.

It was wrong to compare, but my mind reminded me of the difference between his soft, unmarred hands and Liam's calloused ones.

I tried to pull back for a breath, but he reeled me in and used my open mouth as a gateway for his tongue. His teeth clicked against mine, and I wanted to scream. Gooseflesh climbed my skin at his wandering touch. I had never been so grateful to be wearing so many clothes.

His tongue wandered around my mouth like it was checking for hidden crevices, and I strangled the urge to bite down. When his arms dropped, giving his hands access to my ass, I pushed off his chest. I stumbled back with what I hoped was a promising chuckle. "Until we meet again."

"Right." He grinned, and the skin by his eyes crinkled. "Save some mystery for our next meeting."

When I reached the stables, Liam paced in front of an already saddled and bridled Jett.

His dark curls were mussed like he spent all morning working to pull them out. He didn't wait for me to question his presence before he was babbling. "Scoot and Fox left last night."

"And?" While my stomach pinched with worry for the young novice, I wasn't all that close to him, and I didn't think Liam was either.

"They dressed as servants and joined a traveling party of those fired." He moved closer to me, but his hand was raised as if in his defense.

My brows lifted, and I shrugged. It was a pretty good cover.

"Baltazar sent Driata with them." His words echoed through my skull, and a clanging hammer of fear and anger pounded in me.

"Driata is being sent to Faery?"

He nodded. "Baltazar wasn't going to tell you, but I thought you should know."

Working to calm my rising nerves, I attached my bag to the saddle. I balanced my weight on the stirrup and threw my leg over my mare's back.

Jett trotted forward, and I leaned down, offering Liam my hand.

Liam stared at it blankly.

"Get on the horse." I shook my hand, steeling myself to leave without him. "We don't have time for you to saddle another horse."

He grabbed my forearm with his good hand and hoisted himself behind me with a grunt. I squeezed my calves together.

Liam's hand closed around both of mine as it tangled

around Jett's coarse mane. The wind ripped at my braid as the tie flew from my hair. Her hoofbeats clacking and crunching sounded like battle drums as we sped away from Ellesmere castle.

We had to cut them off. I had to stop her. Driata was in no way prepared for a mission. What was Baltazar thinking? My only hope relied on our one horse. They left before us, but their party was much larger.

I tried to focus my mind on the ride. Not on the morning or the night prior, but on keeping my mount even as my thighs burned. But the day moved forward, and the wind picked up around us, shrieking in an echo of my internal rage.

The afternoon sunlight dimmed as rumbling grey and black clouds promised an unforgiving storm. Raindrops seethed as they pelted my face, hair, and clothes. Sharp wind bit through our sodden clothes and set my teeth to chatter even as my muscles tightened to stay astride.

Liam's voice was muffled when he spoke. "What now?"

"There's a cave by the Nera." I knew the area near the great river well. The cavern was our nearest source of shelter. The trees of the Elwood were dense on the trail, but they would only provide a temporary reprieve. The storm grew colder, and the lightning and thunder warred for dominance in the sky. If we could just travel a bit further...

Jett cleared a stone and nearly threw me from her back. Liam must have felt me grip him tighter. His arm slid up higher, trying to fasten us to Jett's back.

I tried not to recoil. Get to the cave, I thought. Then we could reconvene and go save Dri from her own stupidity.

After a day's travel, I should have heard the rushing water of Nera. But the storm ripped open a flood from the sky. Lightning crackled, and the earth was cast in a watery, grey haze. Jett threw mud as she ran, not stopping, not slowing down. Her back and sides were slick with rain and sweat.

Just a little farther.

She released a snort that I could feel in her neck muscles as though in response to my thoughts.

We finally crested a hill, and I saw that the ordinarily night-black water of the river was full of white, frothing rapids.

The cave was on the other side.

I yanked back on Jett's mane, but she was already slowing, and her hooves dug into the mud-caked ground.

"Where's the cave?" Liam pulled away, sliding down and offering me his hand. I knocked it out of my way, dismounting. The mud sucked my boots into the earth. My legs and ass were numb yet somehow still sore from the long ride.

"Behind the falls." I pointed to the jagged rocks on the other side of the river and the water plummeting over them, feeding into the river. It looked as if the mountain itself wept for my failures. "There's a passage."

It was narrow and formed of rocks that would be soaked and slippery from the rain. But there was no need to warn him. He would see it for himself.

We scanned the area and the river's edge as the rain assaulted us. Falling so hard, I was sure it would leave welts.

As we neared the bank of Nera, Jett stopped moving, digging her hooves into the sopping ground. I patted her face. "We've done this a thousand times over, girl. Would you rather stay in the storm?"

She gave me an indignant huff as if she would certainly rather risk getting struck by lightning.

Liam looked between me and the water crashing on the rocks warily. "I'm with the horse."

My hands balled into tight, determined fists at my side. "If you both will let some rocks scare you, that's fine. But I'm going."

Not the rousing speech I thought it was, neither moved. Determined to prove them both wrong, I turned on my heel.

Crouching to level my center of gravity, I stepped onto the rocks. My boot slid, and I lowered further, placing my palms on the stones. They were smooth, worn from ages of water beating against them. The rock was cold, and my fingers went numb, searching for a handhold.

Twenty feet, I had to make it twenty feet. Thunder and lightning crashed overhead.

Fifteen. The guzzling water slammed into my ribs, pinning me to the rocks. I gasped out a breath, the water washed away, and I dragged myself back to my knees, crawling onward. Nine.

Purple and white light flashed, blinding me as a boom reverberated in my ears. I lost track of my hands, shoulders, and then my head under the bubbling water. My vision fogged as the water filled my eyes. I splashed and battered the water around me.

I coughed as the black water filled my mouth and nose, but a gulp went into my lungs. I kicked my feet down, trying to find the bottom, a rock, anything to drive my head to the surface.

My mouth opened in a scream.

So stupid, I thought as more water rushed into my mouth, and I let out another cough. My body felt weighted as if the stones I searched for tethered my feet. My lungs burned, my vision spotting. Flashes of white and black danced before my shutting eyes.

CHAPTER 17

My eyes fluttered open, still bleary from the watery film over them.

Had I drowned? Was I dead?

I should probably have been alarmed, but I was exhausted. My body was wrecked after being slammed into the rocks.

Do you feel pain when you die? That seemed punishable. I could still hear the rapids rushing and the storm as if it mocked me.

"Drink." Liam's voice was gruff as he pressed a canteen to my lips. The liquid was sweet—too sweet and it burned my raw throat. I choked some down, but most of it pooled out of my mouth.

My eyes adjusted to the darkness, and I realized the sound of water was from the back half of the falls. "How did we…"

I heard the smile in his voice. "I convinced the horse to help."

What?

Jett let out a spiteful snuff somewhere to the side of me, her dark coat blending in with the shadows as if to say it was the last time.

Why would he go through all the trouble?

"We're even." There was no emotion in his voice at that time.

Ah.

I didn't respond. The edges of my vision swam as I regained feeling in my fingers and toes. Heat seeped into my soggy limbs from somewhere to the side of me. He must have started a fire. Smart. I was warm. So deliciously warm, even in my soaked clothes.

The sounds of rustling paper, fabric, and chewing filled the space beyond the crackling wood. It was all too loud. So near the rapids and the rumbling storm brewing behind the booming falls.

Lightning struck as I rose, illuminating the scene in front of me. Liam eating berries, pawing through my things with reddish, purple-stained hands.

"What is all this stuff?" He ran his fingers along with the front cover of a leatherbound journal.

Mine, I wanted to say. The things I started storing after... After she died. But I couldn't find the words. When I discovered the place, I started fantasizing about running away. As far away as the river ran. Doing what my mother had always dreamed of. I started working for Baltazar a year later and made no move to leave. Other than hiding things there a little at a time. When I joined the ring, it only became a good place to regroup, stash things, and take a breather after a mission. No one knew about it except for Jett, who often accompanied me on my travels. *And now Liam,* I thought.

But I couldn't speak. My mouth was dry, and my tongue was too large. I looked at the purple-stained canteen sitting in Liam's lap. Then to the berries he was plopping in his mouth.

My eyes went wide. "Blister berries."

He didn't seem to notice me talking.

My throat was numb, and a sugary taste coated my tongue. "Is that what you poured in my mouth?"

"Yes, and you're welcome, by the way." He smiled as he flipped a page in my journal. I couldn't think of that, though.

"Shit." I had two waterskins in the cave. One I religiously cleaned, and the other I purposely marked with berry stains.

Blister berries were a powerful antiseptic. Good to have on hand—primarily crushed and diluted by water—for cuts or gashes. But they were also a delirium-inducing toxin when ingested.

"How much have you eaten?" My voice was shrill.

The idiot had poisoned us both.

He grabbed another berry. "No need to be greedy. There's plenty more."

"Blister berries," I said again, speaking slowly. My tongue stuck to the roof of my mouth as I reached to smack Liam's hand. The berry rolled across the stone and into the fire. "Poison."

The berry popped, and the flames hissed, turning white, then settled.

"Who..." He let out a chuckle like I told the funniest joke he had ever heard. "Who keeps poison just *lying* around?" The fit of laughter overcame him.

The hallucinations would start soon. A giggle bubbled from my lips at the thought, and I covered my mouth, trying to push it back down.

"What's so funny?" His eyes narrowed, and he cleared his throat. A look that reminded me of Baltazar.

Baltazar. My mentor. My friend. My...more? But he had gone and ruined it. Everything always got ruined. My skin felt hot all over, too hot. The sheer ridiculousness of it sent me into another bout of hilarity.

"*You're Baltazar's brother,*" I whispered as if it were a secret he didn't know.

Liam's eyes went wide, and his face paled as he crawled backward away from me, scattering a pile of berries... That reminded me of something. Something important tugged at my memory.

Why were berries so important? They did look delicious.

"He'll kill her." Liam groaned, his fingers tugging at his hair. "I'm sorry."

What a strange thing to say...

I stood, but my legs wobbled. And I barely caught myself before my face hit the ground. My hands were sticky from berries that squished beneath my hands. Their purple juices coated and stained my fingers and my palms.

"Blister berries," I remembered, but I hadn't had as much as him. Who knew how much the glutton had eaten? The hungry little piggy. Giggles filled my head. Wilboar. How had Arius not found that hilarious? I coached myself to stand even as the cave walls lengthened, then sucked inward. The mountain was breathing.

We had been eaten by a mountain while the sky pissed

around us. The anatomy of the world was too funny. It was going to kill us all.

My head shook. Left. Right. Left again. I could do it—beat the berries.

Blister berry thorns. The antidote was in the stems that nurtured the berries. Where were they? I always had some there. But he rummaged through my things. I looked at the scattered sea of trinkets and items sprawled around him.

Liam let out a low, keening wail, slamming his head against the stone. I would save him from his own idiocy, and then I would kick his ass for going through my stuff. He said we were even. Not a chance.

The stone beneath my feet disappeared, and I was falling. It took me a moment to realize Liam had barreled into me. My right side was in agony where his shoulder had connected. A Giant burst of stars exploded in my vision. The cave contracted. He was pushing his weight down on me.

"Is this what you wanted, Brother?" His nostrils flared with his heavy breaths. The overly fragrant smell of the berries threatened to turn my stomach. That close, I saw his lips were stained. He leaned in toward me, gripping my chin and neck in his hand and tilting it up, so I was looking at him.

Liam's eyes were wild, the beast in him bursting free of his skin, and I ran my fingers through his hair. Even damp, it felt luxurious. I would give anything for him to never stop touching me.

He groaned, and I felt his body stiffen against me, the rugged ridges of him pressing against my soft skin like there were no clothes between us. His face lowered against my neck, and he inhaled.

"You found me." His whispered words ripped me from the toxin-induced trance.

"Get off of me," I ground out. "Liam, I'm trying to help you."

"Help me?" He let out a humorless laugh and brought his lips to my ear. His words were barely a breath. "*You're destroying me.*"

Enough of that. I brought my knee up and slammed it into his groin. He wailed and rolled off me, gripping himself.

My vision tunneled, and the shadows lengthened into reaching, grabbing claws. Focus. I needed to find the satchel I kept my herbs in.

There. Amongst my extra clothes. I rummaged through the bag. Spilling its contents onto the floor and pushing around vials and clothing until I found the leather bag. I undid the string with one hand and grabbed my dagger with the other. I used the flat end of the blade to crush the thorns into a fine powder. Scooping a bit up and dumping it into my throat. I gagged and choked as it coated my tongue. The powder thickened into a paste that I struggled to swallow.

I carried the leather carefully to where Liam lay, screaming —seeing some horror his brain concocted. I gripped his chin and funneled the leather, pouring the dust into his mouth.

He coughed and lashed out but finally went still and silent.

Letting him sleep off the effects, I worked on sorting my things. Making a mental note to gather more blister berry thorns, I carefully tucked the berries into the discarded scrap of leather and bagged them with my herbs. They would spoil, so I would have to get more of those.

I was gathering my notes and the pages that had fallen out of my journal when I saw a browned bit of aged vine tied into a circlet, just large enough to fit my finger. I leaned forward to pick it up, hoping he hadn't seen it pressed in my journal. At some point, I forgot it was there.

It must have been the aftereffects that dragged me into the memory, but more likely, it was aided by my being there with him.

It was my birthday, one I shared with my mother. Each year my father threw his silly little party to commemorate the event. That night, there would be suitors. A long line of them that my father hand-selected for me to wed one day. Even though the most pressure was on Oliver, the newly crowned heir, my father expected his children to take suitors that would benefit the crown.

I didn't want to go. But my mother encouraged me, a rare moment of lucidity for her when she wove my hair into braids atop my head. I looked in the mirror, seeing the tiara and the dress woven with gems and the finest fabrics my father's gold could buy. I told her I looked ridiculous.

"Careful, Princess, it would only take one experienced jewel thief, and you'd be lost forever." I hadn't seen him come in, but Liam was leaning against the door's frame in a suit, his lips parted in a smile.

"Go now, Janie." My mother shooed me out the door. "I'll catch up."

"Do we have to go?" I whispered as soon as I heard the door click closed.

"Let's go for a walk first." He always knew, of course, how much I wanted to be away from my siblings. I returned his smile, and we walked out into the gardens.

The moon was full, casting his eyes a molten silver. I stared at him instead of the flowers, drinking in his beauty, knowing that the gardens couldn't compare. "The only thing I like about this place."

He ran his finger down the night-darkened stem of a rose. "Hmm?"

Though I knew how he felt about me, my stomach always twisted when we spoke about it aloud. "You."

"Lunasa is like this rose." He grinned and used both hands to pluck the thorns from the stem. "Ready to draw blood if you don't remove the thorns."

It made me think of my father and how even a day of the year meant to be special for my mother and me had become a ruse to keep power.

Carefully, he plucked the stem, pulling the flower free from the bush. He pushed my hair back behind my ear, stroking my face with his thumb before tucking the rose there.

Liam laced his fingers in mine, pulling me deeper into the gardens. Far away enough that I no longer heard the music from the ball. Then further still, before he stopped in front of a trellis of jasmine and broke off a bit of vine. "It's not a true ring. But it's a promise of one."

He grabbed my hand, pulling me into his chest. My stomach sank even as my heart swelled. He knew about the suitors then. And knew he wouldn't be an option if my father had a say. His brother had controlled their funds since they had arrived.

My hands wove in his hair. "I don't care for jewelry."

"I will always find my way back to you." He had kissed me then like the world was ending like it was the last time. As if I was his final hope for air.

But when we untangled and made our way to the ball, the music ended, and the revelry stopped. My father's face had grown pale, weary. Whispers wove through the gathered crowd.

I thought perhaps there were brambles in my hair or dirt on my gown from rolling in the gardens. How worried had I been, but my fears proved insufficient.

While I was avoiding the party and my family, my mother had thrown herself from the balcony. Liam vanished that night, taking his love with him.

He left me alone at the time when I needed him most. When I thought I would never live through my grief, my anger. And the next time I saw him, he had changed. Became one of my tormentors. Laughing just as heartily with my siblings when I failed.

Then Baltazar found me, and he taught me how to control my magic and harvest my grief and humanity. How to pluck the thorns from roses, but more importantly, how to become a thorn.

A log snapped in the fire, startling me back to the present. My eyes blurred. I rolled the ring carefully between my fingers. Felt the ridges that had once housed flowers and leaves.

Sitting there, staring into the fire until tangerine bursts danced around the edges of my vision, I let the tears fall. Possibly the first time I had genuinely cried since that night.

"I can't believe you kept that." I don't know how long he stood there watching me. But his words stoked a rage I thought long cooled.

My fingers curled into fists, and I stood, pushing past him. I didn't want to look at his face to see the taunting smirk that would have followed his words.

Once the storm let up, we could go our own ways. I didn't need his help to protect Driata. I could do it alone.

"Jane, I—"

"Don't." I walked to the fire, wishing I could burn away the images of that night—hoping they could be forgotten. So that the years we spent together before that could be erased. "We've both changed."

I tossed the last piece of that night into the flames.

CHAPTER 18

The storm raged through the night, thunder echoing on the stone walls. I hadn't slept—I was too alert, too worried about Driata, and I had grown impatient to the point of pacing.

Our firewood was running low, and any that I would be able to scavenge was likely to be sodden and useless. Even on a mission, there were things to do. To plan. To see.

Liam sat by the fire, silently watching me as I walked back and forth, flipping my dagger in my hand. "You're making my head hurt."

He hadn't responded to what I said or done. He only sat there, gazing into the fire and observing me. I ground my teeth together. "Then stop staring at me."

"I can't." His words hung in the air. A confession or just boredom? I wondered until he cleared his throat. "Don't you have anything to eat here that won't drive me mad?"

"Do you see any food?" I gestured around the cave. "I

236

haven't eaten either."

He looked around, but his eyes landed on the mare, giving me a toothy grin. "The horse."

My lip curled away from my teeth. "I'd rather eat you."

Jett let out a derisive snort.

"My..." He made a noise low in his throat, and his eyes darkened. "What a *wicked* mouth you have."

My heart sped up. Surely the boredom was getting to us both. I was too hot, stifled in my still damp clothes. "You should have let me sink to the bottom of that river."

He huffed a breath. "Perhaps."

Turning away from the fire, I walked to my satchels. I pulled out dry clothes and warmer, waterproof boots.

I moved to the back of the cave when the fire's light couldn't quite reach. The darkened walls were tighter, with less room to move around. I kicked off my sodden shoes.

Shuffling sounded behind. I twisted to see that Liam still hadn't risen but turned to face me. And though it shouldn't have been possible in the darkness, he looked right at me.

His eyes bored into me as I looked back at the stone. I took a steadying breath, gripping the hem of my shirt, and tried to ignore my shaking hands. I pulled it off, tossed it on top of my boots, and tugged on a long-sleeved tunic. I quickly shucked off my pants to replace them with fresh ones. I stepped into my new boots, turning.

Liam absently prodded the embers with an errant stick, but his knuckles had gone white. "No clothes for me?"

Shrugging, I placed the last of our logs on the embers.

His hand flexed, and I was sure the stick would snap. "Wouldn't you love for me to try getting into your pants?"

"You're welcome to strip and string your clothes over the fire." His eyes lit with the challenge. I used all that I learned from Baltazar to keep the emotion from my voice. Uncaring, unfeeling, unbothered. "It won't affect me at all."

He jumped up, and for one panicked moment, I thought he was taking me up on the offer. But he paced to the break in the falls. "I'm going to look for food. Any requests?"

"Anything but berries." I grimaced, still tasting the remnants of the bitter thorns. "And don't eat anything until I tell you it won't kill you."

He ducked into the rain. Jett's hooves clicked against the ground, and she snorted before following him.

Traitor.

"I wasn't the one that threatened to eat you," I shouted after her.

Waiting until the storm devoured the sounds of boots and hooves, I allowed myself one shaking, jagged breath.

I looked down at the glimmering ruby on my finger and wished it meant half as much as that bit of vine once had. Liam and I hadn't spent that much time alone since that night, and it was stirring up emotions I didn't have time for. My heart ached even as I tried to shove the memories away.

That would not break me—I couldn't allow it. Driata was out there, on her way to certain death. I could only hope the storm had stalled their travels as well. Crossing Nera was something a large group wouldn't risk. They would have to go in smaller groups near the mountain where the river thinned.

Footsteps and splashing water had me stuffing down my emotions. "That was fast. Are you sure you're cut out for—" My voice caught in my throat as I looked at the falls.

It was Lux, tapping the back of an axe against his palm.

"A bit obvious for you, isn't it?" As the parting water poured over his cropped hair, I motioned toward the ax. It wasn't a quick or clean weapon.

"Had to blend into the woods." He shrugged his massive shoulders.

"Chop down any trees?" I was rambling...stalling.

"I was planning on chopping down Baltazar's pretty-boy brother, then...the funniest thing happened," he paused, swinging the axe as if testing its weight. "Looked like the boss' favorite pet was runnin' away with the lad."

A new problem...great. "No. That's not what—He's helping me."

"Helping you scratch an itch?" The axe sliced through the air again.

"No—my sister. Baltazar sent Driata over the boundary."

"Tell me something." His breaths were raspy as if he had run the whole way, but I knew the look in his eyes. He was locking in on his target. "What do you think Baltazar had to say when you ran away with Pretty Boy?"

"I didn't run away with him." But I had—temporarily.

"Then he told me to carry you back if I had to."

"Plans change." Sure, I could reason with a murderer. "I'm protecting my sister. He had to know I would do this. That's why he hadn't told me."

"His plans don't change." Lux let out a deep laugh that didn't register with his eyes. "He told me to get you there. He didn't specify the condition I leave you in."

"You call me his pet, and yet it's you that barks when he says fetch." I tightened my hands into fists.

Lux growled as he lunged.

I scraped my boot against the embers, sending them flying toward him. He covered his eyes with his arm, and I dove for his ankles. Hoping to knock him off balance.

He stumbled but didn't fall, and his arm arched down. Metal sang as the axe slammed into stone, barely missing my leg.

Pain ripped through my knees and arms as I skid across the ground, slicing them open on the rocks. My dagger slipped from my hands. "Dammit, Lux, listen to me."

"I've been doing this a long time, kid. A lot longer than you, and I've known Baltazar twice that time." Sparks flew as he dragged the blade on the floor, ambling toward me. "He always gets what he wants."

He aimed the blade at me and motioned with it to the falls. I retreated a step further into the cavern. "What if what he wants gets her killed?"

A dry chuckle, but his pace was slowed. "And you know better than him?"

I couldn't outfight him, not like that—maybe not ever. No, my best bet was to keep him talking. How long had he been out there, waiting for one of us to leave? Was Liam alive?

"So what? You're just going to kill Baltazar's brother. Harm me? How does that play out for you?"

"The orders had nothing to do with the boy." Did that mean he hadn't hurt him? Or that he had?

My shoulders pulled inward, and I let my lower lip quiver as I slowly moved towards where I dropped my dagger. "I'm just trying to do the right thing."

His nostrils flared, and something flashed in his eyes, but it was gone. "There's no such thing."

Something hard and rounded shifted under my foot. Dagger.

Grunting, Lux brought up his axe and sliced it toward my middle. I flinched back and kicked the handle under my boot. My dagger flew up, and I snatched it from the air. He swung again, gaining ground. Metal screamed as the blade of the axe met the dagger. Pain flared down my arm and to my shoulders, but I held.

My foot lashed out and slammed into his stomach. He staggered, and his arm fell back.

His axe is much longer than the dagger and has far more reach, but you are smaller, lighter, and faster. It was as if Baltazar was standing in the cave behind me, whispering in my ear.

I darted forward, slashing at his chest, and backed away, bending at the knees. Lux righted himself, twisting the hilt in his hand.

Catching the wood just below his blade, I shoved my arms up, throwing back his weapon.

I grunted, feeling the weight of the axe and his arms bearing down on me. I couldn't win that way.

Lux must have seen something in my face because he charged with a snarl, slamming the handle of the axe against my wrist. My blade tolled like a death knell as it fell away.

He tipped his weapon down, pressing it into the base of my throat. "Try to speak one bit of magic, and I'll cut first."

I relinquished one step, then two. Lux was too far away to reach with his arm extended. Three. Four. Cold stone bit through my tunic.

The giant man tilted his head to the cave's entrance, where the sun finally peered through the crashing water. He didn't speak, didn't drop the weapon as he pulled something from his pocket.

"Please. Help me get her back, and I promise I'll return."

Lux sighed, the sound of a man who was relenting. He finally lowered his weapon and stepped away a few paces, "Fine. But put this on."

The light caught on links of silver. "A bracelet?"

"He said you'd like it. An apology." Lux held the thing like a viper, about to strike him. Disgust curled his lip from his teeth. He wouldn't look me in the eye, unhappy about delivering such a message. "A parting gift. Until you meet again."

Baltazar had given me gifts before—weapons, potions, always something for jobs. I took it gingerly and felt the diamonds, small but plentiful. Smoothed down to follow each curve. My chest constricted as I readied myself to nod, to tell him we had to go—the cave shook, water misted, scattering the sunlight, and a black blur filled my vision.

Jett's body slammed into the mass of Lux as her hooves scraped against stone, sending him flying into the wall. Rubble tumbled down on top of his sprawled body.

I ran to him, seeing his closed eyelids twitch, but I pressed my fingers to his neck. The slow thump of his pulse responded, even as he lay there.

Whirling on Jett, I screamed, "What the hell was that?"

"Us saving your ass, *again*." Liam walked through the cave's entrance. His arrogant smile was already in place, and his arms crossed over his chest.

"Saving me?" My voice bounced around the cavern. "He wasn't going to hurt me. We came to an agreement."

"An agreement?" Liam's eyes went wide, and his face filled

with rage as he stomped toward me. "And what was this *agreement*? Following him back into my brother's merciless arms?"

Oh, what a card to play. Time to show him my hand. "Why are you even here?"

"Because our *master* has proven—again—he values no one." His words felt like a blow—icy water splashed a flame.

My eyes narrowed, and I ground my teeth together. "I belong to no one."

His eyebrow raised, and he gave me a mockery of a smile. "You do believe that."

"I'm here with you." I gestured around the cavern. "Despite his orders."

Liam's head shook, his curls spilled into his eyes, and he angrily brushed them away. "Not by choice."

"Everything I've done today has been my choice." I prodded his chest at each word, each syllable.

He reached out, trying to snatch the bracelet I'd almost forgotten about. I yanked my arm away.

When he spoke, it was through gritted teeth. "I thought you didn't like jewelry."

I squared my shoulders, meeting his eye. "I told you, we both changed."

So much for honesty.

"It seems you have." His eyes shuttered, any flicker of emotion vanished, and my insides grew cold.

"Why did you even warn me? About Driata? That was a choice you made." He was barely a step away from me, and that close, I saw my own reflection in his eyes. I could hear his sharp intake of breath when I spoke. I caught him off guard. Good. Perhaps we could be honest with each other for once.

"Because he wanted me to." His words were a blow, and I knew he wasn't lying. But why would Baltazar send her and then have Liam tell me? He had to know I would go after her.

Stuffing the bracelet in my pocket, I bit down on my cheek to ward off my tears and leaned down to grab the axe Lux had dropped while tucking my dagger away. His giant back had landed on the sheath holding his sword, so I wouldn't be able to strip him of that. I just had to get away.

Grabbing a bag, I stuffed lighter things in there. Some clothes, a blanket, and herbs for potions. My eyes darted around the cave and back to Lux. The axe was probably useless, but I strapped it to my back and fastened my dagger to my thigh.

"*Jane.*" Liam's voice was choked with a half-assed attempt at emotion. I turned to demand he stop speaking, but my heart fell into my stomach.

Lux had the back of Liam's neck in one hand and a sword in the other. He sliced through the chain holding Liam's talisman and kicked it into the shadows.

I gripped the hilt of my dagger. I could leave them both. But then, there were two liabilities. Even if Lux killed Liam— and he probably would—he would take me back to Baltazar for interrupting his orders. Lux certainly wouldn't help me after what Jett had done. Then I would be back in the castle at square one. And despite what I thought of Liam, I didn't want him to die.

"Let him go." I made a show of releasing the dagger slowly and allowing it to slice through my palm. "And we can leave him."

"No—" Lux clenched down on Liam's neck to silence him.

Lux looked torn. "If I let the boy go, Baltazar would be

disappointed to lose one of his belongings, and you know what happens when he gets disappointed."

He shook his head, bringing up the sword.

Liam flinched, trying to pull his neck from Lux's grasp, but still couldn't move.

I threw up my scraped and bloodied hand and yelled, "ruptus."

Lux's axe-wielding arm snapped—the bone bursting from the skin. He let out a roar, and Liam's face was a mottled red. In anger and in pain, Lux was choking him to death. He wouldn't have much time.

Time.

"Tempus modero." Silence descended. Liam's head looked like it may pop. Lux's arm stuck out to the side, and drops of his blood froze, hanging in the air. But he had dropped the sword.

Lunging for them, I grappled with Lux's fingers, trying to pry them off Liam's neck. I bent and pried and pulled, but they wouldn't budge. He had a death grip on Liam's throat.

I could leave him—should leave him. I glanced at his contorted hand. Broken by the sheer will and malice of his brother. My mentor. My manipulator. His, as well.

"Think about yourself." It's what Baltazar constantly instilled in me during training. *"If it comes down to it, you save yourself."*

Fat, warm tears trailed down my face.

I always knew I couldn't do it.

Lux had been there on my first few missions. I pulled my dagger free and brought my arm up, careful of how far away I stood. It arced down, slicing off Lux's four fingers.

My stomach lurched, and I heaved up all the contents of my stomach. Water sprayed my face from the falls, so cold compared to my tears. I thought how nice it felt as I breathed in the cool spray for a moment. Then, I tucked away my blade and used a cord to string Lux's arms together—careful of his broken one—and kicked out the backs of his knees. He tumbled forward in slow motion.

Shit—things are moving.

I wiped my mouth on my wrist and yanked a slowly blinking Liam forward. He stood, still unseeing. Rocks scraped my hands as I pushed around for his talisman lying by that had fallen during the fight. I stuffed the wolf trinket and the chain into my pocket with the bracelet.

Pulling Liam's arm over my shoulder, I half dragged him, half pushed him toward the entrance.

Lux's roar began anew, with a fresh wave of pain and rage as he realized what I had done, and my ears rang.

Liam stumbled as I strapped my bag to Jett's saddle and slapped her back end.

"Run!" I screamed, dropping his arm.

I knew it was probably disorienting to be in a different place than when time stopped, but he tried to keep up for his part.

The river had calmed, but I couldn't see its bottom through the obsidian-colored surface. And I could tell by the sun's placement that it was around midday. I crossed the rocks without tumbling in and waited for Jett to follow.

Liam ran ahead of her, taking the rocks two at a time. "Where are you going?"

"To get Dri." The fresh air filled my lungs as I sprinted across the gleaming stones.

"You're not going back with him?" Out of the corner of my eye, I saw him tilt his head back toward the cave where Lux was undoubtedly trying to gather his severed bits.

I huffed a breath and shifted on my feet as I waited for Jett to clear the rocks, contemplating leaving them both. "That was the plan until you and killer mare over there knocked him out. Then I chopped his fingers off."

"What's the plan now?" When Jett finished crossing the river, I looked at the water cascading and bubbling down the rocks. I let myself breathe in the scent of the damp grass deeply. My eyes wandered to the cave, and though I couldn't see through the fall, I could smell the smoke of the dying fire.

"No concern of yours." Hopefully, he couldn't tell that was code for I didn't know.

He blocked my view of the cave, his eyebrows raised. "You're going to leave me here with Lumberjackass?"

I shrugged. "We should go our separate ways."

"You're headed to the boundary."

I didn't speak and allowed no emotion to creep into my face.

"It's a two-day ride, and you haven't eaten or slept. You shouldn't travel alone." His voice was gentle as if he were concerned with spooking me in case I chose to run away. I may have considered it.

My brows knitted while I weighed my options, and he tracked that too. "I also have food. Stashed it in some trees down the river after I saw ogre-sized footprints." When he assumed somehow that Lux had been there and came back for me.

My stomach growled in the answer just before it echoed in a roar of ire. Lux was on his way.

I ran. The humid air hit me in the face, shoving its way into my lungs. The ground was already drying in the afternoon sun, but my boots still sank into wet spots as we ran uphill. Liam kept pace with me, not out of breath yet, which was a good sign. My thighs burned, adrenaline finally giving way to exhaustion.

We stopped once we reached the tree line, taking in jagged gulps of the sticky air and near choking on it.

"There." He pointed to a small pile of things, a collection of mushrooms and berries—none of which were blister berries. I picked away the ones I knew would kill us, cause hallucinations, or make us ill. Then I rationed it into two edible piles.

We ate greedily, not caring that the bitterness of the mushroom or the sour and sweet taste of the berries were horrid when combined. Jett grazed on the grass nearby, and I was relieved to see her eating. She needed to be content to make the trek.

He wiped his mouth on the back of his arm as I pulled out a piece of leather from my pack. I wrapped the inedible bits in the scrap and tucked it toward the bottom. The rough tie straps scraped my skin.

"Which way is it from here?" He brushed off his pants as he stood.

"Follow the river, and by tomorrow we should have reached the pass." I pointed in the direction of the mountains.

He nodded. And looking back, I should have probably been suspicious of how quickly he agreed.

CHAPTER 19

It was nearly nightfall when we found a place to camp. I was hopeful that Lux's injuries would slow him down his tracking, but I was still careful to cover our tracks. Just in case. We made it to the edge of the Dreadwood—once known as the king's wood before the curse had killed all life there, leaving only a graveyard of wooden bones.

The trees were knotted and greying things, reaching toward a sun that couldn't save them. They wouldn't provide much cover, but it was our best option. Jett was huffing at the lack of grass, and I had already reassured her four times since our trek began.

My sister's traveling party would likely stay on the road toward Lunasa. The Dreadwood was the only thing between that path and the passage through the mountains to Faery. A passage that followed the bank of the Nera River, created before the laws of my kind, prohibited interaction with the fae. We should have been able to catch up if that was where she and the traveling party were headed.

Dri had no idea what she had gotten herself into. Prepping for dinner parties and getting fitted for dresses wasn't exactly a gateway into the lifestyle. I trained for months before I was even allowed on my first mission. And it damn sure hadn't been with Scoot.

Liam's voice pulled me from my worries. "—sleeping on the ground, then?"

"It seems that way, doesn't it." I dropped my bag onto the ground and started rifling through it.

"Not a fan," he mumbled, kicking at the dirt as if it had offended him.

"Of?"

"The ground."

"Use magic then to—oh wait." I smiled up at him and considered giving the damned talisman back. "You lost your talisman."

His lip pulled back in a grimace. "Now I'm as simple as you."

"So simple that I saved you." That settled it. I would toss it into the river before I gave it back to him. "So simple that you magicked a woman into looking like me."

Watching him tense at my words was almost as satisfying as knowing where his talisman was while he grappled without magic. "It's presumptuous to assume I wanted her to look like anything you."

"Are you dense?" My head tilted. Genuine curiosity trilled through me as I wondered if he really thought I was stupid.

"Why fuck someone who looks like you when I could have the real thing?"

"*Excuse me.*"

"Don't act as though you haven't thought of it." His eyes were like chips of moonlight boring into me.

I snapped the blanket out and took great care to smooth it over the dirt while my jaw worked. *Calm—stay calm. He's trying to get a rise out of you.*

My shoulders relaxed, and I eased open my jaw. "Thought of what?"

Childish and evident as it was to pretend I didn't know, I watched his cocky smile falter as he turned away.

"It was fun," I said to fill the silence despite wishing I could yank the words from the open air. "Meaningless."

"It can mean nothing to you?" His voice was flat, but he stared at me. The question was redundant. It had to be. He had been with other women too. He had to know that it could mean nothing—just a way to fill a need and sate desire.

"Just like with everyone else I've been with since you—" I did force myself to shut up then. I had been in his company for too long. It was making me antsy.

The quiet grew, and I looked over to Nera, noting that the waters had calmed after the storm. They reflected the moonlight and the stars beginning to twinkle in the darkening sky. I had to do something and get away from him for a while.

"Can you make a fire?" I asked, unstrapping my dagger and the axe and tossing them into my bag. "It will only get colder and darker."

"And what will you be doing while you force me into

manual labor?" He turned back to me, crossing his arms over his chest.

"It's nighttime." He stepped in my way. "You shouldn't go into the river when it's dark."

Edging around him, I wondered how hard it could be to evade him and my stirring emotions while we were together.

Then I noted the pinch in his brow. Was he concerned? No—not for me. "Why are you stalling?"

Liam faltered back a step. "Why would you think that?"

My eyes narrowed on him. "Do you not know how to start a fire?"

"Of course, I do." His smirk didn't have its typical bite, though. I shrugged, brushing past him. Then, walking far enough up the river that I thought the shadows would hide my body, I stripped off my clothes.

The chilled water nipped at my skin as I sank into it.

All the tension in my body ebbed away with the muck, grime, and sweat coating my body from our journey. I shoved off any gnawing thoughts of Dri, reminding myself that we would catch them by the following afternoon.

I focused on the feeling of the water lapping up over my breasts, the gentle pull of the current, and the rocky floor below my planted feet.

Tilting my head back to wet my hair, I looked up at the gleaming full moon. A blue and white ring surrounded it, making it look ethereal, which I supposed in many ways it was. There was once a time when even my mother believed in the moon sun's magic. She had told me of mortals who worshiped their greatness with art and celebrations.

Dunking deeper, I willed my eyes to stay open even as my

vision of the sky blurred, seeming to smear like a water painting. I stayed underwater until my lungs ached and burned before bursting back out, only to find Liam too close and staring at me.

"By the gods. What are you doing here?" I rushed to cover my exposed breasts from the cold air and Liam as my nipples hardened. I crouched down in the water and looked up at him.

There was an expression on his face I couldn't read when he didn't answer right away. But then, "I can't start a fire."

"That's why you're creeping up on me naked?" Of course, I meant while *I was naked*, but there were rivulets of water dripping down his hard, shirtless chest, and I wondered what the dark water surrounding him was hiding. Did he take his clothes off to come out there and retrieve me?

"No." His voice was rough, and he wasn't looking at my face...but beneath it. I craned my neck up to look at him in the low light and recognized the look he offered me. It was the same greedy one he gave me when I caught him with the servant. Hunger. Lust. Excitement.

Gods smite me for my stupidity, but I liked it. I bit down on my lip as I rose a fraction from the water and met the air. The chill sank into my bones immediately and with no remorse. Gooseflesh coated my skin, and his eyes tracked it all.

"I was thinking about what you said." Liam's voice was gruff and timid—unexpected. He may as well have reached out and touched me because his words were a caress all over. "It doesn't have to mean anything."

If I had sense, I would've been offended—but instead, my legs stretched more, and my upper half came out of the water, fully revealing my chest to him. I knew I was lying to myself, even as my head signaled an agreement.

"I barely like your company," I agreed quickly... Too quickly.

"And watching over you is tedious," he added. The smirk tugging at his lips told me he knew he was about to have his request granted.

"Not nearly as annoying as a man who can't function without mag—" His fingers tangled in my hair, tugging hard enough to tilt my chin toward him, and I hissed in pain. He devoured the sound as his soft lips—cushioned in comparison to the crushing kiss—pressed against mine.

His tongue teased my mouth open, and I gave in without pause, raking my nails over the ridges in his shoulders. I moaned into his mouth as our tongues met and marveled at how our mingling breaths warmed my cheeks.

Fuck's sake, he was a good kisser.

My toes curled against the sandy river bed, and my mind filled with the terrible thought that it definitely meant...something.

The rough pads of his fingers pinched around my nipple as he broke our kiss, and his lips and teeth explored the flesh of my neck.

His hand slipped down, following the curves of my stomach, then lower still, stroking my inner thighs and caressing them open until he reached their apex. His thumb swirled around the most sensitive part of me once, twice, and a third time before he picked up his pace.

I gripped his neck, my body tensing as he brought me close, too close, without really having done much.

He stopped so suddenly that it felt like he'd stolen the air.

My breaths were jagged, huffing nonsense when I asked, "what's wrong?"

I thought my heart may explode from my body if it ended there.

Liam reached up and pulled my hand free of him. I told myself it was an insignificant lapse of judgment.

We definitely had taken things too far.

But then his hand molded over mine as he used it to cup my breast and follow the same trail he had taken. Down, down, down.

"You said you're an expert at making yourself cum." He shifted behind me, pressing his dick against my back.

His gravelly voice vibrated in my ear as his breath caressed me. Our joined hands dipped between my legs. "I want to see who you scream louder for. Me or you."

"Obviously me." But there was no conviction in my words, and his deep chuckle rumbling through me proved that he heard it.

Our thumbs teased over the bundle of nerves, and I gasped at the contact. Liam urged my fingers down until two pressed into me with his, and I bucked against the pressure.

My head kicked back and landed on his chest while I let out a breathless moan. He sucked in a breath behind me when I rolled my hips against our fingers and hands. I ground down on them as pleasure coiled deeper, lower. It built, sweeping through the muscles in my stomach, legs, and finally, the center of me. I pulsed around our joined fingers, biting the inside of my cheek, but a small whimper escaped.

His breath was on the swell of my cheek, hot in contrast to

the night air. "When you come for me, you moan and cry out but don't ever think you get to be silent."

My free hand found the nape of his neck, and I dragged him toward me, lining his body up behind mine. He dipped his head, biting and licking at my flesh.

Tension wound tighter until all my nerves were strung out inside me. The cold water, his warm skin, and the press of our fingers inside me were delectable torture.

"My only goal is to ruin you." His voice vibrated against my lips and sent chills skittering up my spine.

"Ruin me?" The question was breathless, the muscles in my body taut as I tensed with the implication.

"For other men—for future prospects. Anytime you touch yourself or have another kneel before you, I want you to hear the echoes of your moans for me." With each word, he pumped our fingers inside me, and I gasped, gritting my teeth together against the cursed building in my throat. My core pulsed around our fingers, squeezing, tightening, and stealing away my sanity.

I tilted my chin back and up, wanting to see him, feeling confused by the fervor in his tone, but he caught my mouth with his. He nipped at my lip, and I came undone.

The walls of my wet pussy tensed and quivered while I came for him, moaning his name. He lapped the sound like it was the best thing he had ever sampled.

Only when my body was trembling did he break our kiss and slide our fingers out of me, using his new grip on my waist to turn me.

Moving to slide my hands around him, but he caught my fingers with his mouth. The act of him tasting me was so shocking and sensual. He smiled, and that need was cinching in me again. The pad of his tongue played with the tips of my fingers, and I squeezed my thighs together again. My chest grew heavy with want, and I needed him to fill me.

"Delicious." Liam's groan of pleasure that followed threatened the ruination he promised, and we were colliding again.

I needed him right then. I wanted to explore every plane of his body with my mouth and teeth. I wanted him to make that noise on repeat for the rest of the time.

The frigid air whipped into me when he lifted me up and pressed me against the rigid planes of his body. With my legs splayed and hooked around his hips, I felt his hard dick between my thighs. I ground down on the length of him, wishing he would just pump into me until I was sick of it and my body was no more than a shell.

Water dripped off us as Liam carried me to land, barely jostling me but still not feeding my need.

I groaned in frustration, dropping my ass. The wetness at my center coated his twitching cock. A muscle in his jaw ticked, and I sensed him losing control. We barely made it to the blanket. He placed me on the ground and pinned me with his hand curved around my throat. "Tell me you want me to stop."

"I—what?" My brain was foggy, but I wanted anything other than that.

He throbbed at my entrance, and his voice was barely a whisper. "If you want this to stop, it does."

"No." I was panting, trying to calm down my thumping heart. "Just don't be gentle."

If he were, I would convince myself that it was more than what it was. More than what it could be.

"That I can do." Liam grinned, bumping my legs apart with his own. He slammed into me without warning down to the hilt, and I gasped his name.

Dirt and rocks bit into my back when I arched into him, my breasts pressing into his chest and the raised skin from the cold on my nipples brought me back to the edge. He lifted one of my calves over his shoulder and thrust forward harder, lifting my ass off the ground.

It was ecstasy as he dragged his hand down my neck, thrusting his hips forward and burying deep inside me. I used one hand to claw at his chest and the other to ease some of the tension building lower.

Liam grumbled something that sounded like my name as his thumb and forefinger swirled and pinched at my nipple.

I met his thrusts until our heavy breaths and the sounds of our bodies colliding were all I could hear. I closed my eyes for a second, but his hand left my breast and was at my chin, forcing me to meet his gaze.

Easing my leg down, he posted a hand by my head and slid himself almost all the way out of me. "I want you to feel the power you have over me."

Bobbing my head in a nod, he drove his hips forward and seated himself inside me. His lashes lowered as he pulled back again, casting his silver eyes in shadow.

His muscles flexed as our hips slammed into each other. My body tensed as he plunged a final time and pulsed inside me, so full of him. I bit down against the corded muscle of his forearm. Unable to look him in the face as I followed him into oblivion.

Liam rolled off me and folded the blanket around me while

he stood. I thought it served me right to be disappointed as he walked toward the water's edge.

What did I think—he would lay there with me?

I watched his moonlit form grow smaller as he neared the water. He crouched, picked something up, and returned to our makeshift camp with a bundle in his arms.

When he reached the edge of the blanket, he laid down my clothes. I bit back a laugh at my dramatic thoughts as I rushed against the cold to dress quickly. I stopped myself from thanking him, knowing the cocky bastard would assume I was talking about the orgasms he had given me.

What did strike me into utter silence was when Liam squatted and nudged me over so that he could climb under the blanket with me and tucked me into his side. The muscles in his arm flexed below my head, and I thought perhaps I had forgotten to breathe.

I shuffled deeper under the fleece, pulling it over my face. Trying to ignore Liam's woodsy scent and focus only on the warmth seeping into my bones.

There was a time I wouldn't have questioned an act like that from him, but that was before. And maybe it was only because the idiot didn't know how to start a fire, and I grew too tired to do it myself. But perhaps it was something more despite what we said.

Did he do that with everyone? Men I slept with since often left right after, or I would, depending on where we met. Would Liam have done it with that woman he fucked by the apple trees?

"Why would you make her look like me?" I didn't clarify,

thinking he would deny it again or maybe even feign sleep. Though that close, I could hear his heart rate kick up.

Time stretched, and I could feel my breaths slow to an even pattern. When Liam finally answered, his voice was a muffled whisper above the blanket. His finger traced gentle circles on my shoulder while I started to doze.

"I couldn't stop thinking about you." A deep sigh followed the murmured words. "But I thought—she'll never let it happen again. She's gone. Then I thought maybe if I fucked someone else... I would be fine. But I wasn't. Every time she looked up at me, I saw a face that wasn't yours. Brown eyes instead of green. Gods, I love your eyes."

I'm not sure when I fell asleep, but I woke to the sun casting hues of red on the inside of my eyelids and the sound of metal tinkling and fabric rustling.

Stretching, I reached for a body that wasn't beside me and jerked back from the cold spot where Liam had been. My lids flew open, and the too-bright sun seared my eyes. I blinked away the rainbow flecks clouding my gaze, noting Liam hunched over a canvas bag while rummaging through it.

My bag.

"What are you doing?" My tone hadn't been accusatory, but he started, dropping the bag and spilling its contents on the dewy earth.

"Nothing."

Well, that was just obviously not true. "Are you looking for something?"

Had he figured out somehow that I had his talisman? The last of the sleepy fog peeled away from my brain, and I touched the pocket in my pants where I stowed it away with the bracelet.

They were there, and I grew even more confused.

"I'm looking for—" He paused, clearly trying to think up a lie on the spot. "Food. I'm starving."

"You know there's no food left." My eyes narrowed on him. "Unless you'd like to poison us again."

"Fine." He threw up his hands and spun on me. "I'm looking for the bracelet that Baltazar gave you."

I tucked a hand into my pocket, feeling the crystals bite into my fingers before yanking the dainty thing out and holding it up. "This one?"

He dove at me, arms outstretched with a feral look in his eyes. I tried to slam my feet into his chest, but they tangled in the blanket.

Instead, one caught him on the hip, and he tumbled forward. I twisted onto my stomach and stretched my arms away as he yanked me by the hair. My neck snapped backward as his long body pressed against my back.

He whispered words brushed my ear. "Give it to me, Jane."

My pulse jerked to a sprint, and I cursed myself for the memories washing over me of the night prior. But I forced myself to calm down. "Get off of me."

"Not until you give me the bracelet."

He couldn't reach for it with one good hand locked in my hair. I wrestled the clasp as I snapped it onto my wrist, and he let out a curse.

"Sonofabitch." His fingers loosened their grip, and I slammed my head back into his face.

Pain exploded in my skull as it connected with his jaw. His teeth clacked together, and he leaped away from me. I rolled, watching him grip his face. His hand pulled away, blood glistening at the corner of his mouth as he glared at me.

"What the fuck is wrong with you?" My voice echoed around us as I screamed.

"Abso-fucking-lutely nothing." He kicked at my fallen things. His boot slammed into the axe's handle, and it flew into the river with a splash. "Let's just go."

He didn't pick up my things or even look back as he walked off in the direction we were headed.

Jett snorted by the tree I tied her to the night prior. My face flushed when I realized she was there the entire time. "Apparently, we'll be walking for a bit today."

CHAPTER 20

We reached the mountain's base by the pass, and I looked up at the serrated ridges of the peaks. They disappeared beyond the clouds.

"We're going to climb this?" Liam's eyebrows rose in question as he helped me down from Jett's back.

"Gods, no." It was massive, even if it was its lowest, natural point. Craning my neck, I looked at the dense trees and vegetation climbing up the side of it. The only part of the woods that wasn't dead, as if the mountain itself breathed life into it.

Liam laughed. The sound, low in his throat, made my cheeks burn. "Scaling buildings made of stone, but not mountains."

"What's that?" My face scrunched. "What are you doing?"

"Compiling a list of your strengths and weaknesses." He tapped a finger against his head.

"You were there?" I thought of the night we went to Blair's ship and how I had climbed from my balcony.

He shrugged, his face giving nothing away. "Orders."

"I fell into a mess of brambles from a three-story drop." My mouth gaped. I never thought so much about pummeling somebody. What their face would look like as it met the earth and bled. "And you were what? *Watching me*?"

He looked down at his hand, anger pulling at his features. "Whatever you think you know...you don't."

I would never understand what it was about those words... Or what came over me, even as his voice broke—but my hand lashed out. He caught it with his own just before it connected with his cheek. Our bodies close, the air between us suffocating as we stood there, breath mingling. My head tilted up just a fraction. He let go of my wrist, and it dropped to my side, but neither of us moved.

Looking into his eyes—the same ones I pictured every time mine closed—I wondered if things would have been different. If my mother had told me stories about great loves instead of tragic loss. But she hadn't. And though I lived in a world of royals, I knew that princes weren't noble and that love didn't prevail. "When?"

He started as if he forgot words existed or as if he forgot everything but that—is standing there. He hadn't even realized that the chasm had reformed between us.

"When did you heal your hand?" If my mother hadn't told me her stories, perhaps I wouldn't have noticed. Maybe I wouldn't have waited for him to falter, aware of his every movement. But when he grabbed my hand, it was with the one that was supposed to be broken.

And I still had his talisman.

Reaching for my dagger, I realized it was gone. My eyes left his face long enough to see that he gripped it in his hand, his knuckles white.

Liam's voice was raw, ragged, his chest heaving. "There is nothing he hasn't planned for."

A moment of clarity washed over me. "What were your orders?"

His muscles flexed, his hand twitching.

I trained my eye on his chest, watching the dagger and his face as I took a step back, and he followed me. "What are you supposed to do with me now?"

"*Betray you.*" It was a whisper, and I wished, for a moment, I imagined it. But he swiped with the dagger, and I ducked away and kicked up into his chest, but he caught my boot.

Yanking my foot and nearly losing my balance, I pushed away from the thoughts of what we had done and of his orders to betray me. Had it all been lies?

"Jane, listen to me." He gritted his teeth as if in pain, but I barely landed my blow.

My free foot slid in the dirt as I threw my fist into his face, my fist cracking open on his teeth. He dropped my leg as he clutched his mouth. "Why do you always go for the face?"

His knuckles whitened around the dagger's hilt—*my dagger*—and rage stirred within me as I kicked at his wrist, but he leaped away.

"You think I care about damaging your face?" I didn't recognize my voice when I shrieked, but Liam flinched like I hit him.

"Just hear me out." He winced again, and I noted how tense his entire body was, like he was trying to remain still.

Bouncing on the balls of my feet, I tried to anticipate his next move. "Give me the dagger."

"I *can't*." His voice broke, and the jerky movements of his body reminded me of a marionette.

He lunged forward, and I tried to duck out of the way, but my ankle twisted, and he was falling on top of me.

I threw my hands up and screamed, "tempus modero."

But rather than stopping time, I was met with the full weight of his body landing on me. The air rushed from my lungs as my body slammed against the damp earth. White spots clouded my vision as his hand pinned mine above my head.

Panic lanced through me, turning my veins to ice and threatening to destroy everything. Finally, I managed to gasp out, "how?"

He didn't respond, but his eyes widened like he couldn't understand what he was doing. They flicked above my head at my wrists. The bracelet was—what? A tool to sap my magic? I felt warm yet cold as my vital fluids leaked from my chest and pooled beneath me, taking my consciousness with them.

Liam looked down, and his face looked strained. His eyes slammed shut, and he backed off me. I heard a soft thunk as something fell to the ground. "No—*fuck*. No!"

"Why?" I wasn't sure if I spoke the word or if it was just reverberating in my skull—clanging like the clapper of a bell.

"I never wanted this." His voice was fading, distant, and the incessant white spots vanished before my vision darkened.

Like a message in a bottle, my mind drifted out to sea.

Colorful orbs of light cut across the sky and flickered out before rising again. A glowing arch that held illegible symbols. A giant iron circle soured through the sky above billowing red and gold tents. Banners waved on soaring flag poles and flapped in the sea breeze. Cheerful but discordant music of differing tunes played a hypnotic beat. The scent of butter and sweets danced in the air.

What was that place? Had I...died? My pack was slung over my shoulders, but my dagger was still missing. Liam had probably taken it when he killed me.

He killed me with my own dagger.

Why?

In front of me, I saw colorful strung bulbs filled with fireflies framing crowds of misshapen creatures I didn't recognize pouring in on each side. In the distance, a great blue tower of light flung riders in screeching circles, laughter and cheers mixed with music to create a symphony of confusion.

We had been to a faire once—though it was many years ago. It was a long trip out to the isles surrounding Weylin, but my mother assured me it was worth it. She told me it was the only place in my world that reminded her of home. Though I had never seen the mortal realm, I wondered how a place without magic could conjure something so amazing.

I wondered how she got passage and thought that her descriptions of the fun we would have were a ruse. In truth, I thought she was finally leaving my father, but he sent my siblings with us.

But we gorged on fun, nearly puking on rides made of iron and magic.

This? I wondered. *This was death? A carnival?*

A familiar voice interrupted my thoughts, causing me to start. "Jane!"

"Mom?"

Drawing my eyes from the faire, I looked to the center of the archway where my mother walked toward me, her copper tresses spilling over her shoulders. An oversized stuffed toy filled her arms, a white horse with golden hooves. She looked... happy, sane. But I recognized her face—so like my own—even in death.

She dropped the horse, and I barreled into her waiting arms.

"Mom?" I asked again, trying to calm my voice, but it broke despite my efforts. Was I in shock? The aftereffects of dying, I supposed.

And I must've been dead—to be there, with her.

She pulled away, giving me a disarming smile that lit up her face. "You made it."

Though she didn't seem torn up about the reason for my being there.

"What is this place?" I asked, looking around at the lights. "How did I get here?"

She shook her head, not answering, and started walking toward the carnival. Leaving me to catch up.

It wasn't until we reached the orange and pink arch that she finally slowed for me to reach her. The blinding array of lights and lanterns washed away any sign of night, forcing feigned dawn upon the world. Carts bore sigils and symbols I couldn't comprehend and bodies just as foreign. A male with the legs of a goat turned suspicious-looking meat over coals. A female with cropped blue hair and gills sold live fish with human eyes. Flittering golden creatures beat their wings against the bars of a birdcage as oil popped and bubbled in a pot behind them. A giant spider spun sparkling cotton candy webs around white cones.

The deeper we moved into the fair, a strange numbness set in. "Mom."

Again, she didn't answer, only kept moving, her head swiveling as she walked, waving politely to passersby.

My feet felt leaden, and I stopped moving. "Mom, I feel strange."

"Of course you do, Jane." She giggled, but her words sounded strange too. I shook off the feeling, wondering if I would ever get as comfortable there as she obviously had.

"Let's stop here." She clapped her hands together. "I want you to play a game."

"What? Why?"

"For fun, don't you love fun?"

"I—" I didn't know what to say. I wanted nothing more than to see my mother again, and there she was... More vibrant than she was when she was alive.

"Humor me." She turned to the game in front of her. A

row of bowls was filled with water, each a different size and shape, sitting atop a green table.

"Step on up, folks!" One of the carnies with a braided yellow beard hollered at a young man passing by. He juggled four white balls that dangled in the air just a second too long before falling back to his hands. "Toss the ball into the fishbowl and get one night with a mermaid!" He threw a ball into the collection of fishbowls, where it landed with a plunk. "This is a no-brainer, folks. It's as easy as my mermaid is on the eyes!"

"Not this one." She shook her head and skipped ahead.

"Pop, pop, pop!" Another worker with fuchsia hair down to her ankles sang as we walked by. "Three darts, unlimited potential. Pop three balloons: win your very own Sefar, a true replica!"

She stopped and turned to me with a wicked smirk. "Play this."

Of course, she chose that one. I sighed and turned toward the booth.

That close, the female carnie looked haggard, with greying hair knotted with vines, a necklace of finger bones hanging around her neck. Brightly colored balloons were pinned to the wall behind her, with splashes of what I hoped was red paint splattered where balloons had once been.

"Ah. Back for more?" Her eye twitched as she bared her snaggletooth grin.

"Quiet, witch. I'm not playing your rigged game. She is." She nodded to me as the carnie held out three darts. I feel her disdain for the carnie rolling off her. Perhaps she lost the game before. But more likely, even dead, my mother had no love for witches.

I narrowed my eyes at her, thinking about how she had said the game was rigged. "If I'm sure to lose, why would I play?"

"That's the point of the game."

"To lose?"

"To *play*." My mother nodded her head at the wall of balloons. I shook mine in response.

"Here, dearie. Best of luck." The witch dropped three darts on the counter and motioned for me to back up to the line marking the ground. I looked at my mother and tried not to roll my eyes.

I snatched the darts, rolling the cool metal against my fingers, feeling their weight and balance. They were much lighter than the throwing knives I had practiced with Lux and even more so than my dagger. I stood at the line and lifted my eyes to the balloons, trying to tune out the racket of the faire. I had never done target practice under that much duress. All the people, lights, and sounds were distracting. The most annoying thing at practice had been Lux's banter.

I flung one of the darts at the wall.

It bounced off a balloon rather than puncturing it, then plopped onto the ground behind the witch, who let out a cackle. "Two more chances. You won't win the sword, but perhaps I can find the little girl a stuffed toy."

I kicked the grass with my boot and jabbed my thumb into the dart's tip. It was dull. No wonder it had bounced off the balloon. I had to practically stab myself to feel even the slightest prick.

Strength then, as well as technique.

I aimed, lunging again and throwing my arm forward. The metal flicked out of my fingers, landing in a balloon with a satisfying bang, splashing red liquid all over the wall and ground.

The witch whined as I let the third dart go and popped the purple balloon right above the last.

My mother sucked in a breath. "Impressive."

I realized then that she died before I learned how to carry a weapon. "You should see what I can do with a blade."

The witch sighed and handed me a stuffed green pig the size of my palm.

Handing it to my mother, I offered her a small smile.

"Let's go." She led me deeper into the carnival, and I heard rides: big metal and wooden contraptions, zooming and clacking along tracks.

Screams and laughter chorused with the sounds of carnies and vendors trying to convince people to play their games and buy their wares. Running children chased each other around with glowing wands and swords that played a familiar song. A man carried a rose and a bucket of spilling popcorn as a woman near him ogled a giant teddy bear. A grandmother sat drawing at a picnic table as two little girls rushed past with their funnel cakes, giggling about the friendly centaur running one of the rides.

"Lift it, toss it, swish it in the net! Make a basket, win a prize!" A carnie's voice buzzed from a stretch of games piled on top of each other between two iron rides. Metal screeched behind him as a cart shaped like a dragon roared to a stop behind the booth, and a chorus of laughter ensued.

A girl stumbled out of the exit, her face a pale shade of green as she emptied the contents of her stomach, not quite making it to the trash can in time. A group of friends looked on in excitement as they neared the front of the line, shoving each other and laughing.

Assholes.

I turned away, watching the parents cheering at their children as they rode the blue and white-dyed horses around a ribbon-laden pole. Sitting side saddle on a pale pink mare was a hunched little man with thinning hair and giant painted lips spreading to his ears. His face paint ran in sweaty lines down his face, and he held a deflated heart balloon with yellow string. We locked eyes just before the horse rounded the pole and took him away.

"Close call, y'all!" Another carnie barked. "He went for the win but ended up whining."

My mother stopped so quickly that I nearly ran into her. "She'd like to play for the biggest prize."

The carnie had blue eyes as clear as a morning sky, framed by a wrinkled and spotted face. "If the pretty girl wins, she can pick from any prize I have." He gestured to the side of the booth, where prizes lined the wall.

A rose stood in a glass jar, lit by its own light, glowing a lilac color. Polished metal weapons and shields, stuffed animals, jars of liquids, and herbs. There was much to choose from and nicer prizes than I saw anywhere else.

Picking up the orange ball, I bounced it between my hands and the ground. It was firm and returned to my hands easily. I hadn't played the game before—had never even watched others play, but it was throwing things. How much harder could it be than weapons?

I placed my hands on each side of the ball and crouched, feeling my leg and arm muscles tense. Narrowing my eyes on the net, I imagined the lines of travel, the arc that a knife would make as it flipped and cut into its target. Throwing it, I visualized it sinking into the waiting net.

Instead, it bounced off the metal rim and slammed into the tarp underneath with a flop.

The worker let out a snicker and waved. "You should see your face. Better luck next time, kid."

I held out my hands in anticipation of him placing another ball in them, but my mom shook her head.

"There were three chances with the darts." My head swiveled between the still laughing carnie and her.

"Sometimes, you only get one chance," the carnie said. "And sometimes you *lose*."

His words gave me pause, and I stared blankly at him.

"You blew it!" yelled the carnie. "Now, move along before you scare away my next customers." A group of teenagers pushed past me, snatching the ball and sinking it in the net as I watched on furiously.

My mother grabbed my arm to lead me away, but I wrenched it from her grasp. "This is stupid."

"We have more to see," she countered, walking away again.

I wanted to stand firm, but even at that distance, I longed to be nearer. I had never seen her that content—so peaceful and so full of laughter. She stopped short in front of a building that took the shape of an oversized painted face, with a rolling tongue bent into stairs that led into the dark abyss of its mouth. Without a word, she bounded up the stairs.

Sighing, I followed her.

Inside I was greeted by a hundred versions of myself, all looking confused. Their brows pulled down in the middle, and their foreheads wrinkled. Then they shifted. One turning angry, another sad, another giggled in excitement, and so on as their expressions morphed in each reflection.

Laughter—my own laughter but a hundred versions of it—rang in my ears. Then it swelled, met with a screech of rage, a wail of horror mixing with the hundred laughs.

What was that? Had I gone mad? Where was my mother? I plugged my ears against the roar of my own voices echoing in the small space.

I looked back for the exit, but it was gone, its place filled by yet another mirror, that one blank, reflecting only an empty spot where I stood. I reached out to touch it, to make sure it was indeed there, feeling the cool hard surface.

So forward then, I thought.

I dragged my hands across the mirrors, trying to feel a path through the glass maze since my eyes were deceived by the images laughing and screaming back at me.

"Nothing is ever as it seems." My mother's muffled voice came from behind me.

I whirled around to find her standing alongside my reflection—one of them. A version of me squatted down to the floor, lifting the glass panel to reveal my mother and only her. My image stayed in the mirror as it rose.

"What the hell is this place?" I breathed as I crossed the threshold. I turned back and saw only clear glass at a series of angles, no reflections of myself or anyone else.

"The Hall of Probability. Everything and nothing that could be."

"Well, what does *that* mean?" My voice raised a pitch, filling the small, dark space like my other selves had filled the mirrored room. "Those crazy versions are what I could be?"

"I suppose it's you who decides what you'll be."

"I hate it here," I said, and my mother only let out a derisive snort. She led us deeper into the funhouse, climbing stairs twisted underfoot, dodging padded battering rams that punched at us through walls. We pulled ourselves through webs of rope—how she managed so nimbly was a mystery—and plunged blindly into a spiraling slide.

We were dropped at the final obstacle, a giant spinning tube that took my feet out from under me as I tried to walk out. She laughed as I crawled from the mouth.

Before I could ask my mother for a break to see if there was a quiet place in the chaotic hell for us to talk, she ushered me onward. "Come, there's more to see."

She dragged me to a food stall, where I was greeted by orange and yellow lanterns casting a weird hue on people's faces. A hand-carved sign offered cotton candy.

"You should eat something." She didn't face me, but she sounded breathless. I told myself it was the excitement finally wearing her down, but a strange feeling clawed at my insides.

"I'm not hungry," I said, thinking of the strange wares at the entrance, and any appetite I could've had for sweets vanished.

Her head tilted, and still, she didn't turn. "Don't you want to stay with me, Jane?"

It was the way she said my name slowly that finally made me hear it. *Jane*, not Janie—the pet name she had used since my birth. The same name my father called me, not understanding how it mocked me.

"Of course, let me just get my coins." I let my bag slide off my shoulders. Slowly, to not alert her of my alarm. She hummed, unbothered and out of tune with the music.

Squatting to the ground, I shuffled through my bag. I didn't know if I was dead or if it was some hallucination, but I could at least rule one thing out.

Finding what I was looking for—a vial of coarse salt, not gold. My mother screamed as the granules spilled into my hand. She dove for me, but not fast enough.

She is not your mother. This isn't real, I warned myself as I felt the fear of losing her again and the weight that was left in my chest. I slapped my hand into my eyes.

The salt burned and cut my eyes, and the world frayed at the edges. Iridescent lines fragmented like shattering glass as the film of the glamour shredded.

The music came to a screeching halt, and the lights flickered out.

CHAPTER 21

The sudden silence was an assault on my senses. I was blinded—but seeing, deaf—but voices crept in through the darkness. I had been glamoured before, though it was at a much smaller scale, by a lesser pixie who had tried to make me drown myself.

Think. What do you hear? There were three hushed voices.

"She dreams of the queen while he dreams of her."

"The queen?"

"They're both in agony."

"The delicious taint of loss."

"Yes, yes...but the queen?"

"How does she know her?"

I smelled smoke, the scent of savory meat, and a tint of sweetness that nearly made me gag. I held it down—barely— and kept my eyes softly closed as if I were dreaming.

The delicious taint of loss. Behind my closed eyes, around the reddish tinge from what had to be the fire...I saw my mother's

278

face. Smiling and carefree as it had been, how I had wanted it to be, created from my memories of her.

I wanted to be back there for a moment, to ask her the questions that would forever go unanswered. Even if it were my own subconscious that created those responses.

Shuffling sounded beside me, and pain cut through my chest as one of the fae lifted my arm and sniffed. It was everything I could do not to recoil. I forced my body limp, even as every nerve in my body screamed at me to run.

No, I told myself as a rough tongue lashed out and trailed its way down my forearm toward my wrist. I needed to get my bearings. I focused on the ground. The earth below me was dry, parched as if after a drought. Someone lowered parted lips to my wrist. Hot breath scorched my clammy skin. It was all I could think about. The images and possibilities of what the creature could be raked my mind like sharpened talons.

Serrated teeth met skin, and I almost screamed. But instead, the creature did, recoiling and throwing my arm.

"Devil's Nettle," the creature croaked.

"You said you checked her shoes."

"I did."

The sickening sound of a slap meeting skin.

A retching noise then, "Her wrist."

"The little witch has fastened a chain with it?"

"Take it off then. I'm famished."

Hags. They had to be Hags. Fae that lived in the waters below the boundary and...feasted on witches that ventured into the wood. First their emotions, then their bodies. My father used to have hunting parties that searched for them. Until his curse took hold, and he was barely strong enough to wander the castle.

"There's no clasp."

There had been a fastener when I put it on... Maybe they didn't see it. *Perhaps they would leave me be.*

"Don't be shy then. Break it. I can't say she'll miss it."

A yank at my wrist as the metal bit into my skin but didn't give way. I couldn't take much more of it. *Think.* I just needed to think—

"Cut off her hand."

"That should do it."

I shot up, and my forehead slammed into the wrinkled face of one of the fae. She went sprawling, and her companions shrieked as blackness filled my eyes, then vanished. My chest ached, but no longer from loss. No, it was a real stabbing pain right above my heart. Cold night air nipped at exposed skin, where a moss-filled poultice was packed into the hole in my chest. The sweet smell...blister berries.

Had they healed me just to eat me? I sprung to my feet, the ground below me unsteady.

The Hag nearest me lunged, her nails scraping my arm. But I was faster. I rammed my shoulder into her middle, shoving her into the flames they were probably planning to cook with.

I scrambled back as her body puffed into vapor, leaving nothing but the echo of her screams. That was the reason they glamoured their prey, the same reason they got their name. Their haggard, waterlogged bodies were weak.

"Tell me, witch..." The last one advanced slowly, more cautious than the others, and looked far angrier. "How is it that you've come to know the queen?"

She had been so concerned with the glamour—my visions of my mother. But why was that of any consequence to her? "Why do you care so much about my mom?"

The Hag cackled, spreading gooseflesh up my neck. "The High Queen of Faery is not your mother."

"Of—of course not."

"But those," she gestured to the black smoke rising from the fire and to the ground near it where the other Hag lay, with a pale green fluid oozing below her head. "Were my sisters."

Her last word was no more than a snarl as she threw herself at me. I jumped away, stumbling over another body, just far away enough from the fire that I hadn't noticed him. But as I toppled, I saw his face.

Liam.

"He thinks you dead. How right he's about to be." The Hag lifted a curved knife from a stump. "Though I hate to waste a perfectly good meal."

Climbing over him, I put my body between his and the Hags. "Excuse me for not knowing the proper etiquette for being eaten."

"Can you hear it too—him screaming your name?" Her eyes flicked to him as her tongue dashed out to taste her lips. "The delectable torment of a broken heart."

"I never wanted this." His words echoed in my mind.

"Broken heart?" I let out a dry laugh and bent my knees, readying myself for her attack. "He tried to kill me."

"Ah. But wouldn't you like to know why?" Nimbler than her sisters, she danced around me and to my side, where she slashed out with her knife and claws.

I jerked away, gasping as the poultice shifted. Blood dripped down onto my stomach, seeping through what was left of my shirt.

Feinting to her right, I kicked my boot out, and her wrist made a popping sound as it connected. Her blade skittered into the dead bushes behind her. Her screech of pain and rage echoed in the empty sky around us as she lunged. Sharp teeth and nails like talons clamped down on my arm. I slammed my fist into the side of her head, and the wound on my chest split open.

A scream rang out as another body lunged into the fray. Fiery red locks blew back into my face as the attacker took down the Hag and crushed their body before stabbing an arrow through the raggedy bitch's head.

My breaths were labored—lead weights had taken residence in my chest.

I looked to the woman who saved me. Dressed in black leathers coated in muck and leaves, she wiped the tip of her arrow off on her pants and tucked it into the quiver sticking out over her shoulder. The woman tugged off the mask covering the lower half of her face.

The bushes behind me rattled, followed by a garbled curse, and I turned to see a poorly bandaged Lux breaking through the foliage with Jett.

"I told you to fucking wait," he yelled at the woman, and I felt for her, whoever she was.

"That thing was going to kill her while you were dawdling." The woman's voice changed as she released her face from the cover and—

"Dri?" I narrowed my eyes as if her presence was another

glamour, and I considered grabbing the salt from my bag. "Where are Scoot and Fox?"

She sighed, and I noted how gaunt her face looked. It made her appear much older—covered in grime and not dressed in pastels. "There were raiders near the end of the Dreadwood. Scoot disappeared. Many others were lost. Then Lux showed up."

I turned to Lux as movement caught my eye off to the side. "You helped her?"

"We made a deal." The giant of a man flicked an invisible piece of dust from his sleeve. "I'm a man of my word."

A head of dark curls popped up in the corner of my vision, and I lunged at Liam as he sat up.

"You asshole." I cracked my fist cracked into his cheekbone, snarling. A large hand caught my arm when I reared back to punch him again.

"Can't let you do that." Lux pulled me back, and I slammed my head against the solid wall of his chest. More warmth dribbled down my front.

A pained sound left me, and Driata rushed over. "Did those things do this to you?"

"Liam stabbed me." I attempted again—despite the pain—to yank out of Lux's hold. He only wrapped a solid leg around the front of mine.

"That's why you've gone a bit rabid?" Lux asked, inching us away from Liam.

"I can't heal it all the way, but this should help ease some of your pain." Driata gripped her talisman and pressed her fingers into my chest, not even flinching at the blood. "You won't be in fighting shape for a while."

As she spoke, she glanced at Liam. And she was right, though I would rather just kill him. The wound was drying, and parts of my skin wove back together. But it was still open, and while the pain ebbed, it was still there.

"This is not done," I said through gritted teeth, even though he wouldn't look at me. "Just keep him away from me."

He walked further away, moving toward Jett, and rubbed his once ruined hand down her face. But she backed away and snapped her teeth at his hands like they were a juicy apple.

Somehow that angered me more. He hadn't wanted to, right? Those were his words. Then why? Why does it at all?

I ground my teeth against my pressing questions for him and turned to Dri. "Who the fuck gave you a bow and arrow?"

"I've been taking archery lessons with the twins for years." She shrugged as she wiped her hand on a cloth Lux handed her from a pack. "Baltazar thought it would be the best fit."

Baltazar.

"What are you supposed to do with me now?"

"Betray you."

There was a growing pressure in my chest, and my eyes burned. And while Liam could have been wrong or lying, I had been stabbed because of Baltazar's command. My gaze moved to Liam, still standing with his back turned away from me and his head hanging in...resignation? I didn't know anymore. It felt like I had never known him at all.

How did he manage without his hand so well? When we fought Lux...when he and I...

No, I wouldn't allow my mind to travel along that path. Those were questions for our leader. But— "Lux, did you know what the outcome of this was?"

"I was told to retrieve you. And I want it to be clear now that I didn't hurt you. I won't have Lord Tellyk thinking I've done that." Lux gestured at my chest, and I realized he wasn't really looking at me either. I looked down and noted that my shirt was ripped down the middle—my left breast fully on display.

Tugging the panels of torn fabric, I covered myself as best as possible. Driata shucked off her jacket and helped me into it, so I didn't jostle the injury.

"You can come out now." Lux sighed, turning to face the bushes that he came from.

My brow furrowed in question at the silence that answered, and I looked at my sister, who shared my confusion.

"Don't be shy now. You certainly haven't been subtle," Lux coaxed at the brush. I was about to ask him if he had lost his head when the low-hanging branches he was staring at rattled. The mud-coated, pale yellow mantle stood out like the sun peeking out of clouds as Lou lowered her hood.

She let out an awkward chuckle as she tucked loose strands falling from her braids behind her ears. "How did you know?"

"I noticed you trailing me as soon as I left Ellesmere's gates." Lux raised a brow at her—I recognized the look. Reproach. "Maybe go for a darker cloak next time. And watch your feet."

"You didn't stop me." Her voice pitched in question even while she nodded in agreement.

The assassin shrugged and tucked his thumbs into his belt. "You didn't cause me any bother. But you did slow me down."

Had he...let her follow him? And let her keep up?

Lou didn't respond but closed the distance between us and

tossed her arms around me in an embrace. "You sure love coming close to death."

"The problem is trusting the wrong people." My eyes narrowed over her thin shoulder at the back of Liam's head. I noted how the curls were matted and looked wet. And he still hadn't spoken.

Driata cleared her throat, and Lou released me, giving my sister a thin-lipped grin.

"We should get going," Lux suggested. "Without Scoot and Fox, your mission is compromised."

"My mission ended the moment all of those lives did." Driata's face pinched in memory, and her eyes were wet with unshed tears.

"What were your orders?" I asked, but my eyes stayed on Liam, not wanting to be caught off guard again. He flinched in response to my question.

Her voice was thick when she answered. "We were transporting the servants over the boundary."

"You were taking them to Faery?" I couldn't hide my anger as my fists balled at my sides. "They were dead the minute you left Ellesmere then."

"There's a village there." Driata paused, and her lips pursed. "Well...a rumored one, beyond the pass."

"And?" Lou shouted at my sister, goading her on with it.

"That's all I know." Dri's shoulders drooped, and I knew she couldn't give any more information. Baltazar would have given her the bare minimum.

But the sadness I saw racking her—that was real. I looked at Lou and thought of what she had said the morning I left to find Driata.

All the new servants were fired when Oliver decided to sail to Weylin. Lou had stayed behind. But Agatha and Edera had gone. And what my sister recounted meant that they all died. For what—the scraps of food they carried with them for travel?

Rumors of raiders had started reaching the castle, but my father had simply upped the guards he placed on imports. He did nothing to make the roads safer.

The fact that my sister lived was only thanks to Lux arriving when he had. And I cut off his damn fingers.

"—take us back to the castle?" Liam speaking brought me out of my thoughts, and fury raced through me again.

"We must get closer—past the barrens at least." Dri perked up, her shoulders straightening. "But you and I could work together."

I kept my eyes on the ground, but I could feel him staring at me. "I don't have my talisman."

Guilt warred with my rage. I didn't want to travel days to get back to the castle. And giving him the damned talisman back could speed that up. But if I was without magic, I certainly wasn't offering any to the man who just tried to murder me.

"Great." Lux heaved a sigh and pinched the bridge of his nose. "We'll be walking then."

"We should go quickly if we don't want to meet up with any other of Faery's nasties." Driata tightened the strap holding her bow to her back, nodding.

I looked around again, noting the dense foliage around us. The trees were thick with verdant life and the sounds of animals rustling and squawking. "Oh, for fuck's sake. We're in Faery?"

"Just past the boundary, about a hundred yards from the

river." Lou offered, seeming to realize quickly that I was far past my limit of vague answers.

"The Hags must've been hunting in the river when you two had it out." Lux pushed past Liam and grabbed Jett's reins.

"We did not *have it out*. Liam *stabbed* me. *In the chest*." My words were clipped, my jaw aching from the pressure of clenching my teeth.

The assassin laughed as he walked my mare toward me and offered me his large, functional hand. Could I go a week without damaging someone's appendage? Probably not in that lifetime.

"Where are your horses?" Lux had a heavy pack secured to his back and his sword attached to his belt.

He lifted me up carefully onto Jett's back, and I bit back a yelp as my chest ached with the movement. "We don't have any. You ride, and the others can take turns riding with you."

"I can walk," I offered, though I would have been stupid to think he would agree.

I needed a healer. There was only so much Driata could do with her magic.

Lux shook his head.

"It's fine, Jane. You need to rest." Driata gave me a weary smile.

Fallen leaves kicked up around Liam as he stumbled, arms pinwheeling as he tried to catch himself and fell forward on his face.

Driata and Lou rushed to him while I chortled from atop Jett. "Little help did both hands do you when you can't manage your feet."

"Lie still." My sister urged as she placed his head in her lap. "You've been bashed in the head."

"Did Jane do this—when you fought?" Lou looked at me, then down. Her eyes marked me where I felt the blister berries burning away infection and my sister's magic working to piece together my wound.

"Serves him right." Lux winked at me like we shared a joke.

Shaking my head, I scrubbed a hand down my face, muttering, "I wish it had been me."

"He'll be the first to ride with Jane," Driata said as she and Lou tried to help him rise. Lux, who had lifted me with ease, stood by and watched.

Over my cold, dead body. And even then, I would come back to refuse. "Don't bring him anywhere near me."

Lou tilted her head to the side, and her eyes went wide. "The injury is closed, but he probably has a concussion."

"I'll walk," Liam mumbled, pulling away from the women and staggered again.

"You certainly will not." Dri put on her privileged voice. One full of snark and indignation. "Lux, help him onto the horse."

If I were any closer to the ground, my jaw would have hit it when Lux lifted Liam by his collar and dragged him to Jett's back. "Behind or in front of you?"

"Really?" I asked. His disloyalty sank into my bones as I looked at the man who trained me while he ignored my wishes and met Driata's.

"When I found her, she thought I was a raider and threatened to carve out my organs if I got any closer to her." He gave my apparently savage sister a pointed look. "Then she reattached my fingers."

He wiggled them slightly from inside his bandages and lifted Liam off the ground. Jett sidestepped just before Liam could kick his leg over her back.

She let out an irritated huff and trotted forward a few paces. I bit down on my lip to stifle the manic laughter bubbling up, but we didn't have time. Logic washed over me as I realized the predicament we were in. We killed three Hags, but there could be more. And there could be much worse hidden among those trees.

"Let him on, girl." I patted her neck. "If he tries anything, you can trample him."

Lux helped Liam once more, and we hightailed it out of the deadliest part of Anwyn. and we hightailed it out of the deadliest part of Anwyn.

CHAPTER 22

We made it to the pass quickly with only the sounds of skittering creatures following us. The dense brush covered our footfalls and Jett's hoof beats while we trekked a nonexistent path.

I was desperate to learn more about a supposed hidden village and the raiders who had taken down the traveling party. Still, we had to be wary of the risk of being seen or heard, so I kept my eyes silently tracking Dri as she walked.

Liam's body slumped against my back, and I jabbed my elbow into his ribs to rouse him.

"Fuck," he grunted and scooted further away. "Stop doing that."

Grinding my teeth together to prevent a spiteful response, I marked Lux's eyes narrowing on Liam. He shrank behind me under the weight of the assassin's glare.

I wasn't aware of whatever was going on between the two of them. Though friendly didn't really describe their relationship.

Well, friendly didn't describe Lux at all. Sometimes, I was sure he only tolerated me. But there was something more there. A tension rumbled in the air as the large man stared down Liam, his expression taut, like a band about to snap.

One thing I was sure of was I wouldn't get involved. I was injured, without my magic, and weaponless.

What had happened to my dagger anyway? Did Liam still have it? Remembering my blade being buried in my chest only made me seethe, wishing to clear the damned passageway so Dri could heal me a bit more. I would leave Jett with Liam and walk for a bit. The horse would be pissed, but nothing a few sugar cubes or fat carrots couldn't solve.

Driata's voice was low, almost humming in the wind when she spoke. I might have missed it if my ears hadn't been on high alert, scanning for dangers. "We didn't have time to break down camp. We only concealed it. Once we get over the pass, we can rest there."

Nodding, despite her back turned to me, I thanked the silent gods that she said it. It was as if they were answering my unspoken prayer. Just a little bit longer.

Liam leaned into me then, and my knuckles turned white around Jett's reins. "Can we talk... When we stop?"

His whispered breath brushed against the curve of my ear, and it was all I could do to keep my body from relaxing against him. *He stabbed you, idiot.*

The rocks underfoot sloped down, and I focused my attention on that. No reaction was better than risking anything else. Especially one someone would have when they were a fool in love. And in that silence, as we descended, I realized the unfortunate part of that truth. I still loved him.

How could my heart betray me like that?

The wound of realization was far worse in some ways than the actual stabbing. It felt like the dumb organ tore me in half. Hurt flared in my chest, swelling to a monstrous size. I didn't know how my body wasn't combusting.

Utilizing my training had never been such a necessity. Silently steadying my breathing and blinking away the haze in my eyes, I shoved Liam back again.

He would not hold power over me. I knew the emotion was there, the shameful thing lying in wait—and I would carve it from my body myself if the need arose.

Tangy copper burst in my mouth when I bit down on my cheek hard enough to draw blood.

Fuck him. I would find a way to make him pay for using me.

Perhaps I could make him fall for me and then have him fall on my blade. Mine will be the last face he sees, and he will know his betrayal was what ended him. Then, and only then, I would go after Baltazar. I would break that man until he spilled his secrets at my feet. Yes, they would both regret manipulating me.

I had grown tired of being a pawn.

Driata's camp wasn't far at all. We arrived at a patch of dirt shrouded by the Dreadwood's barren trees, and she sighed, gripping her talisman.

Watching magic concealments peel away was fascinating. It always reminded me of the time a nobleman had been visiting the castle. His courtesan and my mother sneaked me into a brothel to watch a performance. There had been beautiful people backstage caked in kohl, rouge, mystery, and in all states of undress. When they introduced me with a fake name, the women and men doted on me. Placing extravagant, colorful wigs on my head and painting my face.

The makeup coming off was like a large concealment lifting. It melted down a canvas you didn't realize was there until it peeled. The thicker the spells used, the more you had to work at undoing them.

The greying trees dripped away first, then the patch of dirt gave way to a fire pit where the embers had gone cold. Unfurled sleeping mats followed, weighted down by two heavy-looking bags. Then, finally, a pair of covered, short swords, another axe —the curved edge looking much sharper than the one Lux had in the cave—and a crossbow.

What was he planning on encountering out there? I tilted my head at him, and the brute shrugged. "Always be prepared."

I shook my head in disbelief and snickered at the assassin. Leave it to him to come ready for warfare.

Driata stepped in front of him and took care with the bindings wrapped around his hand while she held her talisman. Lux's face relaxed a fraction as more of his unseen pain left him.

Damn, I should probably apologize for that.

"You're next," she said when her gaze connected with mine.

I got the first good look at her since she came to my rescue, and I noted how different she looked outside a castle's walls.

Sure, she wasn't wearing a gown, and her hair wasn't perfectly pinned, but that wasn't the only difference. There was something off with her face, and her posture was rigid. Purplish bags had formed under her hazel eyes too. *What was going on with her?*

She turned away from my apparent scrutiny to face Lou. "There are clean bandages in one of the satchels. Will you help him?"

"Don't need—" Lux started, but whatever look of reproach Dri gave him made him slam his mouth shut.

My brows raised at the sight of a trained killer fumbling for words because of my sister. Lou coughed out a raspy laugh, motioning for Lux to sit so she could assist him. Even sitting, his head was above her waist.

Dri approached with her chin lowered slightly, not looking me in the eye.

"Are you alright?"

Her head bobbed—fast enough that it was suspicious, paired with an overly broad smile. "Just a bit tired."

Perhaps being away from her scented baths and having the polish on her nails chip away gave way to crisis. I wriggled out of the jacket she loaned me and exposed my front.

Dried blood had mixed with the poultice in the wound, and I curled my lip back. Gross, but practical. The injury would mend, and whatever remained of the blister berry mixture would dissolve with a good wash.

Gentle hands pressed into the flesh near it, and I looked again at my sister while she worked to close it more.

Her nose wrinkled. "Why does it smell...sweet?"

"An antiseptic made of berries." I thought of how the fae had been basically preparing me for their next meal and grimaced. "The Hags were thorough."

"Whatever you do, don't eat them." Liam's voice was less strained since he had rested during the trip.

Realizing that my skills in masking my emotions had been successful in even fooling me was a shock that I couldn't afford then. How was I supposed to ensure the guise didn't falter if I didn't know it was in place? Was it obvious to others? Dri? My father? Oh, Gods...Baltazar or Arius?

If they had, I would figure out how to fix it. Finding the right angle would help. But I couldn't cover it up with hatred. One, it hadn't worked before, and two, it was far too easy to mistake the emotion for passion.

No. To accomplish it, I would have to dismiss Liam entirely. I couldn't let him provoke me. I could rage internally while appearing utterly unbothered by his existence. But I couldn't be pleasant. It would be suspicious after he stabbed me.

It would help me with my own personal mission too. How did that saying go? *The heart wants what it can't have.* I would make myself unobtainable until he was panting after me, begging for scraps of my attention. Then, and only then, I would destroy him.

"You can eat all of them you want." I smiled, and I knew it was a cruel thing. Just a slash of teeth with my lips pulled thin before looking away.

"We need to talk."

"I'm not bored enough to talk to you." My face was an unreadable mask.

Driata sighed and fixed the panels of my ripped shirt before helping me to cover up again. She backed away with her forehead wrinkling, pointing between Liam and me. "I'll leave you to whatever this is."

Shit on it. I couldn't beg her to stay. It would be obvious there was something wrong, though the rules I was concocting for the plan were already getting out of hand. What would a normal person do after one impaled them? Be fearful, I supposed. But I would sooner profess my infuriating love than act afraid of Liam Tellyk.

"What is it you want?"

He rubbed the back of his neck and didn't speak.

Waiting while he opened his mouth and closed it again was infuriating. But I coached my face to stay relaxed, picturing the image of clay drying—simple boredom.

Finally, praise above, Liam spoke before I gave any sign he was irritating me. "It's not what you think."

Weighing my options and knowing that playing dumb simply didn't suit me, I rolled my eyes at him. "Then what is it?"

"I...I can't explain." Liam gritted his jaw, pausing and starting again. "But I was—I didn't want...*fuck*."

"Are you having a stroke?"

"No."

Jett had a sudden spell on the other side of the logs Lux worked on lighting. She reared up, stomping her hooves on the dry earth while making horrendous braying noises. Shoving past the tongue-tied ass, I ran toward her.

"Easy girl." I grabbed her reins, calming her and rubbing the center of her face. Then, leaning, I looked for anything around her that could have caused her reaction.

Liam reached a hand, and Jett yanked her head away, pinning her ears. The leather reins tore at my hands as she bucked. "You've pissed off Jett."

"She adores me."

The horse snorted in a way that proved she, in fact, did not adore him and pressed her face back against my palm.

"Are you going to say whatever it is that you think I haven't already guessed?" I gave him a pointed look before focusing my attention on soothing my mare.

He sputtered again, making me wish I hadn't asked. But then, "There are things you don't know."

"We've had this discussion before." I pinched the bridge of my nose. "Tons of things I don't know, then you got all stabby. Let's say we skip the last part, and you just fill me in?"

No answer. Listening to the crackling fire Lux must have gotten going and the distant voices of our companions on the journey, I counted my breaths before trying again. "You were ordered to betray me?"

"Yes."

"By Baltazar, evidently."

A nod.

"Is that why you slept with me?" Damn my voice for cracking, but I had to know.

"You-fucking-*what*?" Lux's tone was full of condemnation as he barreled into Liam, fists already slamming against unprotected ribs.

Toxic masculinity at its finest, pass.

I backed away a few steps before twisting to face the

deserted fire. Sitting in front of it, hands outstretched, the warmth filled me. I ignored the grunts and shouts of rage from where the two men brawled.

Even if Lux had no hands, I couldn't see a world in which Liam won, but I had seen him train. He was fast and could probably get a few good licks in, but Lux was better—and purely *vicious* when pissed off.

Lou grunted as she plopped down next to me. "What happened there?"

"Where were you when it started?"

"Helping Driata find something safe to eat." Lou patted her knees as she talked, none of her usual snark in her voice. "She said if Lux offered her dried meat one more time, she'd be ill."

The same sister who couldn't stand by and watch an innocent animal being eaten was trying to yank Lux off Liam by his collar.

"So?" Lou persisted, and I hummed in turn.

Dri stomped her foot, looking ridiculous near the bulk of the two men. "You'll ruin your hand, you buffoon."

Lux's nose was bleeding, and his brow was split, but I couldn't see the damage Liam was taking under him.

"Why are they fighting?" Lou's voice reminded me I was trying not to care, and I glanced at her. She was staring, not at the ground where the fighting was happening, but at Driata.

"Lux heard I had sex with Liam." Shrugging my shoulders, I tugged at a frayed thread on my sleeve.

"Oh." She sounded confused but not surprised.

I thought of all the times she had seen me with my clothes missing or in disarray after being with Liam. Damn. She was around often enough, I would have to convince her too.

"Are you and Lux..." Lou left the end open in suggestion, and I barked a laugh.

"Not ever." Though the realization that I didn't know why Lux was so angry made my mirth sober up. "I'm not actually sure why he reacted that way."

Lou clicked her tongue. "Men will just never be worth all of this trouble."

I was about to tell her I agreed when Driata finally managed to separate the pair. Instead, I shouted, "if men would just talk, the world's problems could be resolved. Instead, they whip out their *tiny swords* and duel."

"Why don't you pull out a measure and check us for yourself." Liam's eyes drilled into me as he turned his bleeding lip in a grin.

My cheeks burned with the implication, and I narrowed my eyes on the dimple that popped up on Liam's. He would not get a rise out of me.

Lux lunged for him again, but Liam ducked out of the way. Driata stepped between them.

"Jane's right." Driata pointed away from the camp, near the riverbank. "Talk it out."

A muscle feathered in Lux's jaw, but he followed my sister's command with Liam at heel.

While they made their way to have a—hopefully civil, if Driata had anything to say about it—chat, my sister perched next to Lou and me. Her posture straightened as if she were wearing a gown and sitting at a luncheon with royals.

"Don't you want to know what they'll say?" Lou asked before deepening her voice. "No, really, my dick must be bigger than yours."

"Watch this," Dri whispered and gripped her talisman. Suddenly, the men's voices carried over to us.

"—you tried to kill her."

"Correction. I tried *not* to kill her."

"Tell that to the stab wound asshole."

"Orders."

"To betray her?"

"Indeed."

"By fucking her."

"That's how it will be interpreted, I suppose."

"But why would Baltazar send me to retrieve her?"

"My guess?" Liam dragged his hand over his face. "You were far more likely to get her to wear the bracelet than I was."

"But why would he want any of his assets at a disadvantage?"

"Why does Baltazar do anything?"

"Control."

I was vaguely aware of Lou and Driata's hushed tones, but my ears rang with the conversation we were overhearing. One that it was clear I wasn't meant to be privy to. I thought of the underground empire I had seen when Baltazar had taken Liam and me for training. The concealed masses that had bowed for him. The way it had felt when he struck me and later when I realized he was manipulating me. I had gotten too reckless and uncontrollable.

He thought me a beast needing a lesson, but he unwittingly showed his hand. I wasn't an untamed beast. I was a thorn— one that would prick and bleed to see his empire come to ruin.

CHAPTER 23

The sun crested over the mountains as we reached the Barrens.

Farmlands passed down and tilled through generations, back when they were filled with endless rows of orchards and crops that fed all Lunasians, went to waste.

The soil went unturned in the years after the riots, and no one was left to care once their homes burned. So the farmlands laid empty, the curse settling into the roots and soil. But the fields had been unyielding and empty well before being scorched by flames. And our people suffered its devastation, only growing angrier with the king after he limited the allocation of the once ample food supplies in each household. As I walked, the weight in my chest had nothing to do with the healing wound and everything to do with the emptiness surrounding the barrens.

Driata's eyes were wide and scanning from her perch in front of Lou on Jett's back. Shock and horror lined my sister's face as she realized where we were. I stared more at her than our surroundings—watching her sink lower each time we passed a vacated home, though the ones left standing were few and far between.

It must have been jarring for her. My family never traveled out that way. If it weren't a shorter distance between us and the castle than the road from Luhne, we wouldn't have traveled through them that day either. I forced myself to pass through the barrens each time a mission took me in that direction. To memorize the color of the rubble, the shape of the children's toys I found amongst the remains, and the acidic scent of the unfertile lands.

Seeing Driata's reaction made me angrier at my father and his damned curse. His love for his original wife became an obsession after the fae foiled their eternity spell. And that obsession had led to his people suffering every time her incarnation died.

That cycle had been the most trying. When the king killed my grandmother, thinking her daughter was his lost love, the action set off unprecedented reactions throughout his own kingdom.

It was like the land and sky revolted against his selfishness. However, knowing that and being exposed to the backlash his people faced because of his actions were two different things.

And after everything he caused, my father refused to see his people and hear their pleas, only encouraging them to move to bigger cities.

We continued, the hush dragging between us. As though we each knew we carried burdens, it seemed only thoughtless to mention in such a place. But when the sound of a yelling woman peeled back the quiet, I ran.

Clearing the hills of scorched earth and feeling the wind whip at my braided hair would have usually been something that brought me peace. But some unknown fear clawed beyond the new scar on my chest with each thud of my boots. I had never been on that side of the barrens, but I thought everyone had been evacuated.

With every gulp of air, my breath heaved out of me. My lungs burned with the exertion as the acrid smell of the earth coated them.

Who could be out here?

Lou hollered behind me, and dust twisted up around Jett's pounding hooves as the seamstress goaded her on. They quickly cleared the distance, surpassing what progress I had made as she galloped in the direction of distress.

Liam and Lux's longer legs each took up the space at my side as I pumped my arms, and adrenaline coursed through me.

"Raiders?" Liam asked easily. He hadn't even broken a sweat as our feet propelled us forward.

Lux shook his head, jogging to keep up with my pumping legs. "Not this far from the roads."

I worked on lengthening my strides and gained no advantage. Sweat gathered at my brow and a dull ache spasmed in my side.

In through the nose, out through the mouth, Lux's teachings rambled in my mind. Dumbest thing I had ever heard. My nostrils couldn't suck down near as much air as my mouth. *Logic.* The muscle at the back of my thigh cramped, and a slicing pain shot down my leg. I lifted it again, and my body folded.

"*Shitfuckdamnit,*" I wheezed. The earth was hard under my back. White spots flared in my eyes.

"You forgot to stretch," Lux said, stopping. His body blocked out the sky while he leaned over me.

I clutched my leg to my stomach, slamming my eyes closed as my face scrunched. "No time."

"There's always time to be prepared." A sharp, cold response. *Smug asshole.*

"Go help the others. I've got her," Liam said, and I wished a hole would rip open in the earth, so I could fall into it.

A grumbled response under the ringing in my head.

"*I've got her,*" Liam said again, that time firmer.

"It's not far off. Join us quickly." There was a warning in Lux's tone, but his boots skidded on the ground by my head as he turned, padding off.

"Not everything has to be a competition." Liam's voice held a note of humor.

I paused, thinking of how hard I pushed myself after they caught up—and chose to ignore it. "I wasn't aware I was competing."

"You've no competition." Liam cleared his throat before changing the subject. "Can you get up?"

"Yes." The truth was I didn't know. My leg was taut as a bowstring. I should have drank more water, but Lux and Dri each had only one canteen. Mine was lost after dealing with Liam and the hags. It was probably in some graveyard of lost items along with my dagger and the socks I sent to be laundered that never came back.

Instead of complaining, though, I made sure everyone else had a fair share, feigning swigs when they passed it to me. Lux would be furious. Liam would think I was an idiot. Dri and Lou would probably be insulted.

I rubbed my knuckle against the tense muscle, grunting and wrestling myself to sit. Pain flared up my back and ribs.

Calloused fingers wrapped around my wrist and the back of my neck, helping guide me slowly upright.

I smacked at his hand, nearly losing my balance again when he adjusted his grip. "Don't touch me."

Liam laughed, and I realized how close he was standing. "In our language, that's not how you say thank you."

He reached down, pressing his fingers into the back of my thigh, massaging the ache.

My heart, my lungs, and my body froze.

His hands moved in deep, gentle strokes against the pain, and my mind zeroed in on the pressure right under my ass.

The cramp faded, but I couldn't move, not when it felt like a current flowing from his body into mine. My back arched slightly into his chest. Then, as if waking from a fever dream, the noise of my thudding pulse and my too-quick breaths came back into focus. I yanked away from him.

"*Don't do that*," I hissed, stomping after our group.

"You can't say you don't enjoy it," Liam countered.

I squared my shoulders, disinclined to let him see how much he affected me. "And you are an idiot if you think you speak for what I enjoy."

I glanced sideways, and our eyes met. Liam bit his lip, stifling a smile. "I think I'm well versed in what you enjoy, but by all means—feel free to give me another lesson."

Heat spread up from my neck as I burned from outrage and shame. "No."

"Pretty little liar." His silky voice was nothing more than a purr when it reached me, but his laugh was loud as he sprinted off.

His managing so simply to rile me into a rage wasn't a great sign that my plan was going well. I counted my breaths, working to calm my growing nerves as I ran. Finally, I reached a property with a squat cottage sitting pert in the middle.

Jett stood by dulled white fencing, hitched to a post. I gave her a wave, and she snuffed calmly at the dirt surrounding her.

She was there, but where was everyone else? The house was quiet, and no one answered when I knocked. So I edged around the side of it, quietly noting the latched blue shutters, their paint peeling from years of keeping out the overly hot sun.

The metal frame of some kind of shed came into view, and I heard my companions' muffled and rushed voices.

"—mean you no harm," Lux said, his deep timbre and giant size probably not very reassuring.

"What are you doing snooping on my property?" The voice was that of an irate woman.

"Ma'am..." Driata—ever the mediator, was probably giving the woman her brightest smile. "We heard a shout and came to offer aid."

I rounded the corner and saw Lux and the others crowding the entrance of a little building crafted of stained glass and iron.

Over the assassin's head, vines of plump tomatoes climbed up walls. I couldn't make out the woman in front of them, but through the part in their bodies, I saw Driata's petite hands raised with palms forward.

I shoved past Lux, ducking when he tried to stop me. I ran into Dri, whose back was stiffer than the dry earth.

"How many more are there of you—you heathens?" I could see the woman finally and noted her face lined with age—commoners didn't age as well since they weren't given access to magic. A plump little woman who only stood as tall as my chin. Which in and of itself was impressive since I didn't have much height for her to contend with.

Her freckled cheeks were rosy with rage as she waggled a butcher knife in an unsteady hand.

I snaked around Driata and Lou and shielded them with my body. The small space was filled with planters and overflowing with greenery. It was hot in there, though, and I was sweating in the jacket.

"Eyes on me, missy." The woman tutted, lofting the knife only inches away from me.

"Ma'am, wielding sharp objects is no way to have a conversation." I tried, following Dri's lead, contorting my grimace into a smile.

"You barged on my property, covered in filth and what one can only assume is blood. Yet, you don't expect me to protect myself?" Her button nose wrinkled, and she jabbed the knife at me to punctuate her words.

That's enough. Why hadn't anyone disarmed her?

"Listen to me, lady." My sigh was heavy, and she flinched. "I've already been stabbed this week, and I'm not taking any more appointments."

Her little eyebrows scrunched together. "Get off my property."

"You're apparently not in any danger." I took a step back,

giving her a thumbs up. Those behind me moved in turn. "So, can and will do."

I bit my tongue to stop myself from correcting her stance as we made our way—step by step—backing out of the greenhouse. *Probably not best to help someone maim you.*

"What's going on, mama?" A little boy's lisp carried through the crowded bodies at the shed's entrance. I could barely make out his form through the huddle, but I saw a hefty sack of... Something resembling dirt in his arms?

My group parted, readying to leave the property we were very clearly not welcome on.

"Hush up, Kaleb, and go wash." The woman, apparently the boy's mother, shooed him to a little porch at the back of the house. Two rocking chairs sat there, overlooking the family's empty field and beyond, to the mountains dotting the horizon in the distance.

Skinny arms wrapped around my waist and the woman shrieked. My eyes drew away from the property to look down in horror at the small child latched onto me.

But then he bared his missing front teeth in a smile, and his rounded cheeks dimpled.

Oh... I recognized him.

"Did you like the bread?" Kaleb asked, his squeaky voice muffled by the fabric of my shirt. He hadn't smiled brightly in the market, though he had been friendlier than his sister.

Kaleb's mother sputtered, shouting for Gwyn—her daughter and the boy's older sister. The lanky girl banged out of the house holding a limp, wet head of cabbage. She patted her hands on a flower-patterned apron that said, *kiss the chef.*

Gwyn didn't look at her mother, though. Instead, she stared

at Liam, eyes widening, face turning the same shade as a crisp apple.

"Young man, if you don't let that woman go right this—"

Gwyn cut over their mother, looking at me. "You're the woman from the market."

Everyone stared at me as I nodded.

"By the gods." The woman gasped, eyes widening. She slowly tucked the arm holding the butcher knife behind her back. "Forgive me."

"What did you do in the market?" Having apparently made quick work of catching up, Liam feigned a whisper, clearly finding the sudden change in circumstance amusing.

"I bought some bread." I shrugged, not enjoying the attention.

The woman ogled me, something akin to awe lining her face while the boy bounced on the balls of his feet.

"And a carrot," Kaleb added, smiling and showing all his teeth.

"You were too dim to know how much it was actually worth." Gwyn flicked her braid over her shoulder, turning back to the door. *Unimpressed with me... I liked her.*

"Gwyneth—you apologize, right now," the woman demanded.

Hinges screamed when Gwyn slammed the door shut behind her without looking back.

The woman reddened, twisting to me. "I'm sorry about her."

"Teenagers—what are you going to do?" Lux offered when the quiet became awkward.

"You must allow me to make up for my inhospitality." The

woman handed Kaleb the knife, scooting him closer to the house before continuing.

"My name is Tessa Dower. You've met Kaleb and Gwyn. You must be weary and hungry from your..." She paused, poking her tongue in her cheek. She assessed our soiled and bloodied clothes before finishing. "Travels."

"We were just on our way through, actually." I smiled, not wanting to take anything from the family when I saw how excited they were over just a few gold coins.

"Like my friends tried to explain, we thought you were hurt or in danger." Lou narrowed her eyes, unswayed by the newly polite woman.

"No one travels this way other than the raiders." Tessa's eyes lined with silver, her chin trembling. "It's no excuse to assume, but honestly... Look at the state you're all in."

We did, and the results were not good. The panels of my jacket had popped open at the top to reveal my ripped shirt, stiff with blood. Everyone else was covered in scratches, gashes, and scrapes from the journey. Even where they were healed, crimson stains remained.

Lux was the worst of us, with his bandaged hand and giant axe strapped to his back. He had attached our bags with the other weapons to Jett's saddle, but the axe alone, on a man who was already intimidating... Not a great look.

My companions grumbled their acceptance of the truth.

"But we did hear you scream." I prodded, needing to know if anyone was hiding in wait.

"The worms." Tessa patted her cheeks, wiping away her worried tears. "They keep chewing through my tomatoes—tomatoes are my best sellers at the market."

"So that's why you had the knife?" Lux sounded genuinely impressed, and his lips curved in a smirk. "You were threatening the worms."

"Yes, though it sounds silly when it's said aloud." She smoothed the front of her oat-colored dress, her freckles darkening with her blush. "Anyway, I'm not willing to take no for an answer. You will sit down to sup with us—and eat your fill. Then you can rest your sleepy heads."

She gained an inch, straightening and planting her hands on her hips. Daring one of us to argue.

"We will leave first thing in the morning," Driata promised, grinning. Tessa looped their arms, leading my sister inside.

"Wipe your feet," Tessa urged. "And the big one can leave his axe outside. I'm sure he has plenty more hidden weapons to protect himself."

Lux undid the strap fast enough that it seemed his mother had ordered him to, and he risked a whooping. He ducked through the door frame, prowling inside after Tessa with his tongue nearly lolling out.

Luckily, the house was larger inside than it looked, and he barely had to tuck his head once we entered the kitchen.

Dri was already sifting flour into a bowl by the sink while Gwyn chopped the head of cabbage with the same knife her mother had held us up with.

Gwyn looked up just as Liam stepped in behind me, placing his hand on my back. The girl brought the knife down again—harder that time—and the still-rounded half flew off the wooden cutting board, splashing into the bowl of flour. Powder burst from the bowl, covering Dri.

"The big one—" Tessa started, but the assassin corrected her.

"Lux."

"Lux, you're good with blades, I assume. Please chop the vegetables while I show your friend where to wash up. Gwyn, fetch more water from the well."

Lou snorted a laugh at Lux's expense but offered to help with the pails.

Tessa nodded her agreement, somehow seeming fine with having so many filling her home and the lot filed off.

A tug on my sleeve pulled my focus down to two honey-flecked, blue eyes. "I can teach you how to make the rolls. We already have some for dinner, but mama is making some for the market."

He bade me wash my hands and cuff my sleeves before leading me to the counter. They were beautiful, made of pine.

Kaleb noticed me running my fingers along the edge and said, "my Pa made everything in this house before..." He trailed off, his toothy grin fading.

"I heard we're making rolls?" Liam ruffled the boy's hair, seeming to reactivate Kaleb's cheerfulness.

"Don't mind me," Lux grumbled, but I caught that smirk on his mouth again. "Just alone over here chopping the vegetables. Onions, ack. Who needs them?"

"It'll give you a good chance to shed some pent-up tears." Liam chuckled at his joke, but I bit down on my laugh, knowing we would pay for it later.

"So," I focused instead on Kaleb. "Where do we begin?"

We sat down to dinner on mismatched chairs.

Tessa had insisted that I sit at the head of the table, and I refused as politely as possible. But it was her husband's seat before he passed away, and my stomach twisted at the children and their mother's loss.

I tugged at the collar of the gown Tessa loaned me after her family saw that we were all given fresh clothes and cleaned up before we ate.

Luckily Lux brought extras of his own things because Liam barely fit in Tessa's husband's trousers.

The tan material stretched tight around Liam's thighs each time he leaned in to add something to his plate.

I wished he sat further away, where I wouldn't notice, but he stole the seat next to me after I sat. Lux glowered from a rocking chair to his left. Driata was on a quilted ottoman near Tessa, and Lou perched on a step stool between the children.

"Would you mind passing the potatoes, Miss Tessa?" Lux's manners shouldn't have been shocking, but each of our heads turned when he used them.

To her credit, at least, Tessa did seem to expect it. She ladled up a massive scoop and plopped it onto his plate as she hummed a nursery rhyme.

"How do you manage to keep such fresh produce?" Driata asked, biting on a green bean, looking content for the first time in weeks. Given all of the meat offered in Ellesmere—it probably was.

The Dowers looked amongst themselves, without answering, clearly uncomfortable with the topic. Probably because they were farmers wishing for fields of fresh fruits and vegetables.

"Sorry." Driata wasn't used to being the cause of such a lapse in conversation. I could see her fumbling for words as they exited her mouth. "I don't mean to pry. I've never been to this part of Lunasa and was shocked to see how bad it's gotten."

"Where did you say you're all from?" Gwyn asked, exchanging a look with her mother that may have been subtle if I had no eyes.

"We didn't, actually," I cut in, keeping my tone easy and my breathing steady, lifting my water cup. "But we travel from Karhdaro to Anwyn to select wares for the king."

"You're personal with the King of Karhdaro." Tessa arched a brow at me. It should forever be seen as a testament to my skill that I didn't falter or blink despite the indecent place my mind traveled to.

"Very." I nodded, watching the other heads around the table doing the same. "Well, Lux is a hired hand—our guard."

"My father used to sell his woodwork in Karhdaro," Gwyn said. My mistake was evident as the tension in the room spiked. "He came home and told me of their rich markets and glorious accents."

"Ah, yes." Lou smiled, casting a faraway look in her eye as if she were homesick.

"None of you have accents." Gwyn's eyes narrowed, daring me to keep up the lie.

Challenge accepted.

I gulped, letting a mist of unshed tears film my eyes. "Well, originally, we're from Anwyn—which is why Blair trusts us. We know the continent. But when the lands spoiled, we had nothing keeping us here and no job prospects. So, we took to the seas, each on our own journeys that led us together."

Too far, I knew I had gone too far. But I couldn't reel it in now.

"The selfish king and the mad one," Tessa spat. "Pick your poison—they'll let you die either way. At least your new king treats you well?"

"Very." With that, I hoped for the end of the conversation, but Driata couldn't leave it be.

"Has it gotten so bad here?" She needed to stop before she went too far. "That you hate your king?"

"He and his children sit on their gold-encrusted rear ends while their people starve to death." Tessa's grip on her fork threatened to bend it. "The people didn't blame them for a while."

"They blamed the farmers who weren't producing their share." She went on looking at each of us in turn. "Most people who survived it—though many were lost—moved to the cities. It's why our capital is an overpopulated wasteland and unsuitable for any living there."

My throat closed, my stomach tightening as her anger became a palpable thing that sat at the table with us. "But the cities were given the third line of food. With the castle filling its stores, the noblemen were next, then our cities, and only then the people who had kept everyone from going hungry years prior."

"Be glad you got out," Gwyn added, nodding.

Even I had no idea how truly awful it had become. Our tables never went without, and the noblemen and women who showed up to court never looked hungry. I had seen so much go to waste, which enraged me. But learning that the imports weren't making it out to the rest of our people... That people were vacating their homes, giving up everything they knew for a chance at scraps that royals didn't want—it was horrifying.

Driata's eyes brimmed with tears before they free fell down her bronze cheeks. "I—there has to be a way to fix this."

"Ah, child, we're angry enough that eventually, something will give." Tessa's temper had calmed. Possibly because she was so used to living that way, she saw no reason to let it fester constantly. If Baltazar saw the ease at which she controlled her emotions, she may be his next mark in our merry band of misfits. "Besides, my grandmother survived her season. So we'll make it through ours."

"Excuse me—season?" My head tilted to the side.

"Every lifetime, the land hibernates for a season—this is ours." The woman shrugged, and I thought my heartbeat was visible in my neck. *The commoners didn't know about the curse.*

They didn't blame my father at first, but they should have. Perhaps if he were held accountable, he would have searched for a way to end his curse and heal his unfertile lands. Instead, he let his people think that the lands were unforgiving every hundred years. Because Gods forbid, they knew that he let them suffer for his own love.

Kaleb groaned beside me, "This is boring."

Tessa clapped her hands together. "He's right. That talk is far too dark for polite company."

Lux cleared his throat, and I sensed a change of topic in order. "After supper, I'd like to look at your back door, Miss Tessa."

Lou choked on the bite of potato she had bitten into, and Liam howled, nearly falling out of his chair. Lux's face drained of color while he corrected, "It looks as though your hinges have gone crooked."

"Childish," I muttered, dabbing my napkin to my mouth to hide my amusement.

A bony elbow caught me in the ribs, and Kaleb leaned in, his voice hushed, "can you keep a secret?"

"I have a few." I kept my eyes on my plate, playing along.

"Gwyn has a crush on your friend."

The sound that came out of the girl was unnatural. It reached a decibel I had only heard when Gemma got her first haircut, and the servant took off too much.

Gwyn slammed her silverware on the porcelain dish, throwing her chair away from the table before stomping off into the recesses of their home.

"You forgot to whisper," I said, eyes wide as the young boy giggled and bit into a butter-soaked roll. "That's the most important part of a secret."

CHAPTER 24

Perhaps Lux shouldn't have offered to look at the warped hinges on the door because Tessa quickly made use of his efficiency with tools. Once dinner was cleared and the seats back where they belonged, she found out too how many things he could fix without needing a ladder.

Gwyn hadn't emerged from her mother's room—which we found out during dinner was where the pair of children would be sleeping so we could use *their* room. After trying and failing to reassure them it wasn't necessary, we learned the Dowers wouldn't take no for an answer.

So Driata and Lou had retired, claiming dinner had been so filling they were likely to sleep for a year. And Lux was busy fixing lanterns that hadn't been re-oiled in years.

I took up the settee braiding my hair after Kaleb asked to show me card tricks. He shuffled through his deck, apologizing every time they spilled out of his hands.

"It's okay. I thought it was part of the suspense." I winked, and the boy's cheeks flushed.

"With practice, you'll only get better." Liam's voice came from over my shoulder, and with great care, I didn't jump.

"Why don't you help Lux?" I asked, hoping for some space between us. I couldn't trust myself to keep angry when my disturbing thoughts shifted and focused on how he looked in the overly tight clothes.

Think about Baltazar. It didn't cool me off, but the heat of my lust gave way to a boiling rage. But even then, my mind wondered about the things I didn't know. Years of training and working for the man taught me that there was information I hadn't been given. But it always fed his will and his cause. So, what was he withholding that led to me being powerless? And why did he order his brother to betray me?

But Liam wasn't innocent either—not really. He could have ignored the orders or warned me. We could have worked together and convinced Baltazar that he completed whatever task Liam was given.

Instead, he stabbed me. My fingers absently trailed over the new scar on my chest, just above where my heart lay.

Dri had offered to heal it the rest of the way, but I denied her. I have never been a fan of blank canvases, anyway.

"Here," Liam said, rounding the settee and sitting next to Kaleb. His hands curved around the cards, careful of the bent edges as he showed the boy how to shuffle without losing them.

"You're going too fast," Kaleb whined.

"That's the trick. The faster you move, the less your audience sees."

"Oh." Kaleb held his little hands in front of Liam's and copied the movements he made until they were taking turns.

"You gave me a secret, so it's only fair I give you one as well." Liam waggled his brows at the boy who was studiously sifting the cards in hand. "The real magic is knowing who has a queen in their pocket."

He reached over and waved his hand around Kaleb's breast pocket before pulling free a card. A bubble of laughter escaped me before I clapped my hand over my mouth.

Liam had done the very same trick with a rose when we first met at my parent's anniversary ball.

I was eight at the time and clung to my mother's side all night when Liam and Baltazar were announced as they walked in. Liam hadn't been taught how to use his talisman, and I had no success with mine. He told me there was other magic and had seemingly conjured a rose from thin air. Baltazar was hired officially as my father's keeper the next day, and they never left.

My eyes were glazed with memory when they connected with Liam's, and it seemed he thought of the same fateful night. Was he wondering how different our lives would be if we were other people if our duties weren't so misaligned? What if we had just been two ordinary strangers instead of...us?

"Oh!" Tessa's eyes popped wide when she entered the room. "Kaleb, it is well past time for bed."

"But they'll be gone in the morning," he whined, and he was right. We would be leaving by dawn if all went to plan.

"I have to check on the horse anyway." Liam ruffled Kaleb's hair. "If she eats too many of your mama's carrots, she won't be able to carry anyone home."

He better not let Jett hear him talking like that, or it won't be my fists his pretty face had to worry about.

Tessa tutted at the boy, all but lifting him by his ear and leading him to bed.

Liam's mouth popped open when they were nothing more than silhouettes at the end of the darkened hall, but I was already moving. I wouldn't get caught up in conversations about what could have been. If he was going out back where Jett had been moved, I would be out front.

I burst through the door, my scrambled thoughts chasing me. I gulped down the crisp night air.

The barrens were a fraction warmer than the Dreadwood, though the air would only grow warmer the nearer we got to the castle.

The Dowers' home was close enough that we wouldn't have much walking the next day.

Then I could return to my tower and think. Alone.

No longer traveling with so many prying eyes, senseless chatter, and time to breathe before I again had to return to Ellesmere.

And I was glad of it.

The orangey glow of a fire by the fallen fence caught my attention, and I moved toward it.

"Lux?" I asked, seeing his bulky form warming in front of it. "I was just getting some air. Do you mind if I join you?"

"You'll do it even if I say no, right?" His words were followed by a chuckle, and he scooted back from the fire to look at me.

"Are you hiding out here?" I asked, picking up a stick on the fire's edge and prodding the thickest log. A piece of bark sparked and peeled away as the flames billowed up the side before slowly dying in the dirt.

"Are you?" he countered.

"No—" He gave me a pointed look that warned me against my lie. "A little."

He shrugged, glancing at the house. Lanterns lighting the windows gradually flicked off one by one. "The Dowers can only host so many people. So I figured I'd stay out here."

"I don't think Tessa minds having you around."

"She's a tough one." Lux's laugh was hearty and deep, with a clear fondness for the woman. "I offered to stay—there's so much to be done around here."

"What about—you know..." Lowering my voice, I leaned closer to him. "The job."

"Working with Baltazar has never been simple work. But it always made sense. And even when it didn't..." He sighed, rubbing his palm over his face. "It didn't ever involve hurting anyone I—ah. You're a good one. And the situation he's put me in here compromised the morsel of morals I have."

Emotion clogged my throat, and he continued, "you'd do well to get yourself out too."

"So that's it then?" I lobbed a punch at his bicep that he deftly blocked. "You tell me you care about me, then you're going to leave?"

"Well, technically, you'll be leaving, but yes."

I was quiet for a minute before remembering something. "What about your cat?"

"Ginger?" The corners of his mouth turned up in a smile. "She'll find me—always does."

Halfway across the continent? I almost asked, but I didn't

want him to think I was trying to convince him. Instead, I blurted, "I'm sorry about your hand."

He held up his clean bandages and wriggled his fingers. "Your sister said they're almost as good as new."

"Right." I chewed my lower lip. "But I know how it feels to be hurt by someone you care about."

Lux made a sound of realization. "I can't speak on what went down between you and pretty boy, but as far as my hand is concerned, I'm actually proud of you."

My mouth fell open. I cut off his fingers, and he was... proud? Maybe it was good he was retiring. The job was rotting his senses.

"Don't act so surprised." Shadows danced in his eyes, which had nothing to do with the flames. "We both heard what Baltazar said to you that day. But you disarmed me—twice. I wouldn't have done anything differently if our roles had been reversed. You should always be prepared to do whatever you must to win."

"I only bested you because of my magic." I tugged on the damned bracelet as I spoke—feeling powerless.

He placed a heavy hand on my shoulder and forced me to look at him. "Your magic isn't what makes you special, Jane. Take it from the man who trained you—it's your inability to give up."

I nodded, but there was no conviction in it. "There's truly no way to take it off, then?"

"Not that I know of." His brows furrowed as he examined my face like he was searching for something in its lines. "Want to know something?"

"If I say no, you'll tell me anyway, right?" I asked, taking his earlier words.

He smirked, but his mouth flattened when he spoke. "I think you scare him."

"I—"

Lux held up his hand and went on, "for a man who craves control as much as Baltazar does, he's forgotten you came into this without access to magic. And now he's fanned the flames of his own destruction by underestimating you."

Even though I planned on checking on my mare before laying down, I didn't want to risk the potential encounter with Liam. Instead, I reminded myself she had been spoiled with vegetables before Kaleb secured her the fence beyond their greenhouse. She would manage.

I quietly made my way to the room, examining the decorations hanging on the walls in the hall. Filled shelves and frames held intricately carved figurines, handprints, and a child's drawing of the Dower family that included a man floating above those that remained.

An ache filled my chest when I reached the door and turned the knob.

"Turning in?" The lantern was dimmed, but I saw Lou propped up by the headboard, resting her eyes. What was more surprising, though, was Driata's head resting in her lap.

My sister's face was ruddy, and tear tracks lined her cheeks.

"Is she hurt?" I made my way over to the other wooden bed and pulled at the laces of my boots.

"Not physically."

Driata was most likely tired of not having her own chambers, shampoos, and gowns. "Did you remind her we'd be home tomorrow, and she can pamper herself all she wants?"

Lou's head snapped to attention, and she narrowed her eyes at me. "She may have noticed the tax this life has taken on the people later than you, but she's seen it."

"Oh." My mind went to the questions my sister had asked at dinner. I thought she was being insensitive, but she was concerned?

"Have you ever taken a moment to ask her if she was alright after everything she experienced out there?" Lou's voice was nothing more than a breath, but it felt like a slap.

"I meant to—"

"While you and everyone else were busy allowing her to heal all of your wounds, she was carrying many of her own." A muscle feathered in her jaw, and I saw it all at once. Driata's distance and the slight details she had given since she found me frantically pinged around my brain. She had watched all those people die... And she was only alive because Lux saved her.

She must have been terrified—and was so distracted by my own circumstance that it hadn't clicked.

Gods.

Pulling the covers over myself and closing my eyes, I wondered how I could fix it—fix everything. There was no excuse not to find a balance between helping Driata with what she experienced and sorting out my issues.

The door creaked, and my eyes splintered open. Lantern light from the hall flooded in around a silhouette.

Liam.

The pair in the bed across the confined space was snoring softly, so I whispered to avoid waking them, "can I help you?"

Metal snicked, scraping on leather, and I looked down at his hands—he was unfastening his belt. "I'm going to bed—early day and all that."

"Lux has a fire going."

"Driata and Lou are sleeping." He smiled as my face scrunched in confusion. "I thought we were stating facts about our companions."

I pulled the blanket higher around me, though sweat was climbing up the back of my neck. My tongue felt too thick in my mouth while I searched for words.

With one stride, he reached the foot of the bed. With a flick of his wrist, his belt slid free of the loops in his trousers. "Scoot over."

"No," I said, already shaking my head. "Go sleep in the sitting room."

"Sitting rooms are called such because one doesn't sleep there." His damned dimples carved into his cheeks.

"Then sleep outside—there's plenty of room there."

"Honestly," he said, clicking his tongue. "I think Tessa would be disappointed with your inhospitality."

"I don't care. It's not my house to be hospitable in." Fanning my fingers on both sides of me, I judged there were about four inches in either direction of the remaining mattress.

One more step and he was at the side of the bed. His knuckles depressed the bed as he leaned down. "Scooch, or I move you."

"You wouldn't da—"

Liam's hands shot under my calf and shoulder simultaneously, faster than I could react. He rolled me, so I faced away as he landed on the bed behind me. His thigh pinned my legs together while he trapped my arms with his.

"It's not so bad, is it?" He chuckled into my hair, having managed to plant his face above mine on the pillow so I couldn't head butt him.

His forearm pressed against my breasts low enough that I couldn't bite him. I wriggled, trying to slip his grasp and hoping to break any of his bones.

"Fine," I huffed, stretching, moving, and pulling at my body—exasperatedly. "I'll sleep outside. Just let me go."

"Jane." His voice was a husky warning, and I froze. Everything from my collar up to my hairline was hot with embarrassment when I felt what good my struggling did—pressing right against my ass.

He released me, and we rolled onto our backs. We laid there quietly, shoulder to shoulder, each of us hanging a bit off our side of the bed.

Liam's eyes were clamped closed, and I did my part not to look down at the raised bit of blanket at the top of his thighs... but sleep wouldn't come.

I would listen harder to his soft breaths every so often, trying to tell if he was faking it—sleep.

Because I was listening so intently, I heard the splintering sound of wood breaking. Liam tensed beside me, which confirmed he was actually faking it.

"What was—" Liam rolled, clamping a hand over my mouth to silence my murmured words.

My eyes widened, readjusting to the darkness of the room. Then, glancing at him, I nodded, signaling that I understood. He lifted a leg, and the inside of his thigh brushed over the tops of mine. His hand lifted the cuff of his pant leg where he pulled free a dagger—my dagger—and tucked it into my hands before rising from the bed.

Wrapping my hand around the carved pommel gave me a sense of peace and comfort. I didn't realize until that moment how fully I had been missing it. My bare feet padded on the chilled wooden floor when I followed Liam from the bed to the closed door.

I wanted so badly for it to be nothing, one of the broken-down shutters falling in a gale of wind—but the sloppy, drunken sounds of arrogant male laughter filled the home. The intruders stomped, hooted, and broke every fragile thing they got their hands on.

My grip tightened and loosened on the dagger, and I stretched my neck in preparation for a fight.

Liam took a step in front of me and pulled open the door, it creaked, which would draw attention, but we were prepared.

"Back here," one of the men shouted as he barreled down the hall, crashing into Liam's outstretched arm. The man grappled with one of the shelves trying to regain his footing, but it fell. Its contents and the wooden shelf spilled onto his head, knocking him to the floor.

The drunk fool had knocked himself unconscious. His red fabric cap warned me who the men were right before Driata screamed, "Raiders!"

Stepping over the body, I flipped the dagger in my hand and crept along the wall on stealthy feet. The men ransacking the kitchen refocused on finding out who the woman was that screamed. The idiots were talking in exaggerated whispers, seeming to think they could still sneak up on my sister—who clearly knew they were there.

One such raider ambled to the hall's entrance, mumbling something about first dibs when he saw me. He gave me a grin full of greying gums. "Hey, the—"

My foot slammed into his chest, and he bowled into his short friend behind him. Shortie stabilized Toothless, but not before I smashed my palm into his nose. "You wittle bith," he lisped as blood teemed down his face.

"That wasn't very nice, was it?" Shortie said, his voice laced with sugar.

"Do me a favor, Jane?" Liam called back from the room where Driata was whimpering.

Shortie tried to side-step me, his tongue lashing out like he could taste my sister's fear.

"A little busy here," I reminded him, gritting my teeth as my knee met Shortie's groin.

"Do something, Leath, don't just fucking stand there." The little raider gripped himself from the floor while trying to make a grab for my legs.

Toothless—Leath—let go of his bloody nose long enough

to remember he had a sword strapped to his side.

I ducked as he sliced it for my head and jammed my fist into his gut.

He grunted but didn't back down, stepping on Shortie's face to dive for me. Lower still, I slammed my dagger into his thigh—slightly hoping that was the side the nasty asshole was packing on.

Leath's scream filled the house, and the crashing from the kitchen stopped as boot steps echoed and the toothless one fell on top of the short one.

"I was going to say," Liam appeared next to me, holding two of Driata's sharpened arrows. "Show them just how *not nice* you can be?"

He winked and slashed down into Shortie's and Leath's necks, letting blood spray onto the pale flower-dabbled wallpaper.

"We're going to owe Tessa a cleaning fee." I sighed, wiping my dagger on my pant leg.

"If it helps, the raiders don't normally leave any of their victims alive."

"Let's repay the favor then, shall we?"

A skinny man rounded the corner, and I slammed my dagger into his gut, thinking of his people killing my sister's entire traveling party. Leaving her so frightened, she cried herself to sleep.

I bellowed my rage into his face as he fell, already leaping around him to find the others.

Lux was in the kitchen, his rounded axe coming down on a blonde man's shoulder as two more jumped on the retired assassin from behind.

Wrapping one's long hair around my hand, I slammed my knee into his back—the other dove at me with knuckles lined in metal and punched me in the side of my face.

My jaw cracked, and my head snapped back. White spots clouded my vision as I straightened.

"If she wanted it rough—" Liam jerked the man away from me, stabbing the arrows into his shoulder blades and exposing his chest to me. "She would beg for it."

Fighting against nausea caused by the pain in my face, I darted forward, burying my blade in his chest.

"Right." Blinking my eyes to clear the stars, I pulled away.

The Raider slumped onto the swaying floor. Strong arms caught me.

Metal clanged, and Lux cursed a warning as he fell.

A Raider, near Lux's stature, waved a cast iron skillet at Liam and me.

"Driata didn't mention how ugly you all were," Liam murmured—or maybe he shouted as he shoved me behind him.

"*Driata*?" The man's head tilted as he looked at me with hooded eyes. "We've been looking for you."

"Look at her again—and I carve out your eyes before I kill you." Liam's voice held a promise of violence beyond what we had done in the once innocent home.

"Found her!" The man shouted from the hall, followed by Driata and the Dowers' screeches, filling me with unyielding rage. I turned, but Liam must have too because the Raider took the opportunity to grip my hair—yanking me back to him.

He lifted me so that I could barely stand on the balls of my feet, then pressed his tree trunk of a body flush against my back.

"Why'd you run?" His nose dragged along my cheek. "Our fun had only just begun."

He thought I was—oh Gods, what had he done to Driata in those woods?

My hand spiked the dagger to his chest, but he brought the skillet down on my wrist. Bone crunched while metal pinged on the wood floor as my blade hit the ground.

Warmth trailed down my cheek, and the beast of a man tilted his head to the side. Hot breath scorched my jaw bone as he gripped my neck and traced the path of my tears with his tongue.

Bile coated my throat.

"Don't do it," the raider warned. But I was clutching my wrist—I hadn't moved. "Try anything, and I'll snap her pretty neck. Wouldn't that be a shame?"

Oh—Liam.

"Go help." It was slurred as pain sliced my face, and the tang of copper and vomit filled my mouth.

Through watery eyes, I watched him shake his head.

"*Please.*" I choked out.

Liam looked at me, then back at the hall. Then he turned and ran.

Good.

"Now..." A gurgled laugh assaulted my nerves as they all fired warnings. "Where were we?" Then, against my senses, I relaxed my entire body, letting it go limp and feeling the hair rip and snap at my scalp.

The raider lost his balance with the new weight. I planted my feet on the ground, bending at the knees as he tried to pull me back up. I banged my skull as hard as I could into his face.

My head shrieked in agony, but not as loudly as the man wildly swinging his frying pan at my head. Lux groaned from the floor while I bobbed away from the raider. I glanced to see the assassin's eyelids fluttering.

Any day now, Bud.

Lux was still sprawled out, with his fingers loosely curled around the handle of his axe.

You should always be prepared to do whatever you must to win. My mentor's words echoed around in my head with my ringing concussion. I lunged for his fallen axe.

My fingers tightened on the handle as the skillet smashed into my spine. My chest crashed into the floor, but my grip held firm as I rolled. My breaths were sharp rapid things when I heaved the axe up. It plunged between the man's thighs and through his—probably tiny—dick. He reared away, howling like a dying dog and hunching over his wrecked manhood.

Releasing the handle, I dragged myself onto my knees through a growing pool of sticky blood... Toward the man I owed death.

Trembling hands gripped my arms from behind, and I flailed.

"Shh, we've got you." Driata's healing magic rushed into me while Tessa helped right me, examining my face and body.

"How much of this is yours?" Tessa asked, her hands fretting over my clothes covered in blood.

The raider choked on a deep, gasping sob. Turning away from the worried women, I saw Liam standing over him. He aimed my dagger at the raider's face. "I made you a promise, did I not?"

CHAPTER 25

Lunasa's castle grounds bustled with activity when we arrived at the gates. Carriages teemed with well-dressed nobles. The contrast between rich fabrics stitched into gowns and suits and the tanned patches of dead grass busting through fading cobblestones was startling.

Servants moved throughout the crowds, emptying wagons and carts that spilled over with imports like produce and soil.

Ripened apples were kicked and rolled under polished shoes as the painted faces of noblewomen squawked orders about their luggage.

"What's this?" Driata's scanned the drive with weary, alarm-filling eyes. She magicked us straight up to the castle to avoid the glaring guards at the gate.

Even having scrubbed clean all of the blood that had coated us in the fight—we stood out in the borrowed patchwork clothes we wore compared to the busy crowd.

Most nobles would likely think we were the help, but the

workers knew our faces well. Standing there and gawking would do us no favors.

Grabbing Driata's arm, I hauled her to the side of the building, where there was an entrance to the tunnels below the keep.

Lou and Liam kept to our heels as we darted for the cover of the shadows.

The stone bit my fingers as I dragged them along the crevices in the wall. I felt my nerves stretching as I searched for the one that protruded just a bit more than the others.

There.

I looked over my shoulder to ensure no one had seen us and pressed my palm into it. It slid back, releasing a puff of air as the secret door shifted open. Ushering the others inside, I followed —sliding through sideways before it could right itself.

Liam reached overhead and unhooked a lantern from the wall. He spun the creaking knob, and a warm, yellow flame burst to life behind the glass, illuminating the dust motes we roused with our arrival.

Driata let out a tiny gasp as her eyes adjusted to the dim light. "Has this always been here?"

"I think these passages were built when the castle was." I shrugged, trying to decide which of the split tunnels to take. The passages led to all places in the castle and beyond, but I needed to sort out where we would all be most expected.

After the long trip, I only wanted to be alone, but our group couldn't part until I deposited at least Lou and Dri somewhere they wouldn't get lost.

While Lou didn't know her way around the castle, she would be taught. Especially once she was introduced as my seamstress and equally so due to working with Baltazar.

I tapped my lower lip. Dri and I couldn't be seen in the clothes we borrowed from the Dowers—it would only raise suspicion.

"This way," Liam decided for me, taking the opening to the left. His knowledge of the tunnels matched mine, and he could go off on his own.

An irritating part of me was glad he didn't.

We wound through the inner walls of the only home I ever knew, like mice searching for crumbs.

Muffled voices bounced around us from various rooms, which I knew were sitting areas and the grand hall.

My guess rivaled anyone else's as to why the tunnels had been built. Perhaps, in case of an attack or disaster, they were long forgotten by anyone of import when Baltazar discovered them.

His band of misfits and criminals used them to move around the castle unseen. The upper levels' walls were spelled to amplify voices beyond them—allowing Baltazar to steal away important information and objects.

But he found the most use in the levels well below the building. Under the dungeons, tunnels led out of the castle, but also to a chamber Baltazar built for training and quarters for his displaced employees.

"Where are we?" Lou whispered when the lantern didn't serve well to brighten the darkest recesses of the tunnels.

Banging metal and the cursing grievances of overworked servants filtered through the wall, offering me an answer. "Behind the kitchens."

My voice carried, and Dri flinched.

Liam's deep chuckle bounded around the confined space.

"We don't have to whisper. My brother has been thorough in his spell work."

"Oh." Driata tilted her head, listening to the complaining workers. "Then I'll finally ask—why are so many people here?"

"I don't know..." I paused, trying to figure out how many days we had been gone. "Father's traveling party should have been several days out still—at best."

Driata shook her head. "Your family-to-be had the entire group magicked back here as a demonstration of goodwill."

"Servants and all," Lou added, leaning against a dust-ridden wall.

"Maveri made them travel for days—when he had such magic?" Of course, I knew that other kingdoms' magic hadn't suffered the same fate as Lunasa's, but knowing that Maveri was already wielding it as a tool... Didn't sit well with me.

"The mad king didn't think you would show." Lou shrugged, a half-smile tugging at her mouth. "His staff took wagers on it."

"It was a test?" I asked, unsure of why it mattered. Though I was more worried that I had passed it than what would have happened if I failed.

Liam cut in then, catching my eye, "You can fall into crises about the idiocy you're marrying into later—none of this explains those nobles being outside."

"We won't find the answers to anything just standing here." Driata huffed, planting her hands on her hips.

"Then, by all means, *Princess*," Liam gave her an exaggerated bow. "Lead on."

"You've called me by name this whole time. No need to title me now."

"And you've managed to make yourself useful." His eyebrow peaked at the challenge.

Dri crossed her arms over her chest, adjusting to face away from him.

Lou kicked off the wall, squaring her thin shoulders, and I pinched the bridge of my nose. "I'm exhausted. So if you're about to argue, don't."

"I was only going to say, I think we could all use a drink."

Driata cleared her throat, "I don't..."

Liam chuckled when she trailed off, turning on his heel to move further down the corridor.

Lou's eyes locked on Driata, her mouth opening before she snapped it closed.

Glancing between the two, I jerked my head in Liam's direction, where shadows had already started to consume his form. Lou nodded, and we followed the sound of his retreating footsteps.

Finally, the corridor opened to a narrow, winding stairway, and I pieced together the direction Liam was leading us.

"My tower?" I hissed, stomping after him.

"Do you have a better suggestion?" Liam asked, refusing to turn around. "I'd offer up my chambers, but I'm certain Lou would rip my head from my shoulders."

"You've never been there," I said, panic gripping my throat. "How do you even know the way?"

I moved my rooms after...

"If you think that I haven't made it my mission to know how to get to you at all times—you'd assume wrong." His posture was stiff, reminding me of how he had been before he stabbed me.

My heart was an erratic bird trying to escape on broken wings. But I pressed on despite it. Or perhaps, to spite it. "In order to kill me?"

Liam's boots scraped the stone when he faced me, clearing the few steps between us in the span of a breath.

My back slammed against the wall as he pinned me in a cage made from his body. One hand posted above my shoulder, the other tilting my chin so I met his gaze. "If I'd ever been ordered to kill you, Jane, you'd have long been dead."

"You could try." My eyes narrowed on the silver pools of his. *A challenge, perhaps a threat.*

He saw what I could do—even with the bracelet, and he wouldn't catch me off guard again. *But this*, my mind warned. *His being so close was doing something to me that risked everything.*

"My mark has never missed a target."

"You missed my heart." The new scar on my chest ached at the mention, a reminder of his betrayal—a warning that I was betraying myself.

"My mark has never missed a target," he repeated. His calloused fingers were warm at my chin, and his scent settled around me.

I was vaguely aware of Lou and Dri's approaching footfalls. But it didn't matter that they were getting nearer. Nothing mattered but that—the place where his skin met mine. *Fuck.*

"You're admitting to so easily being able to kill me," I said, barely managing to keep my voice even as he nodded. "Then why should I let you touch me?"

Liam's palm slid down my chin until his fingers loosely gripped my throat. He tugged just enough to close the inch of a gap between our chests. My body was a pyre, burning at the contact.

The stubble on his cheek brushed the arch of my ear as he whispered, "*you shouldn't.*"

I didn't move—I couldn't, even when his hand left me, and the cold of the musty cellar draped itself around every part of me that he touched. Even as he turned and descended back down the stairs, and when his departure exposed Driata and Lou's shocked expressions.

"Well..." Driata trailed off, clasping her hands in front of her awkwardly like she didn't know what to do with them.

"That was..." Lou started, but she looked to be grasping for words too.

Shaking my head, I worked to calm the nerves he so easily frayed. "Don't."

The passage narrowed with our ascent until we finally reached the wooden door to my tower.

I chose that tower for its sheer distance, at the farther point of the castle from my family. The servants had moved my belongings just days after... After she died.

Struggling to mentally put the word to it was my own burden. Especially so soon after the mind fuckery caused by the blister berries and the subconscious trip the hags had put me through.

But standing there, staring at the unadorned door to the tower, I realized why all the nobles had come. The days had slipped by me with everything that had happened, and I had forgotten.

My insides hollowed out as my mind ran through the days leading up to that moment. Frantically counting them down and ticking them off in my head while I gripped the iron knob like it was a lifeline.

My birthday was the next day.

The blessings ball—my father's celebration for my mother and I's shared birthdays. He didn't care that it would officially mark the third year she had been gone. The celebrations had gone on despite it, and I was reminded that she killed herself on my sixteenth birthday each year.

Time had moved forward, but I hadn't, I thought, standing in front of the tower door while Driata and Lou waited to be let in.

It was my mother's favorite tower—the one she chose for her private sitting rooms. Nearest to her garden, far enough away from my father. And with its views, she could pretend she wasn't trapped. The window to the right where our kingdom met the gnarled Dreadwood. Beyond that, the boundary between Faerie and us... And the window to the right that looked toward Ellesmere where the land touched the sea. She could pretend those were her escapes. She could and would escape the kingdom and climb aboard a ship or scale that mountain...

"Jane?" Driata asked, her voice soft.

Burning streams seeped down my face. Usually, I would have scrubbed the tears away and brushed her off. But something changed on our travels. I finally saw beyond the princess, beyond the grooming that fit her as a perfect spouse.

"The blessings ball." My voice cracked, and Driata rushed toward me, sweeping the fallen hair from my damp face.

"It's tomorrow," she finished for me, eyes wide. She pulled me into her arms. And for the first time in our lives, I knew she understood.

Lou cleared her throat, choking on the emotion pouring from us. "I think it's time for those drinks."

I didn't wipe away the signs of my distress. I didn't mask it with anger the way I so often did. Instead, I nodded, letting them pull me into my chambers as the stark sense of loss contrasted what I gained. There was peace in it—being with two people who weren't made to stay with you but simply wanted to be there.

"The apartment I have over my bar is bigger than this." Lou snorted and sat down on the stone floor with the bottle of dark liquor I had stashed in a trunk sitting under my window.

It was a small space only filled with necessities.

A plush mattress sat atop layered rugs my mother picked. Next to that, one hobbled nightstand I bought from a servant looking to toss it with the castle wastes. The armoire across from them hung open—the door on it never truly closed, and I hadn't let anyone come in to fix its hinges. So fabrics from gowns my father ordered made, only for me to wear them once, spilled out of it.

Under one window's ledge, there was a trunk I would sit on the sketch. Its false bottom concealed weapons and supplies for my jobs—Hidden by shoes I hated, most useful for weighting down the wood panel below them.

Only two decorations marked the space as mine. A long-dead potted plant sat on a padded stool by the barren window. And a tapestry concealed the hidden door opposite the main exit.

I shrugged, snatching the neck of the bottle and feeling the heavy weight of the thick glass. Then, tipping the bottle back, the warm liquid seared my throat.

Driata's face scrunched when she sniffed the bottle's contents. "This smells of every man that's ever come onto me."

"That's because men need liquid courage to speak to a beautiful woman." Lou winked at my sister, not worried at her boldness. "They use it to cover the stench of desperation and failed dreams."

Dri's face stained red, and her eyes went wide before she cast them at the ground, a faint smile pulling at her lips.

My head tilted while I studied my sister in a new light. Consuming the information I never asked for and having previously made assumptions of my own. "I always thought you liked the attention."

"You were meant to." Driata coughed down a sip before continuing. "Arius showed interest in you early on. Gemma tended to father so he would need her around more than he needed her to wed, and Olivia was being groomed to be an asset to the throne."

"So you were just expected to go along with it? You had no say?" Lou's brow furrowed.

"Look at what they've done to Jane." Driata waved her hand at me. "She didn't get to pick Arius. He was suitable and chose her."

My heart raced a furious beat catching up with what she meant. I thought I had no choice because my pairing would help Lunasa, and Ellesmere was our strongest ally. But if none of us had a choice... How was that fair?

"How have you not wed, then? Or at least received offers?" Lou asked, taking another swig without flinching at its taste.

"Courtly gossip is a strange thing. My father has brought suitors in several times a year. A ball for every occasion—and I would play my part. But rumors would surface just when the men would ready themselves to bend a knee. My barren womb, penchant for talking to animals, or forgetfulness in bathing. Then the suitors would leave." Driata shrugged, staring at an empty wall before taking down a mouthful of the liquor.

She shook it off, holding out the bottle as an offering to me.

For several quiet moments, I only stared at her while she blinked back at me.

Then, her words settled around us, and we each burst into riotous laughter.

"You—made up—stories—about yourself—to avoid..." Each time I tried to speak, my mind would go over what she said again, and I lost myself in a fit all over again.

When we finally settled, I dabbed fat tears from my eyes, and my lungs ached. Looking at Driata again, I saw her in a different light. Forming new respect for the woman I never truly understood.

"Enough of that," Dri said, her words slurring. "I want to know something."

"What's that?"

"Why did you come?" Her eyes bore into Lou, whose thumb circled the rim of the bottle she saved during our spell of amusement.

"I overheard Baltazar ordering Lux to find Jane. He said she was looking for you."

"And..." I led, gesturing for her to continue, knowing there had to be more.

"And nothing. You both went missing, and I came after you."

Driata hummed, showing she didn't really believe it, but Lou turned a sharp expression on me. "Since we're asking prying questions. When will you finally say what's going on between you and Liam?"

"They were together once...before...well before Jane's mother..." Driata searched for the right words so soon after my breakdown.

"Before my mother died." The words were heavy in a way that had nothing to do with the booze thrumming through me.

Lou nodded slowly. "I thought there was a history."

"He proposed," Driata added, her face scrunched in thought. "It was quite romantic in a sense...except then he went away for a while."

I had a chokehold on the bottle, taking a slug of it each time one of the women spoke. "And when he came back, he turned into a prick."

"You love him." It wasn't a question, and the bluntness of Lou speaking my secret aloud made me struggle for breath.

"It doesn't matter," I said finally, hoping that we could just drop it.

"But you do." My sister's voice had lowered as if she just remembered the walls had ears.

"I can learn not to." It was barely a whisper, and it said everything without saying anything at all. Because they didn't need to ask the rest. It was already a question I was asking myself. If it had been three years and I hadn't managed it yet... How would I ever?

Stretching, I stood. Realizing that I couldn't think of it anymore, I had to push it away to a place where the knowledge couldn't hurt me. "I'm going in search of fun."

"You can't go out like that." Driata pointed to the layered dress I borrowed from Tessa and rose on wobbly legs. She ambled like a deer to my armoire and sifted through the gowns.

"It's the whole reason we're hidden away." Lou chimed in though no one asked her. I didn't want to change. But my protests fell on deaf ears as the pair worked to dress me in a way fit to be seen by castle nobles.

CHAPTER 26

I might not have left my chambers had I known the castle walls would be moving as much as they were. But I was well and truly drunk, and I didn't really care about much at all.

The nobles were placed in the usually vacant guest wing, but some floated about like spirits adrift.

Rounding a corner on silent but stumbling feet, I overheard a group of them and slowed.

"The towns have gone to absolute ruin since we've relocated." One woman whined. *Duchess Tilby of the West.* The proud ruler of the Barrens had reason to hate my father and his cursed land. She and her husband took turns showing up each year after they relocated their primary estate to Ellesmere.

"I don't know how the king is even managing to keep up without his taxes." *Lord Weemble, of Luhne.* Yikes—of course, he was concerned with taxes. I was sure even the guards couldn't pry any extra coin from our capital.

"Ellesmere practically owns everything now," Duke Tilby's deep voice added, surprising me by apparently showing up with his wife for a function rather than a courtesan.

Their voices faded as they shuffled down the corridor, but it was a straightway, meaning I couldn't follow them since there would be no place to hide.

"Really?"

"Why do you think Maveri gifted us estates when the crops died?"

"The king is giving up his child to that heathen just to keep his support."

"If Maveri didn't already have that concubine of a wife, I'm sure one of the king's other daughters would be forfeit as well."

"*Gods.*" Duchess Tilby's words caught on a gasp. "Have you seen that man?"

"*The horror,*" her husband agreed, and I had to stifle a snort of laughter despite them being correct at the horror. I thought of my soon-to-be father-in-law and the uncontained drool dribbling from his maw while he spoke of my child-bearing body. That any woman should have to be chained to him even willingly was disturbing. His son was bad enough, his attractive face not making up for his lack of... Well, everything else. A prize-winning boar. I hadn't met the queen during my visit, and she hadn't come to any events in the years prior. Perhaps he feasted on her in his desperate hunger.

"Let's collect our favor and get out of this hellhole as quickly as possible." Lord Weemble offered hopefully.

I waited until their voices faded before staggering around the corner.

My slipper caught on the velvet, blue material of my gown's

train and barely caught myself on the rough fabric of a hanging tapestry. Righting myself, with wide eyes and a slurring giggle, I patted the wall in thanks for catching me. Then, I continued my way to find something—anything—more fun than talking about my old relationship over drinks.

What the nobles said nagged at a distant part of my mind, and I squashed the thoughts away. *Ellesmere practically owned everything on our side of the boundary.* The thought put up a solid fight but lost when I focused on the placement of my feet.

It was strange how similar the halls of the home I spent my whole life in looked to the one I would be soon moving into across the continent. But when I looked down, I noted how the rugs frayed after years of foot traffic and loose stitching where the threads had been repaired. There were also tiny cracks in the stone that we should have hired someone to fix, perhaps opening jobs to some of the out-of-work citizens. After I stepped on one of those fractures, the conversation I'd overheard echoed in my mind.

Had Lunasa reached the dregs of its seemingly endless well of riches? I saw the treasury and knew it was still full of gold and jewels each time I liberated a bit for Lou to pawn to give to those in need. It was beyond what anyone's family required to survive a lifetime. But was it not enough to maintain a kingdom?

Was the mad king behind our continued survival? My mind went to the mass of imports being hauled in when I arrived, and my jaw worked as I thought of the implications. How much debt had my father accrued to maintain his way of life?

If that was happening, and the towns and cities were still starving... Where was all the money going? The thought was sobering to a washed-away mind, but I couldn't piece every-thing together. Finally, I stopped at a window looking out over the front lawn and saw that most of the carriages were gone, having been emptied into our stores.

How much of the food would go to the people? Any?

My hands fisted at my sides as I wondered how much longer he would watch the citizens starve. People who survived a life-time of it—long enough to have supported him before the curse took its root that time.

He was so content to watch them die, apparently.

"What do we have here?" A silky voice reached me from down the hall.

I ignored him, regarding the mountains in the distance, wondering how the Dowers would fare after we left them. Looking at my bare finger where my engagement ring had been and knowing that Driata had left a hefty sack of gold, too, I knew they could make it at least a bit longer.

But then what?

The male from down the hall whistled as he drew nearer, and I finally turned. He was tall, with a thin build, and as he moved closer, I noticed his slanted eyes. They looked familiar, but nothing else about the blonde man did. Though his bright, emerald-colored tunic and smart trousers marked him as a member of the traveling nobles. The strangest thing was his staring right at me, and it seemed... He was trying to capture my attention.

"Can I help you?"

"I certainly hope you will since you've robbed me."

Oh shit—had that man been an unwilling donor to my

cause? I really hoped not. "I don't know what you're talking about."

An unsteady step back and the fogginess around my mind reminded me I was far too drunk for a fight. But I wasn't going to let a strange man blow my cover. Not to mention...

"I've been robbed of my very breath."

A bubble of laughter escaped me. "Oh, no, sir. You must be mistaken."

Please, Gods, don't let the man embarrass himself after the day I had—the week, if I was being honest.

"Sir?" He gripped his chest. "You wound me."

Not as much as I could have if Driata hadn't taken my dagger before I left my chambers.

My chin dipped in apology even while I suppressed the urge to roll my eyes. "That was not my intention." *Sir.*

"Well, politeness never hurt anyone." He propped himself on the wall next to me. "I think I will manage to survive it."

"That's good. It would be improper to have blood on my hands." I wiggled my fingers before fisting them in my skirts. They weren't the supple and unmarked hands of a noble.

"I don't know. I've got a nagging feeling that you would like to be stained." He wagered while giving me a dimpled grin.

My eyebrow peaked as the man finally gained my interest. Every so often, I would find a man that managed not to bore me too thoroughly, and I would have a bit of fun with them. No names, no titles, no history. And though I fretted the first and second time that my honor and reputation would be sullied... They seemed reasonably quick to keep our shared secret.

He stretched and adjusted in front of me when I gave him a smirk in answer. Skinny as he was, he filled my vision with how near he was standing. "Why would a beauty like yourself be walking around unattended?"

He wasn't really my type—friendly, even for a noble, and a bit too old if the slight crinkling around his eyes was any indication. Though it was always hard to tell with witches.

My smile widened, and I looked up through hooded lashes. "I'm not alone."

"Not now, at least. No—now you get the honor of accompanying me to the ball tomorrow, you lucky thing." He winked when he leaned with puckered lips and grabbed my hand like he would place a peck on it.

But I leveraged it to grip his chin, reaching up, so my lips brushed his. It was gentle. His hands feathered my waist. I dragged him closer so I was pressed against the sill, the stone biting into the tops of my thighs.

Gods. I felt...nothing. It was like kissing a block of cheese.

His tongue danced at the part in my mouth, asking for permission.

"You know what they say?" Liam called, appearing behind the man. He yanked the noble back by the collar and made me wish the floor would swallow me into its cavernous belly. "Three is company, four is a crowd."

The man jerked away from Liam's grip, and I could hear him grinding his teeth though there was a body between us, blocking my view.

"Four?"

"Me." Liam flared a hand to indicate himself, then pointed at us in turn. "*Princess Jane*, you, and your overinflated ego."

"You forget your place, boy," the noble spat, showing a bit

of his truth—his entitlement. "And it is well below one where you can speak to me in public."

"I don't want to talk to you." Liam's brow cocked as he spoke. I had seen the expression before. And unfortunately, it usually ended violently for those on the receiving end.

"Then why are you interrupting?" The man's pale face turned red, but his tensing posture indicated that he wasn't embarrassed but pissed. A vulture guarding his meal.

Liam waved a hand to indicate the noble move further away from me. "To offer you a tour of the palace grounds."

The man paused, clearly thrown off by the sudden change. But then, "come find me later?"

"No, no, you misunderstand," Liam spoke quietly, gripping the man by the collar of his shirt and tugging him up so they were nose to nose. "If you don't make your exit, you'll meet the ground from that window."

Liam pointed to the arched window behind me, and I glanced again below. Just high enough that the noble would minimally break several bones. Liam released the fabric of his tunic and smoothed it before removing his hands entirely, "your choice."

The man made a sound of disgust and took several hurried steps back. "Baltazar will be hearing of this."

Before I could wonder how a noble I didn't recognize knew my mentor so casually, the smell of magic announced his departure.

"You just can't keep yourself from getting into trouble?" Liam snapped, turning to me while rubbing his temples.

"I hadn't been in any trouble." I propped my ass on the

window ledge, gauging the distance between myself and the ground in case Liam thought to shove me. Or in case I jumped.

"Are you drunk?" Liam asked, massaging the skin at his temples.

I chose not to answer, but his flaring nostrils told me it was a mistake. His inhale was sharp, and his hands fell away from his face. "*Are you fucking drunk?*"

Shaking my head, I said decisively, "no."

"You smell like a pub." His eyes narrowed, scraping down my face and pausing on my neck like he saw my hurried pulse before they moved back up.

"And you smell—" I stopped myself—barely—from admitting that he smelled delicious if only because my mouth chose that moment to hiccup.

He sighed, but his posture didn't loosen with the breath. "There are too many nobles around for you to be this drunk right now."

"It's unbecoming." I flashed my teeth in a mockery of a smile while I tugged at the hem of my sleeve. "I'm aware, and I truly don't care."

"Not that... Jane, you don't see how they look at you."

"No, Liam—I do. Why do you think I left my chambers?"

"For attention?"

"For *fun.*" Steepling my hands in front of me, I weighed my options. My anger weighed out. "What if I told you I planned on letting him fuck me?"

Something sparked in his eyes before his face became as unreadable as stone. "You wouldn't dare."

My head tilted, and I glared at him. What implications

would make him speak out on my actions? "Why, because it may upset Arius?"

"Because if you ever let him touch you," he said, turning on his heel, already walking away again. "I would have ripped out his spine."

My eyes popped wide, and my mouth fell open. "You're a psychopath."

"For you." I thought I may have imagined his words, though I was sobering up by the second.

"For me?"

"Orders." He shrugged, disappearing around the corner.

If Liam thought that he could dismiss me and disappear that quickly, he was mistaken.

The moment he rounded the corner, I kicked off my slippers—worrying the soles may make a sound and give me away —and followed him.

I stood in a dusty, curtained alcove, repressing a sneeze and suffering the peach-colored settee pressing into my hip. But I couldn't move, not at the risk of being seen or heard.

As it was, Baltazar's wing-tipped shoes clicked a furious beat each pass he took in front of the curtain. I could only imagine his face was pinched in barely concealed rage while Liam did his best at posturing calm.

But the last time I bore witness to my mentor's disappointment in his brother, it resulted in a barely functional hand for a time. Though I figured Baltazar had something to do with it being healed, given that Liam was still using them both. But that time, Liam had his talisman, and I still had it stashed among my things.

"You can't go around threatening nobles." His shoes clacking echoed his words and, further, his displeasure.

"He's an ass," Liam offered, unapologetically paired with an expression, I was sure, he masked in boredom.

"Nevertheless," Baltazar said, surprising me with his agreement. "Now he's become a pain in mine."

"He wouldn't normally show up to these things. So why is he here?" My brows knit together as Liam spoke.

How important was the noble that he had driven the brothers into a strange unity?

"I'm not certain, but you must keep him away from Jane." Baltazar seemed...perturbed. Which was perhaps the most shocking of all. Angry, decisive, self-sure... But never uneasy.

"You're not sure?" Liam voiced my worries, reminding me we both knew the man well.

"That's not your concern." Baltazar was tense, though, alluding to their being more significant problems at bay. "Just keep him away from her. He can't figure out what we're doing."

"He won't touch her again," Liam swore, with something akin to venom laced through the promise.

"Be sure of it." Baltazar stopped just outside of the curtain, and I saw the backs of his polished shoes pointed wherever it was Liam was standing. "And brother, don't think I haven't realized you're pushing boundaries."

"I haven't."

"You have," My mentor said calmly, though there was an undercurrent of violence. "And luckily, they've aided my plan so far, but the moment they hinder it, I will tighten your leash."

Fading footfalls told me Liam had been dismissed, but the backs of Baltazar's feet warned that he remained. And being that near him, with no witnesses—not even his brother to stop me, begged me to confront him. He had caused me much grief in the past several days that my fists ached to lash into him.

Baltazar had manipulated my every action for Gods knew how long, and those last few days had proven it. But he was stronger, faster, better trained... He'd confirmed I understood that each time I sought to show him how much I learned, he easily put me back into my place.

Plus, he was always one step ahead of me, if not ten or twenty. Even Lux and Liam had been confused by his actions, not knowing what he stood to gain from giving them opposing orders. To beat him, I needed to plan without planning, make moves without lifting a finger and manage to catch him off guard, but his slights would not go unpunished.

No, when I won—whatever game we were playing—he would regret picking his game piece up at all.

CHAPTER 27

P eople danced around the party as the music dipped and swelled.

The woman nearest me spun offbeat in a circle of married nobles whose wives were suspiciously absent.

She wore a primitive-looking gown crafted of white fur and red feathers. The combination made her look like she had skinned unsuspecting rabbits and birds before her seamstress sewed them together. Nevertheless, the fabric alone probably cost more than a month's supply of the feast servants were carrying around on polished silver trays.

Everyone was dressed just as gaudy, though there were variations in color and textures. Some even looked like their bodies had been painted with liquid gems and gold.

Driata was amongst the crowd, pleasing, smiling, doting, and collecting favor. She put on quite the spectacle after her argument with our father the day prior.

Having finally escaped the dimly lit corridor where Baltazar and Liam had their exchange, I was corralled by a frantic Driata into a family dinner in my father's chambers.

At first, it was hushed without Oliver and Olivia. Ciaran was pissed he had been left behind, and Gemma was too focused on tending our father to notice me.

But father stiffened when Driata entered behind me. "And just where have you been?"

"I wanted to... I—"

Silencing my sister with a nudge, I gave my father a nod, the only pleasantry he would receive. "I asked her to come with me. So, she wouldn't have to be cooped up for days on end in a carriage."

"You knew Maveri offered to transport us," my father said to Driata, hearing but ignoring me altogether.

"Jane will be leaving us, and I wanted the extra time with her." I stifled my proud grin at her lie.

"Without warning?" His beady, bloodshot eyes narrowed on her. "I expect this behavior from Jane but not from you."

Ouch, that was a cheap shot—true... But still.

Opening my mouth to come to her aid, Driata stepped closer to the round table, her fingers gripping the edge as she leaned toward him. "You should remember that Jane's wedding is saving your sorry ass and this kingdom."

My mouth popped open in disbelief, and Gemma almost fell out of her seat. Driata had never spoken to him like that.

And if the color rushing to his face proved anything, it was that. "You—you will not use that kind of language." He turned that anger on me, his shaking finger raised. "Did you tell her to speak to me this way, Janie?"

"That is not her name!" Driata's voice rose above his as her hands slammed down onto the table in fists rattling the dinnerware. "And if you, for one single second, thought of anyone other than yourself, you would know that. But, instead, you sit there, wasting away but eating your fill while your people—my people—starve to death. And they don't even know why. Do the nobles know about your pathetic curse? Do they know that you've caused all of this?"

Her voice echoed around his sitting room, confronting my father's strained expression from every angle.

"Enough!" He dabbed his splotchy face with his napkin while Gemma and Ciaran only stared on with matching shocked expressions. "You will respect me."

"You may have my hand to pawn off to the highest bidder since that is all your children are good for," Driata said, storming toward the door. "But you will never again have my respect."

But Dri was attending the blessings ball, an event most likely planned hastily to do just what she accused. Marry my remaining siblings off. And if what the Tilbys and Lord Weemble had claimed the day prior was true, our kingdom needed it more than ever.

If that was the case, and Driata didn't scare them off with her brilliant ruse to make herself undesirable, she would surely have several offers by the evening's end.

She looked stunning with her sparkling diadem sitting amongst a crown of curls. Her cheeks had been rouged to make her look more modest, the long column of her neck was covered by pale lace, and her gown was crafted of the finest silks my father could import on such short notice. Its golden tint complimented her eyes each time she focused them on another ill-fitted suitor.

I saw the difference since I knew to look. Her smile wasn't as easy as I once thought it to be, and behind the sparkle in her gaze, there was a dullness like her life drained away each time she was forced to give one attention.

If my father noticed my sister's act from the erected dais to the side of the vaulted room, he didn't show it. Which told me he didn't. Otherwise, he did and couldn't care. There was a ghost of a smile toying at the corners of his face as he sat propped, watching all three siblings mingle amongst the crowd.

He had given me one command—to keep up appearances, so I was loitering along the walls, swiping food as it passed me.

Baltazar was missing, though Liam made his way through the crowd, offering greetings to familiar faces before being swept into an upbeat dance.

A weasel-faced servant cleared his throat at the entrance to the great hall, and I nearly dismissed it before seeing a flash of white hair.

"Duke Vellum Tellyk and his son, Keeper of the Crown, Lord Baltazar Tellyk." The weary butler announced, and my heart swapped places with my stomach.

A noble who put Liam and Baltazar on edge. So much that they were speaking on common ground, one I didn't recognize because he rarely left his manor and had never visited the castle.

And as the shock of blonde hair, only a few shades darker than his eldest son's and eyes the same honey shade. I was an idiot—a stupid, idiotic woman that had kissed Liam's gods damned father.

Kill me... Strike me down where I stand. Liam saw me kissing his father, for fuck's sake.

If there was a time to acknowledge my rightness in not wanting to come to the function, it was at that moment as Lord Tellyk's eyes met mine from across the room.

A server swept by me, and I ducked behind her and into the herded bodies swinging around the woman draped in animal pelts. If I had any say in it, Liam wouldn't have to keep his father away from me as Baltazar requested. I would stay well away all on my own.

The crowd swallowed me as I made it deeper into the room. I was only occasionally stopped by nobles wanting to see the ring, and my excuses for its absence weren't landing well. There were also those annoying few collecting favor by complimenting my ideal match.

Was it, though? Not likely—and the nobles probably knew it too, given how the ones in the hall had spoken. But everyone also seemed to know which direction Lunasa was sliding, which was right into Ellesmere's grip.

"There you are." Driata popped out from between two guards I had shamelessly hidden behind. She gripped my forearm, "can I hide with you for a moment? I won't give you away to whoever you're avoiding, and I'll be gone before—"

"I don't mind," I said with a quiet laugh, if only to stop her explanation. I raised a brow in question, prying her death grip from my arm.

She peeked around the taller of the two guards. "Father has invited every unattached potential match in existence, it seems."

"Is that why Duke Tellyk is here?" I thought about the implications of that... Did he want a wife after all those years?

"Ah, yes." Her nose wrinkled as she turned back to face me. "Baltazar warned me to stay away from that one."

Despite my anger with him, it was hard to entirely erase the bitter sting I got when she mentioned it. It wasn't that I wanted the crime lord to seek me out, but more so that I was used to it. But he hadn't, and I wouldn't go to him until I had a firmer grasp on the knowledge I gained.

"You should stay away from Baltazar," I urged even though I knew she wouldn't listen. Baltazar was a lot of things, but his charisma is what wrapped everyone around his finger. His charm was undoubtedly one reason I had panted after him for so long.

"I thought we were past that." Driata shook her head, wringing her hands in front of her.

Biting my lip to silence my argument, I huffed a sigh. "He's the reason Liam stabbed me."

"Right." I gaped at her, and she held up her hands, rushing on. "That's the story that Liam tells, and you're so quick to believe him after he stabbed you."

"Why would he lie about it?"

She squeezed my hand in her own, and her voice was barely a breath when she finally remembered I was waiting for an answer. Instead, she asked, "why wouldn't he?"

Glancing over her shoulder, I saw one of the older dukes attempting to wave her down and shoving past dozens of spinning bodies to head our way. "You have to go."

Driata peeked, and her eyes went wide. "Catch up with you later."

She ducked away just as I decided that I had made enough

appearances. I was going to head to my room for a nice, quiet rest and most likely drink until I forgot what day it was.

I had been breaking into heavily guarded estates and treasuries for three years. If I could do that, I certainly could sneak out of my father's idea of a party.

I leaped back into the horde of nobles who danced like they would shatter if they stopped. Working to avoid inviting eye contact with them and hoped I wouldn't have to socialize with them for at least another year.

Well, there was the wedding... But that was a guest list problem for another day. I made it about halfway when the servant at the entrance cleared his throat again. That time, the sound was choked like the man was sobbing.

Squinting and leaning around the gasping nobles nearest me, I realized why everyone was stepping back. The music stopped, one of the string instruments screeching as the bow halted mid-note.

I covered my mouth as horror filled me.

Arius dressed in a loose-fitted black tunic and pants, with several Ellesmeran guards fanned out behind him. But the real horror was the burlap bag he was holding so casually. The sack reminded me of a dying rose, still vibrant in the middle but ruined around the browning edges.

"Announce me," the prince hissed at the trembling servant, and one of his guards pressed a long sword to the back of the poor man's neck. Though he spoke low, the words echoed in the silence of the space like a war drum.

"P—Prince Arius of Ellesmere," the man sputtered out as a dark spot spread on his trousers.

"What is the meaning of this?" my father rasped.

The crowd parted, forming an aisle that Arius strolled calmly down.

The prince's boots squeaked on the drippings from his satchel, splashing onto the shining quartz floor. "You'll be happy to know I've learned who stole my father's crown."

"Is that what this display is about?" My father's frail hand was lifted from the arm of his raised throne to encompass Arius and the dramatic act he was putting on.

The incessant dribbling of the blood caught my focus, and I couldn't move my eyes away. He figured it out. *Drip.* I was going to die in the same space my mother had. *Drip.* They hadn't changed the floors. *Drip.* If I looked close enough, the splatters looked like the puddle that had pooled around her. *Drip.*

"Given that we in Ellesmere have been your greatest and only allies, and my pairing with your daughter...I was stunned to find out your children had so cruelly stolen from my father." Arius' pace never slowed. The metal plates of his guard's uniforms scraped together as they formed a tighter semi-circle around him. *Drip.*

My heart would give out. I couldn't let Arius say the words, not in front of everyone.

My shoe inched forward—to do what, I wasn't sure—but a firm hand gripped my bicep, and the smell of pine and spice folded around me.

"Don't," Liam murmured before releasing me and moving into the crowd.

Arius was going to kill us—he had already killed someone. Even an idiot would know that sack didn't contain smashed tomatoes.

Guards poured in from the hall, and I felt a second of relief before seeing the Ellesmeran crest patched onto their chests.

"My children would never do anything to harm our most trusted alliance," my father said. Still, there was more panic in it than conviction. When his eyes darted not to the new wave of guards but around the space, I knew who he was looking for.

Me.

His most defiant child, the one who traveled ahead of everyone else and was unaccounted for during the robbery.

"There must be a mistake." Baltazar offered, coming to my father's side. The look of panic and confusion lining his usually indifferent face was one I had never seen.

Dread washed through me. Drip.

"You *killed* him." I was so sure that I was caught that when Olivia's howl of agony boomed around the room, it took me a few breaths to react—to drag my eyes from the pool of blood forming at Arius' feet.

My eldest sister was hauled in on her knees by the four guards. She was bound. Chains that glowed a shade of orange were cuffed around her ankles and wrists. She lifted one of those rattling chains and pointed a finger of contempt at the prince.

Turning to see Arius' reaction, I noted the cruel slash of teeth he bared at her in a semblance of a smile before once more facing my father. "Would you like to explain why your heir and his twin decided to steal one of my father's most beloved heirlooms?"

I looked back at Olivia, and my sister's eyes narrowed for a moment. I saw the contemplation. She was trying to figure a way out, to kill Arius. Blood for blood.

Members of the gathered crowd inhaled sharply, some

outright gagging as a squishing sound came from the dais. Regretting it already, my head swiveled again.

Oliver's swollen, unseeing head careened for the steps to my father's throne, rolling at a steady, squishy pace.

Olivia's screams echoed throughout the crowd. Her gaze bored into her brother's sightless ones, seeming to look right back. Her twin, her equal, her future king. Her eyes welled with tears. I hadn't ever seen Olivia cry. Not when she broke her arm fighting against two armed guards in a tournament. Not when Oliver was chosen as my father's heir. Never. But now, crystalline tears, fat and full of grief, rolled down her cheeks.

Seconds ticked by, then minutes before she made a decision. Her shoulders sagged forward as she stopped holding her weight, and the four men holding her toppled together, off-balance. She jumped up, dragging them with her as she charged the line, barreling through and dodging the guards surrounding her.

Beelining for the prince who had taken away her twin's life, she dove around a guard poised with a blade to stop her. Boot snapping out and slamming into his wrist. She rolled, snatching the falling dagger from his unclasped hand.

A bellow of terror and sorrow left her lips as she was tackled, but she let the blade go free. It arched through the air twice before Arius lifted his talisman and the dagger vanished.

The prince held up his free hand, and the dagger reappeared there.

Oh, fuck.

He cleared the distance between them in two quick strides, delivering a swift and fatal blow to her heart.

Arius yanked the blade free, dropping it on her slumped

body. He cuffed his bloodied sleeves and whirled on my father. "I was planning to give her a reasonable trial, but she committed treason in front of many witnesses."

My father was still staring at his heir's bloated and blood-spattered head, but he jerked his chin in a nod.

"You'll do nothing?" Ciaran's deep voice boomed across the hall as he questioned the king. Fresh tear tracks discolored his face. "He killed them, and you sit there?"

"Did you not hear me, boy?" Arius' eyes narrowed on my only remaining brother. "They conspired against the crown."

"Your crown. Not ours," Ciaran argued defiantly. He squared his shoulders, preparing for a fight he could not win.

"My crown is why you're able to have this party." Arius' arms went wide to encompass the celebration I never wanted. "My father's generosity is why your nobles have safe residences outside the ones your commoners burned down in raids. It is my father's money that lines your silk-lined pockets. Your father may be a king in title, but my father is the king who owns it all."

Ciaran's face pinched with each truth Arius spoke, and it grew harder for me to breathe. He was insane. And my father had sold me to him like cattle to slaughter.

"Since you have proved to be an unreliable alliance, my father has sent an unbiased third party to offer you two options." Arius gestured with a lazy hand behind him, and a woman barely concealed in gauzy gold fabric appeared.

In the glittering light of the chandelier, I saw all of her through the material. It dragged behind her on the ground through the spatters of the twins' blood that adorned the body-made aisle.

Only as she arrived did I notice the servant had crumpled—hopefully fainted and not been murdered.

Baltazar leveled the new arrival a flat stare, not looking below her neck like most of the other salivating men and women in attendance. "How can we help you, Queen Aurina?"

If I had ever doubted anything, it would have been that Maveri had won over a woman that was so beautiful... But I supposed it explained their son's looks. She was also there when she had never been seen by anyone other than Arius and the mad king. That itself gave me pause.

Her voice was like that of the musical notes that played before the instruments had abruptly stopped. "My husband has sent me to bear witness to your decision as an act of goodwill."

It didn't seem that Maveri's wife could be unbiased, but none of what was happening made much sense.

The knot in Baltazar's throat bobbing was the only sign of his distress, those who didn't know him that well would miss it. "And what are we making a decision on?"

"We can pull our resources entirely," she laced her hands in front of her, keeping her back stiff. Baltazar was already shaking his head at the first option. My father's eyes looked like they might fall from his skull. But she held firm and continued, "or you can crown my son at the wedding and step down."

Oh—*oh, no.*

The crowd chattered around me, stirring. I wished for my bed or anything far enough away that I didn't have to hear the decision.

Arius would be made king, and I—his queen. I was sure he had no proof of any such crimes from the twins. Were they awful people? Certainly. Did they deserve that? Not by that cruel prince's hand, at least.

Baltazar's nod was nearly imperceptible, but I caught it... And when my father spoke, his words filled my body with lead. "Very well."

"Perfect." Arius grinned, stepping in front of his mother. "We wed in two days."

CHAPTER 28

Two days.

My life as I knew it would end in two days. My heart rate—at a steady incline since Arius arrived—was at a lethal pace. My chest was aching, and I had to keep reminding myself to breathe.

In and out.

Arius raised a hand at the band, and though they rushed to pick up their instruments, the blood rushing through my ears made it impossible to hear the notes as they played. People around me chattered, but I only knew it by how quickly their mouths moved.

In and out.

The prince's body turned to me, and each fall of his boots brought him closer. I was overly aware of my clenched hands, my tear-stained face, and my stiff posture—all of which were doing the wrong things.

Smile, Jane. If he demonstrated anything, it was his willingness to kill first and ask questions later.

He would kill me if he found out all I had done. Perhaps though, it would be better than a lifetime shackled to him. Stuck with a madman who would seek to cage me and keep me under his thumb.

Potentially like his mother, whose body was still on display for the entirety of the ballroom to gawk at. Kept unseen for years only to be used as a pawn in a game we didn't know we were playing until we lost.

That had to be their goal all along—Maveri and Arius sought to take over Lunasa. But I saw their people's way of life. They were fed, healthy even—at least in the upper district. What had Arius called those in the lower district? *Undesirable?*

Not to mention, we didn't know if my father giving up his seat on the throne would ease the curse's effects. Or surely, he would have already done it years before. *Right?*

The prince wove around the last body, distancing us. A frown pulled at his mouth while his brows dragged together.

"You didn't think to greet your future king?" Arius asked before even reaching me.

"In fairness," I started, peeling my lips away from my teeth in my worst attempt at a smile. "You've only just become my future king."

Arius clapped his palms against my cheeks—looking every bit to those around us like affection, feeling to me like it would leave bruises. He squished my face between his hands and crushed my lips with a wet kiss.

I hoped it seemed like I was enjoying it, but my stomach

turned with the urge to empty the contents of everything I ate that night.

Finally, he let me come away for air and dragged his hands down my face, then my neck to my forearms. "Did you miss me?"

"It's only been a few days."

His eyes narrowed, and I knew I had said the wrong thing. My mind wasn't moving fast enough to keep up with the demands of the current situation.

"What I meant was," I smiled, but my lips trembled. "Though it's only been a few days, it felt much longer."

Not much better, really. But the crazed glint in his eyes dulled if only by a fraction.

"Come." He dropped one of his hands but kept the other firmly cuffed around my bicep. "I have a surprise for you."

"Great." I pasted on a grin when he gripped his talisman, despite the gnawing feeling that his arrival would only lead to more death.

We arrived by the darkened, ivy-coated stables. The dead

grass had been trampled so thoroughly by hooves and boots it had gone away wholly, leaving behind only broad patches of dirt.

The squealing, snorting sounds of a huge pig carrying from the wooden building told me what my surprise was before I saw it.

Swineston.

"You brought him?" My voice was so sweet and too high-pitched that it sounded foreign to my ears.

Arius was already shaking his head. "He's not the surprise."

"Oh?"

"This is." He grinned, spreading his arms to encompass the stables and the land around them.

Glancing at him, then back over where he had indicated, I tried to gauge how he wanted me to react. "The castle grounds?"

"This will be our wedding venue."

My brow raised in question. He still wore clothes smattered with Olivia's blood and had scared everyone half to death... And he was already in the throes of nuptial planning?

"Before your brother's untimely death, I asked him what he thought another suitable wedding gift for you would be." Arius shrugged.

"You—did what? I'm sorry... I'm not understanding."

"No need to worry about specifics." He waved a casual hand to dismiss my question. "After some questioning, Oliver told me the only two things you care about in the world are drawing and your horse."

I nodded, still not understanding how he gained information about me from my eldest brother... Or how Oliver had any to give. But, I said, "that was thoughtful of you."

Was that what he wanted to hear? I couldn't tell. But I kept that dumb, smitten smile on my face while judging the distance between me and Jett's stall. She was at the far end, by the hay bales, and I was certain Arius would grab a hold of me before I got to her.

That wouldn't do. I would have to come back when I was alone.

No princess, no wedding, no Arius as king. That would have to work. It was my only plan. Maybe I could set aside my grudges against Baltazar and Liam, and we could figure a way around it.

Baltazar had looked just as worried when Arius walked in as I had. When he saw Oliver's head, I watched his skin pale. None of what Arius was doing was part of the keeper's plan.

Long game it was, then—though two days wasn't much time.

"I'm nothing if not considerate," he agreed, showing me all his teeth as if he hadn't just slaughtered two of my siblings. "Now, would you like to see Winston? He's missed you too."

"Sure." My eye twitched with all the effort I put in to manage my facial expressions.

"We'll take him for a walk." Arius reached for my hand, and I took a step back, masking my face with a smile.

"I'm actually exhausted. I was getting ready to retire when you arrived."

"We can go back to my rooms if that's what you prefer." He winked, and revulsion poured through me. I would not be doing that.

Swineston chose that moment to squeal—praise the gods—and I was given a reason to deny the prince. Widening my eyes, I looked to the stables wistfully. "Actually, maybe we should take a walk first."

"Let's not mistake his needs as more important than mine." Arius scratched at his beard, and the skin around his eyes crinkled as he regarded me.

"Of course not, my Prince." Vomit—I was going to throw up everything I had eaten but only after I survived the conversation. "But it is practice. I want to be the best mother I can be to your future heirs."

I would sooner slit my own throat than lay with him, let alone bear him any children. But the way he was leering proved I had strummed the right chord. "We will not coddle them. That should be said now. If your brother had been a stronger man, forced off his mother's teat earlier, he may have stood a chance."

Oliver had been a piece of shit, but he hadn't been weak. I wouldn't have blinked if Arius had admitted it took forty of his men and himself to take down the twins. They trained relentlessly to maintain their power, and together, they were formidable.

"You're right." I lowered my eyes to the ground, then back up to meet his. "But your children will be mighty."

"My *sons.*" He nodded, striding through the wooden entrance. "Daughters are for fools and men with weak seed."

Oh, Gods—the man was the most insufferable piece of— "True."

Swineston rolled in his fifth in the first stall, but he righted himself when I walked in. The pig snuffled, pressing his dirt-dusted nose against the door.

Unhinging it, I let it swing open, and the boar bumped his head into my legs as he walked out, nudging me away from Arius and placing his body between us.

Maybe I could like the rotund animal. That close—and when I actually paid attention—I saw his bristly hair was a dark shade of brown with a few pale pink spots.

Stray strands of hay poked out, and I absently brushed them off. "Do you want to go on a walk with us?"

Swineston grunted as if in answer. A fierce whinny cut through the quiet night down the line of stalls as Jett lost her absolute mind. Her hooves slammed against the door to her stall as she bucked and kicked at it.

I held up a finger to ask the pig and the prince for a moment before rushing to calm her.

"Woah, girl." I raised my hands, palms out, but she didn't notice me. I glanced around in the kicked-up straw to see if I saw what could have spooked her. There wasn't anything.

Moving as slowly as possible while trying to nudge myself into her line of sight, I spoke in gentle tones. "Easy, Jett. Easy. Look at me—that's it—lower your head."

Jett moved her strong neck down. Then, jerking her head to the side and throwing her dark mane in the direction of the entrance, she let out a heavy huff of breath.

"We'll be back shortly. I'm just going for a walk." I looked into her large eyes and tried to stroke my hand down between them. But she reared back, lowering her head so that her muzzle touched my nose and snorted in my face.

Rude.

"Alright," I said, backing away. "I'll come back later with sugar cubes."

Making my way back over to Arius, I jerked my thumb toward the exit. "All set."

I lifted my foot, about to start walking, but he grabbed my hand and yanked me back a step right before Swineston stepped from the wooden floor onto the dirt path.

Crackling and breaking echoed before the boar's shrieking wails of pain caught me up to what happened. Swineston fell, his massive size shaking the ground underfoot. His legs spread away from him at unnatural angles. I moved to run to him, but Arius' grasp on my arm was firm.

"You'll want to wait." I looked at his cruel smirk and watched him grab his talisman, then back at the boar, where the dirt ground lit up with a sigil marking a ward cast there before it faded.

As soon as the blue light faded, I dove for the thrashing pig while his high-pitched barking noises continued.

"*Help him*," I demanded of Arius while I fretted, trying to calm the thing down. "Heal him—you can heal him."

Arius crouched beside me, so his breath warmed my ear, "We do not coddle the weak."

His hand slashed out, and hot blood sprayed my face. I realized what he had done a moment before Swineston's uproars of pain were silenced, and he twitched below my hands.

I turned my head and drained my stomach on the earth until I was retching up water and air.

"You're making a scene, "Arius said as if what I was doing was more distasteful than what he had done. I swiped my sleeve over my mouth and stood, swallowing my words with every gulp of breath.

My wide eyes scanned around us, and sure enough, guards marked with Ellesmere's crest paced around us. They were far enough away that I hadn't noticed them before but close enough that they had seen everything. None of them moved nearer, but I could feel their watchful gazes on us. There were probably more than I could see, hiding just in case I lashed out.

"*What was that*?" My voice was gravelly from straining my throat, and my wet lashes weighed down my eyes. My face felt sticky with gore, but if I thought of it too long, I was sure I would be sick again.

"Wards." The prince turned away from me and nodded to one of his men. "They've been placed all over the grounds. No one enters or exits unscathed until after the wedding aside from those who were invited—even with magic."

Oh... This was a warning and a threat.

He let me see what would happen if I tried to escape and avoided going through our marriage. Had it all been for that end, then? Bringing me there, offering up the stables as a wedding location—just so I could be so close to freedom, without any chance of obtaining it.

The walls of my world crushed in on me, suffocating me and my shaking hand flew over my mouth as warmth trailed down the drying blood staining my cheeks.

Arius whirled on me, surely to warn me against being weak, but his stare reached the hand covering my mouth to trap my sob. He cocked his head.

"*Where is your ring*?" His words were icy, and he snatched my hand, trimmed nails digging into my flesh.

My mouth fell open, but no answer came. All of my lies felt too rushed, too risky. All of my training felt inadequate, with so many guards watching. I was trapped in a nightmare I couldn't wake up from—where the prince was my villain, and no one would save me. There wouldn't be tales of my bravery or my adventures. Instead, they would remember me as the mad prince's wife. The downfall of Lunasa.

The truth was thick on my tongue, and I prepared myself to tell it, but as his eyes cut into me, the scream of a babe cut across the grounds.

Everyone's heads jerked to the interruption. Arius dropped his grip and crossed over to his nearest guard.

He remembered me as an afterthought and tossed over his shoulder, "Jane, go to your rooms and wait for me."

I, of course, had already readied myself for a quick death and would do no such thing.

Boots crunched on the gravel as the men followed Arius toward the sound. I kept my distance, my shoes padding the earth until I saw the men reach a crack in the ancient castle wall. Laying in front of it was a young boy lying on the ground, clutching a leg that was... All wrong.

His toothy lisp carried to me as he cried and begged the guards for help between apologies, and my heart sank to my toes. Even if I couldn't see his skinny frame being hauled up and carried toward the castle, I would recognize his voice anywhere.

Kaleb.

CHAPTER 29

I f ever there was a time for action, it was right then. A scared boy was being hauled off like a felon to the dungeons.

But Arius caught me moments after they ensnared Kaleb. What guards they didn't have treating the babe like an escaped convict, he sent after me. Without a second's thought, I barreled into the largest son of a bitch that had the young boy's mangled leg in a vice grip.

I marked each guard's face to memory—everyone that touched him and those who looked on without a word. All had a space carved in my mind that promised them a long, agonizing death.

If it were under different circumstances, I would have been proud that it took four guards to lug me away. There wasn't an ounce of me that gave a damn about my cover anymore, and I fought in a way that would have made Lux proud if he saw it.

Lux—where was he?

Did he know the boy had traveled all that way? Was Kaleb alone? I couldn't imagine Tess knew, and if she did, would she have sent along with Gwyn?

Questions plagued me as I paced the floor of my tower while the guards who had dragged me away stared straight ahead, having posted themselves, so they surrounded me.

One gift being trapped there had given me was thought—a moment to breathe, to think, and to conspire.

Arius didn't know about the tower's second, secret exit and the tunnels leading off the castle grounds all the way to Luhne.

If I could get Kaleb out, we could get through and circle back to the barrens. Then I could... Well, I would figure out what to do once he was safe.

The sun's movement in the sky told me I had been at it for hours, well into the night and the next day. Which meant I only had one to make everything right.

Step. Step. Observe. The guard to the right had a squared jaw, eyes too small for his face, and stood only a head taller than me. He also favored his left foot, which was hopefully my doing.

Then, before they noticed I stopped, I was back to stomping a rut into the stone floor. I had to get out of there. Then I needed to save Kaleb from what could and would only be an execution if Arius' history proved anything.

Step. Step. Observe. The guard to the left was a blonde with a scar stretching from his temple to his lower lip, giving him a permanent sneer. He sat with his ankles crossed on top of my trunk. That one was dangerous. Anyone that could survive having their face peeled like a potato was a badass. *Avoid pissing him off.*

Wondering if the celebration was still going on, my slipper hissed on the ground as I turned again. Perhaps I could use the revelry, if there was one, as my cover. But, where was Dri—had she made it out after Arius snatched me away?

Step. Step. Observe. The third was a man who looked not much older than me, and his training was probably not half as thorough. Which... If I thought about it for too long, it was insulting.

My heel slid, and I turned about-face and started circling once more.

Were the nobles angry, scared, riotous, or joyous that their cruel prince had been bested?

There were so many variables—too many.

The guard behind me yelled, "can you fucking stop?"

Rotating, I looked at him. Medium build, a sparse patch of grey hair I saw his scalp through, and aged skin told me he hadn't been wearing the talisman dangling around his neck for long.

He was also the only one of four who had one. Recently promoted?

Step. Step. Observe. I was only a foot away from him, and he flinched as I got nearer. Probably because my hair was wrecked, my face was spotted in blood, and I looked like the half-wild beasts I was—not long ago—rumored to be sleeping with. Maybe because women made him nervous. I was betting on both.

"Name?" Short, sweet, and laced with more power than he would want a woman to have. Especially if he was one of Arius' favored. Given the recent appointment to a higher position—I was also wagering on.

His silence told me two things. One, I was right in my assumptions, and two, he definitely had a small dick.

"I asked for your name." My words were clipped, and I took another step toward him, our chests only inches apart. His hand twitched at his side, likely itching to use that talisman on me.

No answer.

"Do you know how many men have been in this room, Commander?" I took a swing at his rank, again doubting I was wrong.

"He's only a captain." Then, looking over my shoulder, I noted the marred face of the guard glaring over me at the captain.

I stood corrected. "And does he have a name?"

"Gialanos, Milady." He nodded before turning and looking back ahead.

"Yours?" I asked, noting he had thoughtful, pale green eyes.

"If it pleases milady, you may call me Zander."

"Well, then, Zander, can you prove another theory I have?" I asked the surprisingly polite guard.

"What's that, Milady?"

"Does he have a sm—"

Lou bursting through the door muzzled me, especially when I noticed Driata was helping the seamstress carry bundles of white fabric.

"You can't be in here." Captain Gialanos said, his tone clipped.

"Correction," Driata curled her lip back, ever the princess. "You can't be in here. My sister has to be fitted for a wedding gown."

"And?" The captain gripped his talisman with all the malice of a newborn babe, and Driata straightened to her full height.

"Do you want to be the one to tell your prince you saw his future wife undressed?"

"By all means." Lou sagged in the door frame, a lazy feline grin grazing her lips. "I'm sure the bloodbath in the grand hall was a one-off, and the prince is *lenient*."

"But just in case," I added, already undoing the buttons at the front of my gown. "Please tell him you were given the option to leave."

The blonde and the boy-man balked and averted their gazes. Zander was already dipping beyond my sister through the door.

"Good day, Milady. I'll just be on the landing."

Captain Gialanos called my bluff, glaring as though he could bore a hole right through me.

My fingers made quick work of the line of fastens while I maintained eye contact with him. And when my bare breasts sprung free, the man turned a shade of pink that was about as unbecoming as my chest on display.

"Out!" He shouted at his men, and they sprinted for the door. He didn't look back when he said, "we will be right here."

The door clicked closed, and I let loose a breath I hadn't realized I was holding.

"We brought you these," Dri whispered, uncovering dark clothes.

"What if they come in here?" I stripped the rest of my gown and tossed it to Lou while Driata handed me a hooded tunic, tugging it over my head.

"Dri will be you." Lou shrugged as if it were that simple while I pulled on the black pants.

"What?" I hissed, not wanting to point out the obvious flaws in the plan.

"Full. Volume. No whispering!" Captain Gialanos' stick up his ass had him screaming at us with what sounded like his lips pressed against the door.

"Ah, I'm beat from such a traumatizing day. I'll just have a rest." Driata flicked her eyes between the tapestry hanging on the wall and me.

I shoved my feet into boots and wished I had more time to plan while Driata tossed my duvet to the bottom of the bed and stuck the down pillows in a line before covering them up.

Lou tossed her a fluffy green robe from my armoire, and Dri stepped onto the padded stool Lou lugged to the center of the room, facing away from the door.

They quickly removed her diadem and pulled the pins from her hair. She dragged her fingers through her perfect ringlets, fluffing them out.

Shuffling around a drawer in my armoire, I pulled out Liam's talisman and tucked it into my pocket.

Tilting my head, I assessed her. My frame was wider than Driata's and a bit shorter, and my hair a few shades lighter—but if one wasn't looking too closely, perhaps she could pass as me from behind.

The seamstress placed the diadem on the bed by what was supposed to be Driata's head, and I stifled a snort. Driata would sleep so close to her title.

But I didn't necessarily believe that anymore. She was stronger than I knew.

"Why is it so quiet in there?" Gods, I was sick of that man.

"*Go,*" Driata mouthed.

"Do I really have to wear a corset? It's a torture device," I cried, ducking beyond the fabric covering the hidden door.

Lou gave me a thumbs up before looking toward the main door. "If the way that guard regarded your breasts was any indication, we should really highlight them as your best asset."

"I wasn't fucking staring!" He was still trying to defend himself when I descended into the belly of the castle.

The castle's dungeons were full of vagrant drunks and those angry enough with their king to attempt storming the gates. Occasionally, a spy or assassin wound up there, but their connections to Baltazar often led to untimely death before trial and sentencing.

Given the lack of altogether dangerous criminals, the staffing of guards below was normally lacking. But with a young boy's bad decision and a tyrant's attempt at overthrowing a kingdom, the guards' number had tripled.

I wove back and forth from the corridor and into passages avoiding the guards at every opportunity. That's not to say there weren't any close calls. The three men waiting at the entrance had been knocked unconscious and would wake up with quite a headache near the kitchens.

Why were they less likely to alert the others? They were also stripped bare and placed carefully into compromising positions.

Luckily, the lower down I went, the fewer guards there were. Baltazar's wards saw to it that anyone not part of his guild would believe they saw moving shadows and heard the telltale signs of wicked spirits.

Insurance.

And, of course, Arius, my malicious husband-to-be, had placed a babe where even the worst criminals begged not to go. *That damned gossip had a way of spreading.*

But fortunately for Kaleb, those rumors peeled the numbers back on the guards like a thin apple skin.

I crept onto his level and along the shadows clinging to the walls, hoping Arius hadn't hurt him any further. What I had seen of his ruined leg told me he wouldn't make it up the steps to my tower, which was probably for the best. But at least if he could, Driata would have been able to heal him.

"Kaleb?" My voice was no more than a whisper, but it echoed around the space, and I flinched.

"Go away!" He sobbed, gasping for breath. "I don't believe in ghosts."

"Kaleb, it's me," I said, rounding a wall of empty cells and zeroing in on his voice. The walls weren't helping, causing the sound to bounce around me.

"Jane?" The sick sound of something wet on metal and stone turned my stomach. "What are you doing here?"

Shit.

"Well," I began, trying to keep the sound of my feet from

389

covering any noises that could lead me to him. I lied when I told your family where we were from."

"I know," he said, though his voice sounded weak.

Worrying at his leg causing him that much pain, I released a breath, keeping my tone even. "How?"

"Lux told us right after you left." He paused, like he was thinking or maybe drifting off to sleep. "When mama found the gold and the ring."

"Oh." I bit my lip, wishing I could take all of that experience away from him. "Listen, I'm sorry, Kaleb. For this and for how my family has failed you."

"I believe you."

"I'm going to get you out of here."

Quiet met me. Only the sound of dripping water from somewhere greeted me, "I don't believe you."

"I promise you, Kaleb." Saying his name was a tether, and even when I wasn't speaking it aloud, I was repeating my promise tied to his name in my mind.

"The bars are really thick, and... I'm hurt."

"I know, but we must get you back to your mama."

"She doesn't know I came here." Another, longer gap. "I'm a week early, but I wanted to give you back your ring."

"Early for what?" I prodded, needing him to keep talking as it grew darker.

"Can you keep a secret?" Kaleb asked the same way he had the night at his mother's dining table.

I decided to give him the same answer I had then. "I have a few."

"We take soil for the greenhouse."

"That's okay. I stole the mad king's crown." Admitting it

aloud didn't scare me as much as I thought it would, and though his voice was strained, he sounded like he was in awe.

"You did?"

I hooked another right, and there he was, a faint smile on his face... But there was a thick, murky puddle around his middle, and after all my years of magic... I would recognize that tangy scent anywhere.

"Who did this to you?" I asked, but he didn't answer, and it looked like the slight frame of his chest had stopped rising and falling. I tried another question. "Can you walk?"

"I don't think so...." His head barely moved as he tried to shake it, and his face paled.

But thankfully, he answered.

Biting my lower lip, I forced back my tears and yanked my rage to the surface. "Kaleb, I need you to get up."

"It hurts."

"I know, but I don't know how much more time we have."
Silence.

"Kaleb...take my hand." I laid on the floor, stretching one arm to reach for his barely twitching fingers through the bar, grinding my bones against the cold metal. I reached in my pocket with the other and pleaded with the gods.

One palm curved around the smooth stone, and my other reached and stretched and grasped until I felt his clammy little hand.

Please, you careless, bastard Gods. I thought of warmth and light and love and healing magic—every lesson I ever learned about the magic that had never taken. I looked at the damned bracelet on my wrist and then shut my eyes.

I thought of his mother and his sister and their love for him and their greenhouse where they managed not just to grow but thrive. I thought about how if anyone deserved to be whole, it was the bright little boy who had smiled even when they had nothing.

Please.

Warmth spilled down my cheeks as his silence echoed around me and filled me with brutal hatred for such a cruel world. He didn't deserve to die in a damp cell so far away from his home. His mother didn't deserve that loss for trying to feed her children. All of Lunasa had deserved better. But, all they got for their faith in us was that... Desperation and death.

"Jane?" Kaleb's voice was strong as he tugged my hand. "You... Made it better."

"What?" I crawled onto my hands and knees, grasped the bars, and watched in awe as he stood. I had...healed him. I used traditional magic. And I could smell the sulfuric hint in the air through my stuffy nose.

Kaleb hopped, showing me his leg was alright and lifted his shirt to show me where his wound had been. A grin split his face as he rushed the bars and did his best to wrap his little arms around me.

"Okay, listen... A loose stone should open up a passage at the back of your cell. I'm going to wait on the other side."

"You're leaving?" His chin trembled.

"No—no, I'm not leaving you. I just have to meet you in a passage."

He stepped back, nodding, and felt around on the wall. Then, finally, one of the stones gave way, and the hiss of air releasing confirmed he had found it.

"Okay, I'm coming." I gripped the bar, hoping he would

carefully listen to my following words. "If we get split up for whatever reason, stay along the left corridors and follow them to Luhne."

"No." He shook his head. "You have to come with me."

"Sure, yea—yes. I will. Just meet me in the passage." I gave him a smile, though it wasn't much of one, it was all he needed as he ducked away.

I made my way to the nearest entrance and felt the stones shift under my fingers before dipping into the pitch-black space. I felt along the wall, knowing I needed to keep left—just like I told Kaleb.

Kaleb...I healed him. With Liam's talisman—traditional magic had worked for me.

The sound of a clicking tongue came from in front of me—too close and too recognizable. It stunted my thoughts just as Baltazar flicked a lantern I hadn't known was overhead.

My heart was a battered bird inside my chest as I saw he stood beside Arius.

The prince's hand lashed out, cracking into my face, and my head snapped back with the impact.

"Jane." Baltazar titled his head like a concerned teacher, full of reproach. "I do believe you were told to stay in your tower."

I lunged away from them—but crashed into a wall of air as sigils lit up around me. No...I had to get to Kaleb.

Arius' hand crossed over the boundary seamlessly and latched around my throat. My nails raked at his forearm, scratching, clawing, digging but all the while, he choked off my air. The magic barrier—the trap they laid for me—grew tighter, crushing my thighs and ribs with each thrashing move of my body.

Baltazar smirked. "That bracelet has a sister."

He held up an identical band attached to chains, and I bucked against Arius' grip while the magic tightened its vise.

"Fuck. You," I bit out, learning finally—unfortunately—whose side Baltazar was on. His own.

"What a nasty thing to say when someone offers you jewelry." Arius spat, leaning in, but the wards kept me from gouging his eyes.

But between the walls of their two bodies, I saw a small child's frame. Kaleb's face was lined with the terror of everything he had seen—and I was certain, at that moment, he would never be the same.

"*Run.*" The words were nothing more than a rasp of breath. Black spots filled my eyes, and the clanging sounds of the chains locking onto my wrists and ankles were all I heard.

But I prayed to the same gods who healed him that he heard me as the black spots won, and I knew nothing for a time.

There was never a moment in the last three years that I let

myself hope for a better future—a tomorrow that I got to choose.

But as I woke, alarm bells rang in my head. An ache raced from my jaw, into my cheekbone, and up through my temple... I felt more hopeless than I ever had before.

My throat burned and scratched as I dragged in a wheezing breath, and something cold pressed against my face.

"Easy." The grogginess in my head caused me to start, but when it peeled away, I recognized Driata's voice.

I tried to sit, but nimble fingers pushed my shoulders back down. "Don't move yet."

One of my eyes was swollen shut, but the other was overly focused on Driata's face.

The reminder of Arius' violent hands crashed into me just as another memory jerked me away from the recesses of the haze.

"Ka—leb?" I coughed out, copper coating my mouth, telling me I must have bit down on my tongue when I went unconscious.

"They haven't found him." My sister reassured me, and a tear slid down her cheek.

Pallid skin and deep purple welts under her eyes told me she hadn't slept much—if at all.

Sucking down another breath, I relished the sting of my bruised neck because I had been there to get confirmation.

I must have been out for a while, and if they hadn't found him, then...he was going to make it. He had to make it.

Racking my boggled brain, I tried to figure out how to get Lux a message. He needed to meet the boy in Luhne and bring him back to their family farm before the guards figured out where he had gone and raided the capital.

"Do you mind?" I pointed to my face, where she was dabbing a cold washcloth, and she let out a shaky breath.

"I—I can't." I caught a glimpse of her chin trembling before she covered my face again with the cloth.

Was it that bad that she had to heal it in increments?

Light spilled in again as it was lifted, and a floral scent made its way through my sore nose. "Arius threatened to kill any who would heal you."

A male voice came from the other side of the room. "She tried it anyway, and he ripped her talisman from her neck, Milady."

"Dri..." I pushed her hand away to look her in the eye fully. "You shouldn't have risked that."

"You wouldn't wake up. I thought—" A sob broke her voice, taking away her voice.

"We thought you were dead, Milady." That man again...the guard. I propped myself up, and Dri was too overwhelmed to stop me.

He stood by the window, looking at the mountains in thought.

"What are you doing here?" The sheet spilled around my waist, and I realized someone had stripped me bare in enough time to cover myself.

"We were ordered to take shifts, Mi—"

"Jane—just Jane, please."

"Right." He nodded, hands locked behind his back, and didn't look toward me, which I supposed was good because I was still fumbling with the sheets around the manacles and chains binding my wrists and ankles. "Jane."

"How long was I out?" I bit my lip when I glanced at Dri and saw she had folded in on herself. Pain scoured my swollen face.

"It's your wedding day," he said, somehow knowing what I was asking, and my gut fell into my toes.

But the sinking feeling only worsened when I looked about my room. The tapestry covering the hidden door was gone, replaced by a large sigil carved into the wood. The few things I owned were gone. The armoire, the plant, the stool, and my—" Where is my trunk?"

"We were ordered to take all your weapons and anything they thought you may make one out of." A clock tower gonged in the distance, and Zander turned to the main door where two guards entered with Lou.

She again held the white satiny fabric in her arms, but the seamstress didn't give me one of her lazy, easy grins. Her brow was split, her lip swollen and bruised, and I saw her bandaged fingers sticking out from the material.

"Milady." Zander tipped his head to me and made his way to the door while one of the other guards took his place.

The other, an escort, apparently glanced at my chest where the sheets were doing a shit job of covering my breasts and smirked before backing out.

The door latching from the outside was a death sentence, and I wished I had made it to Kaleb before they found us.

But then—what if they had found us together? No. It was better that way. I could hope he was safely on his path home.

Maybe once, I could have found my way out of it, found the perfect role, and played it well. But as the tower tolled noon and the final peal of the hammer rang out, that sinking feeling grew that that day wasn't the beginning of something but the end.

Dri and Lou helped me to my feet, and the chains rattled against the floor. They helped me into a gown made almost entirely of clasps and satin. The fasteners lined each half of the dress where a seam would typically be—down the length of my arms and sides. It was easy to assume they were to accommodate the restraints.

"What happened?" I asked, Lou finally while Driata fastened the buttons.

Lou shook her head, glancing at the guard. My vision flashed red as I ground my teeth together and hot agony sliced through my jaw.

"Did you touch my friend?

Metal scraping sounded as I moved toward him.

He didn't turn, lest he risked seeing me naked, and I shoved at his armored back. His hands caught the ledge just before he tumbled out of the window, and he whirled around on me, chocolate eyes flashing.

"You stupid bitch." Spittle hit my face just before the back of his hand cracked out, and my head snapped to the side.

Righting myself, I marked him, just as I had all the others who would die before Arius decided to end me. But I committed his brown—shit-filled—eyes and his rounded jaw to memory and thought of the bronze sheen paling on his skin when he realized how long his death would last.

"Name?" I asked the same way I had Captain Gialanos, and I figured he would give me the same silence-filled answer.

But instead, he squared his shoulders and rose to his full height, so I had to cock my head back to keep meeting his gaze. The gleam he shot back told me everything. "Codis Wallin."

"Proud of what you did then?" I narrowed my one good eye while ice wrapped around my stomach. "You feel like a powerful man?"

"I'm not apologizing, am I?" His lip curled away from his teeth as if the air I breathed disgusted him.

"Keep that same energy when I paint your skin with your entrails." I turned, back stiff, to see the door open. Two more guards were carrying in a framed mirror and a wooden chair.

"If you attempt to break the glass, they are ordered to subdue you. But I'm of the mindset that every bride should see themselves on their wedding day."

Arius' mother was dressed in gossamer, her body on display through the sheer panels, but she held her head high, chin up as if it didn't concern her that the guards leered. She had a firm grip on a woven basket with brushes and combs sticking out the side.

Her pause when she saw my ruined face was nearly imperceptible. When she motioned for the guards to set down the furniture, I almost thought I imagined it. "Sit."

CHAPTER 30

My breathing was sharp when I did as she commanded, not sure what I expected of the woman who raised the monster that was her son.

The mirror reflected the horror marring my face. One side was completely swollen and seemingly made up of a bluish bruise. The lump of skin covering my eye was nearly indistinguishable from the rest of my face save for the smattering of dark lashes that split the skin. The other side was red and still warmed where Wallin struck me.

But the most jarring was the fat blue and grey markings of a handprint that circled the column of my neck.

Queen Aurina hummed behind me as she rummaged through her basket, finding a wide comb and pulling it through the ends of my matted hair. "Did Arius ever tell you about his pet bird?"

Shaking my head, I thought, *this is it. The part where she tries to win me over for her beloved son.*

"Don't move." The comb gliding through my hair and the soft pull on my scalp kept me grounded as she began. "When Arius was a boy, my husband had traveled to Karhdaro. Maveri returned with the most beautiful blue speckled bird and gifted it to our son."

Aurina sighed as she moved on to another section of my hair. "But the bird hated its cage and longed to fly. So we constructed an entire aviary, where gardeners tended real trees and plants. Painters detailed clouds and a bright morning sky. But the bird rebelled and flew so hard at the ceiling that it crashed into the ground."

The queen twisted one of my coils around her finger and met my eye in the glass. "I was going to braid it, but I think it's much too pretty to tuck away."

"What happened to the bird?" I asked, wondering where she was going with the story. "Did it die?"

"Not then." A frown tugged at her full lips. "Arius—too afraid of losing her—clipped her wings. But she resisted still, attacking him each time he went near. He didn't understand she was terrified and away from all the freedoms she had ever known. Finally, one day, he went in to check on her, and she had thrown herself onto the floor in front of the doors."

Aurina paused, switching the comb out for a hair cream and smoothing it into my hair. "When he lamented, the bird flapped her broken wings as hard as she could to reach the open air. He grabbed her and snapped her neck."

Of course, he killed a pet in the name of love. "Is that supposed to be a warning?"

"Loving the men in my family is hard. I recognize that." She shifted in front of me and tugged my curls over my shoulders, looking me head-on, and that close, I noted what I hadn't before. Her high chin wasn't for her pride at being on display. "I just hope you do better than me. Just remember, calm heads prevail."

And when a cold metal key fell into my cleavage as she shifted my hair to cover it, I knew what the story meant. The queen wanted me to do a better job escaping than the bird and to be more successful at it than she had with the king.

Dread pooled inside me when the guards hauled me to the rose-coated arch that made up the altar.

Even knowing I had the key, I couldn't reach my hands above my waist. My sister had been dragged off to be dressed, and Lou wouldn't be allowed to attend. I couldn't even ask them for help. I blinked to clear my burning eyes. If I could help it, I would not let Arius see me broken.

Looking out on the blurred faces of the nobles—seated in chairs on either side of a flower-strewn aisle—I noted that none of them could quite look at me.

Perhaps their privilege had kept them from knowing such

violence that marked my face. But maybe some of them also felt the wrongness of the event. The blight that Arius' ruling would cause our lands would be far worse than the curse.

My father was many things in my lifetime, but he would not once have seen that done to a woman and if he only knew what they had done to Kaleb... I had to think he would have stopped it. But as I stood there, attempting to keep up the ruse of my bravery—even if it was for myself—I realized that though my father hadn't wielded his fists and wasn't the one to lift the blade, he caused the pain too.

Hatred, pure and vile, replaced my lifeblood, and I shook with it, wishing that all of the men in my life would burn for what they triggered. I imagined it as I stood there, and while guests trickled in, I wove the illusion inside my head that I held the match.

Trumpets sounded in the distance, and I squinted to understand what I saw. Women clad in gowns that looked like armor crested the dusty hill, and I recognized Orabelle leading them.

"The other monarchs were invited to recognize the prince being crowned," Duchess Tilby whispered to the man sitting next to her. Not her husband, I noted.

The man balked, showing he was offended by the idea though it was hard to tell if it was the plan to see Arius rise to power or if it was the idea that the other rulers would come.

Something in the thought that Blair would be there made my stomach turn, especially when I was already hoping Liam would keep away.

Not long ago, I thought that marrying someone I didn't love was the worst thing that could happen to me, but spending my life with a man I wished dead was much worse.

Orabelle led her troop of women to the aisle, where they fanned out, finding spots among the gathered nobles. Each was as magnificent as their queen, and they looked at the guests and guards like they hungered to feast.

The foreign queen didn't sit just then, though. Instead, she stood no more than ten feet from where I was chained to the altar and curled her lip back from her too-white teeth. "I expected more from you than this."

"Me too." I forced a shrug but winced when the cuffs dug into my skin.

Her thin brow, dusted in silver cocked, and the metal scales of her gown tinkled like chimes when she spun away. "Let us hope I didn't travel all this way for nothing."

"Will you help me?" I tried, not caring how pathetic it made me sound. Or how the guards stiffened with their hands on the hilts of their swords.

She didn't turn to face me as she turned to walk away. But then she said, loud enough that her voice carried to the sky. "I will never understand why women let men decide if they get to be the villain or the victim in their story."

The band filed into their seats beside the altar and tuned their instruments with shaking hands. Nobles shifted, uncomfortable with their new seatmates, who salivated with every shift of the wind.

The quiet was so loud that I heard fabric rustling from the back of the audience. I wanted to scream, beg, and plead. Briefly, I even considered ripping my own arms off to get out of the cuffs.

But my eyes trailed to the glowing markings underfoot, only set to deactivate once the wedding ended.

A furious whinny rocked me. I watched in terror as armored guards dragged Driata, Lou, and Jett out from the stables. Loaded crossbows pressed into their temples, drawing beads of blood. Bindings wrapped around Lou and Dri's mouths, and I screamed.

No words came—only a tidal wave of sound. It poured out of me as I recognized Captain Gialanos, Wallin, and the scrawny guard from my chambers before I found Kaleb.

Finally, I managed, "if you hurt them, the gods themselves won't stop me from ripping you apart."

Captain Gialanos gave me a malice-lined grin and turned his crossbow, bringing the stock down hard on the top of Driata's head. She crumpled, and I relished my fury as the cold metal of my cuffs sliced into my wrists and ankles. I slammed my body against the wall of air surrounding me, imagining it was his body I was bruising.

The music picked up, but I only beat at the shield harder. I funneled my anger and devastation into my fists with everything I had until their sides were smeared in blood, and my temples throbbed.

"*I'll fucking kill you,*" I swore irrevocably—the words were nothing more than panting breaths, but the nobles gasped at my language. Orabelle's people snickered, feeding on the frantic energy around us.

"Enough!" Arius bellowed from the end of the aisle. I hadn't seen him arrive, but he stood dressed in a pressed white suit behind my father, who walked with Ciaran and Gemma on either arm.

My siblings looked at the wreckage of life like it disturbed them, and they questioned if they ever knew me. Of course, they hadn't—but I need not tell them now.

Gasping, rage-filled breaths heaved out of me as I stared over their heads at Arius, who was being escorted by his mother.

Aurina blinked, once slowly as if urging me. *Calm heads prevail. But how—how could I compose myself in this?*

Gemma and Ciaran transported our father under the arch, facing me. I saw a flicker of recognition in his weary eyes. He could have prevented it, but he said nothing.

"You look—" Ciaran started in the same tone he would normally use to insult me, but the words died in his throat when Gemma smacked him in the back of the head.

"Beautiful," she finished for him and rushed him to the front row next to Orabelle.

The number of guards tripled, filling up any empty space, and I wondered what they thought I would do, what they thought me capable of.

Right in front of Arius, a door ripped open the air, and when the knob turned...I knew. My body weighted with dread.

Baltazar—my mentor, friend, and manipulator—stepped through the bloody portal. He dragged Liam with him, dumping his slumped body at my feet. The crowd chattered at the use of the illegal magic, but Arius silenced them with a commanding hand. Aurina kissed his cheek hurriedly and dove into the nearest seat.

"Your final wedding gift, my love." Arius' voice and words pelted through me as though a round of archers had made their mark. "Once this is through, you're free to do with him as you please."

Orabelle tittered like she was watching some grandiose

production as the panels of my life shattered before me. Even if I found a way out... There was no going back and no shadows to cling to. The pair of them knew how to crawl under my skin.

My lips trembled, and my vision clouded before several warm tears slipped down my face, burning the scrapes and bruises there.

I stared at Arius long and hard before finally, I managed to whisper, "kill me."

Arius *laughed*—the sound cutting into me. "Excuse me?"

"I would sooner die than spend a lifetime submitting to you."

His cinnamon-colored eyes—ones that I thought should have been kind if they weren't flecked with insanity—gleamed as he shook his head. "You will not die today. But you will be the first to kneel."

The prince's polished boot kicked out, slamming into my leg and the damned thing buckled and crushed the petals coating the dirt. My gown caught on the chains, and my face smashed into the magic barrier. I slid, blood filling my mouth, and nearly fell, but Arius gripped my hair so that I looked up to him.

Something akin to a purr rumbled out of him like the heat of his pleasure at my submission warmed the bubble of magic surrounding us. Bile mixed with blood in my throat.

He faced the gathered crowd and roared for their celebration. Sparse applause rang out from his guards, but the guests remained silent. I lifted my arms, gesturing for the guards who saw me to go fuck themselves, and realized the chains had a significant amount of slack.

Keeping my face neutral, I waited for them to look again at

their fearsome soon-to-be king and tipped my chest forward into my hands, digging around for the key.

I freed it, tucking it into my palm, and slowly brought my hands together, so Arius didn't notice the clatter of the restraints.

Working the thin key into the hole of the chains, I prayed again. But as one manacle clicked open, Liam stirred and brought Arius' attention with him.

I couldn't hide the hanging cuff or the key...so I pulled forward the vile liquid in my mouth with my tongue and spit on Arius' bright white pants.

Blood and bile stained them, and he crouched to strike, but I was ready, and with my free hand, I rammed the key into one of his venomous eyes.

I wished to remember the exact note his scream hit so I could play it on repeat until my fingers or lungs gave out. But it was short-lived when he yanked the key from his busted eye and tossed it out of the air shield. His fingers lined up with the marks he left on my throat, and he lifted me onto my toes while I pummeled the side of his face.

The ground below us trembled, and the air strung out taut. A clap resembling thunder crackled with power as suited bodies appeared in the aisle, weapons already cutting down guards. Nobles screamed, clamoring for a way to exit. My vision darkened as Orabelle's people rose into a frenzy, ripping into anyone wearing the Ellesmeran crest.

Arius' hand crushed my windpipe, and stars burst in my eyes when I swung both of my feet up, but I kicked off his chest, breaking his hold just as the chains hooking me to the altar went taut.

The remaining air in my lungs sputtered out of me when my back thudded into the earth. He lunged for me, but I rolled, crashing into the air shield and sweeping his feet from under him. My vision cleared, and I met silver eyes as Liam slammed his fists against the magic containing us.

"Turn around!" he shouted, and I ducked in time to see Arius swinging my carved wooden dagger for my back. I brought up my chain, wrapped it around his wrist, and yanked, snapping the sensitive bones. The dagger—my dagger—padded onto the ground, and I swiped it up.

Arius gripped his wrist to his chest, and I caught a glimpse of Ciaran magicking my shaking father away behind him.

Asshole.

Jabbing the dagger into Arius' thigh, I sliced and ripped and cut until he was tumbling to the ground on top of me. His limbs tangled in my restraints, and he crushed me and my arms underneath him.

Arius slammed his head down, aiming for my face. I just barely dodged him. But Gods, he was heavy. Each expelled breath weighed a ton, and each inhale felt like my chest would never rise again.

Metal clanged around us as the fighting raged and more guards poured into the battle. A booming laugh rang out, and I looked to find the source.

There. The King of Karhdaro wore a dark blue suit, his long hair tied in a bun, and carved his way through guards like they were butter for his morning toast. He made his way toward the altar, not breaking a sweat with a wicked smile on his face each time he cut one of the bastards down.

Arius' head came down again, and light flared and darkened

as my vision shuttered and returned. I growled, shifting underneath him. My hips twisted, and I jerked my legs around him as he scrambled. The chain locked around his ankles, and I leveraged one arm free and blasted it into the side of his nose.

The cartilage crunched, and he squealed. I lifted my head and chomped down with my teeth ripping, tearing, cutting as the *tough man* wailed and recoiled away from me.

The magic barrier shuddered. I gripped my blade, rolling on top of Arius while he cowered and begged.

"Please, I won't make you marry me." But even as he said it, his hands reached for the talisman dangling from his neck. I lunged, slamming the dagger through the meat of his hand and into his cold, bitter, malicious heart.

The barrier gave out, and Liam dove for me, but Baltazar was suddenly there. He yanked him up by his blue-black curls and pulled tight, lining up a blade with the center of Liam's neck.

"Let him go," I said, kicking off Arius' limp body and dragging myself toward them on the ground. The pressure of the remaining chains tried to pull me back to that condemned altar, and I rioted as fighting stormed on beyond us.

"After all these years, after betrayal and heartbreak." Baltazar examined me with a sneer. "You still love him?"

Liam shook his head just a fraction, his silver eyes pleading for me to deny it. But...I couldn't. Fuck—I wanted to.

My head bobbed in a slow nod.

Baltazar's laugh cut me open and bled me out. He pressed the edge of his blade firmer against his brother's throat.

"Please," I begged, and a muscle feathered in Liam's jaw. "I'll do anything."

410

But they couldn't see what I did. Blair crept up behind them, pressing his index finger to his lips, and brought the hilt of his sword up.

My mentor smiled then—a sweet one meant for lovers between night-warmed sheets. "Anything?"

"I swea—" I started as Blair brought the hilt down and Baltazar folded in on himself, the dagger dragging across Liam's neck.

"No!" The king rushed forward, crimson staining the collar of his shirt too, and my brow scrunched. How had I not seen him get injured? But as quickly as I saw the wound, it was gone. Only the already drying blood remained even as Liam and Baltazar fell.

My nails dug into the hard, dry earth. They cracked and broke and dug as I towed myself forward, my cuffs shredding the skin at my wrist and ankles.

I had to get to him, but Blair was already there. His large back bowed as he knelt to heal Liam and rose.

"Shackles," he said, eyeing the magic-sapping cuffs like their existence was offensive. I couldn't say I disagreed. "Romantic."

"There's a key...but I can't—" I pointed to it, just out of reach.

"What do you say we get you out of those?" He grabbed it like it was made of acid between his thumb and forefinger.

"Please?" I scrambled back, giving the metal slack, and he tossed me the key. The sound of them unlocking was even better than Arius' scream. I rubbed at my raw wrists.

Liam rose behind him and rushed over to pull off the chains before dumping them on Arius' unmoving chest.

"Who did this to you?" The backs of Blair's warm knuckles stroked my cheek, and his healing magic surged into me.

Jerking my chin in the direction of Arius, I let them help me stand.

"Are you okay?" I asked Liam, reaching to touch his neck.

"Let's just get out of here," he offered instead of answering, dragging his assessing eyes over my face.

But I turned, remembering my sister as the fighting ebbed, and saw the three trembling guards hadn't left their station despite their fallen men begging for help.

Captain Gialanos' crossbow wavered over a—now sitting—Driata, who was rubbing the crown of her head.

Her eyes widened when she saw me as if she was just coming out of a daze, and the scrawny guard holding the tip of his arrow at Jett pointed it at me.

I felt Liam and Blair's large forms at my back as I stomped forward despite his finger poised on the trigger. Jett reared with a feverish huff and trampled him under her hooves. He fell beneath her, and the captain turned his crossbow on my ferocious mare. Driata punched out before I could react, and her bound fists slammed into his manhood.

He gasped and gagged, doubling over, and I bent to search for a fallen weapon. Blair clicked his tongue behind me to catch my attention and dangled my gifted dagger over my shoulder. I felt its weight settle in my hand as my fist tightened around the hilt.

Blair magicked himself and Liam behind the guards and clonked their heads together. They toppled, begging, screaming, and pleading, trying to drag themselves away, but I didn't stop until their blood mixed on my hands.

Blair's strong hand pulled me back after my dagger slammed to the hilt again. "We have to go."

"Not yet."

"Jane," Liam said, stepping into view. "You've killed the crowned prince of both Ellesmere and Lunasa. More guards are pouring through the gates as we speak."

I shook my head, looking at the carnage created and seeing Orabelle vanish with her people. Blair's clansmen gathered to leave at his command.

"Dri," I said, trying to clear the fog of rage that consumed me.

"I'm here." Her unbound hands grasped mine, despite the gore. "But I can't come with you."

"What?" My lip trembled as my voice broke.

She gave me the faintest smile. "I've learned a lot in the last few days. Our people need someone to look after them."

"I know." But even as I agreed, my head was shaking.

"This isn't goodbye." But she kissed my cheek and walked away.

"We have to go." Blair urged again, his gaze cutting to a rising Baltazar.

"You didn't kill him?" I yelled, whirling on the king.

"We can't." Liam gripped Blair's arm and dragged me against his chest.

I grabbed for Lou, who urged Jett forward and grasped my hand.

"Let's go home," Blair said, and his men vanished as the world faded around us.

His magic emptied us out on a warm sand dune that butted up against crashing waves. The balmy, briny air coated my nose as I looked around at the white sand and our overdressed and blood-coated group and—

One tall, tanned, completely naked woman with dark hair falling down over her breasts. My brow cocked in confusion. "Who are—"

She grinned like we were old friends. "I think it's time we have a chat."

Author's Note

I've spent my entire life falling in love with books and the characters and worlds stored within them. Bringing Jane's story to life was something that started off as a dream in July of last year. Imposter syndrome, paired with a vicious habit of procrastination and writer's block, caused road bumps along the way, but the first book is done! Many people would probably consider me an actual lunatic for how her inner dialog has so easily become my own while writing for her.

ACKNOWLEDGMENTS

Joshua: Thank you for holding down the fort and supporting me through the highs and lows of creating this world. Thank you for the late-night tear fests when you would have much preferred to have been sleeping. Thank you for being my inspiration and the reason I kept going. Thank you for always being my bright side, I love you most.

To my beta readers: You kept me working on book two while I panicked about you reading book one. You are the first two who got to fall in love with these characters. You are the first two who asked questions that I couldn't answer without giving crazy spoilers. You are the first two readers that gave me hope. Thank you for giving this story a shot and thank you for loving it.

And finally and most importantly, to Booktok and my readers: Thank you! Without you, my dream wouldn't be in the process of coming true. I can't wait to continue Jane's story and share the rest of my worlds with you.

-Deanna ♥

ABOUT THE AUTHOR

Deanna Ortega is an emerging fantasy romance author. By day, she's a mother to two little ladies and a wife to a self-proclaimed muscle head veteran. By night, she's an avid reader of all things mysterious, spicy, and fantastic.

Deanna fell in love with writing in a small town outside of Tampa, Florida, where the librarians all knew her by name. She's been hooked ever since.

She's hopeful that her books and the worlds she has created to inspire other people's journeys and vivid imaginations

Printed in Great Britain
by Amazon

10537159R00249